C000088688

The Dogs of Avarice

The Dogs of Avarice

By,
John G Gemmell

ISBNs
978-1-80541-238-0 - Paperback
978-1-80541-239-7 - eBook
978-1-80541-240-3 - Hardback

www.johnnygg.com

Greed is an emotion, but avarice is a behaviour. Sometimes those who want too much end up with nothing at all. Stephen and Tony have hidden their past lives for a decade. They soon discover that they are not the only ones who have secrets. Matty and Christina, in an Anglo-Calabrian marriage, are driven by a desire to prove that they are successful. Christina's loyalty draws them back to the clutches of her family in Italy.

Featuring lorry theft, money-laundering, bribery, witness protection, people smuggling, drugs and family dynamics, this story plays out in the dark and brooding Morecambe Bay, Glasgow, and seductive Catanzaro. Events force everyone to reflect on what they want from life.

Contents

CHAPTER ONE

2022

A mirror can't lie, but we can lie to the mirror. It won't know that you have lived your life with prolonged dishonesty, constantly in fear that if the ones you love find out, it will never be the same again. Stephen Whyte has lived with this dread every single day for more than a decade.

He stares at the image in the mirror, ashamed of the reflection. The steady creep of grey hair, which started with his eyebrows, has now extended to the side of his head. He is contemplating buying himself an electric shaver to avoid the need for seeing his reflection. He has put on weight, probably because of lockdown, which saw him work from home and abandon his routine at the gym. Opening accounts with a wine supplier and several takeaway providers has done nothing to help. He stops wearing his Apple watch as it is embarrassing to see how few steps he has completed compared to his wife.

He contemplates the odds of losing a stone before his 40th birthday, hurtling towards him at pace, and then the family's long-overdue trip to Florida in the summer. The truth is Paddy Power would give lengthy odds against shedding the weight, given his history of dieting. He knows that with his ageing metabolism, every single pound is a hard-fought battle. Every doughnut or packet of crisps laughs at him, mocking him with sugar and fat.

He is too vain to admit that he needs reading glasses; all these years of staring at a computer have taken their toll.

However, he really can't complain.

He is married to his beautiful Lisa and has two adorable children, Cameron and Emily, aged eight and six, respectively. He has carved out a very successful career as a forensic accountant working for Griffiths & Henderson, based in the city centre.

Living in suburbia can be dull for some, but given his previous career, it is just the way he likes it nowadays. Boring is safe.

Having carried out his morning ritual in the bathroom, he pads downstairs in his comfy

slippers to the kitchen. Of course, given his wife's taste, everything in the kitchen is perfectly white. They have spent a fortune on their new kitchen, with a luxurious, modern glass finish. It's a nightmare to keep clean.

Stephen loads up the coffee machine with his favourite pod, the Istanbul Express, bitter roasted with a fruity and almond finish, high in caffeine to kickstart his day. The smell of rich coffee invades the kitchen. He tops up the kettle to make Lisa her camomile tea. Finally, he pours muesli and milk for the children.

He smiles to himself when he looks in the fridge. Every jar and bottle have been arranged so that it is facing perfectly forward. He can see his wife's OCD in all its glory.

'Morning, darling. And how's my big 40-year-old husband?' Lisa says, coming into the kitchen, hair glistening wet from the shower, smelling of lavender.

'You know perfectly well I am still in my thirties,' Stephen replies, giving her a peck on the cheek. 'Just.'

'The children are getting dressed,' says Lisa. 'Mum and Dad are coming over; I've asked them to drop them off at school.'

'Sure, what's up?'

'Got a Teams call early this morning. We have a big pitch to a new client coming up, and I need to know that the team are going to be ready.'

'Babes, I am so proud of you, but does that mean you are not making me breakfast?'

'Aye, right. Maybe on your birthday, if you are a good boy.'

Lisa is 38 years old, a slender brunette with a truly tender and caring personality. She was born and raised in Clydebank, the only child of Davy and Kathy Gavin. Throughout her childhood, her ambition had been to go into teaching or nursing, but somehow, she gravitated to setting up her own business.

It was her father's genes, as she discovered that she had a rather ruthless entrepreneurial streak. Over the last 10 years, she has combined her values and tenacity to establish a full-service PR company in Glasgow, the DK Partnership, named after her parents, of course. Her speciality is digital campaigns and PR support, helping customers establish their green credentials.

Lisa is passionate about many things. She is a huge believer in taking action to protect the climate, calling out bad corporate behaviour. In the workplace, she has striven to create an inclusive and diverse workplace. She wants her children to grow up with no barriers to succeeding.

The Covid years have been tough, for sure, but she has an inkling that the future looks bright, although she constantly stresses over how under-resourced, she is. In the weeks ahead, she needs to address this, or it will be her nemesis.

She loves her beautiful home with her perfect family. Whilst suburbia might not be everyone's cup of tea, she loves the nest that they have carefully built. They have invested a lot of money in their home to make it just the way that they (she) want.

The clatter down the stairs heralds the arrival of Cameron and Emily. Children of that age may have mastered stairs but can only do so in a chaotic way. Why walk downstairs when it is more fun to jump? They are both immaculately dressed for the High School of Glasgow: regulation royal blue blazers, white polo shirts, navy trousers for Cameron and school tartan kilt for Emily.

'Morning, Daddy. I love you,' says Emily, giving him a big, sloppy kiss.

'I don't want cereal,' says Cameron. 'I want a cheese sandwich, and don't even think of giving me a kiss, Dad.'

'Gran and Gramps will be taking you to school this morning,' says Lisa, whilst drinking her tea and putting on her conference call make-up.

'Shotgun!' shouts Cameron, determined to sit up front in the car.

'Your Dad hates that school. He thinks it's far too pretentious for a working-class boy from Yoker,' says Stephen, with a smile.

'I know. God love him; he is so old school. He said to one of the mums at the gates the other day, "Wearing a kilt to school doesn't make you any cleverer, you know." I was mortified, although I don't think she understood a word he said,' says Lisa, on her way back to the bedroom to get dressed.

Stephen settles down at the breakfast bar and fires up his laptop, ready to take on the inevitable barrage of emails. These days, people have forgotten the art of communication. It is now all emails, followed by messages to check that you have received the email. Then you get a call asking you if you have seen the message yet. Sometimes, you even get messages through WhatsApp or LinkedIn.

It has fuelled a culture of always being on, which is never going to be good for your well-being. An impatient workforce creating a frenzy around mundane tasks. Giving a sense of urgency that is not warranted. Convincing themselves of their productivity. The sooner they are all back in the office the better.

The world of forensic accounting is far removed from the day-to-day work of preparing accounts and tax returns. It's the exciting, sexy part. It's all about following the money; it is almost investigative. Companies figuring out if they can survive. Investors wanting to know where the bodies are hidden. Large complex financial institutions setting up complex financial mechanisms to hide away the cash from the tax man or the shareholders, or both.

In a previous life, his expertise was doing the hiding; now it is the classic poacher-turned-gamekeeper scenario, the skill being not only which stone to pick up and look under but when to put the stone swiftly back and ignore what is lurking below.

There is one email that causes him to groan.

Lisa has returned to the kitchen ready for her call: hair and make-up complete, full business attire for the top half and gym pants for the unseen part. The new modern approach to video calls.

'Oh dear, what's that for?' she asks.

'Email from the boss. We've won a major award at this year's British Accountancy Awards. He wants the whole team to go down to London to celebrate.'

'Oh, darling, that's brilliant news! You have worked so hard over the last few years – you deserve it.'

'I hate it. I really don't like anybody to know who I am. I value my privacy, and the idea of pictures being taken gives me the fear.'

'You are married to someone who has a career in PR. I will be your publicist, free of charge. Now stop stressing,' says Lisa, starting to load up the dishwasher with the morning's breakfast stuff.

'Daddy, can I ask you a question?' says Emily.

'Sure.'

'When we go to Florida, can I meet Mickey Mouse and Minnie Mouse? And are they the *real* ones? Milly says they're just actors pretending to be them.'

'You better believe it, kid. You don't think your dad would introduce you to fake ones?' says Stephen, ruffling her mop of blond hair. 'Now go and get your school things together; you need to leave in five minutes.'

Gran and Gramps arrive and let themselves in with their own key.

'Morning, Davy,' says Stephen. 'Morning, Kathy.'

'Too bloody early in the morning for me. I don't like getting up early anymore, now that I am retired,' says Davy, pouring himself a glass of milk.

'Early bird catches the worm and all that,' says Stephen.

'Never really believed in all that shit. Anyway, the owls stay up all night, then prey on the small birds who get up early.'

'Very dark, Davy.'

Davy is approaching seventy and still stands tall and true. Old-school hairstyle, short back, and sides with a spot of Brylcreem. The standard trousers and polo neck look – you will never see Davy in jeans.

Stephen is healthily scared of his father-in-law, without ever knowing why.

'In my day, we walked to school on our own; now the kids have to be driven to school,' says Davy.

'Don't be ridiculous; it's two miles away, down a very busy dual carriageway,' says Kathy. 'Have the wee ones had their breakfast?'

'Yep, they had muesli.'

'Bloody wallpaper paste. At least my ma gave me a sausage and a bit of bacon most mornings.'

'Yes, and that goes some way to explaining your high cholesterol, doesn't it?' says Kathy.

She might be only a diminutive five foot two in her socks, but she is more than capable of keeping Davy on a tight leash.

'Anyway, what's on today?' asks Davy.

'I'm in the office all day, but Lisa is working from home. It's just that she has a very important call first thing.'

'Kids, a couple of minutes and then Gran and Gramps will take you to school,' shouts Stephen up the stairs.

Outside the house, a black car quietly pulls up and parks on the pavement. Last night's rain is still streaking the ground, but slowly drying out. There are small damp patches where the spring sun has not yet reached.

Inside the warmth of the car are two members of the National Crime Agency – Brogan Reilly and Phil Simpson.

'I hate when we get one of these calls telling us there has been a breach in our protection protocols,' says Brogan.

'To be fair, they are few and far between. Our record is not bad.'

'It means that someone has fucked up, though,' replies Brogan, rifling through the file in preparation.

'I don't know Glasgow that well, but this is a rather well-off neighbourhood.'

'Oh, this is money, alright. They even have their own driveway, and in Hillhead that is rare.'

'I see they have one of those Tesla's up the drive. Plugged in like a giant hairdryer.'

'Oh, this boy has done well for himself. According to the file, he makes big money, and his missus has her own thriving business as well.'

'Well, he's in for some surprise in a minute, when we ring his doorbell.'

They walk up the short driveway to the front door and press the button.

Two things happen simultaneously: the front door chimes reverberate through the house, and Stephen's app vibrates on his wrist, informing him that someone is at the front door.

'Cameron, get the front door for me, please,' shouts Stephen. 'It's probably another delivery for Mum.'

The young man opens the door to see two uniformed police officers on the front step. He is so taken aback that he goes as white as a sheet and cannot find any words to say. Thankfully, the whole family arrive in the hallway at the same time, all ready for the day ahead, nobody expecting anything other than normality.

'Are you Mr Stephen Whyte?' asks Brogan.

'Yes, that's me. How can I help?'

'Sir, we are from the National Crime Agency. I am afraid that you need to come with us immediately. We have reason to believe that your life may be at risk.'

The scream from Lisa echoes up and down the street.

'Stephen, what the fuck is going on? What is this all about?'

'Are we still going to go to school?' says Cameron.

'Does this mean I don't get to meet Mickey?' wails Emily, immediately bursting into tears.

'Is he under arrest?' asks Davy, with his arms protectively on his daughter's shoulders. Kathy holds both children tightly to her body.

'No, sir, this is for his own protection.'

CHAPTER TWO

2022

Tony Fowler is one of those guys who lives his life on a day-to-day basis, following the rules of the urban jungle, using his instincts. He has no real family that he is aware of, no employment, no substantial assets, but always has a smile on his face.

He isn't originally from the Northeast, as he grew up in Dublin. Having chucked school as soon as he could at the age of 16, he discovered the one thing in life that he seemed to be very good at was stealing. He had a natural talent for it, with speed and ghostly agility being his forte. Only problem was he pissed off so many people in Dublin that he eventually had to catch the ferry and give England a try. He worked for many years in and around Lancashire for a guy called Matty O'Hare before he had to hastily migrate to Gateshead where he now lives alone in a one-bedroomed flat.

Tony's main source of income comes directly from the government and pays his rent and bills, but he's always on the lookout for petty crime opportunities. These days, it is less about the income stream and more about the habit he has formed over the last twenty years.

He is over the moon that the government is now encouraging people to stop working from home and return to the office. The lockdown for Covid was not very kind to independent thieves as everyone was at home.

His office is not a traditional one. It is, in fact, the Gateshead Social Club where he likes to spend his days.

Isolation was brutal, enduring lockdown on his own. Thankfully, he acquired an 80-inch flat-screen TV and a collection of fake logins for all the streaming apps.

Never blessed with a great dress sense, he tends to wear stuff that is knocked off. Young kids shout abuse at him in the street, but it never bothers him. There are worse crimes than sartorial inelegance.

So, as he pushes open the heavy double door of the social club, just after midday, he is hopeful that life is beginning to return to the old days.

'Awrite, Bill, how you getting on?' asks Tony.

'Canny, man,' replies Bill. 'You want the usual?'

'Yes, please, a pint of Carling, salt and vinegar crisps, and give us a deek at your *Chronicle* . . . and a pair of readers, 2.0 please.'

The club keeps an old, battered shoebox full of reading glasses, discarded and left behind, rescued, and repurposed by the cleaners, just in case any visually challenged bingo players need some help.

The Gateshead Social Club is one of those classic working men's clubs in the North of England. The small bar is the only one open during the day, a spot where the old fellas gather, drink their beer, and complain about anybody and everything.

A full-size snooker table dominates the space, at peace, awaiting the soldiers of the green baize to do battle over its surface. You can play dominos or darts. The television hums quietly in the background with the racing on every afternoon, delivered via a dodgy website from the Middle East. The bookies are conveniently situated next door, a perfect marriage.

Lighting is of the fluorescent variety, bright at all times of the day. Light so harsh it makes your skin porous. The club has a whiff of disinfectant as the cleaners have been giving the floors a scrub.

The club used to be run by a committee, but to be honest, a large group of amateurs rarely gets anything done. Meetings were a shambles, with arguments about how many free pints at Christmas they might expect. Everyone was on the take. Anyone with access to the keys to the fruit machine was accused of fraud.

Today it is the personal fiefdom of Bill, who runs it with a vice-like grip.

In many ways, these clubs manage themselves. Everyone knows everyone; if you misbehaved at the weekend, you get yourself down first thing on a Monday morning to apologise. Drugs are not tolerated; it is pints and bottles of Dog only.

The function bar opens Thursday through to Sunday and can get busy when the karaoke or bingo is on. The bar is dominated by a large stage, with a backdrop of golden streamer curtains that resembles an enormous ra ra skirt.

In the good old days, the club used to be on the comedy circuit. Comedians would brace themselves to face an alcohol-fuelled audience. Recently, they tried running Bongo Bingo to attract the young team, without gaining any traction. The club is now struggling to stay relevant, the great heyday of the social club having passed.

However, the club still plays an important part in the local community, with fundraising for local charities and the famous kids'

Christmas party every year, with Bill playing the role of Santa in a suit that is increasingly threadbare and beginning to have a fusty hum to it.

It is here in the club that Tony gathers some of his best intelligence: guys who are pissed off with their bosses who might reveal something held in a warehouse; people going on holiday, leaving their homes empty; people having a big win at the bookies and splashing their cash.

His only rule is that he never robs anyone from his own community, as that is not part of his moral code.

Tony learned his trade working for Matty O'Hare. He was taught that the successful thief is decided by the quality of their intelligence and homework, above anything else. Do your homework and your ratios go up, otherwise known as the 5Ps: Preparation prevents piss-poor performance, as some business guru once said.

Tony thrives on the persona he has created: he is just a daft, wee, harmless, Irish fella who likes a drink or two. He likes the fact that people underestimate him; it gives him the upper hand. He reads everything and is always up to speed with what is going on in the world. A captain of curiosity.

Bill isn't averse to playing a few naughty games himself. Nothing better than ripping the drayman off with a few kegs or buying cheap vodka and decanting it into Smirnoff bottles. Or taking a small loan from the brewery to build a kitchen.

The kitchen that was eventually finished is in his house and not the club, as it never serves food. If they need catering for a 21st, it comes from the Indian round the corner. If it's a funeral, it's sausage rolls from the bakers on the high street. Local businesses supporting each other.

'Good to see the club up and running again,' says Tony.

'Yep, but not sure for how long, mate. The bloody virus has just about emptied our resources,' says Bill. 'The price of everything is going through the roof; not sure we can cover the costs without a big hike in prices.'

'That won't go down well with the natives. Remember the last time you put a pint up by 10p – they threatened a boycott.'

'The other thing, everyone's expectations have changed after lockdown. Now they come in and ask for a vodka, then they hold it up to the light and say, "Away and shite! Is that a proper measure?" They spent two years free-pouring spirits – they were probably getting quadruples at home.'

'You've been short measuring for years, ya old bugger.' Tony chuckles.

'Fuck you.'

'Fill the glass up with ice first; that's what they do in Benidorm.'

'Also, that bloody Simon Cowell has a lot to answer, in all,' says Bill.

'What's he done to you?'

'Well, it used to be Saturday nights when we were mobbed. We used to have some of the best turns on in the Northeast. Total sell-out. Now they all stay at home and watch *Britain's Got Talent* and those wee dicks, Ant and Dec.'

'But I thought all you Geordies loved them!'

'Not when they stop people coming down the club. Anyway, how you getting on? Are you making a coin?'

'Absolutely shocking, to be honest,' says Tony, before taking a long sip of a second freshly poured lager. 'Everyone's been at home, putting all this bloody technology into their houses: smart video doorbells, CCTV everywhere. It used to be just dugs I feared. Now it feels like I am being watched every time I go into someone's back garden, ready to set off a trip wire.

'I was running through a garden the other day, and there was this bird sunbathing in the nude and on the prosecco at eleven in the morning. I didn't know where to look. She just smiled and gave me a wave. I reckon I could have pulled her if I had stopped.

'Then the nebby ones who set up these little community Facebook sites dedicated to complaining about dog poo and putting up screenshots of burglars. It's no fair, you know; a man is just trying to make a living.'

'Might be time to retrain, get yourself some new skills.'

'What – like become a fucking Amazon delivery driver, delivering parcels at speed, probably on speed, given how many drops they need to make on a shift. Away and shite!'

'You know, you are becoming more and more like a bitter Geordie,' jokes Bill.

'Away man, I'm from Gateshead.'

'Maybe you could go back to Morecambe and work for that guy Matty O'Hare that you are always banging on about.'

'No chance. It's fair to say I wouldn't be very welcome over there.'

As Tony returns to his paper, Bill makes a start on cleaning the beer lines, a job he hates as it feels like he is pouring money down the drain.

In the old days, you could probably re-use it. Fire the slops back in the barrel and make yourself a few quid.

The doors of the club creak open loudly, delivering a cold blast of air, and two uniformed police officers appear at the bar.

'Don't worry, lads, it's all in order in here. The Licensing police and Health and Safety were round last week and gave us a clean bill of health,' says Bill.

Inside he is sweating. He has two pallets of hooky vodka in his cellar, and if they are here to carry out an inspection, he is up shit creek. It could be vodka galore as opposed to *Whisky Galore*.

'It's not you we need; it's Mr Anthony Fowler. You need to come with us straight away,' says the senior policeman.

'After all these years I've been on the run, don't tell me you have finally found me holed up in the Gateshead Social Cub,' he says, barely lifting his eyes from the paper. 'Can I at least finish my pint before you take me away and beat me black and blue?'

'You have been watching too much telly, mate. This time, it's to protect you. Someone is out to get you.'

Tony finishes his pint, grabs his jacket and shouts to Bill, 'If I am not back in a day or so, can you round up some guys and send out a search party, mate?'

CHAPTER THREE

1985

A steady stream of excitable new arrivals begins to form a line outside the nightclub. Having spent a few hours pre-loading at somebody's house, if they were lucky, or in the bushes at the local park if not, they are in a boisterous mood. It is the era of post-punk, the emergence of the New Romantics. The girls are all dressed like Madonna, and some of the boys have discovered eyeliner and double-breasted shirts.

'Not tonight, fellas,' says Matty to two young lads.

'But we're stone-cold sober, mate. We haven't had a drink yet.'

'It's not that. It's just the eyeliner you have put on – it's terrible. You really need to get your little sister to show you how to do it properly. Anyway, I'm only joking. Come on in; have a great night.'

Saturday night, pinnacle of the week. You dreamt of it as the clock ticked painfully slowly through the drudgery of midweek. The thought of a night of debauchery at the local club made you giddy with excitement.

Growing up in simpler times. . . If you wanted to meet your mates, you agreed on a time and a place, under the clock tower or whatever the relevant place was in your town. You always made sure that you were on time, as the fear of missing out was real, not abstract. It hadn't aspired to its own acronym yet.

You still used the public phone box, even though it smelt of pee, and you knew all your mates' phone numbers off by heart. The phone at home was occasionally prone to one of your mad neighbours joining in on their handset, you didn't block people on the dreaded party line; you just left it off the cradle if you didn't want to speak to someone.

If you wanted to find your mates, you needed to hunt up and down the town until you found a collection of bikes, and then you knew where they were.

There were no apps tracking where you were, and what you were up to. In and out of a Ford Sierra in seconds and off with the radio, without any car alarms. Down to the nearest estate pub where you could sell it off for cash to fund the weekend's craziness.

It was tough being brought up in the Northwest of England. No knives or guns, disputes settled with your fists, so you had to be able to scrap and fight for every inch. It was Darwinian: only the strongest survived.

This was the world in which Matty O'Hare entered adulthood in 1985.

He was born Matthew O'Hare in Morecambe, the eldest of four children. Then came two sisters and a baby brother. His dad was a docker and his mum was a school dinner lady. They worked tirelessly to feed the family and instil in their children proper working-class values.

At six foot three, and 195lbs, Matty is a mountain of a young man. His hair is light brown, and he has a slightly sallow complexion, even though he is always outside.

He has shown great promise as an amateur boxer, tipped to go professional if he really wanted, but he doesn't have the patience for the training and would rather make his money in ways that don't involve getting his face smashed.

So, he does what many other 'big units' do and becomes a bouncer at the nightclubs of Lancashire. The owners know that having Big Matty on the door ensures a trouble-free evening. He always works the doors with his two childhood friends. Steven 'Hammy' Hamilton has been his best friend since the age of two when his family moved in next door. He's a man of few words, but when he speaks, you generally listen.

Then there is Benny D'Arcy, whom they picked up when they started junior school: short in stature, fond of a witty response, but don't underestimate his ability to fight. One of those blokes who is desperate for it all to kick off so that he can wade in and crack some skulls. And whatever you do, never poke fun at his surname.

So here they are, just another Saturday night running the door at Bliss Nightclub in Preston.

The entrance is down a cobbled alleyway. Inside it is dark and smoky, all gleaming mirrors and spinning lights, with lots of little alcoves to hide away in and get up to teenage nonsense. And boy, is it loud – decibels that match a plane taking off. It smells of raging hormones as this is the place to meet partners.

'Right boys, another night dealing with Preston's finest scallywags,' says Matty. 'First thing is the cloakroom. It's £1 a jacket. Nobody gets two jackets on one hanger; we're on commission here.'

'What if they don't have a jacket?' says Benny.

'Send them back to their ma and da's to get one; it's going to be cold later,' jokes Matty.

'Secondly, no drugs in any form are allowed. I promised my ma, on the Virgin Mary, that I wouldn't let that shit into any club that I worked at.'

'Ok, gaffer . . . it's bad enough when they are on the Stella; that's fighting juice, that stuff,' shouts Benny.

Inside, the music begins to crank out the crowd's favourites. Billy Idol sings about a White Wedding, the Monochrome Set are climbing Jacob's Ladder and Madonna is acting Like a Virgin, probably not for the very first time.

'Not tonight, lads,' says Hammy to a group of boys.

'How come, mate? We come here every Saturday,' says the cockiest of the three.

'Well, you aren't tonight,' says Hammy, contemplating his fingernails in a bored fashion.

'My big brother is inside. When he hears, he won't be very happy.'

As this minor confrontation is slowing up the flow of new entrants, Matty decides to offer some sage advice.

'Lads, lads . . . your patter is shite, your trainers are manky, your shell suit is probably inflammable, and you look like you have been on the white cider. You have zero chance of pulling anyone tonight, so away up the road before I knock the fuck out of you.' He speaks quietly, not wanting to offend the rest of his customers.

The line gradually shortens until there's a lull, knowing full well that the drunken back shift is much harder. The boys get a chance to talk about the future.

'Hammy, I am bored with this shit these days,' Matty says. 'We can't stand outside in the cold all our lives.'

'It's alright – pays decent money, don't need to be up at the crack of dawn, and there's always some lass that wants to get it on with the bouncers.'

'Never me – they don't like the short ones,' said Benny with a laugh.

'Ah, but you get your thrills when it all kicks off and you get to go back into the ring without your gloves,' says Hammy.

'But can you really see us doing this as we get older? It's a young man's game. Someone will come along one day and claim the crown,' Matty says.

'There must be another pathway to getting rich. I am thinking about a change in career and getting into the haulage business. The only problem is that I don't have any trucks.'

'A mere technical dilemma, gaffer,' declares Benny.

'Oh, very posh, Benny. What do you fucking mean?' says Hammy.

'Well, it's easy. We just go and boost a couple of trucks. I know a guy called Tony; he can break into any vehicle in seconds. We go and lift a few trucks, spray paint them, change the registration plates and boom, we are in the haulage business.'

'You know, let me think this though,' says Matty. 'Let's meet during the week.'

At this point, a new group of young girls appears at the front door. True to form, they are all dressed the same – baggy shirts, leggings, and Converse boots – with huge hair that has been back-combed and then solidified with hairspray. Heavy black eye make-up gives them a faux Goth look.

Apart from the one at the back, who is wearing a smart black dress and high heels. She is tall with clear olive skin and luxurious, long, black hair. High cheekbones and an intense stare. She is clearly not from around these parts and carries an air of Continental mystery. She stands out in the Lancashire gloom like a warm light.

'Haven't seen you here before, my love,' says Matty.

She giggles without saying anything, maintaining eye contact throughout.

'Hey, big boy, settle down. She is well out of your league, handsome. This is Christina de Luca, and you will have her whole Italian family after your balls if you go anywhere near her,' says one of her friends, laughing.

Entirely unfazed by the threat, Matty says, 'Well, just to introduce myself, I am Matthew O'Hare from Morecambe, and if there is anything that my associates or I can do for your party, please let me know.'

The girls burst into laughter at the unexpected formality and chivalry from the big, muscle-bound bouncer. Making little girly faces at them on the way past, they skip through into the sweaty, noisy nightclub, ready to dance the night away.

'Lads, I have something to tell you' says Matty. 'I think I might have a chance with that one.'

* * *

Matty has the good sense to get Christina's contact details before she leaves the club. She is visiting relatives nearby and is still here for another week or two. Enough time for Matty to take her on a couple of dates, nothing too elaborate – a pub in Morecambe, a drive out to Lake Windermere to feed the distinctive black-headed geese that terrorise the town, a gentle trip on the lake in a rowing boat.

By the time her trip is over, they are both smitten. Conducting a long-distance romance in the eighties is not a straightforward task. They both write letters to each other every week. If Matty knew that she would keep every one of them over the next three years, he would be mortified. His love letter writing skills are not something he wants shared with his two best mates.

He tries to phone Christina as often as he can. There he is on the rain-swept promenade in Morecambe, the wind howling its annoyance, making it hard to hear. He fires fifty-pence pieces into a filthy phone box at an alarming rate, just to be able to speak with her for a few minutes at her home in Calabria. He doesn't even know where Calabria is.

However, he is now on the way over to meet her again, this time in Rome. He has caught a flight from Liverpool to Rome with Alitalia. Christina has managed to borrow a friend's studio apartment for the week, near the Jewish Quarter.

He has never flown in his life; in fact, he has never been to another country. He looks out of the window in awe as they cross the snow-topped Alps. As the plane starts its turbulent descent, he looks out at the hills of Lazio, nervously excited.

She is waiting for him in the baggage hall, and they run into each other's arms. Inexplicably, it is the big Northern lad that bursts into tears when he grabs her. Christina finds it very cute but doesn't know whether she should cry or laugh. His gentle, low, broken sound is muffled in her shoulder.

They spend a long time in bed, getting to know each other properly, often not heading off sightseeing until late in the afternoon.

When they do, he is blown away by Rome, the sights and the sounds, the carnival of life. It is a living museum. She takes him to the Colosseum, the Roman Forum and Piazza Navona. They walk everywhere, determined not to miss anything, drinking in every drop of the Eternal City elixir, almost drowning in it.

He falls in love with the Trevi Fountain, marvelling at the craftsmanship that created such a timeless monument. Always busy, but somehow carrying an air of hope. Of course, they oblige by throwing coins into the fountain.

'What did you wish for, my darling?' says Matty.

'Oh no, that would be bad luck! I will keep it to myself, thank you very much.'

He loves just watching Christina full of life in her own country. If she slows down her speech, he can sometimes understand it, but when it is at a hundred miles an hour, with her hands flailing like windmills, it is impossible. He wonders whether an Italian can speak if you tie their hands behind their back.

It takes him a while to realise that she isn't having a full-blown argument with a waiter; they are only having a casual conversation about what is on the menu.

She takes him to little corners of Rome to find the places where the locals eat, rather than the tourist traps near the beauty spots. She orders for him, not telling him what he is getting, and then watches his delight as he tries new flavours.

They hold hands as they walk through the cobbled streets.

Matty loves her vivid personality. On the one hand, she comes across as a sweet, beautiful young girl, but the fiery Italian temperament is always lurking close to the surface. He senses that learning to manage the explosions will test him.

Only on one occasion in Rome does he see her get angry. A drunk man stumbles past her and says, 'Go home, *terroni*.' Christina goes crazy and starts to shout at him, aiming a couple of blows. Matty has to stop her, and only later does she explain the word to him. *Terroni* translates as the southern peasants that work the land.

The North looks down on the South. Christina is not someone to take a slur lying down. She mumbles something about being careful because Mount Etna is thought to be a woman who bubbles slowly before erupting violently.

Matty realises he has a lot to learn about Italian culture.

As the clock continues its inevitable progress, they both realise that their time is coming to an end. Neither of them says anything, but the hours ahead are going to be sad, as they will need to say goodbye.

They are seated outdoors at a small café beside the Pantheon, having a gelato and a coffee.

'Matthew, thank you for a perfect week.'

'No, it was you that sorted it all. Rome has been mind-blowing.'

'I am glad we came here, rather than to Catanzaro. That would have been stifling. Everyone in the village would have wanted to come out to see you, to poke at you like an exhibit in a zoo. It would have been horrible.'

'Well, maybe the next time. I want to be with you, so I am ready to face them.'

'You know, I need to get out of Calabria. It is not a happy place for me.'

'Tell me, what is it that you worry about?'

'You will love the place; it is very beautiful. You will love Mamma and Papa, and their villa. It's just that it is a painfully old-fashioned place. There is no hope for me. Girls are not encouraged to be successful; it is a boy's world, I am afraid. I don't want to be stuck in the family office. My brother has already inherited the business, and when my parents die, he will own the villa. It only passes to the male heir in the family.'

'Oh, that's not fair.'

'It has been like that since medieval times. You won't change it anytime soon.

'My brother is very ambitious. I've been told that he is starting to hang out with some very bad people. He is not only ambitious but also greedy and narcissistic, which is a potent combination.

'I love my family. I believe that I will always be loyal to them. I just want to get out, or I will suffocate,' continues Christina.

The two of them are lost in thought, watching people passing by. The tour guide with a red flag gently shepherds her group along, the clown entertains the children, the young lovers walk hand in hand, lost in each other. The street vendors seamlessly switch from selling sunglasses to umbrellas, depending on the weather. The pickpockets lurk, preying on the vulnerable.

'But do not worry, Matthew, as I know the answer.'

'Ok, tell me.'

'When we get married, we will set up home in England,' says Christina, smiling.

And so, it is settled: no lengthy process, no going down on bended knee, just romantic Rome doing its stuff.

CHAPTER FOUR

2022

Stephen is transferred by car, during the day, down to the Northeast of England. There needs to be a cloak of anonymity, so the meeting is held at the Ramside Hotel in Durham. It is booked under the name of the Northeast Fertiliser Association. The room is upstairs in the older part of the hotel, up the wooden central staircase, with important industrialists of the past smiling down from their portraits.

The meeting room is functional, with a projector and screen for meetings, tea and coffee, and a nice view out over the gardens.

The two members of the National Crime Agency who collected him from Glasgow are present, dressed in smart jeans and polo shirts. Brogan Reilly and Phil Simpson have worked in their roles as Customer Liaison Officers for many years.

Phil is the older of the two and still looks after himself, carrying his gym body well. He appears very laid back. Brogan has short blonde hair and wears small black glasses. It is she who has an air of menace about her. Normally, their role is at the front end of the process. It's about identity creation and placement, making sure that their customers simply disappear from the eyes of their protagonists.

Occasionally, such as today, they are brought together when identity has been compromised. Brogan doesn't like that because it means somebody has screwed up. She is the ambitious one of the two and takes this personally. People are not supposed to be identified on her watch.

'Good morning. Now, do you want to be known as Johnny Rodgers or Stephen Whyte?' says Phil.

'Listen, it's a shit morning. I woke up yesterday with my beautiful family, and then I was abducted by you lot, and nobody is telling me a damn thing. I have taken more than ten years to get used to being Stephen Whyte, so you better call me Stephen.'

'Ok, Stephen it is. Can I get you a coffee perhaps?' asks Phil. 'And abducted is a little bit over the top.'

'Whatever . . . Listen, I need to call my wife. Lisa will be mad with worry. I need her to know everything is ok.'

'Don't worry about that,' says Brogan, 'and for peace of mind, the local police are keeping a discreet watch on your house.'

'Oh, just great – now I should be worrying about something happening to them as well. When are you going to tell me what this is all about?'

'Give us five minutes; we have somebody else that is going to join us.'

The phone at the side of the meeting room interrupts them, ringing loudly. It is one of their police colleagues to inform them that their other guest has arrived and is on the way up. The door of the meeting room opens and the diminutive and very shabby Tony Fowler shuffles into the room like a condemned man unsure what his fate is going to be.

'Fuck me, it's Tony the Snip,' says Stephen. 'I haven't seen you in more than ten years, you little fucker.'

'Well, if it isn't Johnny Cash,' says Tony, genuinely smiling because he knows someone in the room. 'The best laundry man I ever worked with. Making dirty money as clean as whistle.'

'Thanks for the praise, but that life is well behind me, and my name is now Stephen Whyte.'

'Ah, so you went for the change-of-name option. Witness protection schemes are just a kind of grown-up version of hide and seek, you know. At some point, the game comes to an end.'

'At the beginning, it was odd, but as the years have gone by, I have become more used to my new identity.'

'Just as well we don't live in America. There they go all in on facial surgery. Although maybe I could have got my nose fixed. They tried to get me to change my name, too, but I couldn't be arsed. I messed about using Anthony, but nobody has ever called me that, apart from my old mum, whenever I did something wrong.'

'You were still the quickest thief that we ever had. The way you could boost lorries in seconds was some skill. And you have not changed one bit. You are still a skinny little runt and as unfashionable as ever. Does anyone still wear Wrangler jeans?'

'Well, thanks. But you, my friend, have been letting things go. Look at the state of you! At least a couple of stone heavier, and your hair is growing grey. Too much of the good life, methinks.'

'Great, just what I need, a lecture from my long-lost Irish friend.'

The Crime Agency team has retreated from the room to discuss the next steps. They are awaiting further instructions by phone from head office.

'Looks like it might take a couple of days for the Manchester team to work up a plan for what they are going to do to investigate,' says Phil.

'Ok, we can live with that,' says Brogan.

'They are watching the Manchester nightclubs carefully but have asked us not to stir up any shit right now.'

'Well, as long as they don't sit on their hands; the longer this takes, the more risk there is.'

'I think the right call is to place them somewhere safe,' says Phil.

'I also think these boys will know more about the reasons behind this. In our line of work, I always presume guilt over innocence.'

'You never trust anyone, do you?'

'Nope.'

Meanwhile, the boys help themselves to more coffee. Stephen gazes ruefully at the digestive biscuits mocking him quietly, whereas Tony wolfs down four in one go.

'So, where did you end up, anyway? I think I can detect a bit of a Scottish accent there that you didn't have before,' says Tony.

'Well, I now live in Glasgow. I'm married to Lisa, with two adorable kids. I still work in finance, just a bit more legitimate, with a proper accountancy firm. To be honest, I thought all this was behind me.'

'I always knew you were good with numbers. I used to tell Matty you were the bright one in the team.'

'So, how has the last decade treated you?' asks Stephen. 'Because I have to say, this Irish Geordie accent is hilarious.'

'Well, you know, a bit of this and a bit of that. I've lived in Gateshead most of the time, mostly stealing stuff from warehouses, sometimes a few cars, nothing big time. I try to fly under the radar.'

'Well, at least it's what you know best.'

'See, to be honest, I think I need a change of career. I should have stuck in at school. The game is getting harder and harder. You approach a house in the middle of the night, and the bloody app goes off and some bloke is shouting "Fuck off or you're getting it!"'

'Try and hot wire a car these days and see where that gets you. Open the bonnet and there are no wires; it's all sealed up and loaded with software,' the rant continues.

'Just try and boost a fucking Tesla. That Elon Musk has made that a complete no-go. Even if I could get inside, I would be sitting in the driveway for hours trying to figure out how to work the computer, let alone start it. Even if I did, the bastard would be tracking me all the way from his gaff in California.'

'We have a Tesla,' says Stephen politely. 'My wife is trying to save the world.'

'Load of shite. All these people drive electric cars, yet we still burn gas to produce the electricity.'

'Are there many Tesla's in Gateshead?'

'Nope, but I fish in the posh suburbs. I never steal from my own people. I don't shit in me own back garden.'

'Of course; very noble of you.'

'No, if you remember, it was what Matty always taught us: never steal from poor people or people who are not insured.'

'Yes, the big man was always very virtuous in his own mind. Not quite so when it came to us.'

'So, I think I want to get out of physical stealing and maybe move on to internet theft,' says Tony. 'Only problem is I don't know how to work on a computer, so I might enrol at college.'

'Great idea. Maybe the witness protection people can sponsor you, give you a bursary,' says Stephen. 'You should ask Brogan.'

The meeting room door opens and Phil and Brogan stride into the room, beckoning the boys to sit back down at the table.

'So, now that you two have been reacquainted, shall we begin?' says Brogan, clearly in charge.

'As you both know, in 2010 you both gave evidence in a trial against Matthew O'Hare and his two colleagues, relating to numerous crimes including theft, extortion and money laundering. Matthew was convicted at Manchester Crown Court and was given a 15-year jail sentence. He was released in March 2020 for good behaviour.

'At the same time, you were given leniency for your involvement with this syndicate, and it was decided that you would be given support from our office to establish a new identity. At that time, there was a fear that you would be at risk through some form of retribution. Over time, that proved not to be the case, and Matty and his team have shown no desire to follow up. As a result, we have broadly scaled back our operation to the bare minimum, just occasionally checking in on you. For us, this was a successful outcome.

'However, we have recently received very credible information that your participation in this has not been forgotten. We have two separate sources who have advised us that due to a security leak, you are both at risk of serious harm.'

'Hold on a minute,' interrupts Stephen. 'How can there be a breach?'

'Well, back in 2010, when we were regionalised, records were not shared on a central database,' replies Phil. 'After 2013, everything was amalgamated onto a central database, which is much more efficient but is probably not as secure. The data is available on shared drives across the network. We are currently running an investigation as to who has been able to access the data.'

'See, I told you this bloody internet is going to spoil everything!' says Tony.

'We believe that a Manchester-based crime family have declared you both as targets, with a substantial amount of cash on delivery. We can't understand it because there is no link between Matty and this team in Manchester,' says Brogan.

'However, as a result of this, we are serving you with an Osman warning, which is done only when we have intelligence to suggest that there is a real and immediate threat to life. You are not forced to obey the warning, but it ensures that we have done all in our power to protect you.'

'Bet you it's more about protecting yourselves from a lawsuit if it goes wrong,' says Stephen, cynically.

'We simply just don't understand the level of threat that this implies. The serious crime team has determined that, as a precaution, we need to remove you both and hide you somewhere more secure. Hopefully, this is just a short-term thing, it will blow over and we can all go back to normal,' says Brogan.

She steps out of the room to take a phone call, leaving the boys alone with Phil.

'Boys, listen, I know that Brogan can come across very formal, but this is all going to be fine. I have seen this countless times before.'

'How come she is so abrupt and sarcastic, then?' says Tony.

'Well, the difference between her and me is that she is a career cop. She has loads of ambition but will play it very straight, always following the playbook, whereas I am quite content with what I do, not really driven by promotion.'

Brogan returns, shooting Phil a dark look, as she knows full well that the minute she turns her back, he reverts to matey mode with the clients.

'We are going to allow you to make one call to your loved ones by either phone or Zoom, but then we need you to surrender your phones to avoid the risk of mobile phone tracking,' says Brogan.

* * *

Stephen sent an invite to Lisa fifteen minutes earlier, and now he fires up the Zoom app on the police iPad and connects to his wife.

'Hi babes, it's me.'

'Stephen, please tell me what the *fuck* is going on,' says Lisa. 'I've had the worst day ever, worrying about this.'

'I know, I know . . . but I am fine.'

'But where the hell are you?'

'Look, I am not supposed to tell you, but I am near Durham, in the North East of England.'

'Ok, so you have a sudden meeting that you must run off to without telling me what's up. It completely messed up my day. I couldn't sleep a wink last night, and I feel a wreck.'

'How are the kids?'

'Fine. They are just back from hockey and rugby practice. Grandad picked them up . . . again.'

'I thought he didn't do private schools.'

'I think he realised how worried I was, and for the first time, he never mentioned it. In fact, he's here, and he wants a word.'

'Look, as much as I love the Knightswood Bowling Club, a conversation with your old man is not top priority right now.'

'I tell you what top priority is – giving me a fucking explanation!' screams Lisa.

Stephen pauses for a second, realising that he is about to deliver the truth and it will go off like a bomb. Normally, if you have led a serious lie for ten years, especially to your wife, the mother of your two children, and have an amazing future ahead of you, then Zoom might not be the best choice of platform for such a revelation.

On the other hand, it is perhaps good fortune that he is a couple of hundred miles away. Because this is not going to end well.

'So, my name is not Stephen Whyte,' says Stephen, dropping the bombshell. 'Well, it is it's just that it never used to be.'

'*What the fuck!* I don't understand,' says Lisa, now running at Defcon Five on the stress level counter.

'My birth name is Johnny Rodgers. I was born in London in 1978. I have two parents that I have not seen for over 15 years. I don't have any siblings. I worked as an accountant for a bloke who went to prison for 10 years. I was involved in his downfall, so then I had to enter a witness protection scheme, which provided me with an entirely new identity as Stephen Whyte.'

The gap between the exhalation of air and the scream is officially timed at 3 seconds. Although he is on his own, he is pretty sure the whole hotel will have heard the on-line scream. A piercing howl, followed by deep sobbing, Lisa struggling to bring it under control.

'Are you fucking kidding? We met ten years ago; you are Stephen Whyte. We are married with two children, and now you decide to tell me that you are not a Stephen, you are a Johnny. Is this some kind of sick joke or just a nightmare?'

'I know, I know, this is not how I wanted you to find out. I was planning to tell you eventually.'

'Of course. Maybe you were planning a bloody identity reveal party.'

'No, I just thought everything was in the past and we didn't need to confront this. The last ten years have been the happiest of my life. Please forgive me. I will explain it all properly.'

Thankfully, Zoom does its thing, and the call is interrupted by the arrival of the children, children effortlessly adapting to technology without a second thought. They give Stephen time to regroup.

'Daddy!' squeals Emily.

'Hey, little one, how was school?'

'It was super. We have started to learn French. And I have a new best friend called Harper, and we are learning to do cartwheels.'

'Great stuff,' says Stephen. 'Is Cameron there?'

'Yep, he is on the PlayStation as usual, but I will go and get him.'

'I don't know what kind of deep shitstorm you are in, but don't you dare tell the kids; they are far too young to deal with this,' whispers Lisa.

'Hey, Dad, what's up?' says Cameron.

'Well, just maybe to say hello.'

'Well, hello, but if you don't mind, I am right in the middle of a PlayStation game with a boy from Shanghai, and with the time difference, it's close to midnight over there.'

Lisa is back on, and Stephen can see the tears forming in her eyes.

'You have misled me every day for ten years. How can I possibly trust you again?'

'Let me prove it to you.'

'So, what happens next?'

'Me and Tony need to move to a safe house for a week or so.'

'Wait, it's not just you?'

'No, looks like I will be spending time on the road with Tony, lovely fella, appalling dress –'

'Listen, I am really sorry, but Dad wants that word.'

Davy appears on the scene, somewhat haphazardly, so that Stephen can see only half a head.

'I don't get this technology stuff, but I need to speak to you, son. What on earth have you done to my wee lassie?'

'Hi Dad . . . sorry, Dad.'

'No need for sorry; that's a waste of words. We need answers.'

'It's not easy to explain over the internet.'

'You know that I can help you with this sort of stuff –'

'Listen, I appreciate the offer, but I'm not sure you can help me with this.'

'Son, you really don't know me that well, do you?'

'Sorry, Dad, I don't have time for this right now. Can you put Lisa back on, please?'

'So, do I need to cancel your 40th, and what should we do about Florida?' says Lisa.

'Look, give me a week and I will get back in touch.'

* * *

Loners don't have the need to make video calls; no one really cares what they get up to.

However, Tony decides he will hand over only one of his mobile phones to the police. He thinks it might be better to have another phone up his sleeve. It might give him an edge. The movies like to call it a 'burner' phone, but he isn't sure why.

He does need to attend to a little local business before he sets off, so he phones the landline of the Gateshead Social Club.

'Bill, it's me, Tony.'

'Well, well, I though the bizzies had put you in the clink for thieving.'

'Nah, it's alright mate, but I might need to disappear for a week or so. Any chance you could do me a favour?'

'Ok, what do you want?' asks Bill with a groan.

'Well, can you go round to my flat? You will find a key box on the wall. The code is 1234.'

'Very original.'

'Can you feed me cat for me? He doesn't like tinned cat food; he only eats cooked chicken, or tuna, in spring water, not olive oil.'

'Jesus, it's a fecking cat.'

'And I think I need some cash. So go into the bedroom and open the drawer beside the bed. You will find twenty Apple AirPods. I think you can get £1500 for them. If you sell them for me, then take a couple of hundred as commission, and I will be in touch to collect the rest.'

'I won't ask where you got them from,' says Bill. 'Listen, is everything all right?'

'Yeah, it's all fine. I thought they were going to lift me for something serious, but it's just something from years ago. Going to take myself a little holiday, have some fun for once.'

CHAPTER FIVE

1991

The intoxicating scent of jasmine and bougainvillaea lingers seductively in the warmth of a late summer's day in the Villa de Luca in a little village outside Catanzaro. The town is known as the City of Two Seas and is the ancient capital of Calabria, the foot of Italy, the metatarsal to be precise. The villa has the most exquisite location at the foot of the village, gently set amongst the olive and orange groves. The evening light bathes the scene in a cloak of sepia.

Christina knew from a very early age that she would be married at the Immaculate Church of Badolato, with its steep steps and stunning vistas. In her early dreams, it had been to a handsome Italian prince, but the reality is that a big, strapping lad from Lancashire came along and swept her off her feet. She is radiant on her big day.

The summer warmth is enough to allow the wedding reception to take place outside in the courtyard of the family villa.

She had chosen to be married on a Sunday, traditionally seen as being the luckiest day to get wed. The service earlier that day was both romantic and beautiful. The marriage mass was celebrated in front of family and friends, with Father Contardo Agostino presiding. He has been the family's priest for years. He baptised her as a little girl, and she knows him fondly as Father Conte.

Her bespoke designer wedding dress is made of white silk and velvet. The history of the town of Catanzaro is heavily connected to the silk trade, so it is only appropriate that silk forms such an important part of the dress. The tradition is that the length of the veil reflects the number of years that the couple have been engaged. One metre for each year, so it is three metres long.

Her engagement ring is a blue Ceylon Sapphire, surrounding by a cluster of eighteen diamonds, sparkling in the sun.

Of course, it helps that her brother Bruno de Luca owns several fashion distributors across Southern Italy. He is playing the role of host today, accompanied by his wife Maria and their little girls Sofia and Aurelia.

From the UK, a small party has made their way over, including Matty's mother and father and both of his sisters and their partners. His youngest brother is not there as is currently at sea with the Merchant Navy.

Of course, his two best friends, Hammy and Benny, are attending as well.

Christina's bridesmaid is her close friend, Carolina Romano, wearing a pale blue dress. She chose her brother Bruno's children to be her flower girl and ring bearer. Both, of course, steal the show, as children are the only ones who can outshine a bride at her wedding.

Traditionally, at a wedding, the guests are asked who they are with, the bride or the groom. The task is made easier today: the bride's guests are all wearing sunglasses, and the groom's guests are sweating profusely.

The wedding dinner is a sumptuous affair. The primo course is mushroom and truffle ravioli, silky in texture. The secondi, locally caught octopus, char-grilled on the wood-fired barbeque. The main course is rabbit cooked slowly in red wine. To finish, there is tiramisu, or 'pick-me-up' in Italian. It is all washed down with smooth local wine provided by a local vineyard as a gift to Christina and her family.

'My love, this is the happiest day of my life,' says Christina.

'It's been amazing. I'm a lucky boy that someone as beautiful as you happened to be in Preston that night. The gods were looking after me!'

'No, Matty, it's me that is the lucky one.'

'The food has been outstanding. I cannot believe that your mamma organised all of this.'

'She loves it – she was born to feed!'

'The English boys are getting very pissed now. I don't think they realise how strong that red wine is.'

'Leave them – it is traditional to drink so much you fall over drunk at a wedding and fall asleep. Let them sleep it off underneath a tree and get up and start all over again.'

'And the best man is getting very leery with the bridesmaid. He keeps on feeling her arse.'

'Believe me, if Carolina was unhappy, she would have smacked him by now.'

Matty glances over at their parents, sitting in the shade drinking champagne, along with Father Conte. Both couples look elegant, with dark blue suits for the men, and dark blue evening gowns for the ladies.

'It's been perfect, and our families are getting on so well,' says Matty, 'despite challenges with language.'

'The language of parenthood knows no borders, my love,' says Christina with a smile.

'That generation has seen so much; they are so strong. I hope we make it that long.'

'I think the secret is that given everything they have lived through, they are just happy to be alive.'

'Although I wonder what that lot are up to?' says Matty, looking over at Hammy and Benny, who are in deep conversation with Bruno and a couple of his friends. They are all dressed in black, sipping champagne and smoking cigarettes. It looks straight off the set of a gangster movie.

'No business please, on my wedding day.'

Having exchanged wedding rings or *fede* at the church, there are still a couple of Calabrian traditions to be followed. Christina and the flower girls go round all the guests with bomboniere, small gifts of sugared almonds and ribbons.

At the same time, Bruno comes up and puts his arm around Matty's shoulders.

'Well, brother-in-law, not many outsiders come and take one of our women away.'

'I am not taking her away; it is her choice.'

'I am only messing. You will be a beautiful couple, although it will be interesting to see who the boss is.'

'I don't know what you mean.'

'My sister is very good at crafting the image of the nice girl next door. But never forget she is Calabrian: she is stubborn as hell and will expect to get her own way. She has probably fed you a line about wanting to get away. My sister is very ambitious, so you better be ready.'

Matty watches his back as he departs, keeping his thoughts to himself. He has noted the warning signals for another day.

The couple are given a glass vase, which they break; the number of fragments indicates how many years the marriage will last. The omens are favourable as it shatters into hundreds of pieces, giving Christina a happy glow. At the same time, they are showered in rice, which is thrown as a sign of fertility.

It is an unforgettable evening in the hills of Calabria; the children laugh and play, the adults drink and tell stories. Gentle, soulful tunes come from the wedding singer. Darkness arrives, but the courtyard is illuminated by strings of lights and hundreds of candles. Garlands of red chillies hang from the trees to scare away any evil spirits. Every step is taken to ensure happiness for the young couple.

'Bueno sera, ladies and gentlemen,' announces Bruno, grandly clinking his glass with a silver spoon.

'Many of you will not know that the dialect of Calabria is a form of Italian that is heavily influenced by ancient Greece. If I were to speak in my own tongue, it would probably be all Greek to you. So, I will speak in English so that all our guests can understand me. Although, having listened to my new friend, Mr D'Arcy, speaking in his native tongue, I am not confident that I know English as well as I should.

'My father is a very quiet and shy man; he doesn't do a lot of talking. He has asked me to say a few words on behalf of the family.

'Firstly, we welcome you all to the Villa de Luca, home to our family for more than a hundred years, and four generations.

'Secondly, to Father Conte, you were the perfect person to lead the celebration. It wouldn't have been the same without you.

'And of course, to my little sister, Christi, I have to say that I have never seen you look so beautiful in all my life.

'To Matthew, on this very special day, we invite you to be part of our family. I see this as a great collaboration between Calabria and Lancashire, but if it's ok with you, let's leave the food and drink to the Italians.

'I place great faith in you, entrusting my sister's future happiness to you. I am sure that you won't let us down.

'So, ladies and gentlemen, please raise your glasses to Matthew and Christina. May your life be like good wine.'

Then it was time for the groom to reply.

'*A nome di me e mia moglie* (on behalf of my wife and I),' Matty starts in broken Italian, bringing the house down with a deafening cheer.

'I am trying to learn to speak Italian, but so far, Christina has really only taught me the swear words.

'Anyway, I stand before you as the luckiest man in the world. I get to marry the most beautiful, clever and caring person I've ever known. I knew the moment we met that I wanted to spend my life with you.

'Although, given that I am marrying an Italian woman, I was wondering if someone could give me an instruction manual. That would be very helpful.

'When a marriage takes place, it sees two families come together. When I look over at both sets of parents tonight, I see so much in common. I want to thank all of them for bringing us both up to be the people that we are today. Without them, this wedding could not take place. Although, I have to say, having an Italian mother-in-law is another very scary prospect.'

Which prompts Mamma to smile and raise her fist in mock anger.

'Christina wants to set up home with me in Morecambe. I have to say that I think she is mad. She is giving up the Mediterranean climate of Southern Italy for the drizzle of the estuary, the homemade pasta for the gammon and chips, and this beautiful red wine for a pint of bitter.

'To Bruno, I give you my word that I will look after Christina.

'To Christina, I might come from a humble background, but I am determined to build a strong business to provide for us, and hopefully, we can bring some children into this world too.'

This is met with extreme enthusiasm from the crowd, along with the inevitable dirty jokes in both Italian and English.

'So, friends and family, I have two toasts that I would like to make.

'To all of you here tonight, the toast is *La famiglia prima di tutto*.

'To Christina, *La donna piu bella*, in the whole of Calabria,' says Matty with a flourish, before giving her a lingering kiss to the applause of all the guests.

Next up to say a few words is Hammy, normally a man of very few words. You can tell he is not looking forward to this, as his forehead glistens in the evening glow.

'Well, well, the bold boy is a bit of a smoothie, isn't he? I have never spoken in public, so I've been dreading this for weeks. Once it's out the way, I'm getting pissed.

'I was there when Matty and Christina first crossed paths, at the legendary Bliss Nightclub in Preston. Even back then, you could tell the boy was completely smitten. He might look like a big old lad, but inside he is just a big softie.

'Anyway, Matty, having listened to your new brother-in-law speak, the Calabrian mob look like they will be keeping a very close eye on you.'

Feeling emboldened now that he has got the speech up and running, Hammy thinks he might get away with injecting a couple of jokes.

'So, an Italian man with spells of amnesia goes into a bar. The barman asks him what he wants, and he replies, "Affogato."'

The joke is met by complete silence. Undeterred, he chooses to press on.

'Did you hear about the old Italian man?' he says. 'He pasta away.'

'Shocking!' shouts Benny. 'Get him off. Boo!'

Recognising that he might just be losing his audience, Hammy decides to bring it to a close. 'To the De Luca family, I would like to thank you for your hospitality. The setting here is beautiful. Quite why Christina is giving this up is beyond me.

'So please be upstanding and join me in a toast to the bride and groom.'

The band announces that it is time for a traditional dance and invites the bride and groom and all the guests to come onto the dance floor.

'My love, I have two left feet! I can't dance.'

'Don't worry, I will get you through this. It's called the tarantella. Think of "That's Amore". The guests will hold hands and surround us, moving clockwise and anti-clockwise. We just need to look beautiful.'

'Ok, you can do beautiful.'

'But be careful, as it gets boisterous. As the tempo of the tune increases, so does the speed, and it gets quite rough. Your job is to defend me from them all.'

'Now I'm built for that dance,' shouts Matty.

It is danced as a way of wishing the future couple good luck in their future together. Given the amount of wine that has been consumed and the need for the Italians and the English to show who has the most testosterone, this one is not for the faint-hearted, and there are at least a couple of sprained ankles.

Afterwards, having a quiet moment together sitting back at the top table, the happy couple hold hands, looking radiant.

'Darling, can I ask you something?' says Matty.

'Of course. What is it?'

'Thinking about what Hammy said, are you sure you want to give this all up, be away from your family and live in England? If you want, we could live in Italy.'

'Matthew, it is exactly what I want. I want a fresh start. You English come to Italy on holiday and get seduced by the romanticism of it all, but you don't see the other side: poverty, inequality, the way men treat women. There is a dark side to my brother that I want to distance myself from.'

CHAPTER SIX

2022

Following a conference call between the Northumberland Police Force and the Scottish Police Force, it is decided that Stephen and Tony will spend the night at the Ramside Hotel before relocating to a safe house in Edinburgh in the morning.

They decide to have dinner at the legendary carvery within the hotel. Stephen, who is privately smarting over Tony's jibe about his weight, has resolved to stay with a salad and the cold buffet.

Tony, however, is one of those guys blessed with a rampant metabolism; he looks malnourished all the time, but in fact he is a bottomless pit. He comes back with a plate brimming with roast pork, roast beef, steak pie, potatoes, and cauliflower cheese, all smothered in gravy. He has a side portion of chilli con carne (why not, just in case).

Phil and Brogan are remaining with the boys overnight, but they adjourn to a booth and are clearly talking shop, as their laptops are out as if they are playing a game of battleships. The light outside is dwindling, the shadows on the golf course lengthening.

'So, tell me how a nice boy like you ended up getting involved in all of this,' says Tony.

'You know, I ask myself the same question all the time,' says Stephen. 'I grew up in London. Mum and Dad didn't really manage to hold proper jobs down, so they didn't have a lot. When I wanted to go to Manchester University to study, I knew I would have to fund it myself. It was tough. The government had taken away the grants and not yet properly replaced them with student loans. I ended up with horrible debt, owed to some proper nasty people.'

'And here is me thinking you were the man when it came to managing money,' says Tony. 'I always thought of you as the consigliere, like in the *Godfather* movies.'

'Other people's money, not my own. So along comes Matty. I was introduced to him one night, and he offered to sort out all my debts in return for taking on some accountancy work for him. He told me he wanted to spread his empire beyond the haulage business. So, my job was to set up a whole series of new businesses. We bought pubs, tanning salons, car washes, and he started to buy property.'

'And everything paid for in cash, I suppose,' says Tony.

'Of course. Cash was king. Back then, the banks didn't care where the money came from. It wasn't regulated the way it is today. You could take it in black bin bags, and they would accept the deposit without asking any questions. My job was to set up complex structures so that we could move cash around the businesses however we wanted. I used to shit myself carrying around twenty grand in cash in the boot of my car.'

'I never really knew the whole picture. I just kind of put my head down and did what was asked of me,' says Tony.

'We were turning over a hundred grand a week at one point. I ended up getting pretty good at what I did. It sounds complicated, but it was really very easy.'

'Also, Matty was fun to work for; he had such charisma,' says Tony.

'He had both sides to his personality, though. He could be a scary big guy. He once took me with him to visit two guys who hadn't paid for a consignment of televisions. I swear to God, he beat them both to within an inch of their lives. I think he took me along to give me a lesson about the life that he leads.'

Having wolfed down his first pass at the buffet, Tony is back for a second run. He returns with a plate of chips covered in curry sauce.

Stephen's eyebrow lifts slightly when he sees his new friend's latest plate. 'I don't want to be mean, but I am not changing your nappy in the morning,' he jokes.

'Anyway, how did you end up in the Matty O'Hare empire?' asks Stephen.

'Well, I had to get out of Dublin sharpish. I had been shagging the daughter of some heavy, who decided that he wanted my head.

'You see, I left school with nothing; all I have ever been good at was stealing to order. It was Benny D'Arcy that introduced me to Matty and Hammy. I stole a couple of trucks for them outside Liverpool. It was how they started the haulage business.

'To be honest, having spent my life floating about, it was the first time that I ever felt part of a family.

'Of course, the haulage business was never going to provide the cash that would satisfy their ambitions. Especially with Christina spending it at a rate of knots.'

Stephen visits the bar to get them a couple of pints of Guinness, accompanied by a cold stare from Brogan. On his return, he notes that

Tony must have squeezed in another visit, as he is now tucking into a steamed treacle pudding with custard.

'The game was quite simple, really,' says Tony. 'We boosted trucks up and down the motorway network of the North West. We preferred to stay away from the service stations and find those trucks that were parked up in lay-bys. There was much less risk of being disturbed.

'It was always a great result if any of the drivers went to visit one of their many girlfriends for a shag, or they went to the pub. That way, we could avoid any violence. If it was needed, then it was Benny D'Arcy's job to take care of it.

'Most of the time, we just moved the goods onto our trucks, but a couple of times we just unhooked the whole trailer and took it back to base, nice and simple.

'The trick was to be good at targeting a mark to boost. We didn't want perishables like food or flowers; we avoided booze because that brought the duty police out. We wanted stuff that we could sell easily, electronics, things like Gameboys and Walkmans, or designer clothes.'

'Yes, you got to hand it to Matty, he was good at spotting a trend,' says Stephen.

'Yep, he was clever. He always told us to steal from companies, which had insurance. The pencil pushers wouldn't come after you the way someone with a vested interest would. Also don't ever steal from other criminals; that would be bad for business. Finally, stay away from Liverpool and Manchester; they used guns. He didn't like them at all. Stay low under the radar and go about your business quietly.

'Matty built up a huge network of local contacts. In return for lots of small bribes, he had a group of people who could accurately tip him off over the location of goods.'

'Yes, I could explain away most of the cash, but there was always a significant amount of outgoings that I could never balance,' says Stephen.

'And then, of course, Hammy's job in this little gang was to move the goods that we stole – sometimes individually through the pubs and sometimes as a job lot. We used to send a lot of stuff in boats over to Ireland.'

'Ah, both a primary and secondary distribution model,' says Stephen.

'Fuck knows what that means . . . But all in all, simple, you see. I stole it, they moved it, you washed the cash, and Christina spent it.'

After they have enjoyed dinner in reasonable peace and quiet, the restaurant suddenly bursts into life. The carvery has suddenly filled up with two coach parties of older customers, all now plundering the buffet with aggressive intent. When it was inclusive, you made the most of it.

This bothers Phil and Brogan a little, as it was easy for them to keep an eye on the boys when it was quiet. Not that they were fearing an attack from the blue rinse brigade; it would just be easier if they were tucked up in their rooms for the night.

'OK, love birds. On the basis you have had enough to eat,' Brogan says, staring at Tony, 'I think it's about time you boys head off to bed. A car will pick us up at eight am tomorrow, and we will head up to Edinburgh. Don't be late.'

As they head along the corridor to the new wing of the hotel, Tony turns to Stephen and says,

'Although neither of us have said why we chose to turn on them.'

CHAPTER SEVEN

1992

The home of Matty O'Hare Transportation, 'A Family Business, since 1990', is in the coastal town of Heysham overlooking Morecambe Bay, the vast swathe of water and sand on the north-west corner of England. It is a nondescript port town with a regular ferry crossing to Ireland, ideal if you like moving goods back and forward across the Irish Sea and keeping yourself to yourself.

It is a one-road-in and one-road-out type of town, perfectly fitting the bill for their needs.

The depot itself is located at the end of a dusty road in a small industrial unit. It consists of a modest administrative building at the front, behind which are the loading bays for the company's fleet of fourteen trucks.

At the rear is a storage facility. The front half is used to store the legitimate goods that it moves, with the back half hidden behind a false façade. This is invariably where the goods that have been boosted are brought so that Hammy and his team can evaluate how to liquidate them in the most efficient and profitable way.

The three boys gather in the large office that they share. Natural light floods into the room from the large window. Maggie, the PA to Matty, puts her head round the door.

'Do you wanna brew, lads?' She probably doesn't need to ask, as she knows the answer. She returns with Jaffa cakes and steaming tea in a hotchpotch of chipped mugs, stained brown, well used over the years.

'There you go, Mr D'Arcy,' says Maggie, with a little bow.

'Maggie, please, just make it Benny.'

She heads back out, leaving the boys in peace.

'You see, ever since everyone started harping on about that Mr D'Arcy in *Pride and Prejudice*, he has got very twitchy about his name. I think he would look good in riding breeches,' jokes Hammy. 'He might even get lucky for a change.'

'Shut your hole.'

The news plays quietly on the television in the corner. Nelson Mandela has finally been appointed as the first black president of South

Africa, Brazil has won the World Cup (again) and in America, OJ Simpson, suspected of the murder of his wife, has embarked on some crazy live chase from the cops.

'You in court today, or do you have a job interview?' asks Benny, noting the fact that Matty is dressed in an expensive, dark blue, Italian suit.

'Neither,' Matty replies. 'I am having lunch with the Lancaster Chamber of Commerce. I want to keep building my networks within the council as it will help us all in the long run.'

'Well, good to see that the Contessa is now in charge of your wardrobe,' says Benny.

'Hey lads, did you hear the news about the old Bliss Nightclub in Preston?' says Hammy.

'No,' in unison.

'Looks like they have lost their entertainment licence. Five kids were taken to hospital last week after taking ecstasy at the club. One of them was the niece of the local MP, so they are up shit creek.'

'We made the right call to get out of nightclubs. These pills are almost impossible to detect, and the people that make them don't give a fuck about what they do to you,' says Matty.

Firing a Jaffa cake across the room to both of his friends, Benny provides an update on his week ahead.

'We have a nice little one lined up for Thursday night. It's a small van, but it's going to be loaded with Play Stations headed for Scotland. We have already paid the driver off, so it's an easy lift. We are going to take him up in that lay-by beside the Carlisle Garden Centre. I will take Tony with me and a couple of others, and it will be a piece of cake.'

'Great, high in value, small in weight, just the way we like them,' says Matty. 'And you, Mr Hamilton, what are you working on?'

'Well, I tell you what: those Timberland boots went fast. Five hundred pairs and they all went in the blink of an eye. I reckon we'll turn easily twenty-five grand on that lot. In fact, if I had even more size nines, I could have sold more.'

'You see, boys, that is exactly what I have been telling you: we follow the trends. Don't just steal stuff randomly. When people get excited about missing out, they will pay even more for it.'

Matty goes over to the mirror to check his appearance and comb his hair. He has always had the physical looks, but now he is adding self-assurance to the mix, and it makes him look even more powerful, some might even say intimidating. Although the three have known each other for ever, it is very clear that Matty is the boss.

'I have some news as well, boys,' says Matty. 'I want us to buy a few pubs in and around Preston and Morecambe, so I have asked young Johnny to set up a sideline running pubs. I have told him to pick them very carefully. Stay away from the big brewers and the pub companies. Those bastards watch everything. They monitor your beer consumption and put in their own stocktakers, so that every pound is visible. We will stick to independent places, lease them out to some nice, unsuspecting couple, and then we can decide what the turnover of the pub might be.'

'Sounds bob on, and presumably we will get a free tab,' says Benny.

'No, you won't; we don't attract attention, remember. You pay your own way, you tightwad.

'Also, I have agreed to help Christina's family out. They have opened some opportunities to move their fashion products to England. They want to bring a weekly truck over from Italy and get us to distribute their clothing range across the UK,' says Matty.

'Wait a minute, are you really sure you want to jump into bed with Bruno de Marco?' asks Hammy.

'We are not going into a new partnership. I have just agreed to support my wife, that's all.'

'Yeah, but Matty, you always said that one of the golden rules is that we can all get to any of our businesses within the hour if something goes wrong,' says Hammy. 'Seem to remember it was "to think global but act local". It's a long old way to the mountains of Southern Italy.'

'Look, lads, we won't go the whole way; we will meet the delivery in Calais. This is the way forward. It's what the European Union is about, free movement of goods and people.'

'And golden rule number two, we don't carry out jobs in Manchester or Liverpool because there are some naughty fellas there, but hey, Calabria is fine. It's only the fucking mafia bandits we would be dealing with.'

'He is not the mafia, OK? This matter is closed. I have decided that we are doing it,' says Matty, visibly rattled that his friends have pushed back on him.

'Whatever happened to consultation? We always talk it through first.'

'Well, this time we won't. This is about family first, that's all.'

* * *

Later that evening, Matty drives home. For once, the stunning natural beauty of the coastline doesn't capture his attention. As he comes into town, he would normally look out and be pissed off at the lack of proper planning and investment in his hometown. It is a shadow of its former self, which often makes him angry.

But tonight, his mind wanders to the conversation with his best friends. He has known them both forever and he trusts his life with them. He knows that they mean no harm, and deep down he should be open to considering different perspectives. If you look at problems from different angles, you will get rounder decisions.

He knows that Christina has her doubts about them and their willingness to change and adapt to the world around them. They are comfortable in their little world, but he knows he is restless for more. He doesn't want to be known as a bouncer in a nightclub, or a thief who steals from trucks in the middle of the night. He doesn't want to be known as the big dog in Morecambe. He wants more than that.

He has ambitions, he wants respect from his community, he wants the recognition that he is a respected business leader. In time, he wants to play an active role in politics, regenerating the area. Matty wants to take his beautiful Italian wife to events across the North of England, and he wants people to look at the glamorous couple with awe. He wants Christina to be able to show her family back home that moving to England was the right choice.

Matty pulls into the driveway of his house on Happy Mount Court. This is fast becoming the most desirable address in Morecambe due to its spellbinding views over the eponymous bay. He watches a flock of birds trying to fight against the prevailing wind. It is good for his soul.

Since they moved in, the property has been extensively refurbished under Christina's guidance. It now has five bedrooms, three large bathrooms and a six-burner hob in the kitchen, imported from Italy, of course.

Matty takes a moment to reflect on how different this is from his own family upbringing. Six of them had lived in a two-bedroom semi-detached on the outskirts of Liverpool. Ma O'Hare had two electric hobs but still managed to feed the whole family wholesome food, the chip fan hissing with fat, creating an intoxicating aroma in the cramped kitchen.

He spent most of his childhood sharing a bedroom with his brother and one of his sisters. The elder sister slept downstairs in an alcove that doubled as a pantry during the day. Almost inconceivable now.

They only had one bathroom. When his da went for his inevitable Sunday night bath, which lasted for hours, he read his newspaper in the bath, the steam transferring the print to his hands. There was no lock on the door. The old fella had a flannel which he used to cover his dignity if anybody needed to use the loo.

The moment Matty opens the door, his senses are hit with the fragrance. Christina adores flowers and candles. She believes a house is empty of spirit without them. Today it is a mixture of chrysanthemums, lilies and jasmine. The table is set for dinner.

'*Mia caro,*' Christina says, as she kisses him on the cheek.

'Hey, sweetheart, how are you tonight?'

'*Tutti benne, tutti benne.*'

Christina has settled in well to life in England. She loves being by the sea and could never imagine not living beside it. She finds the people in town are welcoming, and she is not treated as an outsider. She loves her home and that Matty has allowed her to do whatever she wants to it.

Of course, she misses her Mamma and Papa and, of course, the warm Calabrian sunshine, but overall, she is happy with the life that she has chosen. Although she loves telling Matty about things that are better in Italy.

'You know what I miss about Calabria? It's shopping for food.'

'What have we done wrong now?'

'Everyone here goes to big supermarkets; everything is pre-packaged from across the world. Nothing is local. At home, I know the butcher and the baker,' she says. 'At home, we use everything. If we kill the pig, we eat it all. Here people don't like the ugly stuff.'

He knows he won't win, so he takes off his suit jacket and carefully hangs it up. As he sits down at the table, he is promptly given a very cold glass of Greco di Tufo, with its subtle flavour of spices, herbs and citrus.

Dinner tonight is one of his favourites, Fusilli al Salmone. She has made it by softening some onions, stirring in smoked salmon and double cream and adding perfectly al dente pasta. Always the Italian way, pasta to sauce, and never the other way around. He had done it wrong only once, and he can still feel her stinging indignation and contempt.

Christina pours a second glass for her husband, and sparkling water for herself.

'Listen, thanks for agreeing to help my brother out.'

'The boys are not happy about not being consulted. Are you sure we're doing the right thing?'

'I think so, although it's complicated. On the one hand, I think my brother is a shit, and on the other hand, I am Italian, and being loyal to my family is very important. I promise to keep an eye on it.'

'It will be fine.'

'And your friends, they need to learn their place a little. You're in charge, not them. This is our family business, and there is a clear hierarchy. You don't need to ask their permission to make decisions.'

'Christina, I have known them all my life.'

'It doesn't matter. If you want to grow this business, then you need to make tough decisions sometimes.'

She returns to the kitchen to serve dinner.

'Tell me about lunch with the Chamber of Commerce?'

'Bunch of old farts, to be honest, but I think they like me. I have offered to sponsor their annual dinner dance, so they love me.'

'Good boy. Remember, it is very important for an Italian family to be seen as pillars of the local community.'

'But I am not Italian, my love.'

'I have been thinking about that. I have looked it up, and I think we should both apply for dual nationality; we are both entitled to it. We can have two passports each: you can become Italian, and I can become English.'

'You are determined, aren't you? Did your Papa put you up to this?'

'Not at all, but I want my children to have an Italian father too. Especially as your first child is on the way.'

* * *

The two boys are born in quick succession. Their entry into the world could not be more different. Christina is in labour for almost twenty hours as Angelo makes a very reluctant entrance. Two years later, it is the turn of Marco, who arrives like a tornado, with a labour lasting less than two hours, as he noisily makes his appearance. It is perhaps a portent of his life.

Angelo de Luca O'Hare is named after the Biblical spirit messengers that God sends to men. He has a mop of blond hair and piercing blue eyes. Every day that he grows, Christina can see him looking more and more like Matty. He is a quiet, laid-back boy, almost painfully shy. As much as Matty wants to play rough with him, he is at his happiest merely following his Mamma around.

Marco de Luca O'Hare is the complete opposite. He is truly a force of nature. He has jet-black hair and a dark olive complexion. He is a bundle of energy that never stops. He races around the house wildly, shouting and screaming. He is the first to rise every morning, generally before six am. There is no off switch, and his parents fight every night to get him to go to sleep. His favourite pastime is to wind up his big brother; it's almost as if he can sense his sensitivity and is always ready to exploit it.

Both boys are taken over to Catanzaro to be baptised at the Immaculate Church of Badolato by Father Conte. On each occasion, they wear the family christening robe handed down through the generations. Her Mamma is bursting with joy on both occasions.

Christina's world has been made; she would do anything for her little princes. As much as she loves Matty, and loves her family back home in Italy, this is her calling. She wants them to have everything in life. Their job as parents is to provide the boys with the best life ever.

CHAPTER EIGHT

2022

The last few days have been tough on Lisa. She hasn't been sleeping at all and has stopped looking in the mirror, scared to see the person that looks back. She prays for it to be a dream and that her husband hasn't just disappeared. She wants to still be married to Stephen Whyte, and certainly not to Johnny Rodgers, whom she doesn't know. What does a Manchester crime mob want with her handsome, but slightly boring, husband? It is either a mistake or she has been duped.

She is triggered by seeing his stuff in the bathroom. His electric toothbrush is fully charged, waiting to be called into action. His lotions and potions lie quietly in his little cabinet, curious that he has not been around recently.

At the same time, work never stops at the DK Partnership. Demand is pouring back in as companies start to reinvest in marketing after the pandemic. She is dealing with the worry, managing the children and working beyond midnight just to try and stay afloat.

Tonight, however, she has the company of her parents, Davy and Kathy Gavin. Despite having a high-tech kitchen, she is in no mood to cook, so dinner tonight is Chinese takeaway from Deliveroo. The children are thrilled that their normal, disciplined midweek diet has been replaced by a more exciting one.

Gramps settles down with Cameron and Emily, happily watching a cartoon on television, another pastime generally frowned upon on a Wednesday school night.

'Darling, you look dreadful!' says Kathy.

'Thanks, Mum, just what I need right now.'

'Sorry, not very nice of me.'

Lisa clinks some ice into glasses and pours her mother and herself a large Tanqueray gin with Fever-Tree tonic.

'So, have you heard anything at all from Stephen?' asks Kathy.

'No, nothing since we had the Zoom call a few days ago. That was when he told me about his past, about his change in identity and having to run away from some bad people.'

'It's such a shock. He is such a lovely man, and a great father; who would have thought it?'

'Ach, it's the wee surprises that keep a marriage alive,' pipes up Davy from the sofa.

'Keep it alive? He will be lucky if *he* is alive when I get my hands on him,' says Lisa.

The doorbell chimes down the corridor, and Davy wanders along to collect the food. Even though it has been ordered and paid for through the app, Davy is old school, so he slips the driver a cheeky wee fiver.

The feast is opened on the central island of the kitchen. Chicken balls glistening with sweet 'n sour sauce and chicken fried rice for the children. Barbeque spareribs and Schezuan chicken for the adults, with the aromatic smell of chilli invading the kitchen. And of course, the obligatory prawn crackers, whose purpose nobody is very sure of. It's like having a packet of crisps with your fish and chips.

'I feel so embarrassed. How could I possibly marry a man and not know about this? I mean it's an absolute betrayal. Is it even legal? Maybe it means we are not married at all. Can you marry someone with a false birth certificate? What am I going to tell our friends? It's a disaster!'

'Don't be hard on yourself, my dear,' says her mum. 'This is not your fault, it's his. Though I always wondered why he insisted on such a small wedding. Your father and I had saved for a much grander affair.'

'He told me that he didn't have any family, that the only people he had at the wedding were his work colleagues. Now I find out that the kids have two other grandparents whom they have never even met,' says Lisa, now getting angry. 'How could he do that to them, deny them the joy of seeing their grandchildren growing up? I think I will cancel his birthday party; there just isn't any point. And to be honest, I am not sure that we will go to Florida.'

'*What?*' screams Cameron. 'Are you kidding? Dad is so bloody selfish!'

'Oi, language,' says Lisa.

'Right, children, let Granny get you upstairs and ready for bed,' declares Kathy, taking control of the situation.

Of course, the process of rounding youngsters up ahead of their normal bedtime is never straightforward. However, Scottish Grannies are blessed with the perfect combination of charming persuasion and menace. The trio head off upstairs, leaving Lisa alone with her dad.

'Right, Lisa . . . Mum isn't here now, so tell me – should I be worried?'

'I don't know, Dad. I just don't know what he did in the past.'

'Do you know anything about this guy that he gave evidence against?'

'No, he didn't give me any information. It's somebody he used to work for before he met me.'

'Well, if he phones again, try and get him to give you more details, and maybe I can look into it.'

'Dad, you're sixty-nine years old. You are far too old to be getting dragged into this stuff. This is my mess, or actually, it is Stephen's mess. It should be him that is cleaning it up.'

'Aw, Lisa hen, it is just a bit boring being retired. I go down to that club and look around and think I am in a care home. All they can talk about is who has just died. Try and find out who it is, and I can have something to get my teeth into.'

'What? And not only have my husband at risk but my dad too?'

'Listen, you know what I did when you were growing up. I know people.'

Even though she has no intention of involving him, it does make her feel better that her old dad thinks that he can still protect her. Normally, her feminist desire to be self-sufficient would rail against this. Tonight, though, it is comforting.

'Ok, I promise,' says Lisa.

'Oh, and another thing . . . Get some sleep – you look like shit.'

CHAPTER NINE

2022

On the morning of their departure from the Ramside to Edinburgh, they begin to gather in the foyer. Stephen, being an accountant, is impeccably on time; Tony, being a renegade, has yet to appear.

'So, Stephen, how was your experience of witness protection?' asks Phil.

'Well, to begin with, it was quite a shock. I agreed to a change of name, and we did all the practical stuff, such as a new National Insurance number, passport and driving licence.'

'All the basics, then.'

'Back then, I didn't do social media, so there was no digital footprint to deal with. I am still paranoid about any of that stuff. My wife thinks I am a Neanderthal.'

'To be honest, in our line of work, social media tends to be the biggest source of a breach in security.'

'After that, it was a case of simply going along to the local police and having a bit of a tame interview every month. Over time, it felt like everyone had lost interest, and I could just get on with life.'

'That's the way we like it.'

'So, you see, the longer I left it, the harder it became to tell my wife about my previous life.'

'What the fuck!' interrupts Brogan, who had been only half listening to the conversation. 'You mean your wife doesn't know?'

'Well, she does now, because I told her on the Zoom call.'

'Holy Moly, that is going to be quite some reunion, once you go back,' says Brogan.

Tony is not a great believer in strict timekeeping and is twenty minutes late when he appears, bizarrely dressed in a lurid purple Balenciaga tracksuit.

'Mate, that is some look!' said Stephen, laughing. 'I don't mean to be cheeky, but do you actually know how to pronounce it?'

'I think it's Ball n' Cigar,' says Tony in his Irish Geordie brogue, setting the others off chuckling. 'All the young team are wearing them these days. I managed to obtain forty pairs. They are fake, by the way, but I still made good money on them, you know.'

'Fake? No, really?' says Brogan. 'Right, let's go; the people carrier is outside.'

The journey is uneventful, and they are taken by the police to an address in the New Town of Edinburgh. Their temporary home is one of the Georgian flats that have been renovated and turned into Airbnb rentals. Increasingly, Edinburgh is becoming overwhelmed by them, to the point that noise is becoming a problem, as the guests do not show any consideration for the community, and they fill up the public bins with their detritus on departure.

The flat has huge ceilings that would need the big ladder to paint. The delicate and ornate cornices painted over with emulsion would offend the craftsman who toiled over them. There are two bedrooms, one with a modern en-suite bathroom, all glass and chrome, the second more modest.

'You take the en-suite one, Stephen,' says Tony.

'Are you sure? I don't mind.'

'Ach, it's no bother. I only have a shower once a week, so it will be lost on me.'

The police have provided a Tesco Direct delivery with enough provisions to last about a week. The instructions are very clear: stay at home, don't go out, lie low. Sounds suspiciously like a government advisory that they heard once or twice before.

Thankfully, the television comes with a Netflix account, so at least they can watch some box sets. The thing about staying in rental properties is that you get some insight into the earlier residents' viewing preferences by looking at the search function. Stephen is not sure he wants to watch *Naked Housewives of Cheshire* or *Boy'z in Leather* with Tony, thanks very much.

Tony wants to watch *Peaky Blinders*, all the way from the very beginning. He likes watching gangster films, and he really admires the big black coats and the caps that they wear. He quite fancies himself in the Cillian Murphy mould, riding moodily on his horse, even though the image could not be further from reality.

'I really can't be bothered watching this,' says Stephen.

'You will watch it. That's an order by the Peaky Fucking Blinders,' says Tony, channelling his inner Arthur Shelby.

'It's just I am worried about Lisa. It's not fair on her.'

'Look, do you want to give her a call? I only handed over one phone to the police; I thought I would keep the other one just in case.'

* * *

Lisa is walking down Byres Road, avoiding the students rushing to class. She has been in town attending a meeting with her finance team. They have spent the day reviewing the annual accounts that need to be submitted and their financial forecasts moving forward.

Normally, she would effortlessly be able to influence them, but today she was listless and lacking in confidence. Not surprising when the love of your life disappears and then reappears as someone else.

Her phone begins to ring from the depths of her bag, with an unknown number. She doesn't usually answer unsolicited calls, but given all her current worries, she makes an exception. She ducks into a closed charity shop doorway so that she can hear properly, trying to avoid the rumbling of traffic and the wailing of an ambulance.

'Lisa Whyte.'

'Lisa, it's me. I borrowed a phone.'

'Oh, thank God, how are you? Where are you? When are you coming home?'

'Look, I cannot tell you where we are. I just want you to know that we are safe. The police are looking after us. Can you phone my boss? Say we have had a bereavement or something.'

'Fuck off. You phone him. And two weeks – are you kidding me?'

'I don't know how long this will last, to be honest, but I promise that I will make it up to you. How are the kids?'

'They are fine. They just think you are away on a business trip. Mum and Dad were round last night. Dad was asking if you could tell us the name of the guy who you gave evidence against.'

'What, so the old boy will round up his cronies from the club, hire a minibus, and go and sort him out?'

'It's me that's asking. If you want me to understand this, you need to open up more and share it with me. Remember . . . your wife who you made your marriage vows to.'

'Ok, here goes. His name is Matty O'Hare. Quite the character; operated a legitimate haulage business out of the North West of England. He was involved in lots of other naughty stuff. I was his accountant for more than ten years. He was like a father to me, but it turned sour. I gave evidence against him, and Matty was sent to jail for fifteen years, finally being released in 2020. The police cannot figure out if this threat is directly linked to Matty, but for now, they want me out of the way.'

'Good Lord, the more I know, the worse it gets.'

'It will be fine – don't stress.'

'And how is your little house-buddy getting on?'

'Oh, just great. Right now, he's trying to work out how to hide a razor blade in his knocked-off Balenciaga baseball cap, just in case the Irish Army come looking for him.'

* * *

After a few days of being confined to the flat, the boys have grown weary and decide to break out for a pint. They trudge up the hill to the Wetherspoons on George Street. The streets are empty, and the weather is gloomy. George Street is a cold and windy corridor most of the year, with rubbish tossed haphazardly in the air. The warm pub is a welcome beacon.

'Two pints of Guinness, please,' says Tony.

'You can pay by card, using our app, and we can bring it straight to the table,' says the barman cheerily.

'But I don't have a card or a phone.'

'Well, we can take cash, I suppose, if you really want,' says the young man, clearly confused by a no phone/no card combo in 2022.

'But you do have a phone,' says Stephen when they are seated at their table.

'Yes, but I don't want that little fucker to know that I don't know how to use that funny wee square thing on the table.'

'I think you will find it is a QR code. It stands for quick response. You just point the camera at it, and it opens their app.'

'Well, he better give me a quick response and get those pints over here, pronto.'

'Do you ever eat in a Spoons?' asks Tony.

'Eh no, Lisa is not a big fan.'

'Oh, I like their Curry Club on a Tuesday and Fish Fridays, but you got to remember to count their chips, as it can vary quite a lot, depending on who is cooking.'

'I must remember to do just that.'

Two perfectly poured pints of Guinness arrive in front of them. Spoons are the marmite of pubs, with their garish carpets and outspoken owner. But say what you want, they pour a very good pint of beer, at a reasonable price. It is made even more pleasurable by the illicit nature of their visit. Both men take a pause to savour that first mouthful, cutting through the foam to the black velvety goodness, finishing the first gulp perfectly on the line of the harp.

'So, mate, we never finished that conversation the other night,' says Tony. 'Why did you end up giving evidence against Matty?'

'Well, to be honest, it wasn't Matty.'

'What do you mean?'

'It was Christina. She threatened to have me bumped off.'

'Fuck off.'

'She said she was going to get her brother to take me out. I found out some stuff about some shipments coming in from Italy that didn't add up. Vehicles that needed their temperature controlled, to deliver clothes, didn't make any sense.'

'Drugs?'

'No, in many ways, it was worse. And Christina didn't want Matty to know about it, or he would go mad. It was strictly between her and her brother. So, we had a blazing row, and she phoned her brother, shouting in Italian. The next minute, she hands the phone to me, and he tells me I am a dead man.'

'Anyway, I never stayed to find out. I ran away and gave evidence to the police about the family, and the rest is history.'

Tony disappears off to the toilets, which, in a Spoons, involves a long trek, and on his return, he has two packets of salt and vinegar crisps that he has pilfered from the corridor through the back. Once a thief, always a thief!

'So, what made Tony cough up?'

'Well, the more I think about it, Christina was probably behind it as well. She hated me from the very beginning; always looked down her nose at me. She used to tell Matty that I should not be part of the inner circle, that I was just a stupid Irish oink. Italians can be very racist when they put their minds to it.

'They wanted to stop the boosting part of the business and concentrate on the other more respectable stuff. She told me that I was not needed any more, that I could disappear to whatever hole I had come from. Matty would never have treated me like that, but she seemed to relish it.

'Eventually, the police came and told me that you had already given them lots of information and if I co-operated, then I wouldn't go to jail, so I thought, "Fuck this for a game of soldiers."'

'You know, sometimes I feel sorry for Matty. He was the one that took the hit, and the Italian princess got off free,' says Stephen.

'No . . . he may have gone to jail, but what hurt Christina the most was the loss of all their assets. Even more important, she could no longer preen about in public. That would have hurt much more,' says Tony.

'And she had to bring up her two boys on her own.'

'The older one was alright, but the younger one had the makings of being an almighty prick.'

'It's what happens when they grow up into some money, and their parents put them on a pedestal.'

'Anyway, I'm clamming,' says Tony.

'Would love to know what language you are speaking.'

'That's Geordie for being hungry,'

'You are always hungry, my friend.'

'Do you fancy a fish supper on the way home?' says Tony.

Conveniently, Mario's Chip Shop is just around the corner on North Frederick Street as they head home. A proper chip shop, none of that fish, kebab and pizza combo. Just focused on deep-fried delights from its oily cavern, and not much else. The seductive aroma teasing them during the short wait was almost unbearable.

'Two fish suppers and four pickled onions, please,' says Tony.

'Salt and vinegar or salt and sauce, love?' says the fryer.

On seeing the uncertainty on his friend's face, Stephen leans in. 'We'll have salt and vinegar please, and we are not playing your odd Edinburgh vs Glasgow game tonight.'

'Oh, look at the size of these pickled onions!' says Tony.

'They are pickled eggs,' says Stephen.

'Eggs – pickled . . . God, that's weird.'

'That will be £22.60, please,' says the fryer.

Stephen pays up as it's clear that his friend is completely lost for words. As they leave the shop, he contemplates the irony of being given a little wooden knife and fork to save the world, whilst the food itself is served in a large polystyrene container and a cheap polythene bag. It makes him think of Lisa, as she would have had plenty to say.

'It's criminal – more than £10 for a fish supper! The world has gone completely mad,' says Tony. 'You have a healthy product, nice white fish, good potatoes, but charge that and all you will do is force the kids to go to the Clown, the King, and the Colonel.'

'What are you talking about?'

'McDonald's, Burger King and KFC. Send the kids there and they will just eat a lot of shite. It's why everyone is getting fat in this country.' The rant continues unabated. 'We are all going to end up like the Americans, waddling along the street, riddled with type two diabetes.

'And whilst I am talking about potatoes, here's another thing. Everyone says this about the Irish, that during the potato famine, why didn't they just catch fish? But we couldn't because the English landowners wouldn't let us cross the land to get to the sea.'

'But the Irish do like potatoes,' says Stephen. 'I was once in a restaurant in County Mayo, and they served me roast potatoes with spaghetti Bolognese.'

'What's wrong with that? It sounds great.'

The streets are deserted as the clock ticks round to eleven pm. Their only companions for the stroll home are the streetlights, dimly covering them in orange light, and the occasional taxi, with drivers weighing up staying out or going home.

As they turn the corner onto Queen Street, they are happily absorbed in eating their chips, oblivious to the powerful 4 x 4 Black Range Rover slowly creeping up on them from the east.

At almost the last minute, the driver floors the accelerator, and it kicks forward violently. It mounts the pavement behind them, its powerful lights illuminating both, framing them as it takes aim. It bears down on them at speed, the engine angrily roaring.

It happens in an instant but feels as if it is being played out in slow motion. They hear the noise of the car about a nanosecond before impact, giving them just enough time to act.

Stephen is the luckier of the two as he hurls himself into the doorway of a gentleman's outfitters, colliding with the window and leaving it with a break like a spider's web. Tony takes the impact on his right side and is thrown against the shop window. Fish and chips are thrown everywhere.

The car careers off, taking out some waste bins on the way and disappearing round the corner. A couple on the other side of the road run across to see if they can help, the young girl screaming in anguish.

'Tony – Tony, mate, are you ok?'

'That fucking hurt,' says Tony, 'but I think I am ok. I think they tried to kill us.'

'No shit, Sherlock.'

'I suppose it could have been worse. If we had gone for the sauce option, it would have made much more mess!'

CHAPTER TEN

1998

This morning's breakfast meeting is being held at Matty's house in Morecambe Bay. The usual team are assembled, Matty, Hammy and Benny. Today they have been joined by Johnny and Tony and are all gathered around the table, reading the papers.

The Sun carries a very lewd review of Bill Clinton's impeachment over the Monica Lewinsky incident. *The Times* is covering the imminent arrival of the Euro across eleven countries. *The Daily Express* continues its coverage of Princess Diana's death, even though it has been over a year. The front cover of the *Westmorland Gazette* carries a story about two grandmothers who needed to be rescued by the fire brigade from a tree as they attempted to rescue their cat.

As an act of team building, Matty has decided to make breakfast. He has rustled up sausages, bacon, fried eggs and lots of hot buttered toast. He has already set the smoke alarm off twice and is in danger of seriously pissing off Christina and her carefully curated, scented kitchen.

'Mamma mia!' says Christina. 'It stinks in here. Open the bloody windows and the back door.'

She has never understood this strange fascination that English men have with a fried breakfast. At least he hasn't gone one step further and added baked beans; that is a mortal sin in her book. She is pretty sure that not one of them could tell her what type of bean is in the jars. They have no idea it is haricot beans. Sad post-war food that, for some reason, the Brits have a romantic relationship with.

Her husband can also put just about anything between two slices of bread and butter. She has even seen him make a sandwich with a banana. She is convinced that if there had been a jug of gravy, he would have dunked it in for good measure.

It had taken her almost five years to work out that a barm is a bread roll thing that you add a filling to.

Italian people like to start the day with a pastry, some fresh juice and the finest of coffees. She resolves never to allow her two young boys to eat that kind of fried food. They may well be English by birth, Irish by surname, but their souls are Italian.

Christina has conflicting thoughts about the gang that has gathered in her kitchen.

Firstly, she knows she was the one that wanted to escape Italy and the actions of her brother. She had not imagined it was to swop that life for one involving low-level crime. She manages to live with it because the money is good, but she does crave more legitimacy.

Secondly, as much as she loves Matty, she knows that he is not willing to be tough with his friends. If this family are going to be successful, then she will need to convince him to be more ruthless.

Thirdly, his friends act as though they are in the school playground, fooling around all the time like naughty schoolboys. They think that she just spends money, without realising she is joint head of the family. They don't treat her with enough respect.

She is particularly irritated by the fact that they have all rocked up in her kitchen this morning and turned it into a roadside café. The presence of Tony does nothing for her mood. She doesn't trust him one bit, as he would be off with the family silver given a chance. Growing up in Calabria, she detested people who were common thieves, without seeing the irony of her situation.

'Tony, how many times must I tell you? Take your shoes off before you come in this house – they are covered in mud,' she says angrily, ignoring the fact that all the others still have theirs on too.

Christina settles the boys down in the living room with some books and returns to the kitchen to make coffee. Not for her is it builders' tea or Nescafe; she wants a fresh cappuccino, made by her pride and joy, her own coffee machine. Only permissible before eleven am; anytime later is sacrilegious.

Secretly though her other purpose is to listen in to what the gang have to say about the business. She needs to know what is happening in case she has to intervene.

Matty is still dressed in his running gear from his early morning run.

'Out running, big fella?' asks Benny.

'Yep, did about six miles or so. You should come out with me sometime.'

'No thanks . . . Chinese doctor once told me heart only has so many beats. If you exercise, you use them up faster. Better to have nap instead.'

'Alright, Confucius.'

Hammy and Benny seem to have inadvertently started to coordinate their look, which today is jeans and black shirts. They look like a couple of book ends.

Johnny, who always seems in denial about the firm's legitimacy, wears a shirt and tie as if he is appearing at a monthly management meeting with the board of directors, pen in hand, poised ready to take the minutes on his pad.

And then there is Tony, easily the most voracious of eaters, hoovering up the sausage and bacon, bizarrely dressed in an oversized Boston Celtics basketball shirt.

'Hey, Tony, you better ease up on the sausage if you plan to play NBA,' says Benny.

'I never knew that the Irish were any good at basketball,' quips Hammy.

'I will have you know that Larry Bird is Irish,' says Tony.

'No, he is not. He is pure American, Indiana I think,' says Hammy.

'Irish heritage. Enough for me. We have exported it all over the world.'

'He's also 6 foot 9 and built like a tank, whereas you are 5 foot 3, a pale skinny runt that would need both of us to lift you up to get anywhere near the hoop,' teases Benny.

'Anyway, the Chicago Bulls have just won the World Series, and Michael Jordan is the greatest of all time,' says Hammy.

With his instinct for business opportunities, Matty has been thinking about basketball recently. Not that he wants to play the sport; it's just what is happening with big brands and sporting associations these days.

'That man will make more money outside of basketball than he does from within. Nike were nothing until they signed Jordan. All the kids wanted Adidas or Converse, but he has changed everything.'

'In fact, a consignment of Air Jordans would be the Holy Grail for truck bandits.'

'And on that note, what on earth happened the other night?' asks Matty.

'Well, the little Irish basketball player over there was sent to do a job and take a consignment of iPods, but instead, he brings back two pallets of books – *Harry Potter and the Philosopher's Stone* by JK Rowling. It's a good read, I hear, possibly better than the first one,' says Benny.

'Aw, fuck off!'

'Anthony, no swearing in this house,' says Christina, 'in case the boys hear.'

'Sorry, love.'

'And I am *not* your love. And for what it is worth, messing up like that is unacceptable.'

'Hold on. Look, everyone in this team has their own job to do. Mine is get in quick and steal what is there. It's not my fault that the intelligence was wrong.'

'Ok, calm down everyone. What's done is done. Now, we move on. I don't suppose we could offload them through our own pubs, Hammy,' says Matty.

'Sorry, Boss, not a lot of Harry Potter fans in our pubs.'

'Ok, let's store them up and keep them till Christmas. We can give them out as a goodwill gift to friends and families,' says Matty.

'Also, we have a tip-off about a warehouse that we know in Manchester that has a load of dishwashers that we could nick,' says Benny.

'A bit heavy to lift, though. You would need forklifts,' says Hammy.

'Where is it?' asks Matty.

'South side of Manchester,' says Benny.

'That's a no from me,' says Matty.

Johnny decides that he would use the time to clear the plates and load the dishwasher. This action is watched by Christina, who even observes that he rinses them and loads them in a neat and orderly fashion.

'Thank you, Johnny. Very kind of you.'

She is pretty sure that none of the others has ever offered to load the dishwasher. He is an enigma to her, clearly a clever young man who has been brought up well. He just seems strangely different from the others lounging about her kitchen. Although she worries more about the clever ones; they are often the hardest to control. The stupid ones just do what they are told.

'Anything else I need to know?' asks Matty.

'Yeah, we have a problem over at the White Horse in Preston,' says Hammy.

'Brendan, our tenant, has stopped buying his beer from us. He says the rent is too high and he can buy his beer much cheaper from the local cash and carry. He says he has been in touch with a few others, and they are thinking of getting some legal advice, possibly forming a buying club.'

'Ok, I will go over and speak with him tomorrow,' says Matty. 'Brendan is a solid guy. I have known him and his family for years; they are good people. I will sort it out.'

'Will you – fuck!' shouts Christina, taking everybody by complete surprise. For a nanosecond, Tony thinks about reminding her of the house rules on swearing but thinks better of it.

'That would be a sign of weakness. They're only running that pub because we gave it to them in good faith. Once these things start, they become like a cancer.

'Benny, you will go see Mr Brendan in the morning, and you will tell him that he has twenty-four hours to commence trading, or we will torch the pub and then send him and his entire family on a road trip to meet my big brother in Calabria.'

The group knows that trying to calm an angry Italian woman is like baptising a cat; it rarely ends well.

A strange silence falls over the kitchen as everyone tries to process what has just gone on. For the first time, Johnny contemplates whether he is now actually involved with the mafia.

Matty's two childhood friends stare intently at their best friend, contemplating whether they have just observed some passing of power. Christina knows that she has provoked a fight and is worried that she has overstepped the mark.

Matty measures his wife's moods like hurricanes, and this one is a four, possibly even a five. After a long pause, he says, 'I think Christina is right. That's what we will do.'

CHAPTER ELEVEN

2022

The NHS is still recovering from the impact of the pandemic. Waiting times are horrendous in A&E.

To make matters worse, some big football match had taken place this evening. Some team from Glasgow had come through to battle some team in Edinburgh. It didn't matter what time the kick-off was, it just meant that they had been drinking since breakfast.

The usual collection of post-match injuries has made its way to the hospital to be patched up and sent back out, hopefully before the pubs shut. So not only having to deal with triage for new arrivals, the front of house team are trying to provide segregation in the waiting room between the warring factions. Occasionally, some break out into angry song, peppered with expletives antagonising the other group.

It is almost five hours before Tony is seen by the doctor. He is extremely lucky that nothing is broken. He has taken most of the impact on his right thigh, receiving the worst dead leg that the staff have ever seen. The bruising is already showing prominently, running from right hip to right knee.

'The bruising is like the fucking map of South America,' says Tony to his friend, who is finally allowed in to see him. 'It's an absolutely lush colour already.'

'Well, at least nothing was broken. It could have been so much worse.'

'It happened so quickly – we never saw it coming.'

'Did you get a chance to clock who was driving?'

'Afraid not; it all happened so quick, and it was dark.'

'This shit's getting real then.'

The police have set up shop in one of the small staff meeting rooms to conclude an immediate debrief with the boys. Phil Simpson is not present tonight as he is off at a family wedding. Brogan Reilly is not at all happy that she is here, as she had plans for drinks with the girls tonight; that is not going to happen now. The Espresso Martini will need to wait until she sorts these two idiots out. She is accompanied tonight by a local police liaison officer, Jennifer Wilson, a recruit learning her trade from someone more experienced. It's clear that Brogan is going to be in full-blown alpha-female mode tonight, hackles bristling.

Of course, Tony detects this in advance and can't resist kicking off the meet with a one-liner.

'Ah, so it's Cagney and Lacey. So which of you is the butch one?'

'You have no idea how insulting that sounds,' says Jennifer. 'Even though I have no fucking clue who they are.'

'Tony, should I presume that they gave you strong painkillers and I should just talk to Stephen?' says Brogan.

'So, right, let's start . . . what the *fuck* did you think you were doing leaving the flat? We told you, very clearly, you had to stay there and await further instructions. The situation is very unclear here, and you are at risk.'

'Well, you see, we had finally finished *Peaky Blinders*, Series Six. Great ending by the way. I hear they might make a feature film next,' says Tony.

'To be honest, Brogan, we were bored stiff, going a bit stir-crazy,' says Stephen. 'We just wanted a quiet pint and a bit of fish and chips on the way home.'

'And do you know how much a fish supper is these days?' asks Tony.

'I don't know, and I really don't care,' snaps Brogan.

'Actually, now you come to mention it, I feel a bit peckish,' says Tony. Looking at Jennifer, he says, 'Go and be a pet, and get me a sandwich and a cup of tea, three sugars, please.'

'Away and fuck yourself.'

'Look, this is important. What can you tell us about what happened?' says Brogan.

'Not much, really. We went for a pint up at the Spoons and were heading back to the flat with the fish and chips. This big black car comes up behind us and sends us flying.'

'Is there anything else that you remember?' asks Jennifer.

'Yes . . . there is another crime that I would like to report. Do you know that they pickle eggs up here? They should be getting jail for that crime,' says Tony.

'Ok, I have had enough of this nonsense. You two simply don't seem to be taking this seriously enough,' says Brogan. 'You are both in a witness protection scheme; you were given new identities.'

'Yeah, but you know if I was to have my time over again, I might have asked for something a bit different,' says Tony. 'You just moved me on as a thief. Next time, I want you to give me an identity as a gigolo in the South of France looking after rich divorcees.'

'Jesus, shall we get a nurse in, Tony? Maybe up the meds and get you to shut up?'

'So,' she continues, 'have either of you had any contact with the three that went to prison?'

'Absolutely not,' says Tony.

'Me neither. Occasionally I would borrow my wife's log-in details for Facebook and try and see what Christina and the boys were up to, but I haven't seen Matty for more than 13 years. I liked Matty a lot. I sometimes have regrets for what I did,' says Stephen.

'In court, the gang were convicted of 12 counts of goods theft, although we know the number was at least four times that, the money laundering of assets, physical intimidation, and bribery of local council officials,' says Brogan.

'Yep, sounds right.'

'Can I ask you both: to the best of your knowledge, did Matty and his team ever get involved in the drugs trade?'

'Absolutely not, no way. If there was one thing that Matty was very clear about, no one was to go anywhere near drugs. He said they destroyed communities,' says Tony.

'Even though you don't need to be a rocket scientist to make a straight-line connection between Matty and Christina's family in Calabria, one of the biggest sources of illicit drugs in the whole of Europe,' continues Brogan.

'I agree with Tony. I never saw any signs of drugs in the entire time that I worked for Matty. And I would know, because all the books went through me.'

'But increasingly more work was being done between Matty and the de Lucas,' she says, refusing to let go.

'It was mostly Christina who organised it. We moved a lot of things, but drugs were not one of them,' says Stephen, irritation rising inside him.

'So, what if I were to tell you that the intelligence we have in our possession is that a Manchester-based crime family, headed up by a Frank Williams, has put a bounty on your heads? A family that has nothing to do with the haulage business, money laundering or pilfering. A family that believes the best way forward is to focus on selling only Cat A drugs,' says Brogan.

'No way! If rule number one from Matty was no drugs, then rule number two was don't go anywhere near Liverpool or Manchester, as that's where the bad boys live. I have never heard this name Frank Williams, so I am not sure where you are going with this,' says Stephen.

'Actually, it makes no sense to me. What would a drug-dealing mob want from an accountant and a two-bit, Irish burglar living in Geordie land?' says Brogan.

'Oi, that's a bit harsh.'

'Well, over the next couple of days, we are organising a visit from our colleagues in Manchester to Mr Williams, to see if he is willing to offer anything up.'

'Good luck with that,' says Tony.

'But here is what we cannot work out. Since Matty left prison, he is back living in Morecambe. By all accounts, he is going straight, trying to set up a small business, supporting one of his sons setting up his digital business,' she says.

'Benny D'Arcy moved to Puerto Pollensa, where he is running a small restaurant with his Spanish girlfriend. Steven Hamilton is still living in and around Morecambe and is working as a landscape gardener. We have zero evidence that any of the three that you helped put away has returned to a life of crime. So back to the pivotal question: why do you have a bounty on your head?'

'I like a Bounty, but I prefer a Marathon; when they changed it to Snickers, I was gutted,' quipped Tony.

'What age are you . . . ten?' says Jennifer.

'Well, we cannot help you find the evidence. It's your job to find out,' says Stephen. 'I have found this meeting to be quite intimidating. We are not accused of anything; your job is to support and help us, not to get all aggressive with us. And tell me this, how did they know where we were in Edinburgh? That leak must have come from within your organisation; your people were the only ones who knew.'

'We don't know yet; we are reviewing the protocols,' says Brogan, going red in the face at being challenged in front of another colleague.

'Protocols . . . total bollocks. Just make sure we stay safe.'

'So, in the absence of any compelling new information, and on the basis that we cannot join the dots between Manchester and Matty, it is decided we will continue to pursue the strategy of safe houses.'

'Now, not teaching you how to do the job, but is following the same strategy not a bit stupid?' says Stephen. 'Doing the same thing over and over and getting the same result.'

'Leave this to us please,' says Brogan. 'You're going to Northumberland.'

A quick trip to Marks and Spencer's to load up on some additional middle-aged, middle-class gear and they are put on a train from Edinburgh to Berwick-upon-Tweed. There they are collected by the local police. The liaison team has found them a secluded farmhouse, two miles outside of Craster. It is beside the coast, mainly in the middle of nowhere.

It's dark by the time they arrive. With little light pollution, the sky is ablaze with twinkling stars all vying for recognition.

The owners are away on a long-term holiday, so many of their personal possessions are still in the house. Stephen can see Tony's eyes lighting up greedily, pretty sure that he will be rifling through their possessions before long. The house smells a little musty as it has not been used for a while. A thin layer of dust covers the coffee table.

Before their arrival, Tony attempted to give the police his personal list of things he wanted, like a rider that a big act might request at a gig. They paid little attention to his requests, and once again, Tesco Direct has provided the delivery. Sadly, the order must have been placed by some student on work experience, as the food supplies include ready meals and Pot Noodles.

However, they have learnt, from their previous mistake, that the boys cannot survive a week without a beer, so they have included a case of Peroni.

'So why is Italian beer so popular in Britain these days?' asks Tony.

'No idea, mate . . . I think it's the romantic vision we have of Italy. The *dolce vita*,' says Stephen, opening a couple of bottles.

'Yeah, but I tell you what, try charging a bunch of Romans £7 per pint and there will be a riot. Do you know that the number one imported beer in Italy is Tennent's Super, which is loopy juice?'

'I don't think that Brogan likes us very much; she has really been bursting our balls.'

'She's alright. She is just showboating for the crowd.'

'But I have been thinking about what she said. Do you think there was any chance that Matty was dealing drugs and we simply just didn't know about it?'

'No, I don't, but somehow, I think that Christina and her family are firmly at the heart of this.'

CHAPTER TWELVE

2022

At just about the same time that the boys are settling down to drink their Italian beer, Lisa is opening a bottle of Cava to share with her best friend, Bella Saad.

Bella is a tall, dark-haired girl born to French and Lebanese parents. She is also remarkably well educated, firstly in Beirut and then Paris, as she followed her parents through their work in the diplomatic corps. She speaks the poshest English imaginable but can pepper it with funny little nuggets of Glaswegian when she needs to. Swearing is much more enjoyable when delivered by a posh person.

The two met on their first day at Glasgow University, both feeling nervous and determined to make a new friend in the first hour, just like toddlers on holiday at the kids club. They immediately fell into each other's company and have been inseparable ever since.

Bella works for a law firm in Glasgow, specialising in human rights. She spends her time challenging discrimination and advising clients whose human rights have been violated.

Lisa decides not to order takeaway for once, determined to rediscover her routine, and has made them all a tuna, borlotti bean and red onion salad. She opens the wine for the grown-ups and makes orange squash for the youngsters.

Cameron and Emily join them for dinner. They both adore Aunty Bella. Emily clambers up onto Bella's knee and is happily playing with her pony tail.

'How is school, my darlings?' asks Bella.

'Boring,' says Cameron.

'Well, you have a long time still to go in education, young man,' says Bella, 'so it's a bit early to be getting bored. You need to get all your studying done early, before the girls start to get interested,' she teased.

'I am learning to speak French,' says Emily.

'Really? In Primary Two? These posh private schools are really something,' says Bella. 'I can help you a little, Emily, because I am half French.'

'Which half?'

Not to be outdone by his little sister, Cameron pipes up, 'Well, I am learning to read and speak Latin.'

'Well, you're on your own there, son. I cannot help you.'

'There you go, best part of twenty grand per year on school fees so that they can speak a language that no one else in the world speaks.' Lisa laughs. 'Maybe Spanish or even Chinese would be more useful.'

Aunty Bella has brought dessert with her. She knows the owners of a fabulous little Lebanese restaurant in Paisley Road West called the Beirut Star. They make the most amazing Baklava: filo pastry filled with chopped nuts, sweetened with honey. Whenever she needs any, she just phones up and the tray is waiting for her. She always argues with them about whether she should pay or not. She rarely wins.

'Children, take your cake and go and read your books. I want to have a gossip with Aunty Bella.'

She splits the remaining Cava between them, wondering about opening a second bottle, but thinks better of it as it is a school night.

'So, tell me, have you heard from Stephen at all?' asks Bella.

'I haven't spoken to him since he phoned me from this guy Tony's phone. The police have taken his phone from him to avoid detection. But I did receive a WhatsApp message yesterday. It just said this:

HAD TO LEAVE EDINBURGH QUICKLY. BEING SENT TO ENGLAND. HOPEFULLY SORTED SOON. S. XXX☺

'I mean who puts a smiley emoji in a message when they are a fugitive on the run?'

'I still cannot believe that Stephen has another identity. He is kind, charming and considerate. You both live this perfect life together; I have always been super jealous.'

'I know. I keep trying to piece it together with hindsight. The lack of any family, or any friends that pre-date us or who are not joint friends. The way he shuns recognition. I once thought about getting him diagnosed by the doctor. His abject hatred of social media. I mean, come on, it's 2022. Who doesn't have Twitter or Insta?'

'And do you believe that he was just caught up by chance or was he up to his ears in mischief?' asks Bella, and takes another mouthful of moist cake.

'Given the way the police are taking this so seriously, he must have been involved somehow.'

'Might have been against his wishes, though.'

'I am going through such conflicting emotions. On the one hand, I want to throttle him for betraying me, and on the other hand, I feel sorry for him and want to know he is ok. It's a bloody nightmare.

'It's like all of a sudden, life is altered. The present makes no sense, and the future is impossible to visualise. I mean, if he can hide something like this, what else has he been hiding?'

Bella can see the tears forming in her friend's eyes, so she reaches over to give her a hug. The tears come in convulsing shakes, and there is nothing they can do but grip each other tightly.

'Are you coping alright, Lisa? Do you think you should go and see a doctor, maybe get something to help?'

'Absolutely not, no way. What would I say? Can you prescribe me something for a misplaced husband? Anyway, they're all far too busy. They would just prescribe me Valium, which would make me sluggish. I think I am going to need my strength.

'My mum and dad have been good helping with the kids. Dad is desperate to help Stephen somehow, but he is just too old now. I don't want him involved.'

'Well, you know that Cameron and Emily can come and stay with me anytime that they want,' says Bella. 'It would be a pleasure.'

'Thanks, babes. Aw, fuck it, let's open the second bottle of Cava.'

She deftly retrieves the bottle from the wine fridge, perfectly chilled to 6.5 degrees, opens it and pours it into two fresh, long-stemmed glasses.

'And how is the DK Partnership?' asks Bella.

'Don't get me started on that subject. It's mental; the amount of new work coming our way is crazy. Everyone is in a race to develop their green credentials, to save the planet.'

'I blame Greta Thunberg,' says Bella.

'And then we had COP in Glasgow last autumn, two weeks of talking hot air, and what did it achieve? Everyone heads back and continues where they were.'

'You know, I was down in Troon, about a month before COP, and there was this procession of huge cargo planes landing at Prestwick Airport. Turns out it was all the armour-plated cars for the USA security team. Pretty good for the environment, not!' says Bella.

'That's the problem, it's just greenwashing.'

'What's that?'

'You know, just painting a thin green façade over your business – reduce plastic, save water, plant trees. Move from plastic to paper, no problem. Put the price up, make the consumer pay for it; just don't think of damaging the shareholders' profits or returns.'

'Then you get "wackaging" or "matewashing".'

'Girl, you are just making words up now.'

'No, it's when they use casual, matey language, pretending to fix the planet. There was this ridiculous animated advert recently by Innocent Drinks. It was about a man and his aquatic best friend, who happened to be an otter, who were both going trying to save the planet. Conveniently not mentioning the fact that Innocent Drinks is majority owned by Coca-Cola, voted the world's worst plastic polluter for four years in a row.'

'Let it all out'-says Bella.

'Sorry, I must sound so boring and woke. I get so enthusiastic about it. The problem is that we are still an incredibly young agency, and we cannot afford to turn down any work based on my principles.'

'And do these principles include flying transatlantic to Florida, to see Mickey and Minnie Mouse?'

'Ha ha . . . yes, you have me there. I was secretly glad last year when it got pushed back because of Covid. Now, with everything going on with Stephen, I just cannot see it happening. I just don't have the heart to tell the children.'

'Tell us what?' asks Emily, stifling a yawn.

'Nothing, darling. Now go and give Aunty Bella a kiss goodnight, and go up and brush your teeth. And tell Cameron that he has another thirty minutes before he is off too.'

Emily wanders off, mischievously telling her brother it is bedtime now, causing a furious argument about the proper time for an eight-year-old to go to bed, and how all his friends regularly stayed up past ten o'clock. Lisa had heard it all before, and after a few glasses of Cava is immune to it.

'Listen, thanks so much for coming tonight. I feel so much better just getting it off my chest.'

'Well, I have some breaking news . . .' says Bella.

'Oh, do tell me!'

'Well, I have met a man. His name is Mikkel. We both attend the same spin class at David Lloyd. We have been out on a few dates recently, and he has asked me to go down to London with him for a weekend. He is Scandinavian, and an architect.'

Momentarily, this news brightens up her best friend, who immediately morphs into a giddy teenager. She needs to know all the juicy facts: what is he like, does he make her laugh, and has she slept with him yet. Always at the back of her mind, though, is her own current predicament.

'He sounds like a keeper. I am made up for you, Bella. But if I were you, I would insist on seeing his driving licence, passport, meet both parents, and all four grandparents, if still alive, just to be on the safe side.' They both dissolve in a fit of giggles.

CHAPTER THIRTEEN

2002

2001 was a dark year, both at home and abroad.

It was not uncommon for Matty to see mounds of animals being burned in funeral pyres in the corner of fields. Not exactly a great look for Visit England to sell to tourists. A major outbreak of foot and mouth disease caused chaos in the agricultural and tourism sectors. The worst-affected areas were Cumbria and Lancashire, where more than six million innocent cows were slaughtered to halt the disease.

Abroad, the news was even more devasting. On the 11th of September, the world watched in abject horror as nineteen militants hijacked four planes, bringing down the Twin Towers in New York, killing almost 3000 innocent souls.

Matty and Christina refused to let the boys see the news that night, but once they were in bed, they both sat for hours watching it on repeat, stunned by the barbarity of it. The world would never be the same again.

Against this backdrop, there was much speculation as to whether Tony Blair would take the country into a war against Iraq. Matty could feel the tensions rising between the white and Muslim communities in the working-class towns of the North West.

Matty hates intolerance at every level. He believes that it is holding the North West back. He is beginning to take much more notice of local politics and has a desire to become actively involved one day. He has started to meet with community leaders from different backgrounds, in his own small way doing whatever he can to encourage harmony.

Against a backdrop of doom, business continues to be as brisk as usual for Matty and the team. The tried and tested business model of stealing from lorries and investing them into more legitimate businesses continues. All criminals crave to be legitimate and to be respected. Matty is no different. Hopefully, over time, it will be only about the legitimate stuff.

However, it still isn't quick enough for Christina, and they have a furious row this morning at breakfast. Having sampled the higher levels of society the previous night, she is becoming impatient for more.

It had started from nowhere, with Matty chiding his wife about her spending habits, but escalated rapidly.

'Darling, we need to be careful about spending. We don't want to attract attention.'

'What do you mean? We run a successful family business. Why can I not spend our money on nice clothes? I hate the mainstream UK fashion brands. I prefer Italian design.'

'You don't need a new outfit for every occasion, though.'

'Every occasion! You don't exactly take me to many exotic locations. Last night was a luxury; it's normally some council event in Blackpool.'

'Your brother is involved in the fashion trade – get him to send you clothes.'

'I certainly will not be relying on the goodwill of my brother.'

'You know where most of the money comes from; we need to be cautious.'

'Well, we need to go faster then, get out of stealing and move into legitimate businesses, don't we? And I keep telling you, it won't be with the current gang that you run with; they are already at their ceiling.'

'I am just saying we need to fly under the radar a little, ok?'

'I don't need a fucking radar to track me.'

Having secured the last word, she storms out, leaving Matty to reflect on what a fiery handful she could be. He fears that he is heading towards a battle of loyalties between his wife and his friends.

After the last meeting at the house, and her assertive intervention, Matty has started to hold meetings with his friends off-site. It isn't that he is unhappy with his wife being there; he just likes to be in control.

The venue for their meeting is the Tickled Trout Hotel, just off the M6, beside the River Ribble. A solid, white-bricked coaching inn. The staff know them well, so they are ensconced at their usual table at the back of the restaurant. The only one not present today is Tony, who is away scoping out a mark on the A69. They order proper butties: ham and pickle, egg and cress, cheese and tomato, and mugs of strong tea, not cups. The girls don't need to ask whether it is white or brown bread, they know already.

Outside, the river is swollen from last night's rain, threatening the banks with violence but not quite brave enough to make it.

'Well, how was it last night? says Hammy.

The previous evening, Matty and Christina had attended the gala opening of the Commonwealth Games in Manchester. It was a gift from the leader of the Lancashire council to thank the O'Hares for their support and help in raising funds to refurbish a local library.

There had been an A-list of influential businesspeople, all excited to be at such an event. Visitors from across the world, with dazzling outfits reflecting their local customs. This was the type of network gold dust that Matty loved, and it almost made the investment in a new Versace dress for Christina worth it.

'You know, it was actually great fun. Christina was in her element, although pissed off she didn't get to meet the Queen. But she did get to say hello to David and Victoria Beckham, so all was not lost.'

'Well, to be fair, they are royalty these days, anyway,' says Hammy.

'So, was Her Maj not there, then?' says Benny.

'Oh, she was there alright, just not quite available for a mere Morecambe haulier and his Italian wife.'

'I can't stand the Royal Family, you know. They cost us all a bloody fortune, and the way that they treated Princess Diana was terrible,' says Benny.

'Well, I actually like the Queen. She believes in loyalty to her family, despite how badly they all behave,' Matty says. 'And anyway, leave her alone – her ma has just died.

'So, with your head filled with all this Commonwealth guff, does that mean we are opening an international office? If so, can you make it Marbella? I will head it up,' says Benny with a laugh.

'Spain is not part of the Commonwealth, you idiot. Anyway, you wouldn't last two weeks – far too hot for you. Also, it's full of gangsters and Russians. You would end up fighting everyone,' says Hammy.

The waitresses arrive to clear the plates. The boys fall quiet, ready to talk the business of the day.

Matty, who never used to pay much attention to reading when he was at school, has now become an avid reader of the papers and magazines. He isn't one for gossip or frivolity; he prefers reading articles about current affairs and the economy. He reckons that he needs to expand his general knowledge if he is going to hang out with other business leaders. He needs a grasp of what is happening in the world, not just the high street in Morecambe.

'I have been reading an interesting article about on-line shopping and the emergence of companies like Amazon,' says Matty.

'That's the mob that delivers books. Remember that time Tony fucked up and stole all those *Harry Potter* Books? We didn't make much coin from that one, so I cannot see what is interesting about Amazon,' says Benny.

Matty decides to press on and ignores his friend. 'The article says that today, more than 60% of the population have access to the internet, and they think that in ten years, this will grow to 98%. In essence, everyone will use the internet in the future.

'It says that it is now expecting companies like Amazon to bet on people buying all sorts of stuff online, not just books. Everything you need at the click of a finger. You know what the wee curly arrow means in their logo? From A to Z. They are just like us, a distribution company that is diversifying.'

'I am confused,' says Benny. 'Are you saying we are going to be opening an internet company? Because there will be no fucking fun in that, sitting away rattling about on a keyboard all day.'

'No, don't be daft. Of course we are not. But think of the implications. Today, if someone wants a pair of shoes, they go to the shop and try them on. If they like them, they hand over their cash and physically take them home. Some even wear them at once if their current shoes are a bit minging. In this future world, the shoes will be delivered from the factory to a warehouse, and then from a warehouse to a customer at home, giving us two opportunities to steal them,' concludes Matty.

'So, this internet thing is a good thing,' says Benny.

'It's the Internet of Things, you will find,' pipes up Johnny. Irony lost on Hammy and Benny.

Feeling that, for once, this is a discussion that he can contribute to, as opposed to the usual boisterous kidology that normally dominates the meetings, Johnny decides to offer further opinion.

'Of course, you need to be aware of the law of unintended consequences,' says Johnny.

'Christ, you two are talking in absolute fucking riddles today. I can't understand any of this shite,' says Benny. 'Can we not talk about football or something?'

'What do you mean, Johnny?' asks Matty.

'I think there are several things that you need to take into consideration when you look at how technology is going to change the world.

'Firstly, these companies have millions or even billions of pounds of resources. They will take security extremely seriously; they will invest in it. Their trucks will be way more secure than they are now. They will put tracking devices in, not just so that the punters can see when their trainers will arrive, but so they can protect their vehicles and stock. It is going to make the noble art of stealing from a truck much harder.

'Secondly, as the technology advances, we will see more and more closed-circuit television appearing on our streets and warehouses. It might make it a bit trickier for Tony to maintain his cloak of invisibility. In the future, you will not be able to drive down the street without being picked up by a camera.

'Thirdly, my job of cleaning the money is going to get even harder. The government and the banks are going to get much stricter on money laundering, especially after 9/11. You used to be able to pay someone cash to buy a property or a business. Soon that will be impossible; money laundering checks are going to be rigid. You never know, one day maybe nobody will use cash – we will go cashless.'

'There will always be cash,' says Matty.

'Don't bet on that, Matty. Maybe, one day, people will invent other forms of currency.'

'So, in this brave new world that you are both imagining, what happens to your trainers if they're delivered when you're not in, maybe at your work?' asks Hammy, playing along.

'Well, maybe your neighbour can accept them for you?' says Matty, without any real confidence.

'That will be shining bright. I fucking hate my neighbour. The big, ugly, baldy bastard would keep the shoes for himself, even if they weren't his size,' says Benny, trying to attract the waitress's attention for a piece of bun to go with his tea.

'Maybe they will just leave them round the back, or in the shed,' says Matty.

'Well, surely, that's when we can lift them,' says Benny.

'That's going to be a slow old process that, following a delivery driver around the estate, hoping that there is no one at home,' says Johnny.

'So that's us back to this internet thing being bad, then,' declares Benny triumphantly. 'I told you all along, no good can come of this thing.'

'No, I disagree. It is just inevitable progress that we need to navigate our way around,' says Matty.

'I just think we need to start to think a little more strategic, have a bit more of a longer-term vision about where we want to go. Think about the external factors, about our future sources of growth. I think, as CEO of this enterprise, I should conduct a strategic review.'

'One bloody night hanging about with the big knobs and the Commonwealth Games and he comes back here harping on about technology and strategic reviews. It's a far cry from the front door of the Bliss boys,' says Hammy.

'I think we need to grow the legitimate part of our business faster. Let's consider taking on more jobs outside the county lines. It'll give us more opportunity and reduce the risk of getting caught. We're hauling back and forward for the de Lucas anyway,' says Matty.

'Ok, let me get started on it,' says Hammy.

'Oh, by the way, how is the Italian job going?' asks Matty.

'Like clockwork. Once a week, we collect from a lorry park twenty miles from Calais and bring the deliveries over to two warehouses outside Birmingham. Import paperwork is always in order, so a piece of cake,' he says, chewing on an Eccles bun.

'Ok, good stuff. We are blessed with a visit from big brother tonight. We are taking him out for dinner.'

As the meeting begins to wind down, Benny has one more declaration to make on the internet.

'There is a fourth consequence that you haven't thought through about this internet thing,' he says.

'Enlighten us then, Einstein,' says Matty, playfully.

'Well, once your Christina figures out how to use a computer and do her shopping online, you are absolutely fucked, gaffer.'

* * *

The O'Hare family home is rarely a quiet one. Having an eight-year-old and a six-year-old can be a noisy affair. As the boys are extremely spoiled, there are toys of all varieties lying around the hall when he comes through the door. He picks his way carefully across the room as there is no pain like standing on a piece of Lego.

The babysitter who has been organised for tonight has not arrived yet, so Matty is at once deployed into action to break up a fight. Once again, it is the younger boy, Marco, who has the upper hand and is standing over his big brother, Angelo, pummelling him with a very expensive blue silk pillow. Matty thinks, for a millisecond, about how his wife would probably rescue the pillow first before her son.

As usual, all the aggression is coming from the younger boy. Angelo rarely retaliates. Sometimes Matty wishes he would, as it might solve the problem.

'Boys, stop this immediately!' booms Matty. The boys know that whenever their dad raises his voice, the game is up.

'Sorry, Dad,' says Marco, 'but he started it,' before turning on the crocodile tears.

'I very much doubt that. Where is your mother, anyway?'

'She is having a bath,' says Angelo.

'Well, go to your own rooms, and don't come out until I tell you it's ok.'

Upstairs in the main bathroom, Christina has lit some lavender candles and is relaxing in a hot foamy bath, enjoying a cold glass of champagne and listening to opera music. She has developed this kind of strange, motherly hearing. She can completely zone out when the boys start to fight, simply not hearing it. However, if there is any possibility of a real threat, she will hear it, crystal clear, the way that mums can pick out their children crying in a busy park, or dog owners know the sound of their pooches' woofs.

Taking a moment to fully admire his wife's body, unblemished by two children, full of curves in all the right places, Matty contemplates jumping in beside her but thinks that the bath might overflow. Instead, he kisses her gently on the forehead, and she gives him a sip of champagne.

'I am sorry for this morning, my love,' says Matty.

'It's fine; it is nothing,' says Christina. 'Anyway, what did Marco do now?'

'How do you know it wasn't Angelo?' He laughs.

'Because Angelo, how do you English say, would not say boo to a goose.'

'Do you have geese in Calabria?'

'No, only in Northern Italy, as it's too hot in the south. Anyway, we would shoot them for the pot, rather than say boo to them.'

'So, when does big brother arrive?'

'He should be here about seven. He has a car bringing him from Manchester.'

'Why did you not offer to let him stay the night?'

John G Gemmell

'Of course I did, but he said something about catching an early flight back to Italy. I don't believe a word of it. He will have some hooker at the hotel waiting for him when he gets back.'

'But your sister-in-law is gorgeous, and they have a couple of lovely girls.'

'Oh, I am sure she knows. It means that he leaves her alone. It's Italy, Matty. The men think that they can behave however they want. The only one that they are truly scared of is Mamma.'

'So, to what do we owe the honour of this visit, anyway?' asks Matty with a sigh.

'To see that his baby sister is being looked after by the big, tough Englishman, Fee-fi-fo-fum, as your William Shakespeare said in *King Lear*. I am sure he will have something to ask. Bruno always has an agenda.'

'Oh great, just what I need.'

'I want you to take him down to the pub first for a drink while I get the boys settled with the babysitter. You know, band of brothers and all that bonding stuff that men do when their women are not around.' She laughs. 'Now be off with you. I want to get out of the bath, and I don't want you getting all horny.'

Exactly at seven pm, a jet-black Mercedes sweeps into the O'Hare driveway. The driver opens the passenger door and Bruno pauses to admire the view over the estuary. It is a pleasant evening, and he must admit that the view over the bay, with the sun setting out to the far west, is stunning.

Not quite as beautiful as looking out across the sea to Sicily, but certainly better than the post-industrial wasteland that he has been staying in for the last two nights. He had ventured out from the Malmaison Hotel just once and thought that he had entered a war zone on the streets of Piccadilly. The place was full of drunken youngsters gorging on kebabs and threatening to fight anyone that they came across. He couldn't understand a word that anyone was saying.

He doesn't understand the culture of binge drinking. In Italy, if you order a second beer, that is allowed, but a third would draw strange looks, as if you had a problem. Of course, that is conveniently ignoring the fact that they all drink wine like water.

Although the sun is still shining, this is Lancashire, so the fine rain and mist are undoubtedly not far away, and he is glad that he has brought a raincoat. His feet crunch on the gravel driveway.

The front door opens, and the two young boys fly down the stairs.

'*Ciao*, Uncle Bruno!'

'My goodness, you boys are growing up so fast. Maybe it's because I don't get to see you as much as I should, as your mother doesn't bring you to Italy enough. Now, I have something for you both, but you have to promise me something,' he says, producing two crisp fifty-pound notes.

The boys' eyes are agog. Neither of them has seen a fifty before.

'Promise me both, if either of you get good at football, that you choose to play for Italy, and not England. And not Ireland, as I am pretty sure your Daddy will have an Irish grandparent somewhere. Now go and put that in your *salvadanaio* and don't tell your mother!' He laughs, enjoying the benevolent moment with his nephews.

'Hello, my *fratello,*' says Christina, kissing him three times on the cheeks.

'*Sorelle,* I have missed you so much that my heart breaks.'

He nods to the driver, who goes into the boot of the car and hands her an enormous bouquet of white lilies. He also produces a small hamper with fresh mozzarella, San Marzano tomatoes and a choice of cured meats.

She smiles and guides him, arm in arm, into the family home.

'Tell me, how are Mamma and Papa?'

'Mamma is fine, her usual self, poking her nose into everyone's business, especially mine. Remember she doesn't just enjoy guilt trips, she runs the travel agency. Papa is not so good; his memory is a real problem now. I'm starting to see the decline. The doctor thinks he might have dementia.'

'I promise to come over for Christmas, once the boys break up from school.'

Matty comes downstairs, dressed in smart jeans, brown shoes and a fitted white shirt. It is straight out of the packet, so you can still see the fold lines. He formally offers his hand to Bruno for the traditional English handshake.

'What? You don't even want to give your brother a kiss?' says Bruno, immediately repeating the three-kiss ritual that Matty has never really got used to. If Benny ever tries that one, he will get a slap, thinks Matty.

'Right, you boys are going to the pub first, whilst I get the boys settled.'

'Great, I will get my man to drive us,' says Bruno.

John G Gemmell

'Nonsense, let's walk into town,' says Matty, determined to wrest control over his brother-in-law. He wants home-field advantage.

'The bay is very different from Calabria. It is so vast and flat,' says Bruno as they step out of the driveway.

'Five times bigger than Sydney Harbour,' says Matty. 'But don't be fooled. It is a dangerous down on the mudflats. The tide rises by almost nine metres in hours at certain high tides. Even though I have lived here forever, I never think of myself as a local, so the number of times I have been down on the sands you can count on one hand. It is best left to those whose generations know how to navigate its challenges.'

As they near the town centre, the housing generally becomes tackier: paint flaking off the walls, window repairs overdue. As Bruno had originally forecast, the drizzle has started, so he is thankful for his coat. Matty is oblivious to it, of course; the big coat only comes out mid-November and is put away by mid-February.

'What season is it these days in England?' asks Bruno.

'It is autumn.'

'I only ask, because you seem to have them all in one day.'

Matty can already tell that this evening is going to be one of those Anglo-Italian comparison nights.

'Tell me, Matty, what are these strange little creatures that people have in their gardens? Bearded little chaps, with red caps.

'They are garden gnomes. Very important historically in these parts.'

'And is there any significance to them? Is it like in Italy where every house has a shrine to the Virgin Mary?'

'I'm told they are custodians of the earth, protectors of buried treasure, and a good luck symbol.' Matty laughs. 'Remember, the English are a weird lot.'

The Old Ship Inn is set one street back from the Esplanade, a narrow commercial street protected from the sea. It isn't his normal choice in pubs, but he has specifically chosen it because he knows that Bruno will find it challenging.

The kind of non-descript, British, old-school boozer where people go to get away from their spouses and have a proper drink. Sticky carpets, an odd kind of smell that is probably air freshener. You are still able to smoke in pubs, although the rumour is it will eventually be outlawed, and the smoke kind of hangs around in the air in a pervasive fashion. Even if you don't smoke, your clothes still stink in the morning. Most of the customers don't really see this as an inconvenience, as it acts as a cover for a multitude of other odours.

The television plays away quietly in the corner, normally used to show the sports during the day to accompany the twin activities of daytime drinking and gambling. Tonight, it is tuned to BBC1 so that the barmaid can keep up with the goings on in *EastEnders*.

Two old fellas cackle away in the corner, playing dominoes. The thud of the dominoes provides a pleasant clucking noise. Having gradually entered old age, this is the most competitive sport that they can manage nowadays. They nod gently in the direction of Matty. Everyone in town knows him, mostly by reputation.

The pub doesn't have a food offering; that's if you don't count Scampi Fries and Pork Scratchings hanging on cards beside the spirits, salty snacks cunningly devised to make you thirsty and buy more beer.

'Well, well, Matty, and who is this ravishing young man that you have brought me?' asks Betty, arching her back to see if she can counter gravity, lifting her enormous boobs upwards, completely oblivious that having a front tooth missing might restrict her ability to flirt.

'Betty, this is Bruno. He is Christina's brother from Italy, so go easy on him.'

'So, what will it be?' she says.

'I will have a pint of cask beer, Theakston's Best, please,' says Matty.

'What's that?' asks Bruno.

'Well, it's a beer, like a bitter, not a lager, and it is still fermenting in the container instead of just at the brewery. It's best served not too cold so that you can taste the hops.'

'Nope, absolutely not. A warm beer? You English are mad. Can I have a Campari and Soda, please?'

Although he is sitting on a stool at the bar facing Betty, Matty is utterly convinced that if he turns around, the domino players will have stopped playing to pick their jaws up from the floor. This is the first time that anyone has ever asked for Campari in the Ship Inn.

'Sorry, love, had a run on Campari lately, so it's run out,' says Betty, deadpan.

'Ok, well, perhaps a glass of red wine, please.

Betty returns with a beautiful pint of Theakston's Best Bitter, served in a branded glass, and a single-serve bottle of red shiraz from somewhere in South America. He holds the cold little bottle of wine in his hands uncertainly. He opens the screw top, upends the contents into a wine glass and sniffs it gently. He notes a strange oily slick to the liquid. He wants to say something but for once is speechless. Instead, inside his head, he says, *'Cheaa schifo.'*

Matty is finding this to be a hugely enjoyable lark, smiling as he takes a deep draught of his pint.

Nothing like getting under the skin of his mildly obnoxious brother-in-law.

'So, is your driver also a bodyguard?' asks Matty.

'Yes, he is, but to be honest, it's just for show. Everything in Calabria is just for show. If you don't have a bodyguard, you are seen as being weak. Do you have one, Matty?'

'Never had any need, mate. Anyone tries it on with me, I have Benny and Matty that will back me up. But it's a long time since I have got into a fight. I am a respectable member of the community these days.

'So, I hear you have a young lady for company in Manchester?'

'Ha ha, not much passes my sister by. It's just recreational, a bit of fun. My wife is very happy being at home, whereas I like adventure and variety. And my God, this one is an absolute stunner. If you want, I can give you the name of the escort agency that I use when I am in town. I highly recommend them.'

'No thanks, not my cup of tea. And you do know that I will tell Christina this?'

'Who cares? What can she do? Anyway, I admire your loyalty. When you married Christina, I was worried. Calabrians don't normally allow their women to marry outside of Calabria.'

'Stop with the mafia talk; it really doesn't scare me.'

'Apologies, it is the Italian ability to dramatize everything. You need to know this, though: I know these people and their families, but I am not part of all of that. We have been there for so long that we have a licence to operate. So, you see, I am just like you, a respectable member of the community.'

'And our transportation relationship is going well, I hear?' asks Matty.

'Yes, all is good. Your boys have been perfect. Always on time, no issues, no problems. In fact, a pleasure to do business with,' he says. 'Which is why I have a proposal to make to you.'

'Well, I have been waiting for it, so on you go.'

'No, we wait for my sister. This is a family matter.'

Matty sighs at the extravagant hand gesture that went with the last sentence. The door flies open, and three teenagers come noisily in. Two boys and one girl, dressed in nondescript leisurewear. They take one look at the bar to see Matty O'Hare, local legend, and a decidedly menacing Mediterranean chap, and retreat to the pool table in the back of the pub. They are now so quiet it is as if someone has pressed the mute button on the remote control.

'Betty, do me a favour. Send a couple of pints over to the old fellas from me, and ask the young uns what they would like to drink.' He then looks at his brother-in-law and his half-full glass of red and asks, 'Do you want another one?'

'Actually, can I try a pint of that warm beer? It can't be worse than the red wine.'

Christina is dropped off by the chauffeur/bodyguard. She normally likes walking into town, but not tonight with these heels on. She whisks them both around the corner to the Morecambe Bay Brasserie. It is busy tonight, with a small group of would-be diners waiting patiently in an orderly line outside. Politely queuing, as the British do so well.

Christina doesn't really understand queuing and immediately takes them inside, demanding a good table at the window overlooking the bay. She's oblivious to the looks and whispers.

'Bruno, dear, I hope you don't mind, but quite frankly, there is not an Italian restaurant in this town that I can take you to. There is a pizza place, but oh my God, you have never seen anything like it. You can build your own topping, including pineapple . . . can you believe that? And then people eat it with a knife and fork.

'Then there is the one called Trattoria Amalfi. *Mio Dio*!' She throws her hands up in mock horror. 'The waiter, who I think was Turkish and not Italian, asked me if I wanted an ice cube in my wine. He then argued with me that Alfredo is an authentic Italian sauce for pasta. I said, "Darling, we have an Uncle Alfredo back home, but we certainly don't have an Alfredo sauce!"' She laughs. 'If I took my Mamma there, she would have gone after the chef with a *mattarello*.'

'The thing I don't understand,' says Bruno, 'is that the English spent so much time conquering the world, finding spices all over the Far East, but then refused to use them in their own cooking. What was the point?'

'To be fair, the food here is pretty good,' says Matty, beginning to get pissed off at the siblings' double act.

At that point, an older, well-dressed gentleman appears at the table to pay his respects. Comfy slacks and a golf club sweater knotted over his shoulders. The air suddenly full of entitlement.

'Mr O'Hare, forgive me for interrupting. I just wanted to say hello.'

'Hello, Charles, good to see you. I think you have met my wife, Christina, and this is my brother-in-law from Italy, Bruno de Luca.' Hands are offered and promptly shaken.

'I just wanted to say thank you so much for your support over the library refurbishment. It is great to see local businessmen giving so much back to the community. Perhaps we should have a spot of dinner sometime.'

'That would be lovely,' says Matty.

After he has left, Bruno asks, 'So who is the big shot?'

'He's Charles Eastwood, local Conservative MP. They are all the same, to be honest, just in it for themselves. He's a bit of a tosser, but I need to keep him onside.'

'But of course you do. 'You never know when the time might come.'

'Indeed.'

The three of them study the menu before deciding what to have. Matty isn't sure why he has bothered to look because he always has the same when he comes here, Lancashire Hot-Pot, arguably better than the one his Mum made him as a little boy, although he would never be brave enough to tell her.

It has all the food groups that he craves, meat and potatoes, cooked long and slow.

Christina opts for the Morecambe Bay mussels and scallops, seared on a grill with lemon butter sauce. The shellfish in this part of the world tends to be outstanding.

'You know, the one thing that the British do exceptionally well is rear beef, so I will have a steak tonight,' says Bruno.

'To be honest, they are all going a bit mad here at the moment; I wouldn't,' mutters Matty under his breath.

'Miss, I would like a sirloin steak, with all of the fat trimmed off, cooked mid-point between rare and medium rare, please. I would like it served with a peppercorn sauce on the side, preferably green peppercorn, not black, some mushrooms with some garlic, and chips, not fries. Proper hand-cut chips, not those skinny fries that they sell at McDonald's.'

A brief glance between the waitress and Matty bonds them together. The waitress looks forward to conveying the order to the chef, who is already in a filthy mood tonight, as God forbid, it is busy, and his team is live on Sky.

Just for fun, Matty decides to order a bottle of Chablis, knowing full well that French wine will annoy both Italians.

'So, your brother has a proposition for us, Christina.'

'Really? You surprise me.'

'Matty, for some time, you have kindly helped our family with the distribution of our fashion products in England,' says Bruno. 'We are very grateful for your support.

'Now, I want to know if you would be willing to expand a little. We have other diversified interests and are keen to start importing some other things over to England, perhaps not completely on the right side of the law.'

'I will tell you right now I won't have anything to do with drugs. That is a red line I will not cross,' whispers Matty firmly.

'I swear on the de Luca family name that it will not be drugs. This is not our way.'

'Matty, I promise you: Bruno is telling the truth. You two are more like each other than you think,' says Christina.

'It is nothing to be concerned about: fake cigarettes from Albania, vodka from Ukraine, watches from China, some electrical products. We are simply the intermediaries facilitating goods making their way from other countries to England.'

'Ok, let me speak to the boys, but I have one condition. It's your responsibility to bring it across the Channel. We will collect it from outside Dover; that way, we limit our risk.'

'*Benne*, that is settled, then. Let's share some wine,' Bruno says, reaching for the bottle. 'But I, too, have one important condition. I like your friends, Mr Hammy and Mr Benny, but I would like Christina to manage these arrangements; keep it in the family, so to speak.'

The waitress arrives to take away the empty plates. She is somewhat relieved that the kitchen has managed to turn out the steak to Bruno's exact requirements.

'How was your steak, sir?' she asks.

'My dear, it was sublime; one of the best I have ever had,' says Bruno. 'Can you ask the chef where he sources his beef?'

'Of course I can,' she replies as she heads off to find the chef.

'He says Brake Brothers,' she says on her return. Matty smiles to himself. The daft Italian thinks that this is a local artisanal butcher as opposed to an industrial frozen food supplier.

The evening is over. Bruno has been collected by his driver and is now speeding down the M61 for another long night of illicit pleasure with his young lady. The evening has turned colder as Matty and Christina walk back home. She, at least, had the foresight to bring a spare pair of trainers to walk in.

There is a chilly wind coming off the sea, and the lack of any moon makes the night look dark and ominous. They can hear and smell the sea, rather than see it. They walk hand in hand, both relieved that they have survived a visit from big brother.

'You knew about this, didn't you?' asks Matty.

'Would you be mad if I told you the answer was, yes? At the end of the day, he is still my brother; I am still loyal. My family is your family.'

'I am only doing this for you. Do you really think that I am like him?'

'Only in the business that you both do, nothing else. As human beings, you could not have more different values. You love your wife and your family and will do anything to help people in need, which is why I love you so much. Whereas he only gives a fuck about himself. He will walk over everybody to get what he wants. That is why I chose England, my love.'

CHAPTER FOURTEEN

2022

The journey south allows the boys to enjoy the views. Northumberland is one of the truly great counties of England: stark coastal beauty with rural farmland, adjacent to the imperious North Sea, before you get down to the industrial plains of the south.

The farmhouse that the police have obtained has a small courtyard with pretty flower planters. The main house is a charming two-storey cottage, painted white, with blue sash windows. The house is secluded from the main road, surrounded by a wall on three sides and screened by shrubbery at the front. It is no longer a working farm, although there are still a large barn and some outbuildings to the side of the cottage, filled with rusting machinery.

'Well, that's a bit shit: no Netflix this time,' says Tony.

'Oh well, we can always just read. It looks like the owners have a wide collection of books.'

'They also have Monopoly.'

'Yeah, right. So, what are the chances that Tony will be able to resist stealing from the bank? How is your leg, anyway?'

'They gave me Arnica for it, and you ought to see the bruising. It's like a fiery sunset. Do you want to see it?'

'No thanks, not before dinner.'

Dinner is disappointing – spaghetti carbonara microwaved to within an inch of its life. The beer, however, has now been chilled, so all is not lost.

'So, what did you do when you moved to Gateshead?' asks Stephen.

'Not a lot, to be honest. I think I wasted away the last twelve years. I decided, after Matty, I didn't really trust working for someone, so I went solo.

'I was with a lass for a good few years, but eventually she couldn't cope with my nocturnal habits, and then she met another fella. Never had any real mates, just people I know down the social club.

'Then Covid came along, and I probably fell even more into a rut, staying in the house for weeks on end, nowhere to go. I thought I liked being a loner, but I realise now that everyone needs people in their lives. So, in a strange kind of way, I am actually finding this whole thing to be good fun.'

'Oh, it's a riot,' says Stephen.

'If I am honest, I kind of miss the old life, the excitement; it felt like we were just part of a big family.'

'We were never part of the family; we were always outsiders.'

'Do you think that Matty would ever turn his back on the others?' says Tony.

'No, he wouldn't; they were his brothers. You and I were disposable once we had outlived our usefulness.'

'What about you – what happened when you went to Glasgow?'

'Well, for me, it was more a sense of freedom to finally get away from it all. Given Matty paid my debts off, I always felt that he had bought me. I felt angry and guilty, so I just wanted a fresh start,' says Stephen.

'I was a fully trained accountant and was lucky to find Griffiths and Henderson. The only person who knows about my background is the Managing Director. He had previously sponsored a couple of others in protection schemes, as part of their commitment to their I&D agenda.

'Then I met Lisa, and we got married and now we have two amazing kids. For sure, Covid was a horrible time. Lisa had just launched her own business and the kids were just starting school, so having to take on the whole home-schooling stuff was tough.

'In fact, I was never busier at work. In my line of work as a forensic accountant, companies wanted to know what they needed to do to stay alive, what mitigations they could implement to protect their cash flow. I used to joke that we were key workers.'

'I never saw rainbow stickers on the windows of accountants,' says Tony, laughing. 'And we certainly never banged our pots and pans for you, either.'

'I worked straight through, no furlough, no holidays.'

'Furlough – first time I heard it I laughed; I thought of the horses. Guess what? I never got any furlough money from the government either. They weren't very keen on looking after the grey economy.'

'So, you see, for us life is going well. We have successful careers, a lovely family, and everything in the world to look forward to,' says Stephen.

'Why did you not tell your wife about your past?'

'I think, to begin with, it was guilt. I thought if she knew about my past, she would not have me in her life. Then as time went by, I began to think that maybe I had got away with it, which made it even harder to tell her. I then thought she would hate me for not telling her, so I just kept delaying it.'

'I've never been married, mate, but even I know that marriages are built on trust. It's going to be a long way back for you,' says Tony.

'I know. I feel as though I have destroyed it all, and I think that's what hurts the most.'

'Mate, do you want to borrow the burner phone again, and give Lisa a call? You will need to go outside, though. Cross over the road and stand beside the gate to the field where the cows are; the signal in the house is rubbish.'

* * *

Lisa sees the call come up on her phone as she is working on her laptop at the kitchen island at home. She saved the number from the last time, so it now comes up as Stephen (or Johnny).

'Stephen, thank God, how are you?'

'We are fine. Tony and I have been moved to another location.'

'I don't understand. What happened?'

'Well, we were in Edinburgh, and someone in a powerful car tried to do a hit and run on us. They missed me but caught Tony in the leg. Thankfully not broken, but badly bruised. We were both very lucky.'

'Jesus Christ, this is serious. What did the police have to say about it? Do they know who did it?'

'Well, to be honest, they are beginning to piss me off. The lead officer you met when they collected me is called Brogan, and she gives the impression of thinking that we are a couple of wide boys. Every interview that we have, it seems as if they think we are the criminals. They keep trying to make a connection to the drugs trade.'

'Stephen, I have real issues with my trust in you. How do I know that you weren't involved in drugs?'

'Lisa, I give you my absolute word. Not once was I ever involved in drugs. I swear on Cameron and Emily's life. I think the police are doing a pretty shit job; I wonder if we are even more at risk letting them call all the shots.'

'You must do what they say; don't make things worse. So where are you now?'

'I really shouldn't tell you, but we are holed up in a farmhouse in Northumberland. You cannot tell anyone.'

'Yeah, of course, like I run around the place with people who carry out hit-and-run murder attempts all the time. Actually, my own business, it's just a big cover-up for my criminal enterprises . .
.

'Also, I have cancelled the holiday to Florida. With everything going on, it just seemed pointless. I just haven't got round to telling Cammy and Emily.'

'We will make it up to them, babe'.

'Yes, *you* will.'

'Can I also ask you to do a favour for me? This stupid Nokia phone of Tony's is rubbish. Can you do some digging for me on Google – investigate Frank Williams and the Manchester drug trade?'

'I don't understand; you said that you had nothing to do with drugs.'

'It's just the police only tell us what they want us to know, and you know me and problem-solving; if I understand it better, then I might be able to figure it all out.'

'Ok, give me a couple of days.'

'So, what are your plans tonight?'

'Oh, you know, picking up Emily from swimming, and then Cameron, making dinner, ironing school clothes, working on a PowerPoint for a pitch tomorrow, and then maybe Bella and I will get glammed up and go to a club until three in the morning.'

'Sorry.'

'And what are you and your best chum Tony getting up to tonight – something nice?'

'Well, we are not allowed out now, so it looks like we are playing Monopoly . . . Tony says that I can have the top hat!'

CHAPTER FIFTEEN

2003

In the end, Christina never made it back for Christmas in 2002. She and Matty were so busy with the boys and a growing number of social occasions to attend that they postponed it. She felt guilty because she knew her Mamma had been telling everyone in the town that her girl was coming back home, and that the boys were the most handsome ever born. She knew her Dad was frail, but she was just so busy.

However, she is finally able to take the boys over at Easter to stay with Nonno and Nonna. It feels wonderful to be back home. Arguably, April is one of the very best times to visit southern Italy. You have the religious significance of Easter, and its countless celebrations and frenetic festivals. It is the start of better spring weather. There is still some snow over on Mount Etna, but the early warmth means that the wildflowers have burst into bloom, their scent strong and vibrant.

Their estate is ablaze with prickly flowering cactus. Everyone has a spring in their step, anticipating the summer months to come.

The sea is still way too cold for most Italians, but Christina has been away so long that she must have a dip. She drives down to the Lido de Catanzaro to swim, with Papa still wearing his big coat, sitting on the sandy beach on a small deckchair. The boys don't like the cold very much and prefer to stay on shore, building sandcastles. The cold shocks her system, but once in, she loves it.

The town is peacefully quiet, with few tourists. Once they have made it this far south, they tend to head for Sicily and trendy resorts such as Taormina, and then on to try and find where Vito Corleone was born.

Growing up in Calabria, Christina understands many families participate in organised crime. In primary school, it was always clear who was and who was not. In many ways, she is immune to it now, no longer seeing it as either a good thing or a bad thing. She knows that Bruno likes to flirt on the edges of it, rather than be part of it. Her big brother is strong on bravado and bullshit, in equal measures. Their family have been here for more than one hundred years, so they are given respect and left alone, without having to pay a *pizzo*.

The deterioration in Papa is pronounced. She hasn't seen him for eighteen months, and she is convinced that he has an aggressive form of either dementia or Alzheimer's. She's grateful that he still knows who she is and loves being with the boys.

He has started to relive the past with a gentle melancholy but cannot remember what he had for lunch.

Father Conte has started to visit him weekly at the villa to hear confession and say Mass.

The problem is that Mamma will not allow any of the family to make an appointment for him at the doctors. Mamma is typically scathing about the fact that he has health problems.

'I think he has Italian Alzheimer's . . . forgets everything apart from his grudges.' She cackles.

She tries to talk to Mamma about the future. She even suggests to her that they come and live with her, knowing that this is probably futile.

'Absolutely no way,' says Mamma. 'We were born in this village, and we will die in this village. Also, where you live is full of kiss-me-quick hats and candy floss.'

Today, Mamma is making dinner and, like any good Italian mother, wants to involve the young ones in the process. As ever, the energetic Marco wants to be involved, so he is given the job of rinsing the fava beans. Even at this young age, he towers over his diminutive grandmother. In the storeroom, she has found one of her old aprons that is already too tight on the young man.

Angelo has no desire to cook and instead buries his face in his Game Boy at the kitchen table.

'So, first of all, we are going to make the salad to go with the fish,' says Nonna.

'We will use eggplant, tomatoes, red onions and the fava beans that you are preparing, Marco.

'For the main course, we will have *pesce spada,* or swordfish, as it's known in English.'

'What? A fish has a sword . . . that's so cool.'

'*Si,* but you don't eat it; far too chewy!' says Nonna, laughing. 'We will cook it with lemon and capers and serve it with a sauce made with olive oil, parsley and oregano. The herbs come straight from my garden. It is a dish that your Mamma used to love as a little girl.

'And to finish, we will have caciocavallo; it's a local cheese which I bought from the market today.'

Happy that her mother is in control of both the cooking and the boys, Christina wanders off down the track behind the house.

The chorus of cicadas rings out, reminding her of summers as a little girl.

Two donkeys stand perfectly still in the field, but she feels their eyes following her.

It was here, growing up as a little girl, that she came to the olive grove to think, to work things out. She has grown up a lot in the last ten years since she left the village. Back then, she was full of spirit and ideology. She knew she wanted to escape Southern Italy, as she found it suffocating.

She loved the thought of living in England. When she visited London, it was everything that she expected. A majestic and historic city, full of life and fervour.

When she visited the Lake District, it was all mountains and stunning scenery; it was green and lush in a way that Italy was not.

In her dreams, she had not expected to find her Prince Charming in Preston, but fate is often unexpected. She is still madly in love with him. He has given her two gorgeous boys, has allowed her to build a beautiful home, and is always faithful to her, unlike any Italian boyfriend that she has ever had.

The only problem is that sometimes his good nature runs close to being soft. She wants him to develop an edge that could make them successful.

She understands she is the one that keeps pushing him to be bolder and faster. He says all the right things, but she knows that at the heart of it, he is struggling with the problem of split loyalties. He wants to be loyal to his own family and to his two lifelong friends. For an Italian, the choice is very clear: you are only loyal to your wife and your blood relatives; you are wary of everyone else.

She resolves to take Matty away for a few days, just the two of them, and talk about moving the business forward with less involvement from the others, perhaps heading in a different direction. At some point, the boys will grow up, and she wants them to take over the business in the future, to keep it within the family.

This makes her contemplate her boys. Angelo is Italian in name only. He has inherited his father's genes and is thoughtful and caring. He is painfully shy; in fact, his teachers have discussed this at parents' night. Academically, he is extremely bright, particularly at mathematics, but socially he is very awkward, and he finds it impossible to make friends. Christina wonders whether she should perhaps get him some therapy.

Marco is the complete opposite, and his personality dwarfs that of his elder brother. He is loud and boisterous, and even in year three, they have been called to the school twice for his starting fights with fellow pupils. He is capable of monumental tantrums if he doesn't get his own way, inevitably taking it out on Angelo. He has a Latin temperament to go with his looks, and Christina knows that the next stage of his growing up is going to be a challenge.

'Hello, sister. Mamma said I would find you here, just like the old times,' says Bruno, no longer dressed like a gangster, but more like a vineyard owner.

'*Ciao*, Bruno. Yeah, it's where I come to sort stuff out in my head.'

'Well, I have bought you a glass of wine,' he says, reaching into his rucksack and producing two glasses and a bottle of red wine. 'Slightly better than the one that your Matthew bought me in the pub. This one is made from grapes on that hill over there, while his had been made in some South American ghetto with leftover grapes and toxic water.'

They sit under an olive tree, with their backs against the trunk.

'So, tell me what problems you are trying to figure out,' says Bruno.

'Nothing serious; just thinking about the life that I have created over in England, and what might be next for us.'

'You have a beautiful family now. I take my hat off to you, and Matty has more than fulfilled his obligations. So, I have stood the assassins down.'

'I know. I would just like him to get out of the stealing business. He is too old for that now. It's time to change direction.'

'I have some news for you, Christi– I am taking on a major hotel development just to the south of the Lido, near Copanello beach.'

Catanzaro is one of those Italian towns that has its main centre inland and up the hill from its seafront, known as the Lido. This was generally to provide safety from various marauders over the years, and there were plenty of them. Now, it means that you get the benefit of both land and sea.

Bruno has long thought that Calabria underperforms when it comes to tourism. Of course, it's hard to compete with the North and its historical monuments, but the South offers a much more authentic version of Italy. One that gives greater insight into the Italy of the past.

Recently, however, Sicily has seen a big uptick in numbers, as it is seen to be safer these days. It also has the romantic history and blockbuster films to promote it.

Nobody thinks very much of poor Calabria, the forgotten toe of Italy. What is needed is investment in infrastructure, with the right modern accommodations and services, and convincing people that rugged Calabria is not only extremely safe but beautiful, too.

Bruno is not driven by altruism; it is his narcissism that motivates him. People think he is a middle-of-the-road businessman, hawking clothes and fashion accessories around Europe. They see him as a middle-league player, not giving him more than a second glance. He finds this deeply offensive, as his enormous ego wants him to be seen at the top table.

For some time now, he has been looking for a break-out investment and meeting potential investors.

'Well, that's going to cost plenty,' Christina says.

'The total project is close to €100 million. We have raised about €10m between three of us, and the Banco de Italia is in for €90million,' Bruno says. 'The banks are awash with money at the moment and are desperate to do the deal.'

'Well, I have to say, you are certainly showing some ambition, alright.'

'There is something that I need to tell you, though. I have asked Mamma and Papa to provide a guarantee for the loan by granting the villa as security.'

'Fuck sake! And you didn't think to ask me if that was ok?'

'With father's health not great, I persuaded them both to give me power of attorney. I could have done it without even telling you, though I have their blessing. They think it's good for the family. The fashion trade is getting harder and harder; margins are being squeezed, with cheaper fashion coming from Asia now.'

'So, you have power of attorney, and I don't?'

'You have chosen a life in the UK. It is me that has remained, and I can make the decisions for them.'

'Well, I can't say that I am happy about it. If anything happens to the family home, I will kill you myself.'

'I also have a business proposition for you,' says Bruno, pouring them both another glass of wine.

John G Gemmell

'Our little arrangement in England is working well for us. We use your distribution network to deliver garments and accessories across England, along with some other products at the same time. In return, Matty has even started to send me some goods back over to Italy, so you see, we have set up our own little European trade deal.'

'I know all of this. It is me that oversees it all, remember.'

'But this new opportunity that has come my way is one that I think Matty would not approve of.'

'You know we don't touch drugs.'

'No, no, you misunderstand. I want to export people. My new partners have a very lucrative business bringing people over from Albania and Kosovo to Italy. Everyone wants to make their way to England, for better social security and job opportunities. I think it can be very lucrative, but I want to keep it in the family now.'

'Bruno, I don't know about this. That is people smuggling.'

'It's very straightforward. Every so often, we will place a small group of people in amongst the goods. We will ensure ventilation and temperature control to make sure that they are safe. Once they get to the UK, you will need to have two drivers who can take them to a safe house as directed. That will be your only involvement; we will be responsible for everything else.

'Think of it as an act of philanthropy and kindness. You will be helping some poor souls start a new life in England. You are helping them escape from a dangerous world, possibly even saving their lives.'

'But it's human trafficking! It's unimaginable that I could say yes to this.'

'Christi, listen. I need you to do this for me and the family. I must ask you to remain loyal to your blood family; loyalty can never waiver. Loyalty to your family is a virtue, not a vice.'

'But I have my own family to think about as well.'

'They will never need to know'

CHAPTER SIXTEEN

2022

The boys have been holed up for four days in their farmhouse and are beginning to go stir-crazy.

They have had no contact with the outside world at all, and Monopoly has run its course. Stephen, surprisingly, won, and he even hopes that Tony might have had an epiphany and given up theft.

Despite the clear warnings from the police, they decide that they need to get out and go for a walk. They find a leaflet in the house recommending a local walk, so they set off.

They walk into the village of Craster, passing it's pretty little harbour. It looks as if it had been a busy dock at some point, but now there are only a few boats sitting mournfully in the silted marshes, awaiting the tide. There is not much fishing these days in this part of the country. The path takes them through farmland, past some nosy cows, with a rocky shoreline off to the right.

'Was Craster not one of the characters in Game of Thrones?' asks Tony

'No idea, mate. I've never seen it.'

'What, one of the greatest television shows ever?'

'It's alright for you, living on your own, watching box sets all through the night. I'm the father of two young children; we live in a CBeebies bubble, I'm afraid.'

'Well, if I remember right, he was a wildling, a bit unsavoury. He ended up getting his throat cut in a grisly end.'

'Lovely, I'm sure.'

This part of England is very peaceful and quite gentrified. It has the air of a conservative voting neighbourhood, full of pensioners with expansive lawns and gold-plated final salary pension pots.

'So, what do you think of Brexit, then?' asks Tony.

'I think it's already been a complete disaster. The morning that we woke up to the news, I simply couldn't believe it. I thought, what have we done? We have collectively gone mad.

'It makes no sense. Why would you make it harder to trade with your biggest market? Why would you take away people's freedom of movement to work in Europe? You know, the British passport used to be the strongest passport in the world, meaning you didn't need visa entry requirements. Now its rating will fall like a stone.

'And our access to labour markets is going to be difficult; people in this country don't want to do the jobs that are vacant.'

'I voted Leave,' says Tony.

They walk past Dunstanburgh Castle, with its ruined staircases and chambers. They continue round the castle and on to the Greymare Rock, made of limestone and shaped by volcanic pressure. There is the shrieking of gulls in the air. Passing a golf course, they come down onto the beach and sit on top of one of the concrete bunkers built generations ago to protect the nation in a time of war.

'So how come you voted Leave?' asks Stephen.

'Not sure, to be honest. Lots of the boys down the club went for it. They said that immigration was out of control, and we couldn't cope with even more of them coming over.'

'But you're an immigrant yourself,' says Stephen with a smile. 'You came over and settled here from Ireland . . . And what about the Northern Ireland protocol?'

'Didn't pay much attention to it, really.'

'And that, my friend, is why it happened – a lack of truthful information and a big dose of apathy. We sleepwalked into it, mate, and a generation will lose out.'

They amble to the far end of Embleton Bay and cross over the little burn. A small group of oystercatchers are having fun on the shore, their high-pitched whoops sounding like the voices of kids on a roller coaster. They approach Newton Haven and then Low Newton. It has a picturesque little square with white fisherman's cottages.

'The problem with both Brexit and Independence is that however you want to round the numbers up, half the people want it, and half the people don't, so a majority will never be happy about the outcome. It's hard to be united when everyone is divided.'

They continue their stroll inland, crossing sand dunes and then a little woodland. They discover two wildlife hikes facing out over the Newton Pool nature reserve. There is a beautiful scent in the air, a mixture of sea salt and marsh, as they continue along the path to Dunstan Steads.

'If you look back over the last few years,' continued Stephen, 'we have had Brexit, then Covid, then rampant inflation, then a war in Ukraine, with possibly another one in Taiwan, a fuel crisis, and the worst cost of living crisis in recent times. The NHS is shot to bits. And we are being led by a group of self-important, narcissistic lunatics who now think it's okay for a politician to tell lies.'

'Loads of people my way switched to Conservative at the last vote. Can you believe that people in Gateshead, of all places, voted Tory?' says Tony. 'The so-called Red Wall fell.'

'It's the young ones that I feel sorry for, held hostage because the older middle classes want to hold on to their secure pensions,' says Stephen, beginning to get wound up, even though he always tries to stay neutral.

'Maybe that's us just getting old now, so we start getting twisty about everything.'

'And here we are with all this stuff happening around us, and we're on the run from gangsters unknown,' says Stephen with a laugh, looking at an older couple out for some birdwatching. 'Do you think they realise that they could be in danger just by being in the same field as the two of us?'

They walk round the golf course again and climb up past the castle before following the track back to Craster. Another twenty minutes and they are back at the farm.

Stephen opens the fridge door and peers in reluctantly. After four nights in a row, he simply cannot face another ready meal.

'Hey, Tony, how about I take you out for something to eat? The tourist brochure says that the Jolly Fisherman in the village is fantastic. Our little police friends don't even need to know.'

'Excellent idea! Count me in. I just want to go and get changed for dinner first.'

He decides that nobody will really mind if he borrows some clothes from the owner of the farm. He tries to carry off the rich farmer look straight from his lurid imagination. When he comes down the stairs, he is wearing dark green tweed trousers, a checked shirt and a lemon-coloured quilted jacket. He has thrown on a flat cap for added effect.

'Fuck me! I don't know if it's landed gentry, or maybe you haven't realised that we have passed the peak hipster era now?'

'Well, I think I look geet lush, and I am now ready for dinner. Let's go,' says Tony, adding a posher lilt to his already strangled dialect.

'Ok, Mr Mumford, to the pub we shall go.'

The Jolly Fisherman is in the centre of the village of Craster. It is a pretty little pub, with a two-story building attached to a single-story building to the right. It has stone floors and beamed ceilings. The menu has been chalked up on the board by someone with good handwriting.

The view out to sea is sensational. The sea is gun-metal grey with white horses galloping towards the shore in formation.

The pub is renowned for its seafood, having won numerous awards. It's reasonably busy this evening, without it being impossible to find a table. The boys pick a table in the corner on the lower floor.

Sat next to them are two older couples, who are currently engaged in a tense stand-off about who is going to drive home tonight and not drink any wine. Eventually, it is settled that no one will drive; they will all drink wine, then they will all walk home, and one of the chaps will come down in the morning to collect the car. The outcome was never in doubt.

Stephen and Tony decide to share the Jolly Fisherman's Fish Board, which has crab, North Sea prawns, salmon, kippers, pate, sweet, cured herring and artisanal sourdough bread. The crab is fantastically fresh, with both white and brown meat.

They have two pints of Estrella Damm at £6.25 a pint, which makes Tony glad that Stephen is paying. He can get two pints of Carling for that back at the club.

'Do you think this is a pub?' asks Tony.

'Yeah, it's a pub which serves great food,' says Stephen, happy to be eating well this evening.

'It's never a pub; it's just a posh restaurant. They are all the same, really. Now they all get painted grey and given some made-up name by combining an adjective and an animal, like the Randy Squirrel or something like that.'

'Although, to be fair, this pub is in a fishing village, and it does specialise in seafood, so its name is not that random.'

'Yes, but it's not that jolly, and I don't see any fishermen, just retirees. There is no jukebox, no fruit machine, no live sports; don't even bother to ask about the pool table or darts board . . . and it's so bloody expensive. That's why people just drink at home these days.'

'The world is changing, my friend. People don't want these things. They want to have nice surroundings, good food, without a bunch of sweaty workers standing at the bar swearing all the time.'

'And they are not even called pubs or bars anymore,' continues Tony. 'They are called inns or taprooms or gin palaces, and people serving beer are not barmen, they are beer mongers.

'Also, whatever happened to the humble beer mat? It was part of our history. It kept the table clear of any spillage and had multiple purposes; you could write a phone number down. It would sort a wonky table. Now they have been consigned to the past, probably by some accountant who reckons you can save money.

'The staff used to be smart, black trousers and a white shirt. Now they wear those silly aprons, either denim or leather.'

Stephen laughs at that one before diving into the sharing plate. Tony is doing so much talking that, for once, he is not hoovering up the food, which is good, as the walk has made him hungry.

'And another thing, don't get me started on places that don't use proper plates. They use ones that are on an angle, so that your soup runs into your lap, or serve your dinner on a slate plate, with your beer in a jam jar. Or that craft beer shit that tastes so hoppy you can't have more than one pint because you are too busy scraping it off your teeth.

'It's all a big con . . . You can't just have a loaf of bread; you must have an artisanal sourdough bread. You can still have a ginger beer, but you must have the one with ginger from the sunny uplands of Sri Lanka. I may be uneducated, but it's all just marketing, so you end up paying through the nose.'

Stephen is stuffed, but Tony manages to put away a sticky toffee pudding, made with caramel sauce and Madagascar vanilla ice cream, which he eats without recognising the irony. The pub is just about ready to close when the boys start their walk home.

It's dark with a clear sky. The moon is just one day short of being full and as omnipresent as ever, puffing itself up one last time for its big monthly moment.

After an uneventful walk home, they turn round the final bend towards their farmhouse.

'Oh shit,' says Stephen, 'I have left my jacket in the pub. I'm going to run back and get it. I will see you at the house.'

He is just in time as they are locking up. Before long, he has made the journey back, although something is not right.

'Fuck, I smell smoke,' mutters Stephen. 'Tony?'

The farmhouse erupts in huge columns of smoke and flames. A brisk breeze fans the flames so they quickly take hold and reach the timber roof, which crackles as it catches. The wind helps to accelerate the fire, so within minutes, the building is fully ablaze.

Choking black smoke spirals upwards, forcing many of the birds in the trees to flee their nests, screeching their unhappiness at being disturbed from their slumbers. An owl hoots its displeasure.

Filthy, acrid fumes burn the back of his throat as he watches the scene unfold from a distance.

He feels helpless, watching on from safety, unable get any nearer because of the heat and the smoke. His heart is beating not just in his chest, but in his head.

Then there is rustling to his right as Tony emerges from the bushes.

'Well, that was a close call!' says Tony, before he is grabbed in a bear hug.

'I thought you were inside.'

'Nah, came round the corner and saw two blokes in a van, so I dived in the bushes instead.'

'Fuck me, now they have tried to burn us to death,' says Stephen. 'This is becoming ridiculous. I've had enough of the bloody police. Why don't we take off on our own this time?'

'Agreed, mate. Let's go back to the pub.'

When they arrive back at the pub, it is cloaked in darkness. Looking back in the direction of the farm, they can see a warm glow on the horizon. Stephen is feeling guilty that they have run and not phoned the fire brigade.

'We need wheels,' says Tony.

'You're the one that told me it is almost impossible to hot rod a car anymore, that under the bonnet was all sealed.'

'Yes, but I don't need to. Remember the two couples sitting beside us? Well, one of them left their car keys on the table, so I just picked them up, and now it's easy: press the button, and hey presto, beep-beep. It looks like the BMW is our ride tonight!'

'Bloody hell, mate, you haven't lost your touch.'

They dive into the car, but it takes them ten minutes to figure out how to start it and locate the handbrake. Once that is resolved, they are on their way.

'I think we should go under the radar and not tell the police where we are. I want to go back to see my family,' says Stephen. 'I need to explain things to Lisa.'

'Ok, a road trip it is, but let's not make it too obvious. This car will have a tracker on it, for sure. We only have the cover of tonight before we need to dump it. Rather than go north, I suggest we go south. And I need to visit Gateshead on the way. Then we take it to some random town and dump it in a quiet street, not in any station car park as they all have CCTV.'

'You have got this all figured out.'

'It's my job. It's what I was born to do . . . I told you this was going to be fun. I have never been to Glasgow before. Will I be safe enough?'

'You might want to change your clothes.'

CHAPTER SEVENTEEN

5th February 2004

Matty rises early on the morning of the 5th of February and heads out for his morning run. He has been persuaded to run the Morecambe half marathon later this year, raising money for Cancer Awareness, so he is trying to maintain a level of fitness.

He heads from his home in Happy Mount southwards along the shore to the town centre, past the Morecambe Hotel and then along the Esplanade.

He passes the art deco Midland Hotel. It closed its doors four years ago and is now a metaphor for the town. Neglected and derelict, at the mercy of the elements. There are rumours that developers want to buy it, so fingers crossed.

He reaches the Eric Morecambe statue and reflects that in a few hours' time, it will be busy with people wanting to get their picture taken with it. It was unveiled five years earlier by the Queen, paying homage to the town's favourite son. With its backdrop of the sea, with the tide fully in this morning, and the mountains of the Lake District, it is a spectacular statue.

These are the sort of civic initiatives that should be applauded but are not the norm

as the local council are generally bereft of good ideas.

He looks at the shops and retail businesses on his left. A lack of vision and leadership means that it is now the charity pound shops, takeaways and cheap cafes that occupy the space. Matty hopes that Morecambe won't go the way of Blackpool, which has become a dumping ground for the socially excluded, with high levels of drug and alcohol abuse. Once it takes hold, it is almost impossible to reverse.

If the decision-making was only in the hands of ambitious private entrepreneurs, rather than the council charlatans, they might make some progress at bringing growth to their little town.

The seagulls are up and about early but bored and unhappy, with no humans around to prey on. They are fatter than normal seagulls, a reflection of their high-cholesterol diet of chips and kebabs.

Down on the beach, two men are battling nature, flying kites in formation on a strong wind.

He stops off at the Stone Jetty to admire the vista and enjoy a bottle of water. This was originally part of the former harbour and has been rebuilt in recent years.

His run continues round onto Marine Road West, down to the west end gardens, before he reaches Whinnysty Lane where he turns around to follow the same route back. He notes thankfully that the wind is now helping him from behind. Inevitably, it has started to rain.

By the time he reaches home, the endorphins have kicked in, and he feels good. He is even happier to note that not only are the boys already at school, but Christina has left a note to say that she has gone to Manchester for the day, meaning he has the house to himself. Today he wants to sit down with young Johnny and take stock of his business.

Johnny arrives and they set themselves up in the dining room.

'So, let's start with the haulage business,' says Matty.

'You know, the core business is really strong. We will turn over something like £2m this year, and maybe a net profit of £200k.'

'Does that include the Italian deal?'

'Nope. Bruno pays Christina directly, and then she passes a dividend to the company; it will be another £200k.

And if I can remind you of the ownership structure here – it is through Matty O'Hare Ltd; you own 50% and Hammy and Benny own 25% each – which, as you know, I don't recommend. If you ever disagree with them, you will have a stalemate.'

'It's fine. I trust them with my life.'

'Ok, the company owns the freehold over the site out at Heysham. You also own 14 HGVs; eight are owned outright and six are on lease.

'You own four tanning salons outright – in Preston, Morecambe, Lancaster and Blackpool. You know, I was sceptical about this approach, but boy, I was wrong. I make each of them show a turnover of £2k per week; sometimes they don't have any customers at all, yet we can pass the money through and make it clean.

'You own three car washes, which you have leased out to Deniz, that Turkish bloke. I think he is from one of the "stans" but just cannot be bothered explaining to Brits where it is. Again, we do the books for him, so we can massage the numbers any way we want, and then we give him an agreed percentage back.

'Then you have the six pubs. These are owned by the Bliss Pub Company (a little nod back to where it all began). The freehold properties are all held under Christina's name and have leases agreed with each tenant, where they pay you rent, and we control the discount from the breweries.

'And finally, there are the flats. Over the years, they have now increased to 12, mostly within Morecambe. They have all been refurbished to a high level and have tenants who are paying the rent on time. Of course, if they don't, we just send Benny round for a word.'

'Good. So, all in, what do you think the net worth is?' asks Matty.

'Well, the tanning salons and the carwashes aren't really assets, but I reckon the rest is probably worth about £5m.'

'And the other part of the business that is not spoken about?'

'Well, as you know, we don't keep books for that one, but it still generates about £2m per year. When you decided to open it up to cover more of the country, that helped with revenue,' says Johnny. 'The problem is one of control. It's no longer just the three of you meeting to agree on the jobs. This is a problem that could bite you one day.'

'I want us to be out of this line of work in the next two years. It might have been where we started, but it's not where I want to go. I want to get more involved in property development, more than anything else. It strikes me that property is the most secure investment, and it doesn't come with violence or the risk of jail.'

'You will need to find something for Tony to do, then.'

'Who cares about him? He can go and retire somewhere nice. There is one other matter that I would like you to attend to.

'This house is in my name only; I would like to transfer it in its entirety to Christina. It will spread the risk for her in case anything ever happens to me.'

'Ok, will do. It carries a mortgage with it, so we will need to get the bank's consent.'

'Fine, ask the bank to transfer the mortgage to her, but I will still function as a guarantor.'

Matty picks the boys up from school as Christina is not yet back from Manchester. It's good for him to get some time with his sons, and they kick a ball about the back garden until it begins to get too cold. It doesn't surprise him that Marco dives about the place, making slide tackles and playing with passion, whereas Angelo's heart is never really in it.

They eventually call it off, as the rain has now started to pour down and darkness is beginning to fall. It's time to get the boys in a hot shower and into their PJs early before Mum comes home.

On her return home, they all enjoy a family dinner, cooked for once by Matty, albeit of the frozen variety. Christina is tired from her day in the city so is willing to eat anything.

'How was Manchester? Did you get what you want?' asks Matty.

'Yes, new school clothes for the boys.'

Matty clocks the fact that one of the bags is from Gucci and one from Prada, and he is pretty sure they don't have a range of school uniforms. However, he chooses silence tonight to avoid any confrontation. He will pick this up at another time.

'We played football today, and I won,' says Marco.

'We weren't counting, you idiot,' says Angelo.

'Well, I was.'

'Right, how about we all watch a DVD before bed?' says Matty.

For once, they all enjoy the film in peace, without any drama. With the boys now in bed, Matty decides to make himself and Christina a cup of tea and is flicking through the post from earlier in the day when the phone rings.

'Matty, is that you? It's Joe Smith from Morecambe Taxis.'

'Hey, Joe, what's up?' says Matty, sensing the urgency.

'Matty, something horrible is happening down at the Sands. It sounds like a large group of cockle pickers have been cut off from the land and are now stranded. The police are here, but we are trying to get them some extra help.'

'Ok, I am on my way, and I will phone the boys. Where is it?'

'It's where the Keel Channel meets the Kent Channel.'

He hangs up the landline, dives for his mobile phone and phones Hammy.

'Hammy, listen, something big is going down in the bay tonight. Could be lots of people stuck out in the sand. Get hold of Benny and as many men as you can. See if you can bring ropes and the winch truck and a couple of 4 x 4s as well in case we need them.'

'Ok, will do, boss, but it's pitch black out there and freezing cold. Don't even contemplate going out onto the sands – that would be lunacy.'

Matt shouts up to Christina that there is an emergency, before running out of the front door and jumping into his car. Just over two miles down the road, he comes upon the bright lights of the search and rescue operation.

One of the old-timer British cockle pickers is standing beside the cars, and Matty recognises him from the pub.

'There are Chinese people out there,' he says. 'About 40 of them went out at four pm. On our way back, we tried to tell them that they needed to leave; we were tapping our watches and pointing to the shore. The heavy rain all day has made it much worse. I think they have made a mistake about the tides, and you don't want to do that on the bay in early February.'

The local police sergeant comes over to speak to Matty.

'This isn't looking good, Matty. We got a call about nine-thirty pm from one of the workers. They couldn't speak much English, but all we heard was "sinking water" before the call was cut off. We have managed to rescue about 10 people so far, and they are all suffering hypothermia.'

'I have rounded up some guys, and some equipment. Tell me what you want me to do,' says Matty.

'I cannot let any of you go out onto the bay. It's treacherous. We need the hovercraft and lifeboats for the ones that go out. They have infrared detectors. ETA of 15 minutes for a chopper.'

'Fuck that, we cannot wait. We are going out.'

'Matty, it's pitch dark, the water is freezing and there is a Force 6 wind out there. It's also fair to say you are no expert.'

'I might be no expert, but 15 minutes could be the difference between life and death.'

'Leave it to the professionals, son,' says the sergeant.

'Fuck off.'

'I could arrest you for interfering with a police operation.'

'You just fucking try and do that if you want.'

Matty and Hammy jump into one of the 4 x 4s and head out into the darkness, their heavy-duty spotlight helping guide them. Although they can see little through the dark, the biggest problem is the vastness of the bay. They don't have any sense of where they should be focusing.

They make slow progress through the liquid sand. They can sense the violence of the bay at night.

'Matty, the water is three feet deep here, and we have no idea where there might be quicksand,' says Hammy.

'Ten more minutes. Let's not give up yet.'

They continue their slow and futile search. The sea is like a wet desert. The wind is howling and whipping up a spray of salty water onto their windscreen. The cloud cover means that visibility is appalling. There are tantalising glimpses of moonlight when there is a little break in the clouds. It dances on the windscreen, teasing them momentarily, before plunging them back into darkness.

Sometimes they think they can hear a scream, but it's just the wind playing tricks on their senses.

'Matty, please, this is not safe. I get you want to be a hero, but let's not leave your boys without a dad.'

'Look, what is that out to the right?'

Hammy adjusts the arc light, and it picks up the shape of a human body. It's in an upright position, but they cannot tell whether it's a male or a female.

'I'm going in – you take over the driving,' shouts Matty.

'Oh Jesus, Matty. This is totally fucked up.'

'I can't leave them.'

'Ok, one piece of advice. If you get stuck on the sand, don't kick or fight it. Lean back as it helps redistribute your weight.'

Matty leaps out of the car into the shallow water, instantly flooding his Wellington boots. His clothes are wet and have lost their purpose of keeping him warm. He is immediately swallowed up from view. Both men are now out in the bay alone, one in a car and one on his own.

He reaches out and grabs what looks to be a young woman. The wet sand has acted like cement, pinning her in an upright position. Waves have ripped her clothing. He instantly knows that she has not made it, and the look on her face will haunt him for the rest of his life.

Hammy continues to point the arc light in the direction he thinks they are, but he is now beginning to have doubts, to be disorientated. Visibility is down to yards. He knows that Matty has been away for ten minutes now, and the fear is palpable. He can feel his heartbeat in both his chest and his head.

Suddenly, out of the mist, appears Matty.

He gently lifts the body into the rear of the car and places a couple of jackets over it. Neither of them says a word, the tears gently trickling down their cheeks, as they return to the shore.

The hovercraft has arrived and is preparing to launch, but deep down Matty knows this is now about retrieval rather than rescue.

Some of the neighbours have made flasks of hot tea and coffee and have brought blankets and extra clothes for the survivors. There are now multiple ambulances on site dealing with the injured, most suffering from hypothermia and shock over what fate might have befallen those who have not made it to shore.

'Hammy, go and get one of the ambulance people to come over and take the body. We will need to give a statement to the police, but keep that sergeant away from me,' says Matty.

It is confirmed that the bodies of 21 men and women, aged between 21 and 45, have been retrieved from the bay. It is a dark night for the town of Morecambe. They were people who gave up their lives on the other side of the world to come to this tiny corner of an island. They had been hired to collect cockles and were being paid just £20 per tonne.

It is five am by the time the boys return to his house to try and get some warmth back into their bones and have a cup of tea. Christina comes down in her dressing gown and immediately bursts into tears when she hears the news.

'I cannot believe that something so horrific and inhumane has taken place on our doorstep,'

says Matty. 'All the workers were untrained farmers from China, who have been people trafficked through Liverpool by criminal enterprises and were completely inexperienced in dealing with the unpredictable tides of Morecambe Bay.

'We brought ashore a young girl who couldn't have been much more than twenty., her face will haunt me forever'-says Matty.' She looked like she was sleeping, but she was gone; it was only three feet deep, but it was hypothermia.'

'I have lived here all my life,' says Hammy. 'That's the last time you will ever catch me out there in the dark.'

'Nobody should be out there in the dark,' says Benny.

'This has been going on for years, and we simply choose to ignore it,' says Matty. 'There are a lot of people here with blood on their hands tonight. The people traffickers who bring them into Liverpool, the gangs that control them when they are here, the bastards that pay them fuck all for cockles that get sent abroad because no one here in England eats them . . .

'We have known that they have been living in flats in the area, up to ten mattresses in a room, with no other services. By turning a blind eye, we are all complicit. First thing tomorrow, I want you to go round all our flats and make sure none of them are participating in this.

'I want you all to put out feelers as to what their set-up is here. I want to know everything about their networks, as I am going to blow it all to fuck.'

The group recognises that Matty rarely blows, but when he does, you are best to be well out of the blast range.

'We will have nothing to do with people trafficking, ever,' he declares.

Listening in from the hallway, her head in her hands, Christina says a little prayer.

CHAPTER EIGHTEEN

2022

Within an hour of discovering the burning shell of their temporary abode, the boys are on the road south. Having stupidly agreed to let Tony drive, Stephen finds himself holding tightly onto his seatbelt. It is not that they are driving particularly fast; it's just that he doesn't believe in staying in line, preferring to straddle the central reservation. This is fine on the dual carriageway parts of the A1, but not the single carriage section, and on more than one occasion, a large overnight express has threatened to collect the bounty on their heads for nothing.

Tony also finds it impossible to stay quiet and wants to talk incessantly.

'So, do you think that was them having another go at us?'

'What do you think? It just so happened that the house self-combusted?' says Stephen. 'Of course it was them.'

'But maybe we left the gas on, or an iron on.'

'We went out for dinner, remember, and do you even know how to use an iron?'

'You know, they don't seem very good at their jobs; that's twice they've missed.'

'Also, I feel a bit bad about swiping that bloke's car. He and his wife seemed like such a lovely couple. When he gets down there later this morning, he will be upset. I think when we dump it, I will post his keys back to the Jolly Fisherman, with a map of where to find it. Maybe put £100 in an envelope for him, to take his wife out for lunch on us.'

They join the A1 at Alnwick and given the lack of traffic in the early hours of the morning, make good time down the road. They fly past Morpeth and come off the A1 just at Gosforth Park beside the racecourse.

'Shall I put some music on?' says Stephen, rummaging through the glove compartment. 'What about Coldplay?'

'Oh God no, do you want to make this night even worse?'

'Got the Lady Gaga album here, *A Star is Born*.'

'Perfect. I need to play the part of Bradley Cooper because I canny get up the high notes that the Gaga can,' says Tony.

They drive right into the centre of Newcastle, ready to cross the Tyne. With seven bridges to choose from, they pick the forerunner of the Sydney Harbour Bridge.

'If there is one way to wind up anyone from Gateshead, it is to suggest that they come from Newcastle,' says Tony. 'In times gone past, it was described as a "dirty lane leading to Newcastle" or "Newcastle's Wife".'

'Charming.'

'Anyway, what do you think we should do about the police?' asks Tony as they pull up at a red light and a police patrol car shoots past them, heading back into town to deal with the usual problems, probably at the Bigg Market.

'Nothing. They have hardly helped us at all; that's twice they have known where we were. The police are a leaky bucket. This Osman warning is optional.'

'We could give them a call from the mobile, just to let them know we are ok.'

'No, we don't want them to have this number; best to keep it to ourselves for now until we figure out what to do.'

'We could call them from a phone box or something?' suggests Tony.

'A phone box? Have you gone completely mad? When was the last time you were in one of them? They don't work anymore. Can you imagine telling a teenager to use a phone box? It would be like you have been sent down from Mars.'

'Ok, that's us here at my flat.'

Tony's flat is in a small and shabby street in the centre of Gateshead. The buildings are two storeys high, in what can only be called distressed red brick. In Islington, it would be super cool, but here it just looks like it is flaking away slowly.

A long time ago, these properties would have had little, well-tended front gardens, but over time, they have all been concreted over. A few have cars parked in them at such alarming angles that you wonder how it is even possible.

Most residents have done it to accommodate the four different types of bins that the council give you these days, as it is much easier to keep them there than dragging them through the house. The refuse planners in the council are in denial about terraced houses and multiple bins, and how difficult it is to get them to the front.

The street is carefully decorated with a used mattress, some laminate flooring and a shopping trolley from Asda. Sometimes it is worth the loss of a pound just to get your shopping to the front door. A couple of the streetlights are out, so half the street is in the dark.

'In you come. Home sweet home, as they say,' says Tony.

As no one had been in over the last week, there is little by way of ventilation. The flat is a complete mess. The living room is scattered with empty newspapers, takeaway cartons, empty bottles of Diet Coke. It is completely dominated by the monster flat-screen television. The kitchen is no better; a collection of fourteen dirty coffee mugs is impressive for a man who lives on his own.

Tony notes that the cat's bowl has cat food in it, which means that Bill did not follow his instructions. The cat has probably gone completely feral by now.

'Do you want anything? I could make you tea, but I don't have any milk.'

'No, all good,' says Stephen, unsure where he might sit.

'Well, I am off to grab a bag and some more clothes, and then we can get going.'

'Any chance that I could borrow the mobile again? I want to message Lisa before the police get to her. And bring the charger; it's going low on juice.'

Hi L, it's me. Listen, we had to leave again in a hurry. This time the police don't know where we are, we are under the radar. We are planning to come up home. Don't tell the police we have been in touch. S. XXX

When he returns, Stephen notes that he has not changed his clothes and is now also carrying two Sports Direct bags.

'So, I see that you are still holding out with your Farmer Giles act,' says Stephen, laughing.

'All part of my disguise. And anyway, they were fresh on this evening, so I can get another good few days out of them before I change. I will withstand the inevitable abuse from the Glaswegians.'

'So, dare I ask what's in the other bag?'

Tony opens the bag to reveal it is full of the oddest collection of stuff. Fifty boxes of Viagra tablets, thirty pairs of Nordic Socks and ten Apple watches. He is working on the principle that he might need some cash to survive the next few weeks on the run, so he plans to liquidate them in Glasgow.

'Do you want some?' asks Tony.

'Eh, no thanks. I'm not even forty yet, and anyway, my feet are perfectly warm enough, thank you.'

'Ok, I'm ready. We just need to pop round to Bill's place first so that I can collect the grand that he has for me.'

'At two in the morning? Will he be up?'

'Oh yes, he always is. He doesn't get in from the club till late, and then he will be up half the night. I think he is addicted to online poker. Right, let's go. It's Bonnie and Clyde time.'

'I don't suppose there is any chance that I could drive this time?'

Bill is awake, as had been predicted. Tony dives in to collect his money, although instead of a grand, it is only £500, with Bill saying that market conditions had driven the price down.

'All ok?'

'Yep, but that dirty fucker ripped me off,' says Tony. 'Also, it seems a couple of fellas came looking for me on the same day that the police took me. I think Bill gave them my mobile number, but no one has called, so it might be just a coincidence.'

'Right, can we go now, or are there any other stops you need to make?'

'No, all good. Let's hit the road, Jack, and don't you come back . . .'

CHAPTER NINETEEN

2006

Christina looks wistfully out of the window of the plane as the Alitalia flight leaves Rome, headed for Lamezia Terme Airport. Her two boys sit beside her and are tucking into Coca-Cola and soured cream and chive Pringles.

Her husband sits across the aisle from them. He is accompanied by his best friends, Hammy and Benny. There is no direct flight from the UK to Calabria, so they have all flown on an early morning flight from Liverpool to Rome and are now aboard their second flight of the day.

It has been six days since her brother called her to say that their father had passed away. She feels sadness and guilt. Sadness that she was not with him in his last few hours, and guilt that she thinks it is probably for the best, as his quality of life had not been good for some time.

Her boys are growing up fast, now aged twelve and ten. They have never been to a funeral, especially not an Italian one. She notes that the grownups on the other side of the aisle are playing cards and are getting a little bit loud, so she gives Matty a look, which he does not fail to misinterpret.

On arrival at the airport, they collect their baggage and are met outside by a minibus driver, who drives them the twenty miles to the family villa where they are met by Bruno.

'Where is Mamma?' says Christina, in a hurry to see her mother.

'In the kitchen,' says Bruno. 'She is cooking up a storm. Not sure how many people are coming to the viewing tonight, but she looks like she is cooking for an army.'

'Mamma, I am here. Let me hug you,' says Christina, grabbing hold of her mother all dressed in black, but with a little covering of flour, with a rolling pin in her hands to make pasta. 'I am sorry I wasn't here for you, but I am now.'

The tears flow from Christina, and the two hold each other for a long time. Christina relishes the smell of her mum, perfume and flour.

'No time for tears, *bella*, we have a lot to do. Your Papa would not want people crying at his funeral. Go and grab an apron and you can help me. And where are my beautiful grandsons? I can't wait to see them.'

Although a death in Italy is a sad and sombre affair, it is also a very communal affair. Since early that day, a steady stream of relatives and neighbours has been arriving at the house, bringing all sorts of different food. There is hearty beef stew, pasta made with vegetables, salamis and prosciutto, fresh bread of all varieties, sandwiches, and all manner of different cakes.

The house smells of garlic and basil. Outside, the wood-fired oven, lovingly hand-built by Nonno, is pressed into action, delivering a tantalising aroma tinged with nostalgia.

There is lots of red wine, which you can tell is local, as it has been poured into five-litre plastic water containers.

Over the course of the evening, the viewing of the body is set to take place. The people who come to visit are very important for Italian people, as they are showing that they are there to love and support you. Food is a big part of that, as it gives you the strength to continue.

More than a hundred people come to pay their respects to Nonno and then visit the kitchen for food and drinks; they spill out into the garden.

At the end of the evening, Christina visits the coffin with her mother and brother. The body that now lies in front of her looks like someone else, like someone she doesn't know. She reaches forward and kisses her papa on the forehead. He is dressed in his best suit, complete with a bow tie. It almost looks as if he is smiling. She places her rosary beads and a picture of her family beside him. The three of them hold hands together as the heavy casket is closed.

The next day, the coffin is taken by car to the Immaculate Church of Badolato. It is carried into the church by several pallbearers, including Bruno and Matty.

Nonna wants to walk into the church with both of her grandsons and her two granddaughters as a show of comfort. Christina, dressed in a long-sleeved black dress, with a short black veil, walks beside Maria.

More than five hundred people turn up at the church, such was the esteem in which Nonno was held. The service, once again, is presided over by Father Conte, the family priest.

'He does everything,' says Hammy.

'Hatches, matches and despatches,' whispers Benny to his friend.

A local singer performs *Con to Partiro* made famous by Andrea Bocelli. The mayor and dignitaries from the local council attend to pay their respects to the family.

At the end of the service, the ornate casket is carried back to the car and driven to the cemetery. A single, poignant bell tolls very slowly, echoing across the valley.

On reaching his final resting place, each of the four grandchildren places a white rose on the coffin, and Bruno and Christina add red roses. Mamma simply places her hand on the coffin, closes her eyes and says a few words to herself. He has been a wonderful husband to her, and she will cry for him every day, but never in front of her family.

After the interment, everyone returns to the family villa to continue paying their respects. This time, however, Bruno has taken charge and has brought in the caterers, as he doesn't want his mamma to be in the kitchen tonight.

It has been agreed that this time Christina should say a few words, instead of her brother. She clinks her glass with a little spoon to gather people's attention.

She speaks entirely in Italian, so the English listen politely, without knowing what she is saying.

'Dear family and friends, I would like to say a few words about my dear Papa. He was born here in this very house in 1936, living through the horrors of the Second World War as a child. It taught him great lessons in life that he passed on to us. A good father and mother are worth a hundred teachers,' she says, raising her glass to her mother.

'Loving one's parents is fundamentally the greatest virtue in life, so I ask you to go and see them as soon as you can and give them an extra hug; they won't be with you forever. Family is everything. It will help us live with our grief.

'He loved this house. It meant everything to him to be the fourth generation of the family to live here. He used to say every bird finds its own nest the most beautiful,' she says, looking directly at her brother.

'He was a man of very few words. If you asked him why, he said you don't need words to be a great listener. When I moved to England after getting married, he said to me, no matter where you go or turn, you will end up home.

'I would like to thank you all for coming, the kind words, and the mountain of food that you brought. And now I would like to propose a toast to Vincente de Luca – God rest your soul,' she concludes, raising her glass to everyone.

Mamma has settled at the kitchen table, surrounded by her grandsons and granddaughters. She has still not cried, and no one expects her to. She is happy to be in the company of the young ones, the future of her family.

Christina seeks out Father Conte, to say hello and to thank him for the service.

'Father Conte, it means a lot for me to have you here to say goodbye to Papa.'

'Christi, you know that I am very fond of your family. It was a pleasure.'

'I am going to miss him, so much.'

'My dear, he will always walk by your side. He may have been a man of few words, but I know that he was very proud of you.'

'Do you think Mamma will be ok?'

'Of course. She is made of tough stuff. She also has her faith. She attends mass every day, and if I ever make a mistake, she is the first to correct me. I worry whenever the bishop visits, in case she submits my report card.'

Christina joins her husband and brother outside in the garden.

'Beautiful words, sis. Thank you,' says Bruno.

'I agree, even though I understood very little. When you are back home, you speak so much faster that I struggle to follow you.' Matty smiles.

'Well, I am buying you lessons when we get back, my love,' says Christina. 'Bruno, how do you think Mamma will get on?'

'I don't know. She has this tough exterior, lived through the war, seen it all before. But you just don't know about grief; it hits everyone in a different way. Anyway, Maria and I are here in Calabria, so we will look after her.'

'Do you think she would come over and stay with us in England for a while?'

'I don't think that wild horses would get her on a plane now, to be honest. This is home, this is where her memories are. She will want to be with Papa.'

'I suppose so.'

'Listen, are you guys free tomorrow? I would like to take you down to the hotel site. It's really starting to come together, and I want you to see it before you head back.'

***

The morning after the funeral, Mamma decides to stay in bed and rest after a tough few days. Maria has agreed to look after the boys, and they are planning a visit to a local park with their cousins.

This allows Bruno to show off his hotel development down the coast, so they set off in his Range Rover. They drive down from Catanzaro to Lido de Catanzaro, before heading through Roccelletta and out to the Copanello beach, which has the perfect combination of fine white sand and clear turquoise water.

The Bai del Copanello Hotel is planned to be an upmarket beachfront hotel, with 200 rooms and several larger suites. There are to be two restaurants, one based on the beach, selling informal pasta and seafood, and a more formal one within the main hotel. There are to be two swimming pools, one for adults and the other for families. Italian law means that they also directly own the beach access, and the public cannot set up in that area.

Construction work is well underway and is due to be completed in time for the start of the holiday season next year. With today being a public holiday, there are no construction workers on site, so they can roam freely.

'Well, what do you think? Welcome to my hotel,' says Bruno.

'I love the location. The beach looks beautiful, and the sea looks tempting,' says Christina.

'The sound of the ocean is wonderful,' says Matty.

'Ah, there is a lovely legend passed down through the generations,' says Christina. 'A beautiful Calabrian wife was kidnapped by the Turks to be taken to the Sultan's harem. She refused and gave herself up to the sea, and it is her sad song that you can hear in the wind.'

'*Bellissima*, sister. We must incorporate that into our marketing plans.'

'What we want to do here is to create a special place where people don't want to leave,' says Bruno. 'We are not Amalfi or Taormina; we don't have Etna or Vesuvius, the fiery sisters. We must cast our own spells around Calabria to capture the guest's imagination.

'If we are to persuade people to come to Calabria, we have to offer them something special. We need to have a big-name chef for the restaurant. We are going to be the first hotel to offer a Thalassos Spa.

'The rooms need to be bigger than people would normally expect. We will have double bathrooms, with his and hers wash basins. We will give them products with a bit of luxury, maybe Acqua di Parma or Dolce & Gabbana, or something like that.'

They wander past the main swimming pool that has been completed already but is lying patiently waiting to be filled up. They look in on the development bedroom that has been created to assess different concepts, admiring the tiling and size of the triple-king mattress. Christina has a bounce on it to test the firmness.

They head down to the beach where the restaurant is partially complete. The three of them sit on a small wall overlooking the beach.

'When the sun slowly sinks, the sunset here is magical. I want people to be back at the hotel, not heading out into town. It's the cruise ship approach: give them everything they need right here, and you capture every cent.'

'Tell me, has it been difficult getting building permissions?' asks Matty.

'This is Italy, my friend Sometimes you need a bit of this,' Bruno says, clenching his fist like a boxer. 'Italy is a country obsessed with bureaucracy. Thankfully, my partners are very good at making things happen smoothly.'

'You mean bribes.'

'That's a little crass, if I might say. Sometimes the planning people have some problems or issues in their lives, and we can help them. It's about mutual benefit, you see. Although it costs more and more these days. When Italy suffered serious earthquakes, the building permit laws were tightened significantly. But where there is a will, there is a way, as the English might say.'

'Christina told me how much it is costing. You are into the banks for €90m.'

'The banks are awash with cash now; I don't ever intend to pay it back. Once we get it up and running profitably, we will flip it and make millions.'

'I don't like debt. I don't want to rely on any bank manager; you are in big trouble if they change them.'

'Very noble, but you see, to do something as impressive as this, you need the financial backing. It is how you play the game, Matty.

'We are also skimming off the building project. The banks think we are using contractors, but we are supplying the labour force ourselves. One of my partners has access to lots of low-cost workers from outside Italy. We pay them only half the going rate, but they are still very happy as it is better than where they come from.'

'You shouldn't do that, Bruno. It is immoral,' says Christina, watching the reaction from Matty.

'Morality doesn't always pay the bills, my dear.'

'Well, the hotel looks great. Put us down for a fortnight next August, please . . . and make sure it's mate rates,' jokes Matty. 'I'm off to take some photos so I can show the council boys back in Morecambe what real ambition looks like.'

'So, sis, what do you think? It's going to be amazing, isn't it?'

'Yes, but you cannot bullshit your little sister. Is it coming in on budget?'

He laughs. 'Not quite. I think we are about €10m over budget now, but don't worry, I have a plan.'

'Remember what I said: if anything happens to the family home, I will fucking kill you.'

'I know, I know. Don't worry, it's fine. It will be fine. Now, while Matty is busy taking pretty pictures, I must tell you that we are ready to go with another shipment into the UK of some new citizens.'

'Bruno, I am not comfortable with this. After what happened that night in Morecambe Bay, I feel very uneasy about using Matty's business to bring people into the UK. I have never seen him so angry.'

'I am afraid we have no other option now, my dear. If I don't do this for my partner, he will remove his support for this project, and our family will lose everything. Imagine Mamma losing her family home after losing her husband. I am sorry that I am putting you in such a predicament, but we have no alternative.'

'*Vaffanculo.* If your greed becomes our downfall, we will lose everything.'

CHAPTER TWENTY

2022

During the pandemic, the DK Partnership started to support a homeless charity and its weekly soup kitchen in Argyle Street.

Lisa likes to be directly involved and makes stews, curries, or soups in large containers that she can drop off for other volunteers to hand out from the temporary trestle tables, through the cold of a weekday night.

This afternoon she is making a huge pot of traditional Scotch broth, made to her grandma's recipe.

It has all the usual suspects – carrots, leeks and turnips all boiled in a ham stock. She used to use several ham hocks, which she then shredded and added at the end, but she has now discovered that Waitrose sells a pre-cooked and shredded version. For her, this is a game changer, albeit a rather ironic one, given where the soup is destined to go.

She makes a mental note to see whether Waitrose would like to be a sponsor.

The children are home from school, and Emily is helping her prepare the leeks. Cameron won't be seen dead in the kitchen, cooking with his sister, so he is messing about on his iPad.

He is still in a filthy mood after being told that the Florida trip is now off. He has spent months bragging about it to his friends, and now they will all be laughing at him. Playgrounds are hostile environments, even at fee-paying schools. He is threatening to call Childline but has not followed through on it yet.

'Mummy why can some people not afford to eat?' asks Emily.

Emily and Cameron are largely immune to poverty, but for Lisa, it is very important to talk about these issues.

'Well, there might be lots of reasons, sweetie. They might have lost their job, or maybe they have other problems that they are dealing with in their lives. The important thing is not to judge anyone.'

'But why doesn't the government or the army sort the problem out? Or the Kardashians? They have lots of money.'

'You know, you might just be onto something. We should give Kim K a call.'

Just then, the landline bursts into action with its distinctive ringtone. It is such a rarity these days that when it does, it makes you jump.

'Lisa Whyte, speaking.'

'Mrs Whyte, this is Brogan Simpson from the Police Liaison team. Are you free to speak?'

'Yes, I am. We are just making soup, of all things. Do you have any news? Has something happened?'

'I need to ask you, has your husband been in touch since last night?'

'No, he hasn't. I haven't heard from him since he was in Edinburgh and was going to be moved south.'

'It's just that we have kind of lost contact with him.'

'What do you mean, you have lost him? You are supposed to oversee his safety and well-being!'

'Well, after what happened in Edinburgh, we moved them to another property in a rural location down in Northumberland. We told him and his bloody friend that no matter what, they were not to leave the property.'

'And I suppose they left, then.'

'Yes, they went to the pub, surprise, surprise. Then the farmhouse was burnt down, by parties that are unclear at this stage.'

'Well, I am glad that they left, then. That probably saved them.'

'Then they just disappeared into the middle of the night. We believe they stole a car and headed south to Newcastle. We have had a couple of sightings on the A1, but then we lost them.'

'Well, that's a bit careless of you, isn't it?'

'We still think that there is a considerable risk of harm to them and that the Osman notice that we served is still valid. Do you think there is any way that your husband was involved in drugs?'

'Listen, love, up until last week, I thought he was just an accountant. Then we have a new identity, a probable car thief, and a man on the run from the police. I don't know anything anymore.'

'And the name Frankie Williams from Manchester means nothing to you?'

'Nope, means nothing,' (mentally noting that she was supposed to have checked him out on Google).

'Well, I must insist that you reach out to me if you hear anything from him. The police have spent a lot of money here trying to protect your husband. He must realise that he cannot behave in such an irresponsible fashion; we must apprehend him.'

'Apprehend . . . Listen, Miss PC Big Boots, he is not guilty of anything – well, maybe the car, but I am sure they will return it. You just concentrate on doing your job and keeping him safe because you have made some hash of it up until now.'

* * *

Thankfully, making a pot of soup is relatively low maintenance. Emily becomes bored and heads to her room to play with her dolls. The broth is coming along nicely, so she turns the heat down to the lowest level to let it bubble away nicely. She then dials her best friend's mobile.

'Hey, Bella, how are you?'

'Hello, gorgeous. Crazy busy at work, as usual, and then trying to break in Mikkel. Feel a bit like a cowboy and he is a wild horse that I am trying to tame.'

'Enough detail about your love life, thanks.'

'He he . . . any news of your missing lover boy?'

'Well, guess what? He has now gone missing and is on the run. I have just had the police on the phone. She was a bit of a bitch, to be honest, but apparently their house was burned down, so he and this new little friend he has have gone AWOL.'

'Oh, God . . . this just seems to get worse and worse.'

'And I get the feeling that the police don't trust any of us, that they think we are all caught up in criminal activity.'

'I am sure they don't.'

'It's alright for him, he seems to be on a sightseeing tour of the UK, while I must carry on as if nothing has happened.'

'Is there anything that you need me to do?'

'Yes, any chance you can take a pot of soup down to Argyle Street for me?'

* * *

She puts the phone down and looks around the kitchen and through the arch to the living room. There is no doubt that bringing up young children is much easier when there are two of you. Just to be able to spell each other and give each other a break.

She contemplates that single parents, of either sex, who bring up children on their own are heroes. They should be given more support from society, not less.

Once again, her phone goes off. She fleetingly thinks of the bus analogy.

'Lisa?'

'Oh, it's the boys on tour?'

'Sorry, sorry, I know that it must be frustrating for you.'

'Frustrating, no . . . fucking unbelievable, yes. I am convinced that this is all some big, bad dream and that I will wake up soon.'

'They tried to burn us down. We went out for something to eat and drink. I only had the one pint. When we came back, the whole farm was ablaze.'

'I know; I heard.'

'What are you talking about? How can you know?'

'I had your police chum, Brogan Simpson, on the phone half an hour ago.'

'You didn't tell her anything, did you?'

'On the basis that you have told me fuck all, I am entirely in the dark.'

'Well, we have had enough of all this bullshit. We are going native, under the radar. We are coming up to Scotland. I want to see you and the kids.'

'Is that wise . . .? When will you be here? How are you travelling?'

'Tomorrow sometime. Tony thinks we should be in disguise to avoid detection.'

'I can't wait to meet this little fella.'

'You will absolutely hate him, but I bet he grows on you.'

'They were asking about that Frankie Williams that you told me about.'

'Did you manage to find out anything?'

'No yet, I have been a bit busy, remember.'

'Ok, listen, got to go. See you tomorrow.'

The soup is now ready for collection by Aunty Bella. The only thing she needs to do is add a little bit of parsley, the curly stuff, not the flat-leafed weed. She fondly remembers that when Grandma made this, her grandpa always used to put white pepper on it, and on special occasions, some HP brown sauce, because why not.

Once again, the phone rings. This time it is her mobile, and this time, she knows at once that it is her mum, as she has given her a personalised ringtone, A Coat of Many Colours by Dolly Parton, her favourite. She puts in her Apple AirPods, so that she can finish up.

'Hi, Mum.'

'Hello, Lisa darling. Just giving you a ring to see how you are getting on.'

'The phone has never stopped, and I have been trying to make soup for the homeless.'

'Oh good. I take it you have made your own stock from scratch?'

'No, Mum, nobody has time to do that. Knorr stock cubes, I am afraid.'

'Well, I am sure it will be ok.'

'Oh, and I heard from both the police and from Stephen. He is on the run from the police.'

'Oh, good giddy god! Let me get your father.'

'What's up, pumpkin?'

'Well, it appears that there was another attempted hit on them. They burnt their house down, but they were out. He and his mate Tony have now decided to go on the run and not tell the police.'

'Good. At least he has decided to grow a set?'

'He was very cryptic, but I think he said that he was heading home to see us.'

'No, no! Is he out of his mind? That's the first place that both the police and the bad guys will look. Tell him to make their way to our house. I will tell Kathy to make the spare room up.'

'The police called as well – wanted me to tell them where he was.'

'Tell them fuck all. They are a useless shower. It's long overdue that your old dad got himself involved in this little caper.'

At this point, Cameron decides to come into the kitchen. He had left some sweets in his school bag and has now discovered a letter from the school that he should have given to his mum last week.

Apparently, the school is to dress up in fancy dress for Climate Day tomorrow, giving his exasperated mother virtually zero notice. She comes very close to giving Cameron another personal lesson in swearing but manages to pull herself back from the edge. Parenting is not for the faint-hearted.

CHAPTER TWENTY-ONE

2007

Matty and his two best friends are sitting in the dining room at the walnut table. In front of them is a pile of cash, mostly twenties.

This job is incredibly tedious, and frankly quite dirty, as you never know who has touched them. However, it is one that they never delegate to others. These are the proceeds from the week, made up mostly of rental but also a payment for a container of LCD televisions that they sent to Ireland.

'Poor people count cash, but rich people weigh it,' says Benny.

'Still got a way to go then,' says Hammy.

Just at that moment, young Marco passes in the hallway with a friend from school and takes in the scene with bug eyes. Matty rises from his chair, winks at his son and slams the door behind him. Christina arrives through the other door, all dressed in white as if she is off to play tennis.

'Ha ha, the boys counting their ill-gotten gains,' she says.

'It's what keeps you in the lifestyle that you are accustomed to, my love.'

'I thought you were all going to get out of this line of work. None of you are getting any younger, you know. Soon you won't be able to run away from the *polizia*.'

'There you go, lads. You see what I must deal with? Italian women are made of sarcasm and wit.'

'I am sorry, my love, I was born with a mouth I can't control.'

'Anyway, what else would I do?' says Benny.

'Find yourself a woman, have some children, discover the joy of a family. Maybe even go abroad and open that beach restaurant that you always talk about,' says Christina.

'That sounds terrible, and expensive, to be honest,' says Benny with a laugh. He enjoys sparring with her, as her Italian accent is increasingly being mangled with a Northern English tone.

'Speaking of family, how is brother's hotel coming on back home?' asks Hammy.

The hotel had finally opened in the early summer of 2006. The family had travelled over and stayed for a fortnight. Christina had to admit that her brother had done a fantastic job. The hotel looked wonderful.

Its low white building elegantly matched the sand dunes. The colour scheme had a seaside vibe going on, lots of aqua and yellow, representing the sun and the sand. Although a reasonably large hotel, the careful positioning of bedrooms and suites meant that there was plenty of privacy.

The main restaurant was very high-end, not ideal for a young family, so they had spent most of their time at the beach. It had been great to see Matty relax with his boys. Christina and Marco, with their darker complexion developed deep tans, whilst Matty and Angelo stayed in the shade with their high-factor sunscreen on.

They'd even managed to coax her Mamma to come and join them for a few days, the highlight of which was her Italian mother having her first massage in the spa, at the age of seventy. Her description of the disposable pants and wearing nothing else but her towel was very funny.

The hotel was busy enough without it being high season. She wondered about the guests that were staying. In her mind, the target market was to be an international crowd, from London or Rome, and possibly the American market. However, when she looked around, all her fellow guests were from Calabria. She asked herself how many full-paying guests there were and how many were just being paid off for services rendered. Her big brother was relishing his new role as international playboy hotelier, but she knew that the hotel's financials would be a closely guarded secret.

'My brother tells me it is trading very strongly. The occupancy is close to 100%, but then again, it needs to be, given the size of the loan he took on,' says Christina.

'Maybe we'll get a cheeky invite over this summer,' says Benny.

At that point, Johnny arrives at the house to collect the neat bundles of cash and then spread them across the various bank accounts. This is how a tanning shop with no customers can turn over two grand a week.

'Christina, love, any chance you can make the lads a brew?' says Matty, knowing full well that she will think the task of making tea beneath her, but he wants her out of the way so that he can discuss his own property development.

'I have bought a piece of land, just to the north of the golf course. It's a five-acre site, and the plan is to build fourteen five-bedroom villas,' says Matty. 'I want them to be ultra-modern, lots of glass, bi-folding doors, double garages, all kitted out with all the high tech that people need these days. The kind of statement homes that can really put Morecambe on the map.

'We will put up big, fancy fencing, with a security guard at the gates, like one of those gated community resorts you get over in Florida.'

'Sounds fecking awesome,' says Benny. 'Beats boosting a few trucks for a living.'

'Although there is one major problem that Matty hasn't mentioned yet,' says Johnny. 'Planning permission. We are pretty sure that the local council are on side, but planning consent comes from Lancaster. Firstly, they don't like the fact that we want to develop greenfield, as there is plenty of brownfield in the area. Secondly, they need any new building to be in the style of neighbouring properties.'

'No vision, that's their problem,' snorts Matty.

'Our lawyers have investigated it for us and give us slim chance of being successful. The law is on the side of the council,' says Johnny.

'Would be a lot easier if we were over in Calabria: just bung them all a big bag of cash, or better still, put them in a bag, and drop it off at sea,' says Benny.

'So, stereotypical, as ever,' says Christina, returning with a tray of mugs and teas, 'although the problem with stereotypes is that they tend to be true.'

The lads look ruefully at the tray in front of them. The tea in the mugs looks very weak, and she has brought lemon slices and honey, instead of milk and sugar. There is no sign of any chocolate Hob-Nobs.

'So, what's the plan? Are you saying that we are contemplating bribing a public official?' asks Hammy.

'*No*, we are not,' says Christina. 'But every person tends to have a weakness or two. We just need you to find out if there is anything that goes on in the life of the Head of Planning that perhaps he doesn't want anyone to know about.'

'I am sure we can find a way to lean in on the council,' says Matty.

'So, extortion is somehow better than bribery?' says Hammy with a wry smile. 'What with your aspirations to be mayor or something that's going to look great on your CV!'

'Needs must, lads. It's just a question of working out whether we use the carrot or a stick. Can you manage this for me please, Hammy?'

The meeting is declared over, and the others head off to their cars.

Christina grabs her husband by the hand and decides she wants to go for a walk. Not too far, just so they can admire the view across the bay to the Lake District. The gulls are flying high above, and the intoxicating smell of ozone is in the air.

They sit on one of the park benches, dedicated to a late dog walker who sat here every night smoking an illicit cigarette that his wife had been oblivious to. The tide begins its furious ascent, which brings difficult memories back for both.

'*Mi caro*, I need to ask you something,' says Christina.

'Sure, what is it?'

'I want to make sure that this doesn't turn into some contest between my husband and my brother. He builds a luxury hotel, and you need to build luxury houses. I don't know the English expression, but showing each other who has the biggest –'

'Of course, not.' He laughs.

'Sometimes, when men let their egos get in the way of decision-making, it can be disastrous.'

'If we can pull this off, it will allow us to concentrate on respectable property development.'

'Then you can leave your gang behind. You won't need them anymore.'

'They will always be my mates, though.'

'And even if we get planning permission, can we afford it?'

'Yes, we can, and the plan is to do it without the banks, to fund it from cash flow. I don't know how your brother can sleep with a bank loan of that size.'

'I didn't tell you, but he also put up the Villa de Luca as additional security.'

'Well, he is a fucking idiot then.'

'Ok, I trust you, my love.'

Of course, Matty knows how to pull all the right levers to get his wife's attention. 'If you want, we can take one of the plots for ourselves, build you a brand-new modern house, and you can do all the design yourself.'

They watch the tide continue to flood in from the west, with the sun making its slow, predictable journey in the opposite direction.

'Also, whilst I have you to myself for once, what are we going to do about Marco? He is only twelve years old, and I swear to God he is going to be the death of me. I might not make it to see our new house. Do you know what he did last week? He found adult magazines while he was out playing. He cut out all the pictures and stuck them up on his brother's wall, trying to get him into trouble. I was showing one of the mums around the house and imagine her expression when she saw that!'

'I know I shouldn't laugh, but . . .'

'No, there are no buts. You cannot defend him. He reminds me very much of my brother when he was growing up. Everyone thinks it's funny and harmless until they take that arrogance into adulthood, and by then they are stuck with it.'

'He is young and full of mischief.'

CHAPTER TWENTY-TWO

2022

The journey back up to Glasgow has been reasonably uneventful. Stephen and Tony abandon the BMW in a small housing estate in Durham. Being true to his word, he posts the keys back to the Jolly Fisherman, with a scrap of paper.

> *To the bloke who lost his motor, you will find it on Eastfield Street, Durham. Please find enclosed the car keys. Thanks for the use of it. Here is £100 to take your missus out for dinner. PS Lady Gaga CD was lush.*

They pay for their tickets at Durham station using cash, booking standard class tickets all the way through to Glasgow Central. Tony decides he wants to get properly into his role so insists on sitting on the other side of the carriage and buries himself in *The Times*, which he thinks is the right look for a gentleman farmer. Even when visiting the buffet car, he insists on keeping up the pretence.

'A bacon and egg sandwich and a cup of tea, please, young man,' he says to the catering member of staff, who could not look more bored as they rattle relentlessly north.

'Well, hello, sir. Are you going up to the Edinburgh Festival, by any chance?' says Tony to Stephen on his arrival in the buffet car.

'It's in August, you half-wit.'

After a three-hour journey on the CrossCountry mainline, they trundle into Central Station where they both alight. The station is full of commuters walking with purpose to catch their train or disgorging out into the city centre.

'Listen, mate, we got a text from Lisa,' says Tony.

DAD SAID, DON'T GO TO OUR HOUSE, TOO RISKY, GO TO HIS HOUSE INSTEAD. MUM IS MAKING DINNER.

'Oh great, we have to go and visit the in-laws in Clydebank. I don't even get a night in my own bed.'

'But the good news is it looks as if we are getting fed, and I am starving.'

They take the local train from Central to Clydebank, which takes about twenty-five minutes, and walk the rest of the way. Although technically Davy and Kathy's house is in Clydebank, you could equally argue that it is in Hardgate, or at a push, even in Drumchapel.

It is a classic bungalow, built post-war in the 1940s, a traditional stone building, with two living rooms, two bedrooms and a kitchen. The front lawn is perfectly manicured, and the flower bed has a mixture of roses and hydrangeas. These are much-sought-after properties, as they are single-storey, meaning you avoid the cost of a stair lift in later life.

Every room is decorated in pastel wallpaper, which, privately, Lisa thinks is a crime against humanity.

The door is opened by Davy, who ushers them inside.

'Davy, let me introduce you to Tony,' says Stephen.

Tony's right hand is immediately engulfed by Davy's, with the strongest handshake ever, so much so that he gives a wince as his knuckles crack. Up close, Davy is a big old boy, over six feet, with broad shoulders and a well-lived-in face.

'Goodness me,' says Davy, taking in his guest's rather dandy attire. 'You dinnae want to be kicking about the streets of Clydebank dressed like that, son.'

'And you, young man,' says Davy rather ominously to Stephen, 'I need to have a chat with you. I cannot believe that you misled my wee lassie for all these years.'

'It's a long story, but can I give Lisa a call first, get her to come over? I need her to bring me some new clothes. Mine all went up in a puff of smoke.'

Kathy comes out from the kitchen with her good apron on, which shows that she has, indeed, been making dinner. She introduces herself to Tony, and then shows the boys to the spare bedroom. It had been Lisa's childhood bedroom but has now been repurposed for when the grandchildren stay over. The room has two single beds and has been decorated in two discrete halves. One half has a *Star Wars* theme, and the other half is from *Frozen*.

'You be Obi-Wan-Kenobi, and I will be Elsa,' says Tony.

✱ ✱ ✱

Lisa arrives a short time later, with both children and Bella in tow, who doesn't want to miss out on any of the action.

The reunion between Stephen and Lisa is an emotional one. Tears streak down their cheeks. They are given some time together in one of the front rooms to talk it through a little without the others eavesdropping. After all the emotion and stress of the last few days, they just hold each other tight.

'I'm so sorry, Lisa. I never wanted to hurt you; it just became really complicated.'

'Can you imagine, what it feels like to have your world fall apart?'

'I just thought that if I ever told you, it would be the end of the relationship. I fucked up big time. Is there any way you can forgive me?'

'I don't know; I really don't know. Let's see if we can get to the end of this nightmare first.'

Emily gives her dad a huge cuddle, happy to be reunited and oblivious to the drama. Cameron remains very frosty, still holding a deep grudge at the loss of his Florida trip.

With there now being eight for dinner, there is no way that they can all fit round the kitchen table. So, as they do at Christmas, the patio table is brought in from the garden and surrounded by a hotchpotch collection of chairs so that they can all break bread together. After all the excitement, the aroma from the cooking is tantalising.

'So, I see that you are my plus one for the evening,' says Tony to Bella, in the most charming tone that he can deliver.

'In your dreams, pal,' says Bella.

'Actually, Bella has a new fella,' says Emily with a fit of the giggles.

'His name is Mikkel, and he is Scandinavian, we hear,' says Lisa.

'Oh my, you are going to have beautiful kids, Lebanese and Scandi,' says Kathy.

'Steady up, Mrs G, early days so far.'

Kathy has gone to considerable effort in a short time and has made two enormous steak pies, mashed potatoes, carrots, and turnips.

'Kathy, I need to warn you, this boy might look skinny, but boy, can he eat,' says Stephen, slapping his friend on the shoulder.

'Aw Mum, it looks delicious,' says Lisa. 'I presume that the pastry is made from scratch and not shop bought,' – getting one back for the jibe about her ham stock.

Dinner itself is very pleasant. With the children present, the adults don't address the elephant in the room. Most of the time is spent hearing tales from school, news of the bowling club, and details about Bella's new man.

It is decided that Tony and Bella should take the children through to the living room so that the others can talk. Lisa asks her friend to use her iPad and Next account to order some new clothes for Tony. If he is going to be around for a while, he needs to dress better. He is allowed to pick his own, but Bella and Emily are to sign off on the final basket.

'Right, so where are we then?' says Davy, head of the family from the head of the table.

'Dad, we have decided to focus on what we are going to do moving forward, rather look back. Focus on the controllables . . . the other stuff can wait,' says Lisa.

'Ok, fair enough. So, what happened when you were in Edinburgh and Northumberland?'

'Well, on both occasions, the police said that we would be safe. In Edinburgh, they tried to knock us down with a Range Rover, and in Northumberland, they burned the house down. On both occasions, we had simply gone out to get something to eat.'

'Holy Mother of God,' says Kathy.

'So, you were saved by your friend's appetite,' says Davy, laughing.

'After that, we lost confidence in the police and just ran,' says Stephen.

'Well, you know that cannot last forever. They will track you down within days. The other lot will be looking for you too; won't take long for them to look here.'

'Maybe it is best if you just hand yourselves in,' says Lisa.

'No, I don't think so. Next time they will make sure that you are locked up good and proper,' says Davy. 'I think we need to find ourselves our own little place to hide.'

'Dad, I don't want you getting caught up in all of this. You are too old for all this stuff,' says Stephen.

'But I *am* caught up in all of this. This is my daughter, those are my precious grandchildren next door. Anyway, growing old is very boring. If I must listen to one more story about a hip replacement down at the bowling club, I will scream. I miss having some excitement in my life.'

'Not sure how you can help, anyway,' says Stephen.

'I know lots of people.'

Kathy rolls her eyes, rises from the table to put the kettle on for tea and starts to clear the dinner plates. Davy goes over to the sideboard and produces a bottle of malt whisky and three glasses. On seeing his daughter's stare, which says, 'It's 2022, you dinosaur,' he returns to collect another glass.

Bella, who is driving tonight, comes into the kitchen to collect a cup of tea.

'Things ok in there?' asks Lisa.

'Yep, successful shopping mission completed. Jeans and polo shirts, nothing too complicated. You will get it on next day delivery tomorrow.'

'And what are they doing now?'

'He's a funny little chap, isn't he? He decided that he didn't want the kids to watch too much telly, so he put the subtitles on so they could read at the same time to help them with their reading.'

'Jesus,' says Stephen.

'Then they got bored, so Cameron has just beaten Tony ten-nil at FIFA on the PlayStation, and Emily is showing him how to put emojis in his text messages.'

'Tony has a phone?' says Davy.

'I think the kids are rather smitten by him, to be honest. He is rather exotic, compared with what they are normally used to in the posh part of Glasgow,' says Bella, grinning. 'He is like a puppy, rather adorable.'

Tony appears in the kitchen, narrowly missing the compliment but gratefully receiving a glass of whisky.

'Mrs Gavin, your steak pie was wonderful, the best I have ever had. There isn't any left by chance?'

'Human garbage disposal unit,' says Stephen.

Kathy, who quietly relishes the praise, is the type of woman who believes that compliments deserve to be rewarded. 'No, it's all finished, but I do have a nice slice of iced ginger cake if you would like.'

'I tell you what, I will get up early in the morning and go to the shops. Then I will make one of my famous Irish breakfasts, the full works,' says Tony.

'No chance! You two muppets are not leaving my sight,' says Davy.

CHAPTER TWENTY-THREE

2008

As he leaves home in Catanzaro, Bruno has a lot on his mind. He has just had a furious argument with his wife about how he has become an absent father to his two girls. Maria is furious with him for spending the last few days in Rome. Whether she knows about the mistress that he has been entertaining at the Cavalieri Waldorf Hotel she never lets on.

That relationship is becoming increasingly complicated. Juliana is a twenty-two-year-old model from Brazil, who has come to Italy to study. She is stunning to look at, and when they are in bed together, Bruno has the time of his life. He is helped along the way with some medication, but he deserves it: he works hard, he takes risks.

However, she likes to party, go to nightclubs, drink alcohol and take cocaine. The truth is he cannot cope with the pace anymore.

He doesn't find the age gap a problem physically, but they are finding it increasingly hard to hold a conversation together, to find anything that they share in common. She doesn't have a clue about the music he likes, and he finds her fascination with the cult of celebrity to be very dull. They go out for dinner, and inevitably people will note the age difference, giving him the cold stare for being a rich predator. He notices it, but she does not.

At first, she wants for very little, with the assurance of youth, but increasingly her demands are coming in thick and fast.

'I want to go to New York soon.'

'I simply need to go and get a handbag from Armani.'

'Can my best friend from Rio come over for the summer?'

'What's the point of you owning a five-star hotel on the beach if I am not allowed to come and stay? Are you ashamed of me?'

The thought of Juliana visiting the hotel, in the vicinity of his mother and wife, gives him cold shivers. He needs to find a solution here, or this could get out of hand.

He loves being the hotel boss. It makes him feel very important. Although he has been successful in the family fashion business, he always feels that people look down on him, still see him as just a village boy from the mountains, better suited to goats. He knows that Matty's boys think that he is somehow involved in the local mafiosi. In his fertile imagination, he prefers to think of himself as a brigand, a much more romantic view of an Italian criminal. A local hero, willing to take on those who hold all the power.

Opening the hotel has been demanding. He relentlessly pushed the design to ensure a luxury finish, knowing full well that it was going over budget. Now the hotel is up and running, the bookings are solid, and more importantly, the TripAdvisor reviews are all fives. Not only that, but they are from real guests, and not artificially created ones.

He hates the mundane back-office part of hotel work – the cleaning, the laundry, the deliveries, staffing issues. He loves being front of house. Not for him a staff uniform with a badge but a nice pale blue suit with tan leather shoes. He is free to roam around the property, offering pleasantries to his guests. Taking the plaudits, without any of the exertion.

Being the main man at the hotel is his gateway to the higher reaches of society. He just cannot decide whether he wants to be accompanied by Maria or Juliana. Maybe he would be better off on his own, without either giving him perpetual earache. He could easily pick up some new woman along the way.

He drops by his Mamma's house, which he tries to do every day when he is at home, another habit that irritates Maria. She says he spends more time with her than with his wife.

'*Ciao*, Mamma.'

'*Tutti benne*, my good son,' she says, carefully cutting fresh flowers to put in a vase.

'You must come down to the hotel soon for another visit.'

'As long as I don't need to get naked in front of someone again. You don't pay the staff enough to see a wrinkled lady in paper pants. You look tired, my dear.'

'Oh, just a lot going on.'

'How is Maria? I haven't seen the girls in ages. You should bring them for lunch soon.'

'Sure,' he says, making a mental note to make sure that he doesn't. He can cope with both individually, but together they are too much for him. He fleetingly thinks of adding Juliana to that scenario, and a cold shudder rattles through him.

Bruno continues down the mountainside to the coast, admiring the aquamarine sea. The sun is shining brightly, bringing warmth and positive energy. He rolls down the window, inhaling the scent. Despite his challenges, today is a day worth living.

He has two important meetings to attend with his partners, Roberto and Nino. It has been tough, but the worst is over. He is now a successful international hotelier, so he should be allowed to enjoy the spoils.

Firstly, he meets with Roberto privately, as he is also his principal partner in the people smuggling business. Roberto is an Italo-Albanian of close to sixty years of age. He sports a deep, immersive tan, which could only be achieved by someone who has spent most of his adult life at sea. He is covered in tattoos and wears a St Anthony cross to protect him at sea, as well as a small, hooped earring, giving him a mild pirate vibe.

Having started as a commercial fisherman, he moved on to pleasure boats as his primary business. There is no part of the Eastern Mediterranean that he doesn't know. He knows where to fish, but more importantly, he knows where to hide.

They have their meeting in a small private suite, with doors that open out onto the sea. There are cold sparkling mineral water and a platter of fresh fruit on the table. You can hear the murmur of happy guests on the beach, their voices muffled by the breeze. The sound comes in waves, matching that of the sea.

For the first time since they started transporting groups of people across to England, one of the shipments has been stopped by French customs. Sixteen people from Albania, Syria and Iraq have been discovered behind a false façade in the rear of the truck. The two lorry drivers, who are Polish, have been arrested at the scene and are now being interviewed by the police at a detention centre.

'So, we lost a shipment then?' says Roberto.

'Yes, we did. First time in two years,' says Bruno.

'Well, shit happens, I suppose. At least they all paid upfront, so we don't lose out. They will probably give it a few weeks and then try again. We like return customers – good for the bottom line.'

'But do you think we will be compromised in any way? Do the drivers know how this is organised?'

'They don't know anything. It's all done through third parties; there is no risk of tracking it back. It's a very porous border, you know, and customs are totally under-resourced, so by the time they finish interviewing those two, there will be another dozen new cases.'

'Yeah, but they seized the vehicle, and it belongs to Matty.'

'Well, you better get on the phone to Christina, and tell her to manage it.'

'I was wondering if we should stop this for a while, let it all calm down. Do we still need to do this now that we have the hotel?'

'No, no . . . we are fine. Listen, there is lots of money to be made from this. With the war in Iraq, people are being displaced and are desperate. It is easy to get to Italy from Albania, but not so easy to get into the UK.'

Although Bruno has known Roberto since he was a little boy, he isn't as well acquainted with Nino. He is a tall, thin man, perhaps six feet, with a shaved head, a somewhat angular face, and round black glasses.

He carries an air of confidence, and he speaks English like a diminutive version of Stanley Tucci, with a deep, plummy voice. He is dressed in a light summer suit and a Panama hat and carries a briefcase. He is a masterful combination of charisma and a perpetual air of menace. It is hard to put an age on him. He has clearly seen many skirmishes in his life.

Bruno was introduced to Nino by the financial advisors that brokered the deal with the bank. They said having a third investor with a reputation in property would be helpful for the bank. Bruno knew that it was not Nino's own money but that of several investors across Calabria. Deep down in his heart, he knows that their business is part of the tree that likes to flourish in silence, but he just chooses to ignore it.

He is so besotted with this project that he is happy to live with them as partners. Don't go looking, in case you find something that you don't like. Maybe, one day, he might be able to buy them out. His greed fails to recognise that it rarely ever plays out like that.

'Good afternoon, gentlemen,' says Nino. 'The hotel is looking great, and the revenue numbers are really shaping up.'

'Yes, it's been hard work,' says Bruno. 'I think that we have made it. *Salut*,' he toasts, raising his glass of mineral water.

The *salut* is not replicated by the others, either because they know that you never toast with water, or perhaps as a sign of what is to come.

'However, we are facing a cold wind blowing in from America. We think we are going to experience a financial disaster. As you will be aware, Lehman Brothers, the fourth-largest bank, has been placed in liquidation,' says Nino. 'Everyone said they were too big to fail, the Government wouldn't allow it, but now we know this is not the case.'

'I know all this, but we don't bank with them; we use an Italian bank,' says Bruno, shrugging his shoulders at Roberto, who is listening quietly.

'Sure, but our advisors are telling us that we are about to be hit by a devasting shitstorm which is going to reach all corners of the globe. All the banks around the world are going to have restricted access to cash. Italy doesn't exactly have the greatest banking structures in place, so we think it will be badly hit and maybe worse than others. All loans that are considered high risk, above a 70% debt to asset ratio, will be placed into intensive care.'

'What does this mean for us?' demands Roberto.

'The bank is in discussions with a corporate debt collector called Cerberus. If you know your Greek mythology, Cerberus was the three-headed beast, the monstrous watchdog of the underworld. It doesn't bode well for your banking partner to be named like this.

'There is a strong likelihood that they will recall the loan and sell the hotel for whatever they can get. These guys are corporate sharks; they have no compassion. Our situation is made even worse by all the overspend that we incurred,' says Nino, staring at Bruno.

Bruno has gone chalk white as he takes all this in. A small bead of sweat breaks out on his forehead. He has a broad understanding of financial markets but finds himself in a world he doesn't understand and can't control. He is at the mercy of the man in front of him.

'It would also mean that you might lose that pretty little villa that your Mamma lives in,' says Nino.

'Oh fuck,' says Bruno, with his head now in his hands.

'However, in times of crisis, it is generally those with cash that will survive. The one thing that my organisation excels in is cash generation. Sometimes we don't know what to do with it we have so much coming in every week.'

'What are you suggesting?' says Bruno.

'That we take over 51% of the hotel in return for a cash investment of €30m, which will be used to reduce the bank debt. That will give the bank the comfort they need on their risk profile.'

Visibly shocked, Bruno reacts by sweeping his glass and the water container off the table. The glass shatters into little pieces, water dripping down the table.

'But that's daylight robbery, you bastard! This place is worth €100m, and you want half for €30m.'

'Well, we all have choices, Bruno. It was you that chose to swim in the sea with us, I seem to remember. If you want, you can take your chances with the bank on your own. Let's see what they say.'

'My friend, I think you should consider this carefully,' says Roberto. 'This is not a time to be reckless.'

'You knew about this, didn't you?' spits Bruno.

'Listen, you will still have a healthy shareholding and will continue to be the main frontman for the hotel. Nobody needs to know,' says Roberto.

'Ok, I need to think about it. This is not what I was expecting, being blind-sided by my partners.'

'In time, you will see that it was the right thing to do,' says Nino. He has started to pick up the pieces of glass from the floor. Time to move on. 'But I have some other conditions that we must insist on.

'Firstly, we will put in the financial processes and manage the books. It's not that we don't trust you, but it's better that way for us as the majority shareholder.

'Secondly, when we restructure, we will want to inherit the guarantee over the villa.'

'But that's nothing, in the grand scheme of things,' says Bruno.

'I know, but we think it will keep you honest.

'Thirdly, we want to discuss with both of you what you know about transportation into the UK. We understand that you have some recent experience in this area. My partners are keen to expand their interests, so it makes sense to share our knowledge.

'We might allow you to become involved in that too, if you do what is right.'

CHAPTER TWENTY-FOUR

2022

For the first time in years, Davy Gavin is up at the crack of dawn, just before the sun makes its appearance. He has a purpose, something to get his teeth into. He has made several phone calls already this morning, putting his plan in place. He needs to move the whole family out of Glasgow, somewhere safe that he can control.

He makes a large pot of coffee and a large bowl of scrambled eggs that he keeps to one side to cool. The bread just needs to go in the toaster once his guests arrive.

Unsurprisingly, the first to arrive is Tony, with the nose of a dog, tens of thousands of times more powerful than that of a human, and a voracious appetite to go with it. He has borrowed a pair of paisley pattern pyjamas from Davy, which, given the size difference, are almost comical. He has rolled up the trouser legs and the cuffs and now looks like someone from a Victorian poor house.

'Morning, Mr Gavin,' says Tony, disappointed to see that the old fella is offering only eggs.

'Morning, son. Let's just keep the formalities to Davy,' he says, collecting the toast as it pops.

'So, you were the one that stole lorries and stuff for that fella from Morecambe.'

'Guilty as charged. Once I came over from Ireland, nobody would give me a job. I was told I was just a daft paddy. I kind of stumbled into it, but once Big Matty gave me a chance, I found that I was good at boosting trucks.

'We had a solid set-up to begin with. The problem was Matty was never satisfied; he wanted more and more all the time. He was being driven on by his Italian wife.'

'Do you think he is behind all this, then?'

'I know it all points to him being behind this, but I really don't think he would do that. He was a man of integrity. I don't think he is involved.'

'But you ratted on him. He spent ten years in Strangeways, I believe.'

'We didn't have any choice. It was all falling apart in different ways; we were spread too wide, and they were closing in on us.'

'Well, the golden rule from the jungle that I grew up in was you never turned the tables on your own people, ever!'

'So, what did you do as a younger man?' asks Tony, while buttering his third slice of toast.

'Oh, this and that. Was in the shipyards when I was young, then most of my time in the building business and property stuff.'

'Well, you're looking well for it, still in good shape.'

'Son, I would like to say that I am ageing like a fine wine, but sadly it is more like a ripe banana,' quips Davy.

'Listen, if that's the case, I have brought up a wee stash of Viagra. If you want, I can give you some.'

Timing, they say, is everything, and at that very moment, Kathy chose to enter the kitchen in her dressing gown and slippers.

She merely pats Tony on the head and says, 'It's alright son, we are good. That ship has well sailed. Don't give the auld fella any ideas,' returning to her room with her morning cuppa.

Stephen is the last one to appear for breakfast. He doesn't look great and slept badly, owing to a combination of sleeping in a single bed for the first time in years and the cacophony of snoring from underneath the Frozen duvet.

Again, he makes the mistake of looking in the mirror and reflects that it is like watching the news on TV, knowing that there will be developments that he doesn't like.

He arrives in the kitchen and goes to the fridge to pour himself some fresh orange juice.

'Kathy tells me the bold boy was trying to offload some of his Viagra on you. You better watch out because it will be Nordic Socks next,' says Stephen.

'Right, whilst you boys have been having a long lie-in, I have been up making arrangements,' says Davy.

'We are all going on a wee road trip. A friend of mine owns a large, secluded house down at Loch Lomond. He is letting us use it for however long it takes. I have booked a seven-seater van from Avis, which I am going to collect in an hour.'

'Yesss!' says Tony. 'Don't get me wrong, but Clydebank is like Gateshead. I want to see the mountains and the lochs on this holiday.'

'I keep telling you, this is not a fucking holiday; it's a continual nightmare that never ends. I need to fix my marriage. I want to be at home, with my kids, not a fugitive on the run with you lot,' says Stephen.

'Well, tough shite, because this is how it's going to be. Tony, you go to Tesco with Kathy and get a big shop in, enough to last a week; Stephen will pay. Give him your credit card,' says Davy.

'Yes, Captain,' says Tony, looking forward to menu planning with Kathy.

'Stephen, you will stay here. Lisa is on her way over in a taxi. Once we are all back, we will get going.'

* * *

Lisa arrives at the house, weighed down by bags containing clothes for the family and packages from Next for Tony.

The children are, for once, in extremely high spirits. They are being allowed to miss school, which has never happened before. It now appears that they are going on a family holiday after all. And Mum has shown no sign of packing any homework materials. Then to top it off, it appears that the funny guy, Tony, is coming along too. The kids skip out to the back garden to play with a frisbee, with an extra spring in their step.

'I need to borrow your iPhone, Lisa,' says Stephen. 'The police took mine. I need to email my boss.'

Stephen's boss is surprisingly relaxed about it all, telling him to just take it out of his holiday entitlement. He also confirms that the police had called round at the office, asking if anyone had heard from him.

He hands the phone back to his wife and asks, 'Did you manage to find out anything about this Frank Williams guy I asked you about?'

'Yes, I did,' she says, scrolling through her phone. 'He seems to be quite a character and well-known in the Manchester criminal world. Here's an article about him I downloaded . . .' She passes the phone back to him

Frank Williams is a notorious criminal based in Salford, Manchester. He is in his late sixties now, but still very much the head of the family. He has two sons, Francis and Kenny, who now run the active part of the business. They also have a half-sister, Josie, who is significantly younger, having just turned twenty, and who consistently manages to drive him nuts.

After his wife was tragically killed in a car crash, Frank embarked on a relationship with a Canadian divorcee. They had Josie, and when the relationship had run its course, her mother decided to return to Canada.

Josie chose to remain with her father to study in Manchester. Although studying takes much application, she prefers to be on the party scene, hunting professional footballers and pretty boys.

Frank is extremely well-known to the police and has served two prison sentences, one for assault and battery and the other for possession of a firearm. The police now look on him with the benign respect that they have for the old-school boys who never hide away and play to the rules, unlike the new breed of criminals that they must deal with. The police know they can call on him at his house, although he does go to extraordinary lengths to ensure that they can never pin anything on him.

The family business was originally based on the provision of gaming machines and jukeboxes to the hospitality industry, with his reach covering from Manchester up to Scotland. It was a lucrative business before being completely disrupted by music apps and online gambling. It was a tough game, though, completely unregulated, and you literally had to fight to secure your listings. In doing so, he built strong networks across the business, and now his sons are taking it in a different direction.

In the late nineties, dance music exploded in cities like Liverpool and Manchester. With it emerged some notorious nightclubs, such as the Hacienda. As a result, the demand for Class A drugs went through the roof. To begin with, ecstasy was the drug of choice, but due to lots of publicity involving some tragic deaths, the product that was fast becoming unstoppable was cocaine.

The boys turned their attention to the security side of nightclubs. They had no desire to be bouncers, but they wanted control. This was based on the philosophy of 'Control the doors, control the floors', or he who owns the front door controls who sells drugs on the premises. They would use extreme violence and intimidation to buy up existing security teams. This then allowed them to approve the dealers that could operate and ensure that no competitors were allowed in.

They now use encrypted devices to talk to their contacts to avoid detection. The beauty of their business is the simplicity of it all. They are never physically connected to drugs, never in possession of them; they are just facilitators. Usually, the police remain silent because what the brothers ensure is law and order in the dance clubs. They know that when violence erupts in the clubs, their bosses back at police HQ feel the heat.

Francis and Kenny have made enormous amounts of money, which allows them to live the life. They both own apartments in The Deansgate, with luxury cars, jewellery, and holidays to Dubai. The family has finally taken a box at Old Trafford, which is Frank's pride and joy. He is on first-name terms with Sir Alex, who regularly pops in for a glass of red wine.

He is proud of his boys. They have inherited their father's work ethic and attention to detail. They have adapted and spotted a gap in the market. He can now enjoy his semi-retirement, safe in the knowledge that if they ever run into problems, they will come to him for his counsel.

All that worries him now is to make sure that his daughter doesn't splash herself across the front page of the tabloids.

Stephen reads it carefully.

'Ok, thanks, but it still doesn't make any sense. 'There is no obvious connection between Matty and Frank Williams. Their businesses don't cross over, so why would they be involved?'

'Listen, we should talk to Dad when we get a chance.'

'There is even less chance that he can connect the dots, unless maybe Frank plays bowls too.'

CHAPTER TWENTY-FIVE

2008

Matty spends the afternoon at the gym. He does his usual routine of ten minutes on the bike, thirty minutes on the cross-trainer, followed by weights and a long session in the pool.

After that, he heads to the steam room. Through the mist of steam, it appears he is not alone. None other than his local MP, Charles Eastwood, sits up on the top bench where the temperature is at its hottest. He is wrapped in a white cotton towel; Matty hopes that he has trunks on underneath.

'Hey, Charles. Nice to see you again. How are you getting on?'

'Very good, Matthew. Taking the opportunity to get a little fitter before the next general election comes round again.'

'Yes, that must be exhausting.'

'I hope I can rely on your vote?'

'Well, of course, but I might need some help with a bit of lobbying for a property development that I am working on.'

Once he is dressed, he makes his way to the café for an Americano, which he enjoys outside as it is a pleasant afternoon.

He picks up a copy of the newspaper on the way outside.

The newspapers are all reporting on the two main stories of the day. There is now a strong likelihood that America is going to vote in its first Black American President. If so, Barack Obama is going to face a baptism of fire and a monumental crisis as financial problems continue to rock the world. In the UK, the first warning sign of a problem is the collapse of Northern Rock bank.

Matty doesn't really understand the world of subprime lending or shadow banking, but his intuition tells him this is going to be a massive problem. He feels relieved that he has always resisted taking on debt. He could never have done a deal like Bruno; he's not sure that he would be able to sleep at night. For him, it will always be cash and property, nothing else.

However, he believes that one person's crisis is another's opportunity. He has resources available to him, and if he can get this property deal over the line, it will be the gateway to serious property development, and he might be able to leave the other stuff behind him. He still loves his best friends, but in his heart, he knows that, at some point, he will need to break away.

Hammy and Benny are not members at David Lloyd, but they are well known to the girls at the front desk for their cheeky chat. As usual, they bring them a giant pack of Haribo and are buzzed straight through without the need to fill out a guest form.

'You don't look a very happy couple,' comments Matty, catching their stern faces. 'Did the girls see through your pathetic chat-up lines as usual?'

'Do you want the good news or the bad news?' says Benny.

'I hate this game; whoever in history invented it should be shot. Give me the bad news,' says Matty, ominously.

'Well, we organised a little job on the M4 near Reading. It was bread and butter, to be honest; same old weekly route, high probability that he was carrying laptops and computer accessories. Tony was supposed to do it himself, but he decided to sub it out to a couple of other guys.'

'So, they didn't pull it off?' says Matty.

'Oh no, they were successful alright. They managed to cut the sides of the truck and get a load of stuff.'

'So, I don't understand what the problem is, then.'

'The problem is that the dozy bastards decided to stop off on the way back home to get a Burger King or something, and somebody stole our fucking truck.'

'Oh, for fuck's sake!' shouts Matty. 'Beaten at our own game.'

'I'm afraid there is more bad news,' says Hammy. 'When the boys were stealing the initial load, the driver disturbed them. They beat him black and blue – one of them was jagged up on something. It looks like he has a fractured skull and is now in hospital. The police are going to be all over this one.'

'Oh great . . . and what does Tony have to say about it? asks Matty.

'He is shitting himself.'

'Well, Christina might be right. Maybe he has outlasted his purpose.'

Initially, they enjoy the outdoor space on their own, but now a young couple have come to play tennis on one of the outside courts. The girl can clearly play, and she is enjoying thundering serves past her male playing partner, winning each point and puncturing his ego at the same time. Their friends have come out to watch his demise, enjoying the weather and the tennis. The boys still have more to discuss but need to speak in more muffled tones.

'Now that's the bad news gone, boss. Would you like to hear the good news?' asks Benny.

'We have done some digging into Charlie Wright, the Head of Planning for Lancaster Council,' whispers Hammy.

'Tell me,' says Matty.

'Well, we have found a couple of interesting angles. Appears that the bold boy has been having an affair with his wife's best friend. Being going on for months, lots of regular little trysts up to the Lake District, the dirty little dog.

'We also have it from a very good source that Charlie has been getting some personal payments from a private house builder for favourable planning consent. It has been going on for years, according to our source.'

'So, Christina was right again: look hard enough and you will find the weak spots, the places where you attack first.'

'So, what is it to be then, the carrot or the stick?' asks Benny.

'I think the answer is both,' says Matty. 'It's time to have a meeting with this Charlie Wright.'

On his arrival home, Christina is waiting for him.

'You must go and speak to that boy. Once again, I was called up to the school to collect him. Apparently, he beat up one of the pupils, and then he was caught selling cigarettes.'

Marco has been sent to his room, his PS2 has been disconnected and he is sitting sullenly staring out of the window when his dad comes through the door.

'Marco, this is beginning to become a habit,' Matty says, sitting beside his son on the bed.

'Nah, complete overreaction as usual, Dad. Not sure who is worse – the headmaster or Mum; a couple of drama queens.'

'Mum said you were fighting with another boy.'

'There's a boy who has been picking on Angelo at school, so I sorted him out.'

'Look, fair play for sticking up for your brother, but fighting is not cool.'

'Dad, he then called me a Tally, so I stood up for myself. He won't be doing that again in a hurry. And anyway, I am the only one that is allowed to bully Ange.'

'You can't do that, son. If people call you names, you must simply rise above it.'

'What would you have done, then? All that time running about the clubs, everyone says you were tasty, the big man that nobody would mess with.'

'I would have done whatever my mother said. Not once did I ever not listen to her. If I said anything out of place, she used to turn her rings round before she slapped me, that way causing maximum damage.

'And what on earth were you doing with cigarettes? You're thirteen, for goodness' sake. How on earth did you get your hands on them? Who would sell them to you?'

'Oh, that's easy. Tell one of the old boys that you will buy them a pint if they buy you the cigs. Then sell them at the school for 50p a cig; the mark-up is great.'

'But you can't do that, son.'

'Dad, I am an O'Hare. I just want to be a businessman like you.'

'Well, don't be like me; try and be like your brother.'

'I don't want to be like him – he is a nonce!'

'How do you even know what that means at your age?'

'Well, he hangs around with all the young kids and all the girls, playing stupid computer games.'

'He studies hard, and his results have been excellent.'

'Here we go again. The golden boy can do no wrong, as usual. You lot are so predictable.'

'Son, I love you very much, but if you're not careful, I will send you over to Italy to look after some sheep in the mountains. One of these days you need to start to take some personal responsibility,' says Matty, leaving the room and slamming the door hard behind him.

Matty is not so much angry as thoughtful as he goes downstairs. His son made him think how the teenage Matty would have reacted to someone insulting him or picking on his brother. He knows full well that he would have responded in the same way, probably with more fire. You also can't deny that he is showing some early entrepreneurial flair with his smoke business.

But just like every other parent, he doesn't want them to lead the same life as he has. He wants it to be different; he wants their lives to be better. His boys live in a nice house, attend a good school; they don't need to scrap and fight for survival. They need to get educated and then put that to good use. He has a horrible feeling that Marco doesn't plan to follow that path. He wants it all to be handed to him on a silver platter.

Christina is watching television when he enters the room. She presses the mute button so that she can speak to him about another issue. Instantly, he knows that this day filled with bad news is not over yet.

'Matty, I have just found out that one of our trucks has been seized by the French customs police,' she says.

'What . . . How . . . What happened?'

'I don't know all the details, but it's something to do with the import paperwork having some discrepancies.'

'Bloody hell, this is getting really careless now. That's two trucks we have lost in one day.'

'Where was the other?'

'Tony decided to make a half-arsed attempt at getting a job done. Brought in some others to do the dirty work. Not only did they put the poor driver in hospital, but then some other team robbed us.'

'I have told you before that boy is a liability; you need to get shot of him,' says Christina, quietly happy with the diversion. 'Don't worry about the French one; we will get it sorted. I will make sure Bruno takes care of it.'

Matty pours himself a glass of Ardbeg whisky and sits back down in an armchair.

What a day, he thinks. You never know what you are going to come across in this line of work. One day it is sunny, all the rent comes in, you sell some goods, make a tidy profit . . . The next day it is raining, someone has failed to pay, and you lose a bloody truck, or two.

Although his intuition tells him that something is not quite right about this latest story. You are held up if the paperwork is wrong; they don't impound your vehicle. He decides to ask Johnny to dig about in the French issue.

He trusts his wife without question, but he doesn't trust his brother-in-law, and that's what gives him the fear.

CHAPTER TWENTY-SIX

2022

It occurs to Stephen that it is very odd that with one single telephone call to someone, his father-in-law has sorted them out with a five-bedroom house, just outside of Rowardennan on the shore of Loch Lomond. He has always believed that Davy has a narrow range of friends, centred around Clydebank.

Davy has returned from the car hire company driving a very impressive Volkswagen Tiguan, a seven-seater SUV, in gunmetal grey. They need all the room that it provides, given the amount of luggage that Lisa has turned up with and the number of bags that have come back from Kathy's shopping trip.

'Nice wheels, Captain,' says Tony.

To the children he says, 'This is a Tiguan. Its name is a combination of two animals, the tiger and the iguana.' They are both in awe that he knows such stuff.

'Nicked a few in my time,' he whispers to Davy.

'Why am I not surprised?' replies Davy.

Lisa and Stephen start to load everything into the car. Although most of the stuff will go into the boot, it is obvious that everyone will be sitting with something on their lap.

'I hear you drive one of those Teslas, Lisa,' comments Tony.

'Yes, I am trying to do my bit for the environment.'

'Is it true that a new Tesla doesn't have a new car smell? They just smell of Musk.'

Lisa thumps him on the shoulder, but with a small smile, as she is slowly getting used to his dreadful repertoire by now.

'Right, boys,' says Davy. 'See, to be honest, my eyesight is not so good these days. Can I get one of you to drive?'

'I will,' says Stephen instantly. 'I have seen this clown drive.'

They load up the car, Tony sitting in the back row with Cameron and Emily. He is trying his new stand-up routine with them.

'What do you call a Spanish man who can't find his car? . . . Carlos.'

'Right, does anyone need the bathroom before we leave?' says Stephen.

Off they set, up onto the Great Western Road, heading west towards Dumbarton. They don't get very far as they have to stop at the petrol station, as Emily needs the bathroom now. Tony also decides he wants to load up on crisps and snacks.

They continue up the A82, passing through Balloch, before continuing to Drymen where they pick up the loch. The eastern shores of the loch are the first leg of the West Highland Way if you are planning to walk northwards. If you walk the other way, then it would be the victory lap before you sort out your blisters and ruined feet.

Even though it is only a thirty-minute journey, Kathy has dispensed a mini car picnic: corned beef sandwiches, much appreciated by everyone. She has even brought tomato sauce for the kids.

'This is nice, isn't it, getting to spend time together as one big family? We don't do this enough,' says Kathy.

'Oh, it's just great, Mum,' says Lisa. 'It certainly beats Disneyland and Universal Studios, escaping from the law and criminals unknown.'

'Well, I am having fun, getting time away with the children. Not every treat in life needs to cost a fortune, you know.'

'Kids, shall we play guess the colour of the next car? First to five wins,' says Davy.

'I'm taking pink,' shouts Emily.

Having just passed the Rowardennan Hotel, they pull off left and head through a gate, crunching down the gravel driveway. The garden is covered in rhododendrons with their large, oval leaves, dark green and glossy. The house is a substantial stone property. It has a double garage off to the left, with a traditional entranceway into the house, complete with a collection of walking sticks and fishing rods and other outdoor paraphernalia.

A serious amount of money has been spent on refurbishing it to a very high standard. Even Lisa, who is quite particular when it comes to kitchens, is impressed with the quality.

The house has five bedrooms, all en suite. There is a games room with a pool table, dart board and jukebox. The kids are ecstatic and are running around singing the Bruno Mars number, 'I wanna be a billionaire, so freakin' bad'.

The open-plan kitchen has bi-folding windows that open onto a wooden deck. Light floods into the living space. There is a hot tub in the corner, with its protective cover on. Lisa decides that there is no way anyone is going in it, as you never know what germs might be lurking below.

A long garden gently slopes down towards the water, where there is a little shingle beach. A small protective fire pit is surrounded by a rough stone circle where you can have a barbeque or simply keep warm as the evening falls. Or maybe hold a pagan celebration if you're that way inclined.

Tony wanders down the garden, listening to the happy, excited noises from the children. He looks out across the vast expanse of water and feels a calmness and peace that he has never felt before.

He is genuinely enjoying himself. Kathy loves the fact that he is so keen on eating, and he thinks Lisa is beginning to warm to him; she has even started to smile at his jokes. Stephen is carrying so much stress on his shoulders that he is worried for him. Then there is strange old Davy, a retired builder, who can rustle up a million-pound home. There is something not quite right about the old fella; he just cannot put his finger on it.

Tony knows that the personal brand that he has created is just a façade. The petty thief, the bad jokes – it all hides the fact that he is desperately lonely. The lockdowns for Covid have taken their toll, but now it feels like a fresh start is round the corner. He vows to go straight and not steal anything from the house.

On reflection, he blames himself for the job that went wrong with Matty and the team. He feels guilty about the poor fella who was ambushed. He feels guilty, for the rest of the gang, that the job went disastrously wrong. But he was made a scapegoat . . .

CHAPTER TWENTY-SEVEN

2009

He wanted to hold the meeting at a venue of his choice. A place where he could manipulate the setting to shift the balance of power in his favour. But he must tread carefully. This is a meeting with a council official, and it would not be right to dictate where the meeting should take place. He wants to convey a casual and relaxed attitude.

He has personally requested the meeting with Charlie Wright, the Head of Planning at the Lancashire Council. At first, Charlie rejected the meeting, saying that this was highly unusual and not how the process worked. However, Charles Eastwood had leaned in on him to take the meeting. This sort of political lobbying pissed him off, so he is already wary.

Hammy has taken on the role of driver and coach for the day as he drives Matty to Lancaster city centre.

'Okay, boss,' says Hammy. 'Run me through your plan?'

'I want to play it very cool at first, nice and calm. I will start with an emotional plea about how I want to do this to help the community of Morecambe.'

'Ok, nice one, pull on those heartstrings.'

'If, however, he starts to get a bit arsey with me, I will casually drop in that I know he has had a couple of nice personal wins before, and then if that doesn't work, that he has been having an affair with his wife's best friend.'

'Please, do me a favour, make sure that there is no one else present if you go down that route. Nobody can hear that conversation.'

'Mate, you make me laugh. You make it sound like CSI Lancaster – this is a low-level council employee and a local haulier having a meeting. The minute he hears what I have to say about his stuff, he will shit himself.'

Matty gazes out the window as they drive into town. Lancaster itself is a busy university town with a vibrant arts centre, quite different from the shabby Victorian coastal town that Matty lives in.

The venue for the meeting is the Toll House Inn, a hotel based in a historic building in the city centre. They sit in the main bar, underneath the stained-glass window, at a wooden table.

Matty has decided to power up for the occasion and is immaculate in a three-piece herringbone suit that Christina had made in Milan. His fellow guest is much more casual, dressed in chinos and a pale blue shirt and carrying a leather satchel like one that you would take to school.

'You know, I really shouldn't be meeting an applicant on a one-to-one basis. It is very irregular,' says Charlie.

'Relax, it's fine. I'm just Matty, a wee fella from Morecambe, no airs or pretences. I just want to get to know you a little. I have heard good things.'

'So how can I help?'

'I'd like to explain my proposed development in my own words so that you get a sense of what we are trying to do and, more importantly, why.'

He pauses momentarily, as the staff have arrived at the table with coffee for Matty and a Diet Coke for Charlie.

'I have lived in Morecambe all my life. I have a family business that supplies much-needed employment to the local community. I started out in the haulage business but have now moved more towards property development.'

'I know this. My colleagues at the local council office speak very highly of you.'

'That's good. You see, I am also very passionate about my town. Every day when I am out running, I feel it could be so much more. It saddens me when I see what the seafront has become. I don't want it to be like Blackpool, full of desperate souls. I don't want it to be remembered for that awful disaster out on the bay.

'I think with the right strategic vision investment, we could bring the sleeping giant to life again. It needs the right ambitious people, a powerful mix of both private and public investment into the infrastructure.'

'This is all very admirable, but I am not sure that I follow you.'

'I want to put out a statement, to put down an anchor investment of fourteen properties that will make people re-appraise our little town,' says Matty. 'At the gateway to the town, this would be the first thing that you see, a town that means business.'

'I think your people know that we have already given our preliminary view and that we have two major reasons for our objection.

'Firstly, this is a greenfield site and there are plenty of other locations available. Secondly, all new buildings must be in the style of existing properties, which is a clear part of our planning mandate, which is made available to all.'

'Mandate? But that is bullshit! You just end up with more of the same. The definition of madness is to keep doing the same thing over and over and expect a different outcome. People don't want Victorian or Georgian properties anymore; that is from a bygone age. They want modern housing; they need glamour. Look at what they are doing over in Dubai.'

'For what it's worth, in my humble opinion, Dubai is immoral when it comes to both planning and workers' rights.'

'Have you ever been?'

'Also, the focus of the council is on the provision of affordable housing,' says Charlie, opting to ignore the question. 'We have a growing homeless problem in this town, and we need to provide the right type of affordable housing, not just luxury housing at the top end.'

'Yeah, that will really help the town, filling it up with homeless people and junkies. I don't think we will persuade people to come back to the town off the back of that strategy.'

'Mr O'Hare, my job is to review this from a planning perspective only. It is not my job to handle strategic regeneration, which is the job of the full council, who, as you know, are elected by the public.'

Charlie excuses himself so that he can go and use the bathroom. Matty is beginning to feel furious that this council employee could thwart his ambitions. He hates people who speak in soundbites and who hide behind words like process and mandate. He wants to banjo him right here and now. A violent beating would be pleasurable in the moment but unlikely to get him the right outcome.

The bar has quietened down considerably, and they are now on their own.

On his return, Charlie sits down and continues where he left off. 'Also, although I am Head of the Planning Department, I do not make decisions on my own. We follow a strict process to ensure that we have integrity and full transparency in our decision-making.'

'Yes, but you are a very influential person,' says Matty. 'In fact, I hear that there have been two residential developments where you personally intervened to get them through. Thornwood and Lethem Hills, if I am not mistaken.'

'They were approved, you are correct.'

'And were the substantial payments that you received from the developers approved? Did your little committee who make all the decisions all weigh in on it, or was it just you? I thought you said you operated with integrity?' says Matty, leaving it hanging in the air.

Charlie takes off his glasses and rubs his eyes. He looks Matty straight in the eye, lowers his voice and speaks. 'Mr O'Hare, be very careful. I have no idea where you get your information, or what your intent is, but you are seriously barking up the wrong tree.'

'Then the other interesting thing I discovered was how you have been treating your dear wife, Chloe. I am sure she would be surprised to know that you have been shagging her best friend!'

The silence is so profound that they can hear the clock on the wall slowly ticking.

Both men stare intently at each other, realising that shots have been fired, but neither knows whether any have landed. There is no metaphorical sight of blood, so the stalemate continues.

'So here is a proposal for you. I won't say anything about the bribes you have already taken. I won't tell your pretty wife about what you have been up to. In return, you will make sure that our little planning permission gets resolved, and because I am a nice fella, I will book you all a family holiday, anywhere in the world you want to go, although clearly not Dubai.

'Of course, there is another option which we could follow, and believe me, you don't want to see my angry side.'

Charlie stands up and slowly pulls on his coat. He seems relaxed and unperturbed as he picks up his satchel. He takes out ten pounds, which he leaves on the table to cover the cost of the drinks.

'You have made a serious error of judgement, Mr O'Hare.'

'Is that right?'

'Not sure where you get your information from, but you might want to check it out. You should also know I owned up to my wife about a year ago about the affair. She was devastated, of course; it was an unforgivable mistake on my part, and we are trying to work through it for the sake of our family.'

* * *

Five days later, Matty receives a recorded delivery letter to his home in Morecambe. It is from a firm of solicitors in Manchester. Charlie has instructed them to write a statement to function as a written record of their meeting. It confirms that his understanding was that he had been offered both a bribe and a threat of blackmail.

It confirms that as the meeting was not witnessed by anyone at that stage, they do not intend to take it any further. It confirms that if Matty attempts to have any further contact with Charlie Wright, the matter will be referred to the police.

The letter also confirms that any requests for planning permission should follow the guidelines that are freely available on the council's website.

He then takes a call from an irate Charles Eastwood.

'Are you out of your mind?' he says. 'I went out of my way to help you secure a meeting with young Charlie, and you start to threaten him. This is totally unacceptable. I am afraid I will not be able to help you any further.'

'Shit,' says Matty, throwing the phone down in disgust. 'Short-sighted bunch of fuckers.'

Another two added to his list of people who will get their comeuppance. Front row on the perfect plane crash. Although, for the first time, he has pangs of doubt. He wonders whether his instinct and judgement have let him down.

CHAPTER TWENTY-EIGHT

2009

Bruno de Luca relaxes in his favourite cabana beside the swimming pool, enjoying a Sea Breeze cocktail. He reaches for his sunglasses as the sun is now arcing high in the sky. A little suntan lotion to make sure he doesn't burn.

He admits to himself that there had been a degree of inevitability that he would end up peddling drugs. He knows his father would turn in his grave at the path he has chosen. He knows he must also keep this from his mother. The truth is the amount of money he can earn is just too alluring.

His wife, Maria, knows, but it is not a subject that he speaks to her about; in fact, they rarely talk at all these days. She protects her girls from this, so the two of them have become even more distant than before. He believes that these are the sacrifices you need to make to get to the top. He wisely ditched the Brazilian lover in Rome, as that was a headache he could do without.

He still likes the company of young women and finds it is much better if he keeps these activities to the confines of the hotel resort. Increasingly, he finds that a small amount of cocaine makes him more charismatic and appealing. He no longer risks rejection and prefers to pay for his assignations. On these occasions, he sleeps at the hotel, rather than going back to his wife.

He has told his sister, although wasn't sure why; perhaps he was showing off a little. They have suspended the people smuggling business as, quite frankly, it was hardly profitable and carried too much risk. He knows his sister was very uncomfortable with it, and that Matty holds strong views.

He wants the whole family to benefit from his future wealth. He wants to be the patriarchal head of the family, spreading his wealth and good nature to everyone. He doesn't necessarily see Matty as a rival; he just wants the crown for himself. His time has come.

Nino has taken Bruno under his wing as a mentor, giving him valuable advice. The most important is never to show signs of sudden wealth. There are to be no fancy sports cars, no jewellery or expensive holidays abroad. In Calabria, the key is to look as though you live your life in the mountains as a shepherd. Let everyone in the North think you are just a simple businessperson. Any partying is confined to within the resort, away from prying eyes.

As a result of their connections in the world of international narcotics, the hotel has taken a slight detour when it comes to the clientele it attracts. Originally, the vision had been international visitors, British and American, all coming to enjoy five-star luxury with their families, in the hope that everyone would fall in love with the beauty of the region, the incredible history and the sensational scenery.

The hotel is certainly getting international visitors, but mostly from Russia, Albania, Bulgaria and Central America. They don't leave the resort very much and are not up for tourist tours. As a result, there has been a significant increase in security, some provided by the hotel and some by the guests. You can no longer walk straight off the beach for a cold beer or glass of wine at the bar.

Bruno does think his guests are lacking in class, though. They all want private cabanas, where they order litre bottles of Grey Goose Vodka and many bottles of Veuve Clique. They order huge plates of fresh fruit (which they rarely eat), just to show that they can.

The restaurant has abandoned any idea of having a dress code because they simply ignore it. They never eat a dish as it appears on the menu; they de-construct it to suit their every whim, just to show everyone who is the boss. They don't want fresh, local Calabrian dishes; they want tomahawk steaks, club sandwiches and French fries, international food for international playboys.

The hotel has spent a great deal of time attracting glamour to the resort, whether by photoshoots for *Sports Illustrated* or launches of new albums. They want the beautiful people to be there, just in case any of their international travellers need some entertainment. The hotel carries a large roster of girls who can be guaranteed to keep the party vibe going.

In truth, the hotel has become a gangster's paradise, like a trade conference at the beach, where they come to hear the latest market developments and strike up new trading partnerships. A kind of criminal version of Davos, with equally as much money at stake.

Nino comes over to join Bruno at his cabana. He is resplendent in a pair of pink shorts, white polo neck and dark tan sliders. Of course, he has the obligatory dark glasses, possibly Armani, and carries a large glass of Aperol Spritz.

'You look down your nose at your customers, my friend,' says Nino.

'I know, but I try not to. Just for once, could they not just try and dress better? Just for once, might they have a girlfriend without surgically enhanced boobs and inflated lips? And just for once, could they be prepared to try the octopus without making the face of a five-year-old?

'I know, I know . . . but they can't all be Italian like us. But the most important thing is that they are happy and they pay well. Our reputation is building nicely, and we will deliver a good profit this year, so your bonus will be good.'

'Well, I suppose I will survive,' says Bruno, flashing a smile.

'Also, the investors are keen to open another three or four of these hotels. Are you up for it, my friend?' says Nino.

Nino and his associates also supply other goods across Italy, Germany and Spain but have yet to make a lucrative move to the UK market. He is keen to give Bruno a lesson on the economics of cocaine.

'There is no market in the world that brings in revenue like cocaine. There is no investment that gives you a better return than cocaine. If you make your bet and are successful, you will accumulate a staggering amount of wealth, although there are many who want to win and many that want to thwart you.'

'I like the idea of staggering wealth,' says Bruno.

'Not everyone makes big returns at every point of the chain. It is relatively easy, if not comically rustic, to make the product in the foothills of Columbia. The people who make the real money are those who control the route to the consumer. The final yard of the journey is where the price is highest.

'The way that it accelerates in value is the key. In Italy, a kilo of Snow White is worth more than fifty times what it is worth in Columbia. In the UK, that rises to almost one hundred times in value.'

'No wonder you are keen to enter the UK market.'

'The value is increased by cutting it with lots of other agents so that one kilo becomes three very quickly. You must watch your ratios, or as they say in Italy, don't put too much sauce in the pasta. By the time it reaches the consumer, the amount of active ingredient is much lower, yet they are prepared to pay a higher price.

'It's an economic miracle,' Nino continues. 'Imagine pouring half a glass of beer, and then topping it up with water and charging a higher price. There is unstoppable demand in places like London and Manchester where the young professionals live. It is no longer restricted to the elite, or nightclubs and music venues; it is everywhere.'

'What about getting it here in the first place?'

'We don't like dealing with the South Americans, so the route that our product generally follows is via Turkey, Albania or Bulgaria. We avoid the "Hail Mary" approach to bringing in hundreds of tonnes through shipping ports. This is where the international scrutiny and cooperation are, and to be honest, we are still too small to contemplate that kind of risk. Fundamentally, we are fishermen; we know and understand the sea.

'Therefore, the loads tend to be small, brought by sea to a rendezvous point and met by Roberto's fishermen, who bring it ashore with the anchovies and the sardines. Small and often is our mantra.'

'Do you get much attention from the Narcos police?'

'Let's just say a regular flow of money passes through to the customs officials, but remember, we have all known each other since the schoolyard.

'Thereafter, by land across Europe is easy, with virtually no border checks. It is the final leg into the UK that is problematic.

'We have had a look at how you were bringing people into the UK,' says Nino. 'To be honest, I am surprised that you didn't get caught more often. It was all a little amateurish.'

'Didn't really think about it much. We were going once a week with fashion garments, and we just added them on to the drop.'

'Well, it won't work for us; there is too much risk. The sad fact is that if you lose people, they don't have any value, but if you lose a consignment of Snow White, it completely fucks your cash flow.'

'So, what are you suggesting?'

'Firstly, we stay away from the main ports and traffic routes. We are thinking of copying our playbook here, maybe bringing it in through Ireland or the North West. Now where do we stand with that sister of yours – would she like to participate?'

'No, not this time. I cannot get her involved in this stuff; her husband will not allow it.'

'Ah, I need to meet this Matty O'Hare. Perhaps we should invite him out to a meeting.'

* * *

Four weeks later, Matty and Christina travel over to Italy, leaving the boys behind with a babysitter. It should have been an armed guard that they needed, given the way that Marco has been behaving.

Christina doesn't want to go anywhere near the hotel this time, as it gives her a bad vibe. She just wants to have some mum-and-daughter time. She knows her mother has found it difficult to clear out her father's stuff. Never an easy task, when you can smell them on every item of clothing.

She wants to be ruthless and chuck everything out, but she knows that it might be a very slow process. The discovery of long-lost photographs can trigger memories craving to be explored.

Her Mamma is very frugal, so disposing of things is against her nature. Christina knows that taking stuff to the church might be the best course of action. She has recruited the help of Father Conte to plant the seed so that she might think it is her idea. If all else fails, turn to Catholicism as the lever to win her Mamma over.

Matty takes a taxi down the mountain to the hotel on his own. When he enters Reception, he immediately feels the difference from his last visit. There is an air of menace. Given his line of work, his radar for criminality is pronounced.

He watches four extremely overweight men loudly splashing around in the pool with four young women who are clearly not their daughters. They have crew-cut hairstyles and are covered in tattoos. He has them down for Russians, but he cannot be sure. They are all on the champagne, and it is not yet midday. Matty thinks that he would be deeply uncomfortable if his wife and boys were trying to enjoy the pool at the same time.

Nino has arranged for them to go out on a short sail on the Ionian Sea. The sea is exquisitely turquoise and intensely reflective. A small motor tender comes to the hotel mooring to collect him, piloted by what can only be one of his security detail. Matty feels as if he is entering the villain's lair.

The yacht is called *Il Pastore* (the shepherd). It is a Horizon 94, sleek and sophisticated. It features a generous walnut interior lounge and large upper deck with a bar and sunbathing area. Inside, the ceiling windows give a view out over the horizon, with remote-controlled blinds for privacy. Brimming with technology, it is more than just a pleasure boat.

It has half a dozen crew, all dressed in matching red shorts, white polo necks and caps embroidered with the ship's name.

'*Ciao*, Matty!' shouts Bruno from the deck, offering his hand to his brother-in-law to help him up on deck.

'Hello, Bruno. Are you well?'

'*Tutti benne.* We are living the good life, my brother. Please let me introduce you to my business partner and good friend, Nino.'

'Hello, Matty. I finally get to meet you! You come with quite a reputation. Settle yourself in and I will tell the crew to make a start.'

'And this is our other partner, Roberto,' says Nino.

'Ciao, Matty. I am but a fisherman, not in the same league as these two. Anyway, I am skippering today, so I hope you enjoy,' says Roberto.

'He ain't no fisherman,' says Matty to his brother-in-law.

The anchor makes a crunching noise as it is raised and they effortlessly glide away, heading north, hugging the shoreline. Matty can make out Catanzaro, high up on the hill.

The table has been set for lunch, and Matty thinks that if they are trying to make an impression, they have succeeded. It certainly is better than the Irish Sea.

'So, Matty, I hear that you run a successful business back in the UK, starting with trucking but moving more into property these days?' says Nino.

'We have done alright with the business so far.'

'And now I hear that you are planning a luxury housing development?'

'Well, we are trying really hard. We have complications over planning which are causing me a headache, but I haven't given up hope yet.'

'We don't like bureaucracy either; it slows us creative entrepreneurs down too much. And of course, you took an Italian wife – you are a brave man, my friend,' says Nino, patting the back of his hand.

'Are you married, Nino?' asks Matty.

'No, my friend. You see, marriages should be based on compromise, and I don't like to compromise.'

'I presume no children, either?'

'None that I know of. The problem in my line of work is that children can be used as leverage against you. Maybe one day, but for now I am on my own. I only share the bed with my dreams.'

The crew have prepared a light lunch of garlic and lemon prawns, Calabrian ravioli and a large mixed green salad. This is accompanied by a very cold glass of Sicilian white wine from the fertile foothills of Etna.

'I see that you are attracting a different kind of crowd at the hotel, Bruno,' says Matty. 'I detect an air of gangsters and their molls in your lavish seaside retreat.'

'The truth is that they pay extremely well. The hotel is flourishing. In fact, we are in talks with Nino about another three hotels.'

'So, Nino, you know about me, but what about you? I am at a disadvantage as I don't know anything about you,' says Matty.

'Well, I am just a simple businessperson. I look for investment opportunities for my backers. Like that *Dragons' Den* TV programme you have in England.'

'And who are these people that like to live in the shadows?'

'Matty, don't let your imagination take over. They are just ordinary people like you and me. The media like to write a lot about organised crime in Calabria. Not all of it is true, you know. We consider ourselves just like you; we are in the transportation business.'

'And I suppose that you have brought me here, with the whole red-carpet treatment, because you have a proposal to make.'

Nino chuckled. 'Very direct, Matty. I hear it is a very Northern English thing. Yes, we want to explore a mutual opportunity with you. We want to start shipping a product into the UK, and we are looking for a local partner at the UK end.'

'May I ask what this product is?'

'Cocaine,' says Nino, without any change in his persona, as if he has said tins of tomatoes.

'You brought me over here for this?' says Matty, pointing his finger at Bruno. 'You know where I stand on this, and the answer is *no*, over my dead body.'

'I was the same as you,' says Bruno, 'but the opportunity and the potential returns are astronomical. The money we are making is through the roof. It will make your little housing development look minuscule in comparison.'

'If you get involved in that kind of stuff, you run into some very bad people. The people who trade in this in Liverpool and Manchester are nasty; they won't just let you come in and take over.'

'Nothing that we haven't handled in any of our other markets around the world,' says Nino. 'We are well equipped to handle a few desperados.'

'Anyway, I am not only driven by money. I also care about my community. Those who trade in drugs don't give a fuck about the damage they cause. Now, I am not naïve enough to think that I can stop it on my own, but I can stick to my principles.'

'You wouldn't be selling it; you would simply be moving it,' says Bruno.

'I don't care. I am the father of two young boys; you are the father of two young girls, my nieces. Would you want them to grow up and take drugs?' says Matty angrily.

'No, of course not,' says Bruno.

'Do you two ever take cocaine?'

Nino firmly shakes his head, but Bruno cannot make eye contact and looks at his shoes instead.

'Look, I am very sorry, but I want to be very clear: this is not a business opportunity for me. This is a red line that I will not cross . . . and please don't try to get round that by appealing to Christina. The answer will still be no.'

'Ok, Matty, I respect your decision. I trust that, for Bruno's sake, this matter will be kept confidential,' says Nino.

'I know how this works; you will have no problems with my confidentiality.'

The small tender takes Bruno and Matty ashore before returning to the boat, which is due to leave to take Nino to another meeting, further down the coastline. It's his floating office where he never stops working.

'Bruno, are you sure you know what you are doing? In the criminal pecking order, this lot are right up at the top of the tree. This is international drug money; this is not a game,' says Matty.

'Relax, it's fine. There is a lot of money to be made and girls to impress,' replies Bruno with a grin.

'If anything goes wrong, this lot will drop you like a stone, whenever it suits them.'

'What can possibly go wrong? Look around. I own an international hotel in the most beautiful part of the world. When I can afford a boat like Nino's, I will have you over. We can sit and drink champagne, and I will remind you that you missed out on one of life's big opportunities.'

***

Later that night, he is lying in bed with Christina back at the Villa de Luca, listening to the nocturnal sounds from the gardens.

'They asked me to get involved in pedalling drugs.'

'My love, if I had known I would never have brought you over. I am sorry.'

'It's fine, though I would like to make a prediction.'

'What is it?'

'Well, it's your brother. When he implodes, it is going to be quite the event.'

CHAPTER TWENTY-NINE

2022

Davy Gavin joins Tony on the little shingle beach beside the loch. The water is like glass tonight as there is no wind. Without even thinking about it, they both start playing the international sport of skimming stones. Picking ones with the right size and shape is the key to success. It's the constant pursuit of that one stone that will give you double-digit skips. An informal sport played by millions across the world, without any recognition from the Olympic committee.

'Do you know what the world record is for skimming stones?' asks Tony.

'Nope.'

'88 skips, by some American dude.'

'You don't half know some weird stuff, lad.'

The freshwater loch lies over the ancient highland boundary fault, long and narrow, deep and mysterious, enormous and opaque.

'It's beautiful, isn't it?' says Davy.

'It's amazing. The colours of the hill reflecting in the water are so soothing. I could live here alright.'

'There used to be monsters here as well, you know, probably kelpies,' says Davy.

'Maybe they weren't as good at marketing as the Loch Ness team.'

'I hate those speedboats and jet skis that they allow on the loch now. My old man used to take me and my pals camping here. He used to bring cans of lager and a bottle of whisky, tie them to a long string and put them in the water to keep cold. We would wait until he got pissed and fell asleep, then we would steal the rest before cutting the string so that in the morning he thought he had lost them.'

'Ha ha. Sort of thing that I would do,' says Tony.

'Then another time, he collapsed asleep and left his light on in the tent, with the flap open. Every insect on the loch feasted on him that night, and by morning it looked like he had an extreme bout of chicken pox.' Davy laughs. 'Simpler times back then.'

'Your dad sounds a character.'

'Do you have family, son?'

'No, not really. Lost touch with my mum and dad when I was a kid; mostly been on my own.'

'Well, you can be part of our family now,' says Davy, with one final, mighty throw, which sadly sinks without skimming. 'C'mon, let's go up to the house and see what they are all up to. Hopefully they have some dinner on the go.'

Dinner is indeed on the go. Kathy is making her famous spaghetti Bolognese from scratch. It is to be accompanied by garlic bread because you need plenty of carbs when you are on the run from the law. She has eventually managed to conquer the hi-tech hob and the Aga oven, and so she is now motoring.

Lisa observes curiously that Cameron is helping to cook with his grandma. He has been given the task of browning the minced beef, a highly honoured role. Since Cameron has arrived, he has been much calmer and more relaxed. Not once has she seen him using anything electronic; the TV has yet to be turned on. Maybe the break is what he needs; maybe this trip isn't going to turn out so bad after all.

'You know, no one really knows the origin of spag bol, although it is thought to be a bastardised version of tagliatelle al ragu. You would outrage the mayor of Bologna if you said it came from his city,' says Lisa.

'The contention from the purists is over the pasta, not the sauce,' she continues.

'Jesus, another one from the school of useless information,' says Davy

'Spaghetti does not hold the ragu as well as its chunkier cousins, fettuccine or tagliatelle. If you opt for spaghetti, you will be left with a puddle of soup in your bowl. It's a complicated business, this pasta thing.'

Either way, it is a much-loved dish served by everyone,' says Kathy, 'especially the hungry of Loch Lomond.'

Dinner is a noisy and messy affair, a proper family dinner. Kathy has never been good at measuring quantities, so it is a huge bowl of pasta, served country style, placed in the middle of the table to be devoured.

Emily has managed to happily smear much of it on her nice white t-shirt. Food should be a joy; nights like this can be memories that last forever; a t-shirt is replaceable.

Again, the adults have agreed that they will not discuss what is going on whilst the children are around.

'So, Cameron, what do you want to be when you grow up?' asks Tony.

'Well, Dad wants me to be a lawyer, but it sounds very dull. I want to be a detective and solve murders and stuff.'

'You follow your dreams, son. If that's what you want, just go for it,' says Kathy.

'Yeah, but the police –' objects Davy with a laugh. 'Never had one of them in the family.'

'And Emily here wants to be a doctor,' says Lisa.

'Or a nurse, or a teacher. I want to help people,' says Emily. 'I used to want to be a mermaid, but it would be too cold in the water, and I don't know how they walk on land.'

'All different when I was at school,' says Davy. 'I was hardly ever there; couldn't wait to get out of school. The only thing I liked was playing football.'

'I want to play football after watching the women's Euros,' says Emily, 'but the school says we must play hockey.'

'Bloody fee-paying schools,' whispers Davy. 'Let the girls play fitba.'

'And you look like you have been having fun, Cameron. I haven't seen you on the computer once,' says Stephen.

'Well, it's nice just to be able to chat as a family. At home, it's always do this and do that, go to clubs, do your homework, go to bed. Mum spends all her time on Twitter, checking on social media, and Dad locks himself away on video calls, with Do Not Disturb on the door. That's why I just get on the computer.'

The children sit up for ages, way later than normal. Emily wraps herself contently around her grandma. They listen to stories from across the generations, both Tony and Davy playing off each other all the time. The kids become so tired they are ready for bed. With them tucked in, the adults sit on the couch and open a couple of bottles of wine.

'I feel terrible listening to the kids describe us,' says Lisa. 'It's like we are so busy ourselves, we are not present for them.'

'It's not easy these days; lots more distractions,' says Davy. 'Don't be hard on yourself; you have done a great job so far, kiddo.'

'You know, it's strange looking back at the whole Covid thing. It seems somehow so surreal that maybe it never happened,' says Stephen. 'Can you get your head round the fact that the whole world got locked up? We had no idea what was happening; it was frightening. Watching the news on an endless loop, hearing the sirens of ambulances, out clapping hands and banging pots and pans for the NHS . . .'

'They would have preferred a better wage,' says Tony.

'I found the whole working from home thing tough. It was even harder on the children, having to try to do classes online,' says Lisa. 'Especially Emily. Imagine starting school and not getting to form friendships; it was heart-breaking.'

'You were lucky, though; you had the room at your place,' says Kathy. 'Imagine if you lived in a flat or you were a single parent.'

'I was on my own for months on end,' says Tony. 'There was nothing to do but buy a load of cans and watch television. I never thought about it until now, but I realise I was struggling. I never had anyone to speak to, just the demons in my head. I know everyone thinks I am just a thief, but I got feelings too. The world didn't really care about people like me. The government weren't exactly providing support; nobody missed me.'

Lisa pours him another glass of wine, sits beside him and gives him a hug.

'You are not the only one, Tony. Most people would say that they struggled at some stage; it's entirely normal,' says Lisa. 'I struggled with the whole perfect mum thing. The old imposter syndrome kicked in when I was setting up my business, coupled with trying to bring up young children and have a nice home.

'I used to agonise over getting the perfect backdrop for my Zoom calls. You know – carefully curated books in the background, by politically correct authors . . .' She laughs.

'Alright for you. I was up in the attic room; I needed the books to balance my laptop,' says Stephen.

'Then if you went onto social media, you'd see people taking on all these challenges: building a garden bar, laser-printing PPE masks, baking banana bread, or learning to speak Spanish. I was just trying to survive day by day.'

'We did alright, babes. We did survive.'

'It's alright for men, though,' says Lisa. 'Stiff upper lip, old chap, and carry on. It's still women who carry the weight of parenthood on their shoulders.'

'They don't know the half of it,' says Kathy.

Davy has decided that they needed to put some music on, so goes over to the CD player and puts on some Leonard Cohen, easily his favourite. He loves his poetic lyrics and soulful voice.

'It's not going to get any easier, you know,' says Stephen. 'We now have a fractured government, a war in Ukraine and rampant inflation, and we might just be staring down the barrel of another recession.'

'You know, when you compare our generations, it's funny,' says Davy. 'When we grew up, we had nothing. I didn't fly in a plane until I was twenty-four. Your Ma and I went on holiday every year to a caravan park in North Wales.

'Your generation is so digitally connected. Need a taxi? Get an Uber; need a curry? go to Just Eat; buy stuff that you don't need to be delivered next day – it's Amazon. You don't need to learn a language or use a map anymore because you have apps for that.

'Nobody fixes stuff anymore; nobody buys shoes that last forever – just throw them away and buy another pair. People complain about not affording their bills but then boast about their new Apple watch. So, although you have all this material stuff, you are less happy than we were.'

'Your old dad is not wrong on this one, you know,' says Tony.

'Well, I booked to go to Florida because I wanted to reward the kids, even though it flies against every value I have when it comes to the environment,' says Lisa.

'I didn't want to go to Florida either,' says Stephen. 'The thought of having to go on a roller coaster makes me feel sick.'

'So why did we book it, then?'

'Because we were chasing the fantasy lifestyle that doesn't actually exist,' replies Stephen. 'We wanted everyone to look at our pictures and make banal comments like "Gorgeous" or "Beautiful" to make us feel happy.'

'Once we get through this, I want to go and find my mum and dad. I have been so selfish that I cannot imagine how they must have been feeling. Imagine denying them access to their grandchildren – I should be ashamed of myself.'

'Did they know what had happened?' says Lisa.

'I sat them down and told them the whole story before going into witness protection. They say that the most common breakdown in security is your parents, so we agreed that I would stay out of contact.

'I used to write to them every three months, so they know what happened. They know about Cameron and Emily; I have sent photographs. I just stopped a few years ago and feel guilty. Do you think they will forgive me?'

'It would be good for the kids, too. Look at them tonight: they have been at their happiest. Good food, parents who were present for once, surrounded by Grandma and Grandpa and their Uncle Tony.'

'Yesss . . . I am an uncle now!' says Tony. 'What a result! Never had the pleasure until now.'

CHAPTER THIRTY

2009

It is one of those wet, drizzly days on the bay that Christina hates. The clouds are so low in the sky that you feel that the ceiling is slowly compressing down on top of you. It isn't really raining, but there is so much moisture in the air it is wetter than rain. It's not that she misses the Italian sunshine; it's just that this always feels like a dark and ominous portent. It makes her feel anxious.

Christina is at home alone; the boys are at school and Matty is down at the office. The doorbell chimes, and it is Johnny at the door.

'Johnny, come in. Can I get you something to drink?'

'No thanks, Christina. Listen, we need to talk.'

'Of course we can. Come through to the kitchen.'

They both take a stool at the island bar.

'Christina, I need to talk to you about something that I have discovered. I am afraid it is a somewhat delicate matter.'

'Sure, but is it not best to wait for Matty? He will be back home soon.'

'No, I want to discuss this with you before I talk to Matty. 'Do you remember last year when we had the problem over in France, when the customs people took one of our trucks off us? At the time, we were told that there were problems related to the import licences.'

'I think I remember, although it is a little hazy.'

'Christina, the vehicle was stopped because it was being used for people trafficking into the UK. They found fourteen people on board in a hidden section. Thankfully, they were all alive; many have lost their lives this way. Your brother was using the route to bring in refugees from all over Europe. You knew about this all along, didn't you?'

Christina lowers her eyes and then looks at him for a few seconds before unleashing a powerful slap across his face, like the crack of a whip.

'You are a little fucking *bastardo*. You come into my house, where my children live, and you say this shit to my face! How dare you?'

'Matty asked me to investigate it. Seems like you lot have pulled this off on several occasions.'

'Listen to you, *pezzo di merda*, describing my family as you lot. How dare you? You are nothing . . . We lifted you up out of nowhere, paid your debts, and this is how you fucking pay us back.'

'I work for Matty.'

'This is a family business. In Italy, you would not dare show me such disrespect, *capiche*.'

'I do respect you. But you remember that night that all the Chinese drowned on the bay? I don't think I have ever seen Matty so upset in my life. He would never have sanctioned this.'

'Let me tell you this very slowly so you understand,' says Christina, angrily. 'If you breathe one word of this to Matty, I will have you killed. I will tell my brother to send people over to take care of it. You will end up in a bag out in that fucking bay.'

The noise in the hallway announces the arrival of Matty, Hammy and Benny. They come into the kitchen, grabbing cans of soft drinks from the fridge and biscuits from the cupboard. Matty detects an air of awkwardness between the pair, and a slight flush on Christina's face. He wonders for a second whether Johnny has tried it on with his wife. Surely, he wouldn't, would he?

'Hey, you two look a bit awkward. We haven't caught you up to something, have we?' says Benny, never one to be tactful.

'Shut up, Benny. I am not in the mood for your nonsense today,' says Christina.

'Right, boys, let's talk. Where are we with this planning guy?' says Matty.

'Well, it turns out that the intel on those residential developments was not from such a secure source as we thought it was. Turns out it might just be another disgruntled developer making claims without any basis,' says Hammy.

'For fuck's sake, you send me in to bat, accusing a public official of taking a bribe that turns out to be complete bollocks. We are fast turning into an amateur show here,' says Matty. 'And it turns out that yes, he did have an affair, but his wife has already heard his confession, so no leverage there.'

'Oh, great.'

'Anything else?' asks Matty.

'Yes, I am afraid that Tony has fucked up again. We set him up on a job to lift a truck outside Leeds last night. He didn't show up again and no explanation from him,' says Benny.

'Right, I have had enough of this nonsense. He is now officially history,' says Matty angrily. 'Who is going to tell him?'

'I will,' says Christina. 'That piece of shit has had this coming for a long time. It will be a pleasure to make the call.'

She slams the door on the way out, heading to her bedroom to make the call.

'Tony, it's Christina here.'

'Hey, is everything ok?'

'No, everything is not ok.'

'What do you mean?'

'I have never trusted you, Tony. I always thought you would steal from anyone if you thought you could get away with it. The family have had a meeting, and with immediate effect, you no longer work for us.'

'I don't understand. Can I speak with Matty?'

'No, you cannot. He is far too busy to speak with you.'

'But what will I do? It's all I have ever known.'

'I have no idea, and quite frankly, try asking someone that actually gives a fuck. And if I ever see you anywhere near my family . . .'

Just at that point, her two boys arrive back from school. Like all other pupils, the first port of call is the fridge. But Christina doesn't want them to hear what is being discussed in the kitchen, so she intercepts them. This is far from ideal, as she wants to be sure that Johnny is not telling the others about his revelation.

Back in the kitchen, the mood is no lighter. They have experienced a poor run recently. The loss of a couple of trucks and a failed attempt at influencing a public official is in danger of creating unnecessary risk.

Matty remembers the words of an old boss when he was a bouncer: 'If you do something wrong once, it is a mistake. If you do something wrong twice, it's a mistake keeping you.'

Matty and his friends had been successful because of their ability to fly under the radar. Now there is a real risk that they might be drawing attention to themselves.

'Lads, we need to put this behind us now. I am pretty sure that our friend in Planning won't go to the police; he won't want the attention. If he does, everyone will leap to the conclusion that he does take a cut; no smoke without fire, so to speak. So, despite his bravado, I think it will be ok,' says Matty. 'Anyway, we have lots of other influence that we can call on.'

'What do you mean?' asks Hammy.

'I have spent years building up my political networks within the council. All these boring events that we have attended were always about securing goodwill in public office.

'I am not for giving up on this development lightly. We will reach out to all the councillors and talk to them about our plans for the town. If they are worried about affordable housing, we will give them some of the flats. In return for support.

'But we need to control the optics. We have to position ourselves as honest businesspeople with a desire to be benevolent and caring, looking after our community.'

'You mean we don't do that already?' says Benny wryly.

'It means that we suspend all other activities for the time being; we want nothing that can damage our reputation.'

'Well, if that's the case, I am buggering off on holiday for a month or so. I haven't had a holiday in years, and seeing you won't be needing my talents, now is as good a time as any,' says Benny.

With the meeting over, Hammy and Benny head for the door and to their respective cars. The front door bangs closed. Johnny, however, hangs around after they leave, with a serious look on his face.

'Can I have a word, boss?'

'Sure, what is it? Is it to do with the strategy for the development? Have I missed something?'

'No, it's an extremely sensitive issue that I need to tell you about, and you are not going to be happy.'

Matty grabs one of the bar chairs and gives full attention to what is about to be said.

'You asked me several months ago to investigate the problem that we had in France. If you remember, we were told it was to do with import licences. That is simply not true. The vehicle was searched by the French police, following a tip-off. They discovered it was being used for people trafficking into the UK. Fourteen foreign nationals were discovered in a false compartment and were removed to a detention centre. It appears that this was a regular occurrence organised by Bruno de Luca and facilitated by your wife. Christina tried to persuade me not to tell you, but I couldn't do that.'

Johnny senses that Matty's eyes have moved away from his and are almost looking straight through him, focused on the doorway. Johnny turns round slowly to discover that Christina has been listening. Her facial expression was a mixture of distress and terror. He doesn't know whether she is going to burst into tears or vent her rage.

The tension in the air gives the silence more oxygen.

'Christina, my love, what is this nonsense that I am hearing?'

'I am truly sorry; I should have told you,' she says. 'I only went along with this to help Bruno; he is my family.'

'Remember the night that we lost all the Chinese on the bay? It was one of the darkest nights we have ever known. We cried ourselves to sleep that night.'

'I know, I know.'

'You know my views on this subject – the inhumane treatment of people, the fact that people have a price attached to them like a commodity, all the filthy people who make money out of it at each step of the journey . . .'

'I know my love, but if the hotel wasn't successful, my Mamma would end up losing her house. The people Nino represents had control over him.'

'Your brother is a piece of shit; he is too busy taking coke and chasing young girls,' spits Matty.

'It also goes without saying that if you want to position yourself as a benefactor to this town, then having your wife involved in people trafficking does not look good,' says Johnny, sarcastically.

This is enough to set Christina off. She flies wildly at Johnny but is caught around the waist by Matty before she reaches him. Instead, she bursts into tears. They stare intently into each other's eyes, knowing that whatever happens next is a pivotal moment in their relationship.

'Ok, ok, enough. Let me ask you this: is it still happening?'

'No, now that the hotel is up and running, we are no longer doing it. There is too much scrutiny at customs now.'

'And Johnny, can I ask you something? Why did you tell me when Christina explicitly told you not to?'

'Er, I work for you, and you asked me to investigate the problem. I was simply doing my job.'

'Yes, I suppose you were. I wish you hadn't told me, though, because you are forgetting one thing – family is everything to me. In future, if my wife asks you to do something, then you follow her instructions. There should be no debate.'

To Christina, Matty says, 'What should I do now?'

'Get rid of him, or I will,' spits Christina.

CHAPTER THIRTY-ONE

2022

It turns out to be a very pleasant early summer afternoon. With the schools not yet finished for the holidays, it is mostly dog walkers and hikers that are out and about, all dressed up in Barbour jackets and Hunter wellies.

It is decided that Stephen and Tony should continue to stay out of sight as a precaution. Davy and Kathy want to get the kids out into the fresh air and plan to go on a walk northwards. They pack a rucksack with clothes because you never know when the weather might turn. Kathy has taken the liberty of packing a light lunch of sausage rolls, boiled eggs and salt and vinegar crisps.

'Lisa, pet, if those two show any sign of leaving, you have my permission to shoot them,' shouts Davy as he leaves the house.

The three that remain sit in the main living room, with a view over the loch. As much fun as it is having the unbridled energy of young children around the place, the peace and quiet is rather enjoyable.

'So, what was it that made you decide to go to the police?' asks Lisa.

'Well, it all happened suddenly. I confronted his wife about what she was up to with shipments coming in from Italy,' says Stephen. 'We had lost a truck, and something felt wrong.'

'What was it?'

'You are not going to believe this, but she was running a people smuggling business. She said it was her brother, but she sanctioned it, and her husband didn't know. They put them on our trucks.'

'Oh, my God,' says Lisa.

'The pious little bitch, all high and mighty, pretending to be above everyone else. I never knew about any of this,' says Tony.

'So, I told Matty about it. I thought he trusted me and that he deserved to know. But he didn't. It was the exact opposite. He took her side and gave me a lecture about respecting Italian families. He went full-scale Al Pacino on me. That was the last time that I saw Matty and Christina.'

'So, what happened?' asks Lisa.

'Well, just before that, Christina told me that if I told Matty anything, she would have me killed. I was shit scared, so I took off and stayed in hotels for a few days. Matty tried to phone me about half a dozen times. I think he was trying to apologise, but I couldn't be sure.'

'Oh my God, Stephen, that is awful,' says Lisa.

'I think Matty changed, you know, and it was because of Christina. He was always a big, gentle giant; you would find him menacing, but underneath, he really cared about people. She was driving him on, never satisfied, always wanting more and more. He was trying to be ruthless, but he ended up making mistakes. He was becoming more Italian and less English,' says Tony.

'So, I went to the police and gave them an interview. I gave them the details of how we had laundered the money through the pubs, salons and car washes. I told them about the death threat and how I was worried about my safety. The only one that I never told them about was the people trafficking business. I am not sure why, but I wanted to protect Matty from that one. It would have broken him,' says Stephen.

'And Tony, what about you?' says Lisa.

'Well, mine was a little more straightforward. The police tracked me down and told me that Stephen had given evidence against them. They offered me immunity if I would make a statement. I was raging mad at Christina, and Matty never bothered to take my calls. I felt alone, so just thought fuck it, and gave them a list of the jobs that we had done.'

'So then they put you both on the witness protection scheme?' says Lisa.

'Pretty much. I took the full works and changed my identity, and the wonder kid here just went and hid away in Gateshead. Nobody would ever find you there,' says Stephen. 'It just doesn't make sense that they would hold a grudge after twelve years.'

'They offered me a full change, but to be honest, I couldn't be arsed. I messed about with Anthony for a bit, but it didn't really stick, so I just went back to being Tony.'

Lisa wanders off into the kitchen to put the kettle on.

'As much as we owe Davy a huge favour for sorting us out with this place, I think we should give the police a call, give that Brogan a call,' says Tony.

'I think you are right, just to find out if there have been any developments from their end. Do you still have her number?'

'Yep, I saved it on my phone. Let me get it,' says Tony, turning his phone on.

'We should probably run it past Davy, though. I don't fancy going behind his back now.'

Lisa returns, bearing mugs of tea. Tony is disappointed at the lack of accompanying biscuits. It wouldn't have happened on Kathy's watch, so he heads back to the kitchen.

'I got a question that I need to ask you, darling,' says Stephen.

'Sure, what is it?'

'How come your old man can organise a place like this with just one phone call? I mean this place is worth a fortune!'

'Ah ha . . . you haven't solved that little puzzle yet, have you, Mr Fancy Dancy, forensic accountant problem solver? Perhaps there is more to the old man than you think. I can have secrets too, you know.'

* * *

The happy hikers return a few hours later. They have been soaked from a sudden downpour and are happily caked in mud. Lisa reflects on the owner's choice of high gloss white marble floor tiles as she contemplates the muddy footprints before her.

Spirits are high; they had spotted some eagles, rabbits and otters. They had laughed at Grandpa, who still thought he was young enough to jump the stream, only to fall back into it, losing a welly.

Grandparents are supposed to help their children get into mischief, otherwise how do they learn?

They had huddled together, cold but happy, sitting on a tartan rug on top of a rock, and eaten their lunch. The purity of the environment and the quality of the air were good for the soul. For Kathy, the simple act of spending time with her grandchildren was a luxury.

'Davy, we were talking whilst you were out,' says Stephen. 'We think we should probably phone the police and check in with them. It might be better to have them on our side, rather than against us.'

'Ok, but you cannot tell them where we are, and I will join in the call once I get changed. Let's use one of these phones,' says Davy, producing three mobile phones and placing them on the table. 'They all have new SIM cards in them and can't be traced.'

The boys look at each other, without being able to ask the obvious question about the possession of multiple phones.

John G Gemmell

When they phone the police, it takes at least ten minutes before they are connected to Brogan and Phil.

'Brogan and Phil speaking.'

'Hi, it's Stephen and Tony here.'

'Oh, it's the wandering idiots. This is completely unacceptable behaviour from you both. We were very clear that you were both to remain in custody.'

'Custody? We were not under arrest; you said this Osman thing was optional.'

'Oh, don't be pedantic. In our care, then; it's the same thing. We have the right resources and the expertise to keep you safe.'

'Didn't do that very well, did you? Almost got run over and then burnt to death.'

'So where are you now? We will send a car and come and pick you up.'

'Good afternoon, Ms Simpson. This is David Gavin; I am the father of Lisa. I think we met briefly when you picked Stephen up; we just didn't get a chance to acquaint ourselves.'

'Eh, hello.'

'Yes, indeed, hello. Can I possibly help?'

'Listen, Grandad, it's lovely to see you getting involved, but you are well over your head here. Perhaps it's about time you went back to your chums at the club.'

'Oh no, this is much more fun.'

'Listen, I am sure you are a lovely old fella, but any chance I can speak to the boys again, please?'

'Oh, don't worry, we are all here. You are on a speaker phone.'

'Look, here is what happens next: we come and pick you up and end this stupid game.'

'No, it's about time that I tell you what is going to happen next. The boys are perfectly secure, and I am personally looking after them. I don't intend to tell you where they are because, quite frankly, my dear, you can't be trusted, I am afraid. Your batting record is zero for two so far.'

'Listen, sir, with respect, that is not how this works. You are talking to the police here.'

'That is exactly how it is going to be. Now can you also tell me the name of your reporting superintendent? I am quite keen to know if our paths have crossed.'

'Hi, it's Phil. Can we maybe start again? I am glad that you are both safe; we do care about your safety and welfare.'

'Great. Let me pass you back to Stephen.'

'So, tell us, do you have any new information that you can share with us?'

'Well, we are beginning to make a little progress. Can I presume that the name Marco de Luca O'Hare means something to you both?'

'That's Matty's youngest boy, little prick if my memory serves me right. He was just a kid, maybe about fourteen, back then.'

'Well, he is twenty-six now and quite the young playboy around town. We are pretty sure there is a connection here that we are following up on. We think he is moving drugs around the North West, and the senior crime people have him on their radar.'

'The Manchester police have also interviewed Frank Williams. As expected, he claims to know absolutely nothing about it. We want them to interview the two sons, but someone senior on our side has asked us to hold fire, which is very frustrating. They must be on their radar for something.'

'Thanks for that. Keep us informed as to how you get on. Listen, we are safe, Brogan. We promise to phone you every couple of days.'

'You two lunatics are not good for my stress levels.'

As the call ends, Davy rises from the table with a wry smile on his face. He must find Cameron as he has promised to give him a lesson on how to play chess.

'What did you say old Davy did again?' asks Tony.

'You know, I find myself asking the same question,' says Stephen.

That evening, the plan is to walk into the village and have dinner at the Rowardennan Hotel. The only challenge is that the children are dog-tired and don't want to go. Tony has volunteered to stay behind and look after them. He thinks it would be nice for the family to have dinner together. It is a mark of how far he has come that Lisa now trusts him in the role of babysitter.

The Rowardennan Hotel is a lovely little coaching inn, right in the middle of the small village. It has a large outdoor terrace and beer garden with beautiful views over the loch. They decide to eat inside and find a cosy table in the corner, lit with candles. They order fish and chips for the boys, huge chunks of flaky haddock in a batter served with chips and mushy peas. Kathy opts for the Cajun steak ciabatta, and Lisa has chosen the mushroom risotto. Both experience pangs of menu jealousy when they see the fish and chips.

They order a bottle of wine for the girls and two pints of Tennent's lager for the chaps. A small local folk group have arrived and are busily setting up, tuning their instruments, for the evening's entertainment.

'I hope Tony will be ok with the kids,' says Lisa.

'Relax, he will be fine,' says Kathy. 'He is not as stupid as he acts, you know.'

'I suppose so. They were so tired that they will probably be asleep by now.'

'They are having so much fun together; I have never seen them happier.'

'You know, Stephen, son, I am still fucking mad at you. You have misled my daughter and us for almost ten years. It's not really what I expect from a son-in-law.'

'Davy, I'm sorry, but hopefully you are beginning to understand the reasons behind it. The pressure was horrible – I had no choice. I will never let Lisa down; I love her to the moon and back.'

'Bit cheesy, but I will let you off,' says Davy. 'Tell you what, that Brogan is feisty, isn't she?'

'Yeah, she thought she was. Until she collapsed like a pack of cards when you came on the call.'

Stephen regales the others with the details of the conference call. He gives the story an extra layer of polish, building up the menacing part played by his father-in-law.

'So, this kid Marco doesn't mean anything to you?' asks Lisa.

'Not at all; he was just a young boy. He was the boisterous one of the two, always up to mischief and getting into trouble. I think he caused Christina all sorts of problems.'

'I Googled him. You don't get much, but my God, his girlfriend is all over it,' says Lisa.

'Oh, did you tell Dad the other name that the police gave you?'

'Oh yeah, what was his name again . . . ? Frank Williams from Manchester, involved in fruit machines and then security, alleged to be involved in drugs.'

'Bloody hell . . . Frankie Williams, I don't bloody believe it!' exclaims Davy, looking directly at his wife. 'That's a blast from the past.'

* * *

The short walk back to the house takes not much more than fifteen minutes. They decide not to stay and enjoy the local band, which turns out to be more post-punk than traditional folk music. Thankfully, with it being early summer and relatively dry, the fearsome midges are nowhere to be seen. The moon is out, bathing the loch in pale light, and lights are twinkling from the other side. There is no traffic, so they walk down the middle of the road.

As they reach the entranceway to the house, the sense of quiet evaporates as they all smell smoke.

'Oh, bloody hell, not again!' screams Stephen, taking off on a run with his wife close behind him.

They fly through the front door, to discover an empty house. They check the bedrooms, but they are still and untouched.

'Cammy! Emmy! Where are you?' screams Lisa.

Davy and Kathy have caught up with them and are looking out the kitchen window at the scene down by the loch.

Emily is seated on a large stone, beside a roaring campfire, poking it with a large stick and showering the air with orange sparks. Cameron is stripped to the waist and is swimming back to shore, only his head bobbing above the water. He has a rope attached to him, pulling a small red rubber dinghy. Tony has the air of a contented father about him, supervising affairs and enjoying the moment, whilst puffing on a large cigar, the smoke spiralling into the air.

'Oh my God, Tony, what the fuck is going on?' screams Lisa.

'Well, I thought I would teach Emily how to make a fire. We were roasting marshmallows.'

'Tony – she is six years old; this is a National Park. Did you not think that leaving a young girl in charge of a fire is a bit of a risk?'

'Sorry, says Tony, almost shrinking.

'And please tell me what on earth Cameron is doing in the freezing loch, swimming in his underpants, at ten o'clock at night.'

'Well, we saw that dinghy, and I thought we could maybe borrow it for tomorrow and go for a sail in it.'

'Unbelievable. This is one of the coldest lochs in the whole of Scotland. Every year, people lose their lives because of the shock of how cold the water is, and you let an eight-year-old go swimming at night, and you think it's ok to teach him to steal someone else's boat. Sometimes you act like a bigger fucking child than them.'

'I just thought it would be fun.'

Lisa gathers her two children together and marches back to the house. As she passes her husband and dad grinning on the terrace, she snaps, 'And you two can wipe those smiles off your face. Men! They are all hopeless. Mum, can you give me a hand here?'

Davy watches an ashen-faced Tony put out the fire and return to the main house.

'Tony, Tony . . . you were doing so well; that's your credit score taken a right battering,' says Davy. 'But the cigars look great. You got any more?'

'What I want to know is where on earth, in the middle of nowhere, you managed to get marshmallows,' says Stephen.

'Oh, that bit was easy. I nicked them from the Esso garage on the way up here.'

CHAPTER THIRTY-TWO

2009

The day does not start well in the O'Hare household. Troubles with Marco are accelerating, and last night he went missing. Despite having a nine pm curfew from his parents, he had still not appeared by ten. Matty and Christina were out in the car, searching the empty streets for more than an hour, trying to locate him.

Eventually, Christina managed to get a tip-off from some youngsters and they found him down at St Patrick's Chapel, the ruined church that stands on a prominent rock overlooking the bay. The walls of the church are covered in graffiti, crew tags from the local young team.

There were six of them, four boys and two girls, sitting around a little campfire. They were listening to Human by The Killers on someone's phone. Empty cans of Strongbow cider and bottles of Smirnoff Ice were strewn at their feet. There was also the whiff of weed, notes of lemongrass and wood, in the cold still air.

Marco was frog-marched to the car by his dad, to his huge embarrassment. Matty told the other three boys that they were to clear up the mess, and when he came back in the morning, it had better be clear, or he would personally hunt them down. The boys believed him.

Christina decided that they needed to take the two girls home as well, as one of them looked the worse for wear. She was alarmed at how revealing their outfits were. She hoped their parents would be worried about where their fourteen-year-old girls were, but she was not sure that they cared. They, too, were placed in the back of the car.

The pale light now signals the arrival of morning, and Christina is sitting with Angelo having breakfast. Angelo is all set for school already. He has a big year ahead with GCSEs and is finishing off some complicated maths homework while eating toast. She looks at her studious older son and asks herself why two boys, with the same upbringing, can be so different.

Christmas is a week away, so the decorations are up. *Buon Natale* is an important celebration for Christina, a time of year back home that she loved as a little girl. She has bought an enormous nine-foot Christmas tree that dominates the hall. The tree has the sweet smell of pine and is adorned with hundreds of baubles and flashes of tinsel.

Hundreds of exterior lights have been put up so that the house sparkles. The decorations will stay up until *La Befana*, the 6th of January, when legend says that an old witch flies from house to house on her broomstick, delivering the gifts that she didn't give to the Holy Child.

The house is decorated throughout with bright red poinsettias. The house smells of Christmas, as she has flown in special diffusers from Aqua di Elba in Tuscany that she once fell in love with in a hotel in Florence. It smells of cinnamon and cloves.

Matty comes bounding into the room and pats his older son on the top of his head.

'Where is he?' growls Matty.

'He is still in bed sleeping. He says he doesn't feel very well and doesn't want to go to school. He wants one of us to phone it in.'

'Go and get him, please. He needn't think he can hide away in his bed all day,' says Matty, pouring himself a coffee.

A sullen-faced fourteen-year-old slopes into the kitchen and sits down with an exaggerated sigh. They can do whatever they want to him, he isn't going to make it easy for them.

'Marco, what on earth did you think you were up to last night?' asks Matty.

'I was only hanging out with my mates.'

'You were drinking alcohol, and God knows what else. You are only fourteen years old.'

'Everyone else does it.'

'Well, you don't, alright? You live in my house and under my rules. One day, when you are head of your own house, you can set the rules. Right now, you are grounded until after Christmas. And whether you like it or not, you are going to school today. You have important years coming up with exams, so you need to start studying.'

'Whatever.'

'And I will drive you this morning so that I know that you have gone.'

Marco heads back up to his room to get dressed, mortified that his pals will see his dad drop him off at the school gates.

'I wanted Christmas to be special this year, but he is going to spoil it for all of us,' says Christina.

'He won't,' says Matty, kissing his wife and stealing her toast. 'I won't let him. Everything is going to be great this Christmas.'

He is not prepared for what happens next.

The front doorbell rings, and when Matty opens the door, he is met by six police officers. Four of them look as if they are in full-blown riot gear, armed with hardware ready to blow the door off its hinges if there are any problems in gaining access.

The lead police officer is Detective Chief Inspector Mark Bolton, who does all the speaking.

'Mr Matthew O'Hare, I must inform you that I am here to place you under arrest on the grounds of multiple thefts, money laundering from the possession of stolen goods, and the attempted bribery of a public official.

'You do not have to say anything. But it may harm your defence if you do not mention, when questioned, something which you later rely on in court. Anything you do say may be given in evidence,' says DCI Bolton. 'Do you understand?'

'Yes, I do'.

'Good. Now, may we come inside, rather than discussing this on the doorstep?'

'Of course. You two can, but kindly ask the four RoboCops to go back to their van. I have two young boys here,' says Matty. 'It's completely unnecessary.'

Christina has been standing behind him with both boys, listening to the exchange.

'Oh my God, Matty,' she says, 'what is happening?'

'It's ok, Christina. Don't get upset; I am sure it's all a big mistake.'

'I am also in possession of a search warrant for this residential property and your office and buildings down at Heysham,' continues the DCI. 'My officers intend to search this property with immediate effect to avoid the risk of anything being contaminated.'

'What? You think I am going to let you crawl all over my beautiful home in front of my two boys? Go and fuck yourselves,' sneers Christina.

'Mrs O'Hare, I am sorry, but this is fully backed up legally. I promise you we will do our utmost to be respectful.'

'Dad, is there anything that we can do to help you?' says Angelo.

Matty ruffles his son's hair. 'Ange, just look after your mum and your little brother for me. You can start by making sure he gets to school. He still doesn't get a pass on that one.'

'Christina, can you phone the lawyers, Madison and Copland, and tell them we need their help?'

Matty is placed in handcuffs and taken by police car to Lancaster police station on Thurnham Street.

At the same time, the same process is executed which leads to the detention of Benny D'Arcy and Steven Hamilton. All of them are now being held separately at the police station, ahead of rounds of questioning. None of the three is expected to cooperate with the police, who are largely unconcerned, as they feel very confident of the validity of the evidence in their possession.

All three are formally held for thirty-six hours before being charged. Matty is charged with theft, handling stolen goods, money laundering, and VAT evasion. Enquiries are ongoing into a potential blackmail charge of a public official. After careful deliberation, it is agreed that they will all be released on bail, provided they surrender their passports and report weekly to the station. It is likely that the court case will be held early the following year.

Christina is not to get the magical Christmas that she aspires to.

* * *

Twelve weeks later, a meeting is set up at the offices of Madison & Copland in Manchester. They are in the board room of the senior partners. There is a large walnut table which seats up to ten people, with comfortable leather chairs. Matty and Christina are here to meet with Stewart Copland, one of the founding partners in the firm, to discuss the upcoming court case.

'Matty, Christina, thank you both very much for coming into the office this morning,' he says. 'To set expectations upfront, I don't think it looks very clever.'

'Yes, we had a feeling that would be the case,' says Matty, remarkably relaxed, given his fate.

'As you know, you have been charged with multiple crimes and are scheduled to be in court in four weeks' time,' says Mr Copland. 'The prosecution has confirmed that the police have both video and written evidence from two of your employees – Johnny Rodgers and Anthony Fowler. Both have given extensive interviews and statements in return for immunity from prosecution.

'They have identified over twenty instances of theft, which I think we can probably narrow down if we choose to. They also have a list of all the assets acquired over the years and explanations of how you moved illegitimate money through legitimate businesses.'

'I really don't know what kind of defence we can rely on, and there is the possibility that we could make the outcome significantly worse. I think you might want to strongly consider the possibility of pleading guilty.'

'And what would the outcome of that be?'

'Well, I think you would be looking at a prison sentence. It would probably be six to eight years for robbery, and ten to twelve years for handling stolen goods and money laundering. We could probably negotiate the bribery accusation away. If you were to own up to the crime, we could ask for sentence leniency,' says Mr Copland.

'Oh, Matty,' says Christina, bursting into a flood of tears.

'I think the other matter that you face is that the Crown will definitely seek a confiscation order to seize whatever assets they can.'

'What will the damage be?'

'I think you will lose the haulage business and all the flats. They won't be interested in the tanning salons or the car washes, as there is no intrinsic value there. The family home, the pubs and the potential property development should be ok, as they are legally owned by Christina.'

'Is it possible for me to get some time alone with Christina, please?' asks Matty.

'Of course,' says Mr Copland, gathering all his files, and exits quietly.

Matty stands up, dabs his wife's tears with a handkerchief and envelopes her in a large embrace.

'Shh, my love. It will be fine.'

'How is that possible? Our world is falling apart. How will I explain this to my family? How will I be able to go about town and meet other people? Everyone will just love to see our downfall.'

'This is my fault; we shouldn't have chased Johnny and Tony away. We should have looked after them, not scared them off. We forgot that they were part of our family.'

'So, what happens now?'

'I think I have no option but to plead guilty; you got to be able to do the time if you do the crime,' he says, trying some lame humour.

'But up to twenty years . . . I will be stuck with nothing, having to bring up two young boys, one of whom is a liability. I will be an old lady by the time you come out.'

'It will be fine. You have the house; there will be income from the pubs; you will survive.'

'But I won't have you!' she cries. 'That's all I have ever wanted. It's all my fault. It was me that caused all this to happen. I betrayed you by being loyal to my brother – that's what triggered this all off.'

'Everything that we did, we did together. We will be strong, my love.'

In March 2010, at the Crown Court of Manchester, Matty is sentenced to a reduced sentence of fifteen years imprisonment. Benny and Hammy are sentenced to eight years each. The police are ecstatic that they have managed to solve a long-running problem of lorry theft in the region. They organise a press conference at the end of the trial, ensuring that it is carried by all the mainstream news outlets, to the further embarrassment of Christina.

The sentence is to be completed at HM Prison Manchester, previously known as Strangeways.

Although this is a Category A prison, Matty is viewed as a low-risk prisoner. The expectation is that with good behaviour, he might serve ten years in jail.

Matty goes into prison with two ambitions. Firstly, to make sure that from day one, nobody will fuck about with him. Secondly, he wants to use his time wisely to make up for lost opportunities and opts to take a degree in Human Psychology at the Open University.

Matty remains in prison until he is eventually released in March 2020.

CHAPTER THIRTY-THREE

2022

Lisa has secretly invited Bella to come down and surprise the children. She drives herself down in her sporty little white Mini. As ever, she comes bearing gifts, having stopped off at the nearby farm shop and collected some local lamb chops, Ayrshire new potatoes and a sponge cake. For the children, she has brought ice cream and magazines.

'Oh, Bella! How lovely to see you,' says Kathy, who is also very smitten by her. Even more so as she comes bearing gifts.

'Some gaff, you got yourself here, Mrs G,' says Bella, admiring the immaculate kitchen.

'I prefer my own hob, dear.'

'*Aunty Bella!*' screams Emily, jumping into her arms.

Tony arrives in the kitchen like a magic trick.

'Here he is, the man of the moment. I hear your attempt at the boy scouts went well last night,' says Bella, laughing. 'Although, sadly, you didn't earn your babysitting badge.'

'Don't bring that up. I am only just out of the doghouse.'

The children go out to play on the tree swing at the bottom of the garden. Lisa, Stephen and Bella go out to watch them from the deck. Kathy goes to her happy place, the kitchen, to prepare dinner.

'So, I hear there is a new man on the go,' says Stephen. 'You decided not to bring him with you.'

'Given we have had only a handful of dates, I thought it was a bit early to introduce Mikkel to a couple of fugitives who have a bit of a problem with someone trying to chase them all over the country and kill them.'

'Touché,' says Stephen, before heading down to join the children.

'Anyway, what's the goss, girl?' asks Bella.

'I have thought long and hard about it. I don't want to lose Stephen.'

'Good girl, you are both right for each other.'

'I just don't intend to make it very easy for him. He will need to work very hard.'

'Well, obviously. Any news on the case?'

'The police seem to have made some connection between Matty O'Hare's youngest son and a drug-dealing family, headed up by a Frank Williams. Now the strange thing is my dad seemed to recognise the name, but he is keeping his cards to himself.'

'Has Stephen worked it out yet about your dad?'

'No, I don't think so. He is going to have to work that one out himself.'

'Where is the old boy, anyway?'

'I have no idea. A large, blacked-out Range Rover came down early this morning and picked him up; he has been away for hours now. He is defo up to something.'

'How exciting. Although you had told me, I have never seen this side of old Davy – it's super fun.'

It is late into the evening before they hear the crunch on the driveway signalling his return. Bella had left a couple of hours earlier, as she had a date with her new beau. Davy appears in a very good mood, whistling an upbeat little melody as he comes through the door. He seems to be energised and is even already looking younger.

'I presume that Tweedledee and Tweedledum have managed to stay out of trouble for once, Kathy?' says Davy.

'Yes, they have been as good as gold. I have kept you some dinner; it's in that Aga thing, so hopefully won't have dried out. Not going to lie, it might be a fancy piece of kit, but I prefer my own oven.'

Davy picks the tartan armchair beside the fire. He feels a little sad that it isn't cold enough to have the log fire yet. It looks as though he is in his own armchair, in his own home, rather than one that he has borrowed from a friend.

'So where have you been today?' asks Lisa.

'Oh, here and there. I was back up in Glasgow, had a few meetings, this and that.'

'Davy, sorry, but enough is enough. There is some stuff going on here that I simply don't understand. Let me start with this one: how on earth did you manage to rustle up this house in the blink of an eye? It seems completely out of character,' says Stephen.

'This house? Oh, that's nothing. I have a mate called Charlie Sweeney; he owns several hotels throughout central Scotland. He's in America with his missus for three months. Anyway, he owes me a favour or two, from back in the day when he was just getting started. He was delighted to help; said we can stay as long as we like.'

Kathy returns to the room with his dinner on a tray. He is to have the lamb chops that Bella brought, along with roast potatoes and a glass of milk. Tony tries to capture Kathy's attention, but for once she ignores him.

'Have you told them yet?' says Kathy.

'I was enjoying the secrecy, dear,' says Davy with a sigh. 'Ach well, I suppose it's about time that I told you about my younger self . . .'

'Buckle up, boys,' says Lisa. 'You are about to go on a wild ride.'

Davy tells them how he was brought up in Glasgow in the early fifties. The city was an industrial powerhouse, built on shipbuilding and engineering, and hard drinking and occasional violence. There was plenty of employment to be had, but there was still much poverty, too.

Davy followed the well-trodden path of leaving school to start his apprenticeship in the shipyards. He hated it and didn't last very long. Instead, he ended up on the building sites. There was lots of work there, following the war and the bombing of Clydebank. There was also investment in new housing to replace homes that had not been supported during the war.

Clydebank was a rough place during this time, and you needed to be able to handle yourself. Davy was more than capable of doing that and created the reputation of someone not to be messed with.

As his prowess grew, he attracted the attention of some of the criminals and gangs that operated in that part of the city. It was very territorial back then. It was no real surprise that Davy gravitated to supplying security over building sites and debt collection for his masters. He never used weapons of any sort, relying on his own physical ability and a small army of loyal, hard-fisted men. They were always there on a Friday to collect their pay, before it got spent on booze.

That said, he was proper old school; he had been brought up in an era when manners were still important. He did not like people who took advantage of others less fortunate. It is not to say that he was soft; he just insisted that people followed the fraternal guidelines.

At the height of his powers, he was feared equally by the police and criminals. He more or less ran the whole of Clydebank, Yoker and Drumchapel. Nothing happened out on the streets without Davy authorising it.

At the same time, he developed substantial networks with the wider criminal community across the UK. They came to him for advice before they took on something or someone in Glasgow. He became a sort of regional security advisor. His network extended deep into the Glasgow police force, never through financial inducement, but through hospitality and the exchange of knowledge, always politely shared over a pot of tea and china cups.

He became the one that you went to resolve disputes. A de facto tribal leader, holding counsel and laying down the law.

Davy and Kathy then moved into the bungalow which is their current residence and their pride and joy. He decided it was time to give it all up and effectively retired. In his line of work, to have an innings in which you avoided both jail and/or permanent injury was regarded as success. He found it strange, the older he got, that he still carried a fearsome reputation.

Even today, if he visits a pub, tables are cleared, people removed, so that he can have the best seat. The older ones still give him respect wherever he goes; the younger ones just assume that he is somebody's grandad and don't really care. When it is explained to them, they suddenly aren't so cool, his reputation still alive and well.

He joined the local bowling club, which he hated. He referred to it as 'God's Waiting Room', as the number one subject was who had just died and who might be next. They had a numerical membership number scheme, so when someone died, you move up a place. It is like a version of *Deadpool*. He had reached number thirty-one on the list.

The reason for joining was not to play bowls but so that he still knew everything that was going on around town. The old boys furnished him with stories of who was up to what. Sadly, the world had changed; there was no longer a code of conduct to be followed, no more honour among thieves. The behaviour of the new breed was getting out of hand, the use of guns, knives and car-bombing all fuelled by the fight for drug profits.

For him, his real success in life has been seeing his daughter grow up to be a beautiful young woman, a fantastic mother and now a successful businesswoman. Davy dotes on his two grandchildren. He likes to moan about private schools but is secretly happy with the education they are getting. Davy had welcomed Stephen into the family and had liked him from day one. He makes Lisa happy, and that is the only thing that matters. He is annoyed at the deception but is now resolved to sort this all out for the young couple. For him, it is his one last dance.

'Jesus Christ,' says Stephen. 'You think you know someone, then you realise that you don't.'

'Ha ha. Let me remind you, you are the one in a witness protection scheme, with a complete change in identity whilst managing to keep it hidden from your wife of over ten years . . . pots and kettles, son.'

'Some life you have had, big Davy,' says Tony.

'Well, that's all a long time ago. We have moved on from it,' says Kathy. 'He retired, and we now live a respectable life. I never thought we would ever discuss this again.'

'Oh, and don't listen to Miss Goody Two Shoes here,' quips Davy. 'She ran a very tasty little shoplifting team through the eighties until they all got caught stealing blouses from Frasers.'

'What? I never knew that!' says Lisa. So, everyone in my entire family is a criminal. I am the only one who is not some kind of gangster.'

'You didn't need to tell her,' says Kathy.

'Just trying to take the heat off me a little bit,' says Davy. 'Anyway, you were good at it. I was proud of you; you had a talent for it.'

'So, any chance you tell us what you have been up to today?' asks Stephen.

'Not yet . . . but soon,' says Davy.

Later, whilst lying in bed, Stephen is reflecting on what had been a highly revealing evening.

'Why have you never told me this before?'

'When I turned eighteen, Dad sat me down and told me everything from start to finish. I think he found it cathartic. Ever since then, I have tried to bury it. It's not easy to run a PR company based on ethical behaviour when your father has a history of being a gangland enforcer.'

'I can't believe I never worked it out until now. Although I think we heard the romantic and sanitised version of his past, the one he is keeping for his memoirs.'

'He is almost seventy now, and he has been out of this for almost twenty-five years. I don't want any harm to come to Mum or Dad. Perhaps it's time to re-think the offer from the police, rather than letting Dad get back on his horse, in case he falls off it.

'Stephen, I am going to forgive you,' says Lisa. 'We have worked hard – let's not throw it away.'

Stephen reaches over and gives her a warm embrace. For the first time, there might be light at the end of the tunnel.

John G Gemmell

'What is so funny, though, is how much everyone is enjoying themselves. The kids are on an adventure holiday, Kathy is feeding everyone, Davy thinks he is back in the game, and Tony is just happy to be part of the family,' says Stephen.

'Yeah, but let's not forget the key thing . . . There is still a contract out on you both, and we can't go to bed every night wondering when it might happen.'

CHAPTER THIRTY-FOUR

2015

It is five years into Matty's sentence. To her credit, Christina visits him religiously every Friday morning. She very rarely takes the boys, as she doesn't want them to see prison life. She hates the trek into Manchester from Preston by train but is determined never to miss it. Her heart still aches at the thought of not being able to see him every day or to hold him in her arms. The house is empty without his personality, and many nights she has cried herself to sleep.

She honours her commitment to stand by him. When her disloyalty over the people smuggling was discovered, it could have gone either way. Matty chose to stand by her, so now she will do the same.

Matty has taken the whole prison life experience in his stride. He has maintained a powerful physical presence and, if anything, has augmented it through his daily gym routine. From very early on, it was clear that none of the wide lads were going to take advantage of him. In addition, the prison warders love him; he has taken his charm and charismatic personality in with him. Prison guards regularly stop by just for a chat.

As he promised himself the day that he went in, he wanted to make use of time by enrolling in a further education programme, so he is studying Psychology. He doesn't have many regrets in life, but one that he does have is that he didn't go on to further education after school. When he is released, he doesn't want to be a pariah; he still believes that he can pull off the property development that he dreams about.

It is still on the slate, and Christina is making some progress with it. It is looking much more positive from a planning perspective, following a change of leadership at the council. The main problem now is accessing the capital. They know that they will now need to borrow money from the banks, who are still very nervous about risk following the financial meltdown. The loan will need to be secured by Christina, as nobody will lend money to Matty.

Having made her way through the usual security checks, Christina is ushered into the prison visitation room. It is a large square room, with harsh lighting and a nondescript carpet. They have spaced out several visitor pods, with uncomfortable blue chairs and little low-level plastic coffee tables.

It is always cold, as if they never put the heating on. Always very quiet, muted, as if everyone is a little ashamed, and only occasional muffled laughter.

'Ah, the love of my life,' says Matty, giving her a warm embrace.

'Hello, darling. I love you so much.'

'So, what's been happening?' says Matty. 'How are the boys?'

'Oh, I have some great news from Angelo. He has been accepted to do a two-year Masters in coding at Manchester University.'

Angelo graduated this summer with a first-class BSc Honours degree in Computer Science. It was sad that Matty had missed this event, but Nonna had been persuaded to come over from Italy to join the celebrations.

'Brilliant.'

'I also think he might have a girlfriend, but you know him – you can't get him to reveal anything.'

The financial impact of Matty's incarceration has been significant. They still have the house and the income from the pub estate, but nothing like the lifestyle that they had once enjoyed. For the first time in her life, Christina has had to work to a monthly budget. To make ends meet, she has taken on a job at Next, out at the Central Retail Park. She has become more frugal, no more designer brands, no more imported goods or expensive nights out. Strangely, she finds herself starting to enjoy it.

The one who is most upset is Marco. His sense of entitlement and his temper mean that he is enraged about suffering such a drastic decline in his allowance and lifestyle. He is offended by the fact that his mother and father are so stoic about their circumstances. As usual, he takes it out on his brother, declaring that as he is now the head of the household, he should be doing something about it, instead of constantly studying or playing computer games with his nerdy friends.

He hangs out with a group of young lads whose aspirations lie in drinking cider and smoking weed. They have been getting into some petty crime, nothing significant, but it's the trajectory that worries Christina.

'And *principe*, Marco?' says Matty.

'What do you think? Out every night, he and his pals; doesn't get home until the early hours, and sleeps all day.'

'I am sorry my love; I should be there for you.'

'No job, and no interest in getting one.'

'That boy has delusions of adequacy.'

'I have decided to take him with me to Italy for a month. I am going to go out and stay with Mamma, so he can come along. Maybe a change of scenery will do him good.'

'Will you see your big brother?'

'I will, but I give you my word, I'm not going back to what we did before.'

* * *

The atmosphere is one of cold hostility between mother and son as they fly out to Calabria. To save money, they fly EasyJet from Liverpool to Naples, which still means a four-hour drive to Catanzaro. It is not helped by Christina's choice of car hire or music on the journey.

Marco says nothing for the first two hours, staring out the windows as they drive past Salerno and head up into the mountains of the south.

'Marco, tell me. What are you thinking?' asks Christina.

'Just how unfair everything is.'

'What do you mean?'

'Just what happened to Dad. Overnight I went from having a great lifestyle, loads of money and clothes, and now it's shit.'

'Well, it doesn't need to be that way. You have your whole life in front of you. You can be anything that you want.'

'I always thought that I would go and take over Dad's business.'

'Your Dad was trying to get out of it all. He wanted to be respectable. He didn't want you to lead your life the way he led his.'

The traffic is chaotic, and the roads are crumbling.

'Everyone thinks I'm the loser in the family. Ange is the clever one, who has studied hard and done well.'

'Don't say that – it is not true.'

'It's how it feels. I suppose it's made worse with Dad being in jail.'

'I want you to know this. I love you so much. I would do anything for you, my angel. Maybe this trip is what you need; it will give you some space to think.'

It is early evening when they arrive at the villa. Nonna has a surprise waiting for Marco: she has bought him a bright red Vespa scooter. She thinks that he needs to be independent, rather than have two old women driving him all over town. He is twenty years old and has girls to impress. His mother detects a smile she has not seen for years.

Christina smiles to herself when she hears Marco speaking. He has a strong Lancashire accent but is also dialling up his Italian mannerisms and hand gestures, with a comical effect. The girls will either love him or laugh at him.

Christina has set up two wicker chairs and a table outside, at the edge of the orchard. She has prepared tall glasses of Orangello, topped up with ice and some sparkling wine. It was Papa's favourite *aperitivo*.

'That boy will be the death of me,' says Christina.

'You are too hard on him,' says Mamma.

'What do you mean?'

'You both try to break him like a wild horse, and he fights back. He now finds himself angry and without a father figure. Let's give him space, see if he can find something to be passionate about. It would help if he could find a girl; then we would see him change. Shall I try and find him a nice Italian girl whilst he is over?'

'Ha ha, sounds like you are thinking about an arranged marriage! A girl from Calabria would make him wilder, not calmer.'

Her sister-in-law, Maria, drops in at the villa to say hello. She is looking strained and older, with grey hair appearing at the roots, something that was previously unimaginable, as her appearance was always immaculate. She has lost her vitality, and there is a cold sadness behind her eyes.

'*Ciao*, Maria,' says Christina.

'*Ciao*, Christina.'

'Tell me how my beautiful nieces are getting on.'

'They are both fantastic. Sofia has moved to Reggio Calabria and has a job as a journalist. Thankfully, it is in finance and not crime, so it is safer. Aurelia is training to become a teacher and has moved in with her boyfriend. I don't approve, but it is the modern way, I am sure.'

'So just you and Bruno at home in the empty nest, then.'

'Mostly just me on my own, to be honest. I don't need to tell you that your brother cannot keep his dick tucked away. Not really someone I want to spend my time with if I can help it. He asked for a divorce, and I said get lost. He doesn't get rid of me that easily.'

Although this is not news to Christina, she can feel the unhappiness and feels very sad. Maybe it is time for her to have it out with him.

After Maria leaves, she and xxx take in the views and listen to the sounds from across the valley. The villa is truly peaceful on an evening like this. It is the golden hour, the one just before sunset, when everything is bathed in golden light.

'Anyway, how are you getting on, Mamma?' asks Christina.

'Oh, I am doing just fine, although old age doesn't come easy, you know. I miss your Papa hugely. I still go to Mass every day and drop by and visit him in the cemetery. I tell him everything that is going on so he doesn't miss out on all the family news.'

'Aw, that's nice.'

'I miss having someone to cook for; it's not the same when you are on your own.'

'And are you coping with the villa?'

'What do you mean? I clean it every day. Are you saying it is dirty?'

'No, Mamma, but it is a big villa; it is a lot of work.'

'It might have eight bedrooms, but I only use one and the kitchen; the others are mostly locked up. I get some help from Antonio and his two sons with the gardens and the orchards.'

'I suppose there is no point in asking again if you want to come to England with me?'

'You know the answer to that one. This isn't just a villa; it is where I talk to your Papa. I could never be separated from him; it means too much to me. One day soon, I will join him again.'

Mamma had lived through the horrors of the Second World War, which had deeply affected Calabria. The South had been occupied by the Italian Army in a war that none of the local inhabitants had wanted. They were not welcome in the region, and to a young girl like her, it was more like an occupation. The girls had all been warned that the soldiers from the North could not be trusted, so they should not talk to them. Her friends told stories of soldiers forcing themselves on young girls.

The occupation ended in 1943. However, on their spiteful retreat from Calabria, the army sought to ruin the infrastructure and destroyed roads, bridges and important buildings, including the beautiful cathedral in Catanzaro.

Mamma can remember her parents being distraught that the church was attacked, that the savages were willing to attack a place of worship. The villagers had carried out the repairs on the church.

After the war, Calabria was neglected by the North as they prioritised investment to suit the wealthy. It was tough for the de Lucas growing up, as living conditions were very poor. The North did not want to spend money on education for the South, on the grounds that it would lead to the poor challenging the elite. Calabria was nearer to Athens than Milan.

With such weak state control, organised crime flourished into a parallel state. No better example of that is the fifty-five years it took to build a motorway to Salerno, due to the infiltration of organised crime.

The de Luca family were respected and trusted in the region. Given that there had been four generations of the family, they were broadly left alone. Of course, they also knew to allow others to live their lives in whatever way they wanted. It was part of life in this region to always turn a blind eye but never to turn the other cheek.

Mamma had spent all her life dealing with adversity. Her dreams had not been about wealth, just safety and security. It was about survival. She needs few material possessions; her family and her faith are all she needs.

'You know, during and immediately after the war, we had to close the clothes factory business. It was too dangerous and impossible to move our goods to the North. We couldn't afford to pay any of the staff, so we mothballed it,' says Mamma, 'but we needed to survive, we needed to eat.

'People look at Calabria, and they think it is very poor; that is a narrative created by wealthy northerners. Agriculturally, it is one of the richest regions in the whole of Italy. For a number of years, these orchards allowed us to survive.'

At the villa, they had reverted to growing fruit that they could sell at local markets. They farmed oranges, clementines and mandarins. They not only produced fresh fruit, but they made preserves, syrups and candied fruit.

However, the one that they were most proud of was the Bergamot – the queen of citrus fruits. Local legend has it that it is good for 'bad breath and psoriasis'.

'So, you see, the secret sometimes is to know when to reinvent yourself,' says Mamma.

'Why do I have a feeling that you are trying to tell me something, giving me a veiled message?' says Christina.

'I suppose I am. Perhaps it's true that necessity is the mother of invention. It forces you to change. Matty will come out of jail at some point, and his world will have changed; it won't be easy to go back to where you were. Perhaps you will both need to reinvent yourselves.'

'Maybe.'

'You know life will not be the same again. You have grown up now, my darling. Make your choices for you and Matty only.

'Also, you know I am getting older now, and I worry about who will take over the villa when I am gone.'

'Well, my brother still lives in town.'

'Christina, your brother is a piece of shit. He will destroy everything. He is on a dangerous path of self-destruction. The way he has treated his wife and daughters is appalling. God will be unforgiving when that boy meets his fate,' says Mamma, her face darkening at the mention of her son's name. 'Go and see him while you are here. I will let you be the judge as to the state of him.'

* * *

A few days later, she travels down the mountain to visit the resort. Marco accompanies her, more than happy to spend his day at a five-star beach resort. Anywhere there might be hot young girls works for him. The sky is clear, and it is going to be a hot one.

When they have parked the car, Marco skips off to the changing rooms and then to the pool, promising his mum that they will meet for lunch.

She finds her brother at one of the resort's private villas, which has become his permanent residence. When she enters the villa, she is surprised by the fact that the blinds are drawn in the middle of the day. The room is littered with dirty glasses and empty bottles. There is an assortment of clothing lying about, so that it looks more like a teenager's bedroom. The air is stale; it smells of clothes that haven't been cleaned. It smells of failure.

Coming out of the shower is a young girl wrapped in a towel, who hastily dresses and leaves the room. The younger woman has no idea who the older woman is, but she senses that getting the hell out of there is a wise decision.

Bruno looks in terrible condition. He has lost probably a couple of stone in weight and has a strange grey pallor about him. His eyes are bloodshot and his pupils dilated. His frequent sniffing might be caused by a sinus infection, but the real cause is abuse.

'Well, you look like proper shit, big brother,' says Christina.

'Thanks, sis.'

'And how old was she, because she looked mighty young to me?'

'Sis, give me peace. She's old enough.'

'Let's get these blinds and windows open and get some air in here.'

'I can't; they are watching me.'

'Who is watching?'

'Nino and his men. They try and control my every move right now; they no longer let me make my own decisions.'

'Well, given the state of you, neither would I.'

'Every time I leave the resort, they follow me. It's as if I know too much.'

'Why don't you go home to your wife?'

'Because she threw me out of my own house, the bitch. I came home one night, and we had a blazing row. I didn't mean to hit her; it was an accident. Anyway, she threw me out, is refusing to divorce me, and won't let me see Sofia and Aurelia anymore. Anyway, I don't give a fuck about her.'

'Bruno, you are falling apart. I met Maria last night, and she is in pieces. I think you need to get a grip on things.'

'No, I am all good, just a rough patch; still building that chain of hotels. It's just the stress of it all.'

He has lost all interest in his silk and textile business, and without any leadership, it has haemorrhaged cash badly. To try and solve his financial problems, he has sold a further stake in the hotel back to Nino. He now owns less than 20% and is very much the minority shareholder. The likelihood of his being involved in future developments is slim, to say the least. Sadly, his vanity means he can't recognise that; he still believes that he is on the verge of that one big breakthrough.

It is as if his personality has been stolen, and he is now trapped in his imagination.

After an hour of listening to his incoherent tune, with claims of betrayal and opportunity, Christina has had enough and decides to go and have lunch with her son. She discovers, to her mild annoyance, that he has started without her and is enjoying a pizza and a cold Messina beer with Nino.

'Ah, Christina, come and join us,' says Nino.

'Nice for you to wait for me,' says Christina to her son.

Nino hands her a menu. 'So can I suppose you have enjoyed the company of your big brother in the last hour?'

'Yes, I have, and he is completely fucked, all over the place.'

Marco has become distracted by a small group of girls in the pool, so has stripped off and dived in.

'You see, Christina, this life is not for everyone,' says Nino. 'I think he might be indulging too much. What do the Americans say? "Don't get high on your own supply."'

'Is it bad?'

'Yes, I think he has a huge problem. He is becoming more and more irrational, and paranoia is kicking in.

'Also, sadly, we have had a couple of situations where he has acted inappropriately towards young female guests on the property. I am afraid I had to make a financial settlement to one guest to make it go away. He is no longer allowed anywhere near the nightclub after ten pm, as he suffers from wandering hands.'

'Oh my God, that's terrible. He thinks you are following him everywhere.'

'Of course we are, but for his own safety, nothing else. I think that we need to get him into a recovery programme. With your blessing, I can sort that out, although it might be best to get him out of the country, perhaps to America.'

'Thank you, but the family will pay.'

'It's fine. Let's just say that we can offset it as a legitimate expense for tax purposes. You should also know that we cannot take a risk now and involve him in the other hotel developments. We have yet to tell him, though.'

'I don't blame you.'

'There is something else that you should know,' says Nino. 'We have recently bought back more of your brother's shareholding. On the back of that, we have cancelled the guarantee on your Mamma's villa. We can't have her worrying about that with this all going on, can we?'

'Well, that's two favours that I owe you now.'

'Christina, you are a sister of Calabria; there is no debt here. I liked your husband when he came out to see me. He is a strong man, one of principle, and I admire that a lot. I misjudged him with my proposal, which I regret, but he handled it like a man. Please pass on my regards.'

'You know, he is actually thriving in jail. Hopefully, I will get him out soon, before we are too old,' says Christina with a laugh.

'I have another proposal for you,' says Nino.

'Go on.'

'I have had a long chat with young Marco. He tells me he is a bit lost in life, doesn't know what he wants to do. His brother is successful, but he feels that he is lacking a purpose. How about he comes out to work with me for a year? He could stay with his Nonna at the villa.'

'Nino, please don't take this the wrong way, but I know what your main business is all about, and I don't want my son anywhere near drugs. I don't want him ending up like his Uncle Bruno.'

'If I have one regret in this life, it is that I have not had a son. I would enjoy helping him grow up a little bit without pressure from the family bubble,' says Nino, pouring her a glass of white wine. 'I give you my word. We have extensive interests in property and hospitality. His time with us would only be spent there, Christina, on my honour.'

'Ok, let me think about it and talk to him,' she replies, noting that her son is making considerable progress with the cute one in the black bikini.

CHAPTER THIRTY-FIVE

2022

It is just past two in the morning. Outside it shifts between complete darkness and silver light, as the clouds race across the sky, joyfully playing with the moon. It isn't a particularly cold night, but it's not warm enough to leave your windows open. Inside, the house is at perfect peace with everyone asleep, apart from the odd atmospheric, ghostly creak that an old house likes to make.

The first to hear the commotion is Davy, who awakens the minute he hears the scrunch on the pebble driveway. He struggles into a pair of trousers and throws on a zipped hoodie. He has not reached the stairs when he hears loud banging at the front door.

He remains calm as he knows instantly who it will be.

He opens the front door and lets in two young men dressed entirely in black, including gloves and hats, complete with head torches. They are in possession of two other men, both with their hands tied behind their backs by what look like cable ties. They are both stocky, possibly Eastern European, with short haircuts and wearing a rather shoddy attempt at camouflage clothes. They look more like nocturnal fishermen than hired assassins.

One of them is sporting a bruised face and a cut above the eyebrow.

'You better come in, boys,' says Davy and leads them into the kitchen. 'And don't be bleeding over this nice kitchen. I will get you a towel and an Elastoplast.'

The commotion awakens others in the house. Tony is the first to run downstairs, wearing only a pair of white underpants and wielding an old hockey stick.

'Go and get some clothes on, Tony. It's all under control, and you look more frightening in those underpants than they are,' says Davy.

Next down are Stephen and Lisa, both shocked and scared by what is playing out before them. This is the first time that they have been in the direct company of people who are being paid to kill.

'Looks like another pair of tossers came after you,' says Davy.

Finally, Kathy appears in a comfortable dressing gown and slippers. Having seen it all before, she carries her air of defiance into the kitchen, sensing that what is needed is a boiling kettle – the solution to most problems.

The children sleep peacefully through the whole episode. They would no doubt have enjoyed the absurdity of having two thugs tied up in their kitchen. It would have made a nice story for their school journal.

'Firstly, let me introduce you to young Billy and Joe here. They're both ex-forces and are the sons of someone that used to work for me,' says Davy.

They both give little smiles and awkward waves to the audience. Kathy serves them their tea first, as she feels that they have probably earned it more than anyone else.

'Thanks, Kathy,' says Billy.

'No problem, son. How's your Mum?' she says.

'Aye, she is grand; had to get her cataracts done, but apart from that she is on top form.'

'They now run a private security firm; it pays better than the army,' Davy continues. 'A couple of days ago, I decided to put an extra layer of security around us, just to be on the safe side. It looks like they picked up a couple of intruders.'

'You really are some machine, Mr G,' says Tony, thankfully now dressed.

'Every day, I feel like I know this man less and less,' says Stephen. 'He also seems to get more menacing by the hour.'

'So, what happened then, boys?' asks Davy.

Billy and Joe had been there since early that evening. For them, it was a very run-of-the-mill assignment; the only challenge was the boredom. There was only one road up the side of the loch and through the village. Billy had set himself up in a clump of bushes at the edge of the village. Joe had located himself in a little shed at the entrance to the property. They wore night vision goggles to allow them to see effectively and were connected to each other through earpieces.

They had watched the family make their journey back from the pub, without revealing their position.

Billy had picked up the car headlights as it slowly made its way through the village. He watched them kill the lights as they tried to locate the house. Billy had notified Joe of incoming traffic, and he easily picked up a line of sight.

'City boys,' whispered Billy down the earpiece.

The car had pulled into a little passing space, and they both observed the occupants unpacking a holdall and starting to pick their way through the trees towards the house. Although they couldn't be completely certain, they believed they were carrying a long-distance weapon with them.

Although they came bearing arms, they had failed to consider the possibility of anyone behind them, so were hopelessly unprepared when Billy and Joe crept up on them from the rear, springing out of the shadows. The sound of their boots had been muffled by soft pillows of moss.

It was over in seconds; one had put up some fight but had received a couple of brutal blows from Billy. They were secured, with their hands in cable ties, before they were taken down to the house.

'Look at the fucking state of the two of you! It's a disgrace. You are not exactly dressed for a job like this. Where are the standards these days? It's all gone downhill,' says Davy.

'So, you two fellas are up from Manchester?' says Stephen.

They say nothing, both impassively staring into space. Stephen doesn't scare them in any way, but the old guy carries a serious aura of danger.

'What were they carrying, boys?' Davy asks his security detail.

'This is it here,' says Joe. 'It's a long-distance rifle, which has had night sights added to it. It's alright, nothing very sophisticated; you could probably buy it online these days.'

'So, you thought you would sit in the trees all night until one of these two appeared,' thunders Davy, 'knowing full well that my wife, daughter and beautiful grandchildren are here as well.'

For good measure, he proceeds to smack one of them over the head with the back of his hand.

'And all to get paid a few measly quid as a bounty,' he continues. 'What is the going rate for possession of a firearm in Scotland, boys?'

'Well, for possession of a firearm, it's seven years,' answers Billy.

'However, for possession of a firearm with intent to endanger life, it is life imprisonment. Can't see them getting much leniency for this one.'

'Do you want to confirm to us who you are working for, then?' says Davy.

'Not telling you anything, old man,' says one of them.

'Yes, you are, right? I am an old man. But thankfully, these two are not,' he says, nodding at Billy and Joe. At this stage, they are being looked after, as Kathy has broken out the toasted cheese to serve to the boys, for which they are very grateful.

'The thing I cannot work out is how they always know where we are. Even the police don't know,' says Stephen.

'I figured that out a few days ago. It's my fault. I should have worked it out earlier. It's simple really. Every time Tony fires up that stupid old Nokia, this lot get your location. Somebody must have given them the number,' says Davy.

'Oh shit, of course. It must have been Bill that gave it to them the first time they came looking for me at the club.'

'Tony, the whole point of having a burner phone is that you get rid of the sim card every time you use it. You know, you *burn* it. Again, the attention to detail here is very disappointing,' says Davy.

With it being summer in Scotland, the morning is beginning to break already, and it is not yet four am. Across the loch, there is a kind of mist caused by a temperature inversion when the water meets the morning light.

'Dad . . . as much as it's really good fun getting to see you play the big man again, what on earth are we going to do with these two?' asks Lisa.

'So, I think our new friends here have three options,' says Davy.

'Number one. We phone up our good friends in Strathclyde Police, and we hand them over to them. The two boys head off for a long, long stretch at Barlinnie Prison. Of course, we make some calls, spread a few lies and mistruths to some contacts in the nick, just to make sure they get a special welcome. Scottish lads get a bit miffed when others come up to their patch, and if we tell them that you have been messing about with wee boys, it could be very nasty.'

Both men in shackles lift their heads, shaking their heads slowly at the choice presented.

'Number two, we opt not to involve the police and sort it ourselves. We take you back up the road to Yoker and do a little trip round a few of the old pubs. You will love them, a little rustic, I suppose, but very hospitable to visitors. Possibly tell a few folks about how you threatened Davy Gavin's grandchildren with a gun. They'll probably ditch you in the Clyde at high tide; might even make Dunoon before you surface.'

No thanks is the message coming from their body language.

'Number three, my boys here drive you down to Manchester to meet with your boss, and you deliver him a personal letter from me.'

'I think we prefer that option,' says one of them.

'Just to very clear though,' says Davy, 'it's not the two young pups, Francis and Kenny. This letter needs to be put in the hands of Frankie Williams Snr.'

Dear Frankie,

I cannot believe it's been almost forty years since our paths crossed. Those were the days, my friend, not like they are nowadays.

I was truly sorry when I heard about what happened with your missus and the horrible car crash. She was a lovely lady, so please accept belated condolences.

I hear that your boys are doing well and that you have a young daughter, too. Family is important, so I hope they are all looking after you. Mine try their best, but occasionally their old dad must get involved.

I remember you said that you would always be in my debt and that I just needed to ask. Well, that time has come now.

Please find two of your boys returned. Sorry one of them had a bit of a slap, but he was a bit cheeky. Don't take this the wrong way, but they weren't very well organised. I think you would have been disappointed at their lack of preparation.

I need you to get your two lads to call off the hit that is out on Stephen Whyte and Tony Fowler in relation to something that went on with Matty O'Hare.

Stephen is my son-in-law, so he is family and cannot be touched.

The other fella doesn't have a family, although he probably needs one, so we are looking after him for now until we figure out what to do with him.

If it's ok with you, I will give you a call soon. I have an idea about how to bring all this nonsense to a satisfactory close.

I hope one day you might find some time to come up to Glasgow and stay over. Kathy would love to see you again. It would be great to swap stories from the old days.

Yours sincerely,

David Gavin

With the options settled, the boys take the two assailants out to a car for the long drive down south. Everyone has drifted off to bed, leaving behind just Tony and Davy. They make a start on doing the dishes. Despite all the excitement, if Kathy comes down in the morning to discover a mess, she will be raging. Big Davy Gavin might be a legend in his own mind, but he is nothing if he leaves a mess behind.

'Davy, who is this Frankie Williams?' asks Tony, loading the dishwasher.

'He's proper old school. I know him from back in the day. I saved his bacon big time.'

'What do you mean?'

'Well, he and his boys conducted an armed robbery on a jewellery business over on the south side of Glasgow. There was a bit of Barney Rubble, and he was going to go down for it, so I helped him out and supplied an alibi and found someone else to take the hit for it.

'So, you see, Frankie owes me, and he knows how to stick to the code. His boys mostly run his business these days and are probably the ones that put the hit out, so I have sent him a little love letter, just to remind him of the debt.'

'Will he agree to it, though?'

'Of course he will. He knows the rules.

'Well, enough excitement for me for one night – I am off to bed . . . and Tony, stay out of the fridge. If you mess with Kathy's system, it will be me that gets it!'

CHAPTER THIRTY-SIX

2016

Marco finds that he is enjoying life in Italy more than he thought he would. As an act of defiance, he immediately dropped the O'Hare surname as he wants to be known as Marco de Luca. This is principally to impress the girls at the resort where he wants to give the impression that he is going to inherit the villa when his grandmother passes away.

His Nonna recognises that what he needs is freedom, so he comes and goes as he wants. She knows he is bringing girls back at night but chooses to turn a blind eye to it. This is part of growing up. Her only insistence is that they attend Mass together each week, he visits Nonno, and then she cooks Sunday lunch. He never misses it.

She is getting old, for sure; mobility is challenging, but her mind is as sharp as ever. When people become old, they earn the right to be judgemental. She has developed this ability to pay a compliment and take it away with a cutting remark. In an instant. She loves Marco and thinks that there is good in his heart. She is the only one in the family who seems to have the patience for him.

Nino has been true to his word, and he has taken Marco's one-year placement seriously. He spent the first three months at the head office in Catanzaro, involved in the planning and construction of new hotels. He worked with the architects, the finance people and the marketing department. He was keen to learn, so for once, the surliness of his youthful years was kept under control.

With a new summer season looming again, it is decided that he will spend all his time at the resort. He uses the time on rotation, covering various roles including reception and the restaurant. But the area that he falls in love with is onsite entertainment, sourcing expensive European DJs to play one-off sets and coordinating special events at the weekends for the beautiful people.

Bruno is still occasionally around but cuts a rather sad figure these days. He spent a long time in America, trying to get his cocaine addiction under control. This was successful in the beginning, but as with many an addictive personality, it is never far from the surface.

He discovered cosmetic surgery when out in America and has had three or four operations to halt the inevitable onslaught of age, rocket-fuelled by his lifestyle. Men never used to get plastic surgery, but now no one even raises an eyebrow.

Now there is the unedifying sight of a fifty-year-old with a reshaped face wearing a matching shorts and top outfit, like a giant baby. He pretends to enjoy the music. Of course, without cocaine, his confidence is broken, and inevitably, his success rate has collapsed, leaving him even more frustrated.

Marco's success rate, however, has taken a massive uplift. Having lived in Italy for months now, he has developed a deep, luxurious tan. Having swopped the meat and bread fest of North West England for a Mediterranean diet, he is positively blooming.

Of course, it helps that he is the music promoter who can introduce the girls to the DJs and that he has a tab for champagne and shots.

Despite being located far away at the bottom of the foot of Italy, it is somewhat surprising that the girl he falls for comes from Manchester.

Josie Williams is eighteen years of age. She is reasonably tall normally but has added a few inches from towering wedges. She has medium-long brown hair and beautiful dark eyes. She still maintains the innocence of the girl next door and doesn't have the hardness behind the eyes that many of the other girls at the resort have.

She has come out with her friend to attend one of the DJ sets this weekend. Sarah-Lou is very much a party girl who has persuaded two guys from London to spring for the trip. Josie is here for the music and the sun. She is also here to get away from the suffocation of two big brothers and a father, who seem to think they have approval rights on her choice of man.

The DJ sets at the resort start about four in the afternoon and last until after dark, at about eleven. The DJ booth is set up on a small pedestal facing the pool. It is the job of the skilled DJs to take the guests on a sensory journey, starting with mellow music to relax to, building up to the sunset and finishing with a crescendo, backed up with pyrotechnics. It is all carefully choreographed by Marco and his team. The guests don't realise that the drinks gradually increase in price with the tempo of the music.

The private area is actually very small. The resort doesn't really warrant one, as seriously wealthy guests don't use VIP areas; they just create their own with their demands. The VIP area is just for ordinary people and day guests to show off a little. Marco likes to oversee the red rope.

'Hi girls, can I help?' he offers with a smile.

'We are with those two,' says Sarah-Lou, lacking in enthusiasm when she sees how inebriated the Londoners are. They had started on the beers at the check-in back in the UK, so she knows it will be a long night ahead. Not many other nations are as skilled at airport breakfast drinking as the Brits.

'Well, in you come, but try and get them to pace themselves; they are paying plenty to be here.'

'Are you a Manc?' asks Josie.

'Ha ha, is it that obvious, love? No one else here can tell the difference. Actually, I am from Morecambe. Marco de Luca at your service.' The information comes complete with a little bow.

'Oh, that's a very common name in Lancashire,' she quips.

'It's my mother's family name. My uncle has an interest in this hotel. I organise the DJ sets.'

'That's impressive.'

'So, what brings you here? We don't normally see many people from England; most of them just go to Sorrento.'

'Well, I am here with Sarah-Lou,' she says, pointing at her blonde friend, who is hanging all over one of the lads. 'To be honest, I think she might be getting paid for this trip, if you know what I mean.'

'Listen, I have seen everything at this place. I go to Confession with my Nonna every week and tell the priest about all the sins I have seen. Sometimes I am in for an hour. The priest has to go to the bishop afterwards to make his own confession after what he has heard from me.'

'Really?' says Josie. 'I thought this was where the super-cool and super-rich came. I didn't realise it was a bit naughty.'

'My dear, you don't know the half of it. But tell me, what's your story back home?'

'Oh God, that's a long one.'

'Well, I am a very good listener. Let me get a bottle of champagne and we'll go to the beach.'

So, they ditch Sarah-Lou and the London boys and head down to sit on a couple of sunbeds. The parasols are sleeping, all tucked up for the night. The pounding bass is still in their ears, but the sea has its own rhythmic beat, the small waves creating a hypnotic symphony.

'So, Mum lives over in Canada now, but I decided to stay in the UK with my dad,' says Josie. 'Dad is like involved in hospitality. I think he started out in fruit machines and karaoke but migrated to door security. My two brothers run the show now. They know everyone in the clubs.'

'That sounds great,' says Marco, passing her a plastic flute of cold bubbles.

'I love them all; it's just that they smother me. I will always be their little girl. Dad boasts that he will conduct a rigorous interview with any potential boyfriend. He jokes that he has a secret trap door underneath the chair, and if the boy gives the wrong answer, he is gone forever.'

They both giggle at the absurdity of it.

'I better study hard before my interview, then. Are you going to uni?'

'I know I should; it's just that I don't see the point. I like totally love fashion and style and stuff, but I don't know that I want to get a degree in that. I would rather live the best life.'

'You don't need to . . . I didn't go to uni . . . not sure I missed anything, to be honest.'

'So why are you here?'

'Well, my mum comes from Calabria, up there in the mountains just outside Catanzaro. She came to the UK to marry my dad and set up home. Unfortunately, two rats committed the ultimate sin and grassed on my dad. He's in prison, and I am here to learn stuff before I head back home in a few months' time.'

'Sorry about your dad – that's horrible. So, when you're back home, what will you do?'

'I must admit I have loved running these DJ sets here at the hotel. I don't see myself as a DJ, but I am keen to see if I can become a promoter.'

'So why don't we hook up when you get back home? Maybe my brothers can do some intros for you at the clubs.'

'That sounds class. Listen, we better get back. I'm on duty, and you need to check on your friend and the London crew.'

**

A few days later, Marco is holding a staff meeting with the in-house team. They are holding a two-day beach party event in a week's time. Rather than at the resort's swimming pool, this time it is to be held down at the beach. The event is open to hotel guests and ticketed to the public. Hopefully, a few thousand will attend. There is a long list of stuff to be organised, from the talent to the set and all the operational issues.

For the first time, Marco is keen to put a brand to his talents, and this is the first reveal of his concept. The weekend event is being named Bergamot, with a gentle nod to his Nonna and his heritage.

Nino has quietly come over and joined the meeting, listening intently. As ever, he is super coolly dressed in black jeans and a fitted grey shirt. He is impressed by the way Marco runs the meeting. To be a leader, you need to have followers, and the team are totally engaged.

After the meeting closes, Nino invites Marco to have an espresso with him on the terrace and an impromptu catch-up.

'You seem on top of it all,' says Nino. 'I love the artwork for Bergamot – very strong and on point.'

'All under control, *Zio* Nino.' He has started to use this expression as a mark of respect, even though they are not blood relatives.

'So have you enjoyed this part of the placement?'

'This has been the best part for me. I think I have a talent for it; perhaps I have found what I want to do in life.'

'So, I won't be able to persuade you to stay then?'

'You have been so kind to me, *Zio*. But I want to prove to my family that I am not a failure and that I can be successful in England.'

'You have never really talked to me about your father and how he ended up in jail.'

Marco has worked hard over the last few months to be mature and credible. The truth is he is still bitterly upset by what happened, and even more upset with his family's reaction and acceptance of their fate. He now finds himself pouring out his heart to Nino.

'Look, I know that Dad was running a criminal enterprise. I know he wasn't innocent, and I get the fact he got caught and must pay the price. But it's hard. We had everything going for us, big house, loads of money. Everyone in the town looked up to us; then, in the blink of an eye, it was all gone.

'Dad gets shipped off to jail, and most of his assets get taken away. Suddenly, everyone in the town is whispering behind my back like they are laughing at me.'

'It must have been hard on them, too; you need to be kind. They are your Mamma and Papa, remember,' says Nino.

'I know, but they just rolled over and accepted it. Dad hasn't complained once, and Mum has had to get a job working at Next, for God's sake.'

'What else would you expect?'

'To put up a fight. They don't seem fussed about the two dirty fuckers that grassed on them in the first place.'

Nino's mobile phone goes off, so he walks off into the gardens, allowing his new 'nephew' to vent in silence.

'You know, young Marco,' he says on his return, 'I too have worried about this. If I look at it from a Calabrian perspective, your family has lost face. That is not something that we like very much.'

'What do you mean?'

'Your family name cannot be respected if you leave this alone. Revenge is a very primitive and pure emotion. Some people prefer their vendettas to be served cold, but I have always preferred it piping hot, as waiting for revenge can prolong the unpleasantness of the original crime.'

'Well, its Dad's call, I suppose.'

'Perhaps it is you who should act. I love that you are passionate, Marco. Don't ever let the English knock that out of you, with their formal manners. You have shown great maturity and impressed me a lot. Once you return to England, if there is ever anything that I can do, let me know,' says Nino, proffering a handshake.

'I do have a favour right now.'

'Of course, anything.'

'Can you help me keep my Uncle Bruno away from the Bergamot set next week? He is creeping everyone out, and if he rocks up, it will be a disaster.'

'Yes, he is fast becoming a disaster, I am afraid.'

CHAPTER THIRTY-SEVEN

2019

Marco and Josie did hook up when he returned to the UK. So much so, that they have been in a relationship for almost three years. Marco has practically moved in with Josie at her apartment in the Northern Quarter in Manchester. It is in a modern-built four-storey block, with two bedrooms and a kitchen. The kitchen sees lots of entertaining, but little cooking. The fridge is exclusively reserved for booze and face creams.

There hasn't been a formal interview with her dad. He has met him, but the old boy gave very little away. He likes to think he passed the test, he just doesn't know. You can never tell with the old boys; they are so good at the poker face.

They have changed a lot from three years ago when they met in Italy. Josie has transformed herself from the girl next door, full of innocent charm, into a modern-day, glamourous young woman, with carefully shaded hair, determined to forge her own career and take no shit from nobody. She is making a good living influencing other young people on how to lead their lives.

She has worked relentlessly to build a social following as an influencer, with her own channels on both YouTube and TikTok. She is keen to set up an OnlyFans account but knows that this might be a step too far for her dad. After all, he owns the flat in Manchester, so she lives rent-free.

She has reached a certain amount of scale, with more than 85,000 followers. She's still a micro-influencer but expecting to become a mega-influencer shortly. She is now so locked into this career that she only attends events that can further her career.

Her channel, #JosieWills, is mostly focused on her shopping channel where she gives advice about the latest trends. She has paid for partnerships with Hype, Pretty Little Things and Oh Polly.

Josie realised early in the process that she needed to go far beyond just recommending clothes to buy. She needed to carefully create a brand around herself that people could emotionally invest in. It means that she posts about her entire life, every day, and almost every hour.

Whether it is her favourite restaurant, cocktails or going to Coachella in California, everything is carefully curated and beautifully presented to her loyal followers. No photographs ever appear without a rigorous approval process.

This doesn't come that easy. There is an army of people who look after her – hairdressers, nail technicians, epilators and make-up artists. Then there are the technical geeks that help her upload it all in a super-cool way. There is always a steady stream of people coming and going at the flat.

She feels it is important that her boyfriend is part of the story and on-brand. She loves his smouldering Italian look. It's also complementary that he turns out to be the hottest DJ promoter in Manchester, with access to venues and stars alike. They are a very promotable couple.

They are out this morning in the Northern Quarter, at their favourite little artisan coffee shop called Coffee for The Soul. They have their little French bulldog with them, called Freddy. Josie is keen to consider the breeding process, as she has heard it is very lucrative, although she has no intention of being involved in the messy part of it; she will leave that to the mother's owner.

She has ordered avocado and toast with chilli jam, the breakfast of choice for Gen Z, and a fat-free iced caramel latte. She is now photographing the breakfast from every possible angle.

'Do you really need to take a photo of every single part of your day?' says Marco, not a natural for mornings, given his career.

'You see, I have no selfie control,' she jokes.

'And you know perfectly well that my followers need content 24/7. They get totally upset and stressed if they don't know what I am up to. I must share my love with the people.'

Marco orders a double espresso because he is Italian, and a roll in bacon with brown sauce because he is still a Lancashire lad.

'You can take a photograph of this if you want.'

'No thanks, babes. It's not very grammable, and I don't think a bacon butty is particularly #JosieWills now. Anyway, my followers all think that I am vegetarian.'

'But you had a steak last night,' says Marco. 'I cooked it.

'Well, you know, a little deception can be very lucrative.'

Marco returned to the UK determined to see whether he could make it as a music promoter. His parents were lukewarm about the idea but agreed to support him as much as they could. They couldn't offer a lot financially, so he was going to have to make it on his own.

Matty couldn't help but think he was making a mistake as he reminisced about the dark days in the clubs of the eighties, working the door in Preston.

Marco discovers that everything he learned in Italy is wholly transferrable. He has a great instinct for identifying DJs that are unique and ahead of the curve. His music is based on broadening people's understanding of the wider Mediterranean. He wants to showcase acts which go beyond the over-hyped Ibiza vibe. He wants to give it a touch of Italy, a whisper of Greece, a whiff of Croatia. He is convinced that he is onto an untapped opportunity.

Having built up the trust of the club owners, they now trust him to deliver. DJs tend to be terrible at promoting and organising themselves, so having a go-between, someone skilled in taking care of the detail, is welcome.

Marco likes to say to the DJs, 'You concentrate on your creativity, and leave everything else to me.'

He can't deny that Josie has been an important breakthrough for him, too. Her platform is great, and wherever possible, she bigs him up. The brothers gave him their seal of approval and afforded introductions to many of the clubs around Manchester, happy that they could help their sister. It made the process of getting his name out there much easier. The brothers carry a fearsome reputation, which meant that some of the existing promoters just backed off, leaving the door open.

He now has four permanent residences under the Bergamot brand name. He has a stable of around forty DJs from across Europe, who command £5-10K per gig. He takes a 10% cut from the DJs and a fixed fee from the clubs. He loves the fact that his office is such an exciting playground.

He is making proper money, but a recent trip to America has blown him away. He and Josie were flown out for three days to Coachella in California as a guest of AEG, the global promoter. This was where the real money was. If there was a ceiling to his ambition, then this was it.

They flew first class on Virgin from London to LAX. Every single step of the journey was broadcast on #JosieWills. She gained thousands of new followers, and she had never been so happy. She even changed into three different outfits on one flight.

They saw a scale that took their breath away. It was like a party city in the desert. The acts were the very top of the industry. Every music executive was there, every social influencer of note was there, under the hot desert sun. It was nothing like a drunken Brit Fest; it was the epitome of cool.

John G Gemmell

'You know, Josie, after seeing Coach, I'm thinking about dipping my toes next year into an outdoor Bergamot event in Manchester,' says Marco.

'Oh, I love it,' purred Josie. 'We can work together, like a co-lab. Maybe we can set up a crowd funder.'

'Are we still out for dinner with the brothers tonight? I can run it past them.'

'Yes, it's eight pm. We are starting at the Botanist.'

Influencers are not renowned for getting ready quickly. After many hours of testing and rejecting outfits, Josie finally opts for an off-white textile dress, cut showing one shoulder, an oversized long white cardigan, and high heels, all supplied gratis in return for her promoting them.

The Botanist is found on Deansgate. You enter along a vine-covered walkway, through a tunnel of white flowers, and into a large, barn-style room. The group have booked a private alcove for six people, which is supposed to be understated and away from prying eyes.

Francis and Kenneth arrive with their latest respective girlfriends. The contrast between the two could not be starker.

Francis is accompanied by Lexi, a very tall blonde girl with short, bobbed hair. She is a direct copy of Josie. She has the most perfect new white Turkish teeth, a set of perfectly multiple-filled lips and an immense pair of new boobs. She is wearing a gravity-defying pale blue dress that probably shows too much and tops it off with huge, gold, wraparound sunglasses, even though it is now dark.

Kenny is accompanied by someone very different. Maya is half Chinese and half Malaysian and has been brought up in Singapore. After studying law in Manchester, she is now head of a charity aimed at promoting opportunities for young South-East Asian women. She is very modestly dressed in comparison and certainly not fazed by the occasion – in fact, the exact opposite.

Cocktails are ordered, with the glamour girls gravitating to porn star martinis. Marco has managed to persuade Maya to try a Negroni for the first time. He loves them, but the English don't like the bitter taste. The brothers are simply drinking fizzy mineral water, as they have a long night ahead and need to be alert. Always on call.

They all choose the legendary Botanist kebab, presented on a vertical skewer, hovering over hand-cut chips and lots of dips. Josie has ordered an extra portion of the falafel kebab so that she can post on her Insta and keep the vegan storyline going.

'So, Josie, I checked you out on YouTube earlier today. I am very impressed,' says Maya.

'My girl is totally rocking it! I love #JosieWills – she is totally lit!' squeals Lexi, the fan girl.

'Oh, thanks, girls. No one sees the hard work and the hours that go into it, feed curation is everything these days' says Josie. 'It's not easy to be original; there are so many girls out there trying to steal content and your followers.'

'I don't know where you get your aura from,' says Lexi.

'Do you think it will last, though, this influencer culture?' says Maya. 'Do you not think that everyone will eventually see through it all, look for things that are authentic, not fake?'

'I can't see it. Young people are under so much pressure to be successful and are almost overwhelmed by choice.'

'That's surely not a good thing, in the long run, for their mental health?' asks Maya.

'My job is to help them narrow it down a little, take the weight from their shoulders,' says Josie. 'I aspire to inspire. Then for brands, what I give them is traffic. It's up to them to convert it into sales.'

'But do you not think that fast fashion is bad for the world?' asks Maya.

'Babes, I don't even know about fast fashion . . . is that a thing?' says Lexi

'And then when people start to fake it until they make it, that bothers me. Like when Kim K launched her appetite-suppressing lollipops – it just encourages body-shaming,' says Maya.

'Oh, total bollocks. It's hardly a new thing. They said that about Kate Moss over thirty years ago,' says Josie, flouncing off to the bathroom, with Lexi hot on her heels.

'Girl's got a lot to say for herself,' says Josie to the bathroom mirror.

'It's alright for her . . . Daddy is a billionaire over in Singapore. Kenny boy should keep hold of that one, for sure.'

Back at the table, the drinks continue to flow. The noise levels ratchet up a couple of notches as everyone looks to the party ramping up. Marco finds himself huddled together with the brothers.

'Can I run something past you both, boys?' says Marco. 'I am thinking of planning an outdoor music festival in Manchester as lead promoter. Do you think that is a daft idea?'

'No, it's not daft at all. You have a cool reputation now, and the Bergamot brand is well-known in the city. But there are pitfalls that you need to think about,' says Kenny.

'The thing is you need to do this with the support of the existing clubs, not against them,' says Francis. 'You won't get a load of love if you empty their clubs over a weekend and take their customers out to some muddy field. Let them in on the action; give them a deal. Cut it up and give them some of the concessions. Play a long game here, rather than a short one.'

'Good advice. Can I presume that you boys would manage security?'

'Depends on whether you can afford us,' says Kenny, slapping the younger man on the back.

'It will be a huge event; you could run a number on your coke business, too.'

The minute the words leave his mouth he wants them back, given the thunderous looks on the brothers' faces. They look at each other before moving their chairs closer to Marco. The warmth of their breath is on his face.

'Marco . . . you are a nice young man, our sister seems happy, let's not go there,' says Kenny.

'What do you mean?'

'You know full well we don't deal drugs. We control security, we provide licences for the sale of merchandising in the clubs, and that is it. So please don't be disrespectful, or you will get a slap,' says Francis.

The girls are ready to move on. Josie and Lexi are now new best friends, practically hanging off each other.

'Right, my brothers, the King of Clubs, where are we off to?' says Josie.

'Let's go to My Illusion, then,' says Francis. It's one of the four clubs that the boys control.

'Just so you know,' says Josie, grabbing her boyfriend by the arm. 'I am out, out!' She is very loud now, following a couple of bumps in the ladies' toilets with Lexi.

'Yeah, like totally, never look back in life and remember the nights you had an early night,' says Lexi in support.

Maya decides that late-night clubbing is not for her, so she calls an Uber. The rest of the party make their way to My Illusion, a cavernous nightclub on the eighth level. Harsh, industrial design, concrete and steel, more like a crumbling warehouse. A raised dance floor and lots of VIP booths where it is bottle service only, at eye-watering prices.

The brothers stop to briefly check all is under control with the security team. The rest are shown to a premium booth from where they can see the whole club laid out in front of them. Where the whole club can see them, too.

The girls increase the pace of their party and start on shots. First up, they have straightforward Jägermeister and Red Bull. Thick and syrupy, full of black liquorice.

Next up is a Silver Bullet, made with mint liqueur and cucumber vodka, very refreshing, probably nice on a hot summer's day but a bit tame for the evening ahead.

Then they find another gear with the Kamikaze, made with vodka, triple sec and lime juice. Given its name, there is going to be only one outcome.

'Man, the vibe in here is immaculate,' shouts Josie. The sounds are banging, and she and Lexi are determined to get some serious dancing done.

'So how long has your old man got left in the nick?' asks Kenneth, offering the others cold bottles of Asahi beer.

'Well, he has done nine years, so we are hopeful that he might get out next year.'

'And then what? Will he go back to what he did before?'

'Nah, he's finished, bro. The king is dead. Doesn't have the heart anymore. He even let the guys that grassed him up get away without any retribution.'

'He should have asked us for advice on that one.'

Francis has a finely developed antenna for when trouble is brewing and has been watching the girls on the dancefloor. These days, there are predators around waiting to take advantage of the vulnerable. When alcohol and drugs combine, they give huge energy rushes, which means that trouble can blow up quickly. Therefore, he rarely drinks when in the clubs.

Josie and Lexi seem to be having a very animated argument with another couple of glamour girls. With their towering heels, they look like people on stilts gearing up for a fight. It isn't long until one of them will throw a drink or grab some hair. It signals the end of the night.

'Marco, be a good boy – time to get our sister home, please,' says Francis.

Josie is not impressed by the ignominy of her partner escorting her off the dance floor and then home.

'That fucking bitch has been stealing my content for years. Now she thinks she can get a picture so that she can steal my followers. She can go do one, fucking whore!' screams Josie.

It takes a long time for them to get Josie to leave the club, and as a finale, when she gets outside, the sudden rush of fresh air makes her very unsteady and she ends up in a heap at the front door.

This is all captured by a local photographer who is skulking around for pictures of celebrities making fools of themselves.

Unfortunately for him, the brothers watch this and have no desire to see their princess sister splashed across social media. The photographer takes a sore face, and the camera ends up at the bottom of the canal.

CHAPTER THIRTY-EIGHT

2019

Bruno de Luca met his fate on the A18 motorway between Messina and Catania, on the island of Sicily. His car was being chased at 180 km/h by another black vehicle. Witnesses speak of a high-speed dance between the vehicles, weaving across the lanes, over many kilometres.

His car crashed through the central barrier at one of the raised sections of the road, landing at the bottom of a ravine, close to the railway line that runs parallel to the road.

The Carabinieri confirm that it is likely he died immediately on impact, given the velocity. Following an autopsy, they confirm a high alcohol blood count and widespread evidence of amphetamines and cocaine.

Although lots of people saw the other car, it has disappeared. CCTV footage confirmed that it was using false plates, so they have not managed to find it. The cause of death is put down to misadventure.

The phone call to Christina is made by Nino.

'**Christina, good morning. It is Nino calling from Calabria.**'

'**Ciao, Nino . . . what is up?**'

'**I am afraid that I am phoning you with some tragic news. Your brother has been killed outright in a car crash on the Island of Sicily.**'

'**Oh, my God!**'

'**I thought that I should let you know in person. The police will be notifying Maria as the next of kin. I wanted you to know first so that you can break the news to your Mamma.**'

'**So, what exactly happened?**'

'**He came off the motorway at high speed late at night. There is speculation that he was being chased.**'

'**Was he high?**'

'**I am afraid yes, he was. He had become a shadow of himself in recent years. His behaviour was erratic and unpredictable.**'

'**Do you know what he was doing in Sicily anyway?**'

'He was suffering from paranoia. He thought that we were working against him. We believe he reached out to a family in Catania, and he was planning to collaborate with them.'

'Do you think he was killed?'

'I think there is a real possibility that this is the case. Obviously, this is not a matter anyone can discuss with the police, so I don't think you will ever know.'

'I need to ask you, Nino. Did you have him killed?'

'I am offended. He was my friend; he was like a brother. I did many things to help him over the years, but he couldn't fight off his demons. I give you my word, I am not involved.'

'Thank you, I needed to ask.'

'My company will, of course, make an offer to buy his shares from Maria. Your sister-in-law and nieces have nothing to worry about. We will also take care of the funeral arrangements; it will be easier as we are over here.'

'Thank you. I will phone my mamma now, and I will let Matty and the boys know.'

'I offer you my sincere condolences. If there is anything at all I can do, I am at your disposal.'

The call to her mamma is not as traumatic as she expects. Her mamma is devastated by the fact that she has outlived her only son. However, through the agony of grief, there is also a sense of relief that he can't cause any more harm, to either himself or others.

She lost her son years ago. He gave up a successful business and the joy of a family in pursuit of a dream that was beyond him. She understands the desire to better oneself, but she wishes he had settled for a simpler life, one that perhaps would have had a happier outcome.

As a devout Catholic, she absolves her son of all his sins and promises that his memory will live on through his daughters. She resolves to do everything she can to help them.

* * *

The weekly Friday visit to Matty follows the next day. Christina has decided that she will mourn her brother and dresses all in black.

'Oh Matty,' she cries. 'It's Bruno – he was killed in a car crash a few days ago.'

'Oh darling, come here,' he says, giving his wife a supportive cuddle. This is normally frowned on in the prison, but Matty has good credits with the warders, and they can sense the grief in the air. They do the right thing and leave them alone.

She describes the details surrounding his tragic demise on the island of Sicily.

'He has been off the rails for years. I feel so guilty about it. I blame myself for not being there.'

'It's not your fault. This was the path that he chose himself; no one forced him.'

They sit in silence for a few moments before Christina asks, 'Do you believe Nino when he says that he was not involved?'

'Not a word of it. There are no limits to that man's malevolence.'

'I know. I think I agree. I get the feeling that he had become too much of a liability.'

They hold hands but say nothing. Christina tries to recover happy memories of her brother when they were young but cannot retrieve the image. Sadly, she can only remember his dark side, which upsets her.

'So, I have some news. There is a parole board coming up soon; the mood music is that I will be released in March next year,' says Matty, smiling.

'Oh, that makes me happy.' A weak smile breaks on her etched face.

'Will you go to the funeral?'

'Yeah, I will go over and stay with Nonna. Hopefully, the boys will come too.'

'And what news of the boys?'

'Great news from Angelo. He is flying with this tech business that he has set up. He has organised the whole thing from the garage. You ought to see all the monitors and technology he has running. It's all beyond me.'

'That's great. It's where the future is.'

'Marco is also doing well with his music-promoting business. He has created a brand called Bergamot, which is very sweet of him. He is working all over Manchester; I hardly see him these days.'

'You know what I think? Manchester is too dangerous.' Matty frowns.

'Oh, behave. It's nothing like the Manchester of old. It's probably the hottest city outside of London these days. Ever since the sheikhs bought that football club, investment has been pouring into it. You ought to see Manchester Life.'

'He has practically moved in with his girlfriend, Josie. She is adorable. You are going to love her. Completely bonkers, but somehow everyone aspires to be her. If you get a chance, check her out on her YouTube channel, #JosieWills. I can't wait to tell them you'll be out soon; we will throw you a party!'

'Oh no . . . let me just come out quietly. It's going to take time to adjust to it all.'

* * *

In the end, Maria decided that she wanted the funeral to be extremely private, so it was just her and her girls, plus Mamma and Christina. There were two reasons for the desire to keep it so private.

Firstly, the impact of the collision had severely disfigured the body. There was no possibility of an open casket.

Secondly, and probably the real reason, was that she thought that her husband was a complete and utter bastard. He had relentlessly been unfaithful, had knocked her front tooth out once, and had been an abject failure in being there for his daughters.

She decided, completely against his wishes, to have him cremated instead of buried. There would be no memorial for Bruno. She didn't even want his ashes, such was her contempt.

There was no way the sanctimonious prick was getting any kind of celebration of his life; he could go straight to hell. She was over the moon at what had happened, and by inheriting his shares in the hotel, she has immediately become a wealthy woman, determined to start her life over again. After what she had put up with, a few million euros was scant reward.

The day after the funeral, Christina takes her Mamma back to the church for daily mass. Afterwards, Mamma has some work to do organising flowers for a forthcoming wedding, so Christina sits out on the church steps in the sunshine, waiting for her to carry out her saintly deed.

She is joined by Father Conte, someone who has been a constant in her life. He is resplendent in a full-length black cassock, with a red trim and ornate red buttons. Underneath he has his favourite Nike trainers, which are much more comfortable than formal shoes.

'Ah, little Christi, I can't tell you how much pleasure it gives to an old priest to see you sitting here on the steps of our church,' says Conte. 'I am sorry that it is not under different circumstances.'

'You have seen it all with my family, Padre Conte,' says Christina.

'And it has been my immeasurable pleasure. Now what is it that is troubling you?'

'How do you know?

'It is written all over your face. Tell me, Christi. Let's see if we can figure it out together,' he says as he sits beside her.

'I decided, as a young girl, to leave this village, to escape and forge a new life on my own. But I never really managed to escape. I was dragged back by a sense of loyalty to my brother. A path that made me disloyal to my husband.'

'The reason why Italian culture believes in loyalty to the family is that in the past, it was seen as a form of protection. You are being too hard on yourself.'

'I went to England as a normal girl, but somehow, I became more demanding. I wanted more and more. I pushed Matty too far. I think I became greedy, and ultimately, he ended up in jail because of it.'

'There is an old Italian fable called *Chi troppo voule nulla stringem* (those who want too much end up with nothing). In the story, a dog is enjoying a bone at the side of the river. Whilst chewing the bone, he looks down at the water's surface. He mistakes his reflection for another dog chewing what seems like a bigger bone. Eager to get a bigger bone, the dog opens his mouth, dropping his own bone and leaving him with nothing.'

'Yep, pretty much sums it up. I didn't lose a bone; I ended up losing Matty for ten years.'

'You know that in Christian thinking, greed is said to be the one cardinal sin that God really hates. It plunges man into a mire; wealth becomes more important than God himself.'

'I think it just becomes important in your life; you start to chase it, perhaps like a drug.'

'You see, money talks, and when it does, every other voice is hushed.'

'I also think that it was greed that killed my brother.'

'On that one, I think you are wrong. It wasn't greed that killed him; it was avarice, which is even more dangerous.'

'What's the difference?'

'In Italian, it is *avarizia,* historically the pre-eminent word for greed, but it has fallen out of favour these days. It is the extreme end of greed, probably the most sinful of all. It's when a sense of entitlement collides with the need to be wealthy. Slowly, inch by inch, it permeates your world, destroys your perspective in the pursuit of your lifestyle. If you add narcissism into the mix, you enter despot territory. Perhaps the word avarice should make a reappearance, given the modern world that we live in.'

'Padre Conte, is there anything that I could have done to save my brother?'

'No, my dear, I knew from the very beginning that this was the path he was destined to follow.'

The two of them fall silent, thinking about how the lessons from the Bible and fables from long ago are still relevant to modern life thousands of years on.

'Of course, dear Christi, you must remember that in addition to the seven deadly sins, there are seven cardinal virtues, which are known as antidotes.'

'Please tell me,' asks Christina.

'Well, it is believed in Christian thinking that the seven virtues act as complete opposites to the seven sins. For you, I think the ones to think about are Faith, Hope and Charity. Faith entails following the teachings of Christ, which started the day that I baptised you here in this church. Carry your faith with you throughout life.

'Hope is looking to the future with optimism and leaving the past behind. Don't mourn your brother too much.

'Charity really means love. Devote your time to the people that you love, rather than chasing material desires: your Mamma, Matty and your boys.'

'Padre Conte, thank you so much,' she says, giving him a warm embrace, one gentle tear snaking down her cheek. 'It makes sense when I hear it from you, in front of my own church, in my own village. Maybe the problem is I have become too English.'

'Nonsense! As the saying goes, you can take the girl out of Calabria, but not Calabria out of the girl.' Padre Conte laughs.

They both stand and look back towards the church doorway. The huge wooden door creaks open, and her diminutive Mamma appears.

'Here she is. The most devout Catholic in the whole of Catanzaro,' says Conte. 'Nobody is more devoted to God than this woman.'

'Father Contardo, the altar was a complete mess as usual. Once again, you have managed to get candle wax all over the altar cloth. How many times do I need to tell you?' says Mamma.

'You see, Christi, this is my life these days,' he says, with a wink. 'We all have a cross to bear.'

CHAPTER THIRTY-NINE

2022

Just after breakfast, Davy announces to the group that it is time to pack up and return to Stephen and Lisa's house in Glasgow. To be fair, it is met with mixed emotions.

'Aw, Gramps, I don't want to go home,' says Cameron.

'Does that mean we need to go back to school again?' says Emily. 'I don't know if I want to go.'

'I was planning on going fishing today; the forecast is good. Can we not just stay for another few days?' laments Tony.

'Sorry, everyone, time to go,' says Davy.

'Am I coming with you, or do you want me to go back to Gateshead?' asks Tony.

'You can stay with us; we have a spare room,' says Lisa, which is somewhat of a relief for Tony.

'I am just looking forward to sleeping in my own bed again. It's two weeks that we have been on the road,' says Stephen.

So, the extended family pack up all their belongings and make the short journey back home. They are dropped off in the West End, then Davy and Kathy go to drop off the hire car, promising to be back later.

The kids disappear to their respective bedrooms to reacquaint themselves with their belongings. Cameron needs to connect to Fortnite in case the community think that he has gone off-grid.

It doesn't take long for a fight to break out, caused mainly by the fact that Emily now likes hanging out with her brother. Lisa reflects that they didn't have one cross word when they were at the loch, but here it takes just ten minutes.

Lisa is immediately compelled to jump on her emails and is horrified that her inbox has over eight hundred emails awaiting her attention. There is no way that she can cope with that level of stress unless she starts to whittle them down immediately.

Stephen and Tony head out on a shopping run, as there are no provisions in the house. They jump into the Tesla, thankful that it still has some juice.

'How do you keep this thing charged up?' asks Tony.

'Pretty easy. You come home, you plug it in and that's it.'

'I can't even keep my phone charged up; always seems to be just one bar.'

The short journey is pleasant, through the leafy suburbs. There is no litter; everything seems neat and tidy. It's a different part of the city from the one that Tony has seen in Clydebank. In the bad old days, this would have been where he would have done his best work, prowling about in the darkness, skulking for opportunities.

'So, what do you think: are we safe now?' asks Tony.

'I don't know, although from what I have learnt about my father-in-law, he wouldn't allow us to be here if he didn't think it was under control. He probably has snipers on the roof as we speak.'

Tony cannot help but glance skywards before he says, 'So we believe that young Marco persuaded Frank Williams's two sons to take out a contract on us as an act of revenge on the family's name?'

'Pretty much.'

'But neither of us knew Frank Williams, and we definitely didn't do him any wrong.'

'The world we live in, I suppose.'

'Do you know what was in the letter that was sent south?' asks Tony.

'No, I don't. He's keeping that one close to his chest. I think he is quite enjoying playing the audience.'

They park the car upstairs in the overground car park at the top of Byres Road and walk into Waitrose.

Tony is in awe; he has always wanted to shop in a Waitrose but never had the bottle to do it. He tends to shop in Lidl and Aldi. Here, though, he is spending Stephen's money, so he is like a child in a toy shop.

He walks around, gazing at things that he has never seen before – gyozas, bao buns and nduja.

'I enjoy shopping here,' says Stephen. 'Not for the food, just for the people watching. There is a cracking Facebook site called Overheard in Waitrose, where they take the piss out of their customers.

Darling, shall we get some good olive oil for the house? Which house? Oh, both of course.'

Or

Daddy, does Lego have a silent T, like Merlot?

'Although, to be honest, I think I spend less here than in other supermarkets. The rest tend to flog all sorts of multi-deals that you don't need.'

'It's all a bit different when you only shop for yourself; you just end up with bloody ready meals.'

Given that Kathy has spent the last few days catering for everybody, the boys think it only right that they repay the favour and cook dinner. They plan to keep it simple and wholesome and make a nice roast chicken dinner.

Lisa is still sitting on the sofa cross-legged, balancing her laptop. She has managed to work her way through most emails. However, a crisis has blown up with a social enterprise that she works with who are trying to build a more sustainable local food system. They offer boxes of organic vegetables, grown locally and sold online to their customers.

The only problem is that they have just been outed on Twitter for the use of pesticides on their farms. They have been inundated with slugs this season and had thought it acceptable to commit a chemically induced mass genocide of the gastropod community. Lisa is doing that thing of holding an imaginary conversation with herself whilst furiously tapping the keyboard.

'I mean, what on earth were you thinking about,' she says to no one.

The boys are cooking up a storm in the kitchen, albeit a messy one.

'Looks like Lisa is right back on it,' says Tony.

'We won't prise her away from that thing tonight. It's the same when every holiday ends; she needs to start back at 100mph every time.'

'Will you go back to work?'

'I need to, mate. Need to earn enough to pay for this lot.'

'Sounds like you are doing it because you need to, rather than want to. It seems to me that lots of people work for the money and not happiness.'

'Don't get me wrong; I like my job. The company took me on board when I needed help. They have been very good to me.'

'But?' says Tony.

'I think corporate life is not really geared towards work-life balance. It has been and always will be motivated by one thing, to give the shareholders more profit. They can dress it up with fancy Mission and

Vision statements, but it's always about the bottom line. What will you do once this is all over?'

'Mate, it's a good question. I know one thing: I am giving up being a thief. It's not rewarding anymore. The last couple of weeks have been enlightening.'

'Have you ever thought about studying?'

'Me? Are you kidding? Who would take me?'

'Listen, the daft wee Tony thing is an act; it's a façade. I have got to know the real Tony over the last two weeks. You're clever, insightful, almost philosophical. You should think about it.'

Davy and Kathy arrive just in time for dinner. Kathy makes straight for the kitchen, like the head chef checking on the work of the under chefs. She tastes the gravy and immediately adds salt and pepper. It doesn't need it; she just needs to maintain her command of the kitchen. It wouldn't do to give the boys the feeling that they were equal. Protecting the hierarchy in her fiefdom.

Tony makes a very comical entrance, wearing a chef's hat made from newspapers, to much laughter from the kids, sharpens his knife dramatically and carves the chicken. Stephen is close behind with all the vegetables.

After dinner, the kids reluctantly go straight upstairs for a bath and to get their school things ready for the morning. It feels like the dreaded end of the holidays and the first day back.

'Well, I had a very rewarding afternoon,' says Davy, in the hope that someone will take the bait.

'Alright, you are clearly dying to tell us,' says Stephen.

'I had two very interesting phone calls a little while earlier. I spoke at length with Frankie Williams. He received my letter, and he sends his apologies to us all. My instinct was right: he didn't know anything about it at all. He is retired now, so the boys only bother him with the big things nowadays.

'It appears that his daughter is in a relationship with Marco O'Hare, although he seems to prefer the name de Luca these days. That is the connection between the families. He is very concerned with the direction that relationship is heading. He is extremely protective of his little girl, just like me,' says Davy, smiling at his daughter.

'Then I had a second phone call, this time with Matty O'Hare. I have to say, what a lovely fella. We had a long conversation. It was not easy for him, going to prison, but he is past all that now and looking forward. He knows the rules of the game, which I find very refreshing these days because not many do. He took his prison sentence on the chin; never complained about it once.

'It seems his lad Marco has been a handful all his life. They thought that he had grown up when he got into music promotion, but he has gone completely off the rails recently. He seems to be a bit of a one-man wrecking ball at the moment.

'I made a proposal to Matty, but it is going to be a very tough decision for him, as it comes with a personal dilemma that he needs to reflect on.'

'Ok, so what does all this mean?' says Stephen.

'Well, the three of us have discussed a solution that is going to bring all this unpleasantness to an end.'

'And are you going to tell us what this is exactly?' says Stephen.

'Actually, I am not,' says Davy. 'I need to hear Matty's decision first. I have invited Brogan Reilly and Phil Simpson to come out to this house tomorrow, and then we can let them in on the plan as well.'

'Dad, you are getting worse!' says Lisa, still on her laptop. 'You are now going all Agatha Christie on us. And the murderer is . . .'

'Yes, I could see myself as Hercule Poirot,' he says, twiddling an imaginary moustache.

CHAPTER FORTY

2020

Matty O'Hare is released from prison on the 11th of March 2020. Coincidentally, it's the same day that the WHO declares Covid-19 a global pandemic.

The speculation first started to track it in early January, with a sense of growing disbelief. At first, it was a disease that was dismissed as coming from bats and limited to South-East Asia; then it was believed to have been made in a laboratory. Either way, it gathered momentum and was now gaining traction in Europe.

Christina watches in anguish as Italy becomes an early epicentre, although she is somewhat relieved that it seems to be contained in the North, around the ski resorts. So far, her hometown of Catanzaro is unaffected, and her Mamma is safe.

As per his request, Matty's homecoming is very intimate and personal. Christina picks him up from the prison in Manchester and brings him home. She wishes she could have him to herself but feels obliged to have a small gathering.

The boys are both back at the house. Marco has brought his girlfriend, Josie, to meet his dad, whilst Angelo has opted to be on his own. It is also the first time that Hammy and Benny have seen their boss in a decade and are excited to catch up. There is a smattering of neighbours and friends, people who have supported Christina through the darkness of the last ten years.

Christina wanted to put on a big spread and bring in a high-end caterer but submitted to Matty's wishes, so instead of having luxury canapes, one of the local chippies has provided the food. Everything is golden fried and probably very bad for the arteries. For Matty, it is the best meal that he has had in years.

'A proper chippy tea!' he says. 'I have dreamt of this for years.'

There are balloons and a Welcome Home banner, but most of all, he is excited to see his sons.

'Ange, come here give your old man a hug,' he says, grabbing his oldest son. 'I hear the app business has taken off and you have started to employ staff?'

'We are doing alright, just starting. I think we can really blow this thing up, Dad.'

'May I come in, and you can show me around?'

'I would love that. Be prepared to have your mind blown.'

Josie and Marco have gone to considerable effort to dress up for the occasion. Josie has gone for a gym wear look that she is currently promoting for Palm Angels. It is made up of leggings and a crop top and is in a taupe brown.

The material contains so much lycra that it is skin-tight. Matty doesn't know where to look when he is introduced.

'So, you must be Josie. Nice to meet you, love.'

'Aww, nice to meet you,' says Josie. 'And this is Freddy. He is pleased to meet you too.'

'Of course,' he says, bizarrely finding himself shaking the paw of a French bulldog.

'I can't believe that you look so different from Marco! He's all swarthy Italian and good-looking, and you look a bit like my dad.'

'Thanks, I think,' says Matty. 'And I hear that you have a career as an influencer? I have been away for ten years; you will need to teach me what that is. I have a lot to learn.'

'Aww, that's sweet. Of course I will. In fact, this is giving me an idea for a whole new genre. Might call it shabby post-prison chic – going to work on it.'

Marco has gone for black jeans and a Stone Island top, coupled with a black leather jacket. He is sporting two unmissable neck chains, one in gold and one studded with diamonds.

'Hello, son,' says Matty, giving his younger son a hug. 'Goes without saying, you have sure grown up fast . . . and very bling!'

'If you got, you got to flaunt it, Dad.'

'I hear the music business is going well for you. Now that I am out and about, I must come to one of the clubs.'

'Nah, you're fine, bro. I don't think they will let someone your age in.'

Christina grabs him by the hand to take him to meet the others.

'You never told me he was a paid-up member of the hood!' he says. 'He called me bro, for fuck's sake.'

Matty soon finds himself in the company of his two best friends. They have both been out of the nick for about four years now. They have all aged over the last decade. Matty has a few grey streaks in his hair, Benny has developed a little paunch and Hammy has a receding hairline.

As with all true friendships forged at an early age, they slip back into the usual routine very easily. You can't bullshit the friends that you have known all your life.

'So let me get this straight,' says Matty. 'You lot commit all these terrible crimes, but it's me that does the longest stretch. How does that work?'

'That's because you were the cunning criminal mastermind, co-ordinating it all,' says Benny, laughing.

'How did you both find it?' says Matty.

'It was like a university for crooks. If you weren't a criminal before you went in, you would be when you came out. The level of experience in naughtiness was incredible. I managed to keep my head down and stay clear,' says Hammy.

'I just found it claustrophobic being locked up for hours on end,' says Benny. 'You know, I'm not afraid to admit, I can't get into a lift nowadays without having a panic.'

'I found that time was a strange concept. On the one hand, the days were ridiculously long, but often the months passed very quickly,' says Hammy.

'It was the nights I hated,' says Matty. 'The echo of the guards' steel-tipped boots as they did their rounds. I could never get back to sleep.'

The one thing that all three friends agree on is that they never want to go back.

'So, what the hell do we do now?' asks Matty, looking around at the collection of guests in his living room.

'I have got myself into landscaping gardens. My plan is to stay local but work outside. I'm loving it,' says Hammy.

'Me too. I have had enough of all the nonsense,' says Benny. 'Also, I have a new Spanish girlfriend. We are planning to open a bar in Majorca. The problem is this pandemic thing might be a real problem.'

'What about you, Matty?' says Hammy.

'Well, the plan was to complete the property development, but you know what? I am not sure I care about it as much as I did before I went in.'

John G Gemmell

'Oh, I meant to tell you,' says Hammy. 'We were right all along about that Charlie boy from the council. He was on the take and got done for taking bribes. He was also still shagging the wife's best friend, so she is taking him to the cleaners.'

'The dirty little fucker! I knew it,' says Matty. 'That day I met him, I knew there was something about him. I should have battered him.'

It feels like a lifetime since he stared the Head of Planning down at the hotel in Lancaster. On the one hand, he is pleasantly pleased that his instincts were right; on the other, it just showed how futile an operation he was trying to run back then.

* * *

Christina's anxiety is getting worse and worse. There is huge concern for the elderly, which heightens her anxiety for her mother. She is on the phone practically daily to make sure she is ok. Thankfully, Maria is being a superstar and has moved into the villa to be with her, along with her two daughters.

Matty and Christina are watching the television when Boris Johnson makes an unprecedented announcement. Everything non-essential is to close. There is going to be a national lockdown.

Everyone should 'Stay at Home – Protect the NHS – Save Lives'.

'Brilliant,' says Matty. 'Locked up for ten years in jail, get out and then get locked up in my own bleeding house.'

Lockdown doesn't have much of an impact on Angelo. For someone who is intensely introverted, it is a gift from heaven. He doesn't need to meet people in person. He retreats to the garage and only interacts with people online. He is so much happier in the virtual world than the real world.

His business is one that is thriving because suddenly everyone needs technical solutions for when they eventually come out the other end. Many businesses have pissed around with tech, thinking it was cool but not worth the investment. Overnight, every retail business in the world needs solutions to abide within lockdown rules. Everyone needs a solution that will allow customers to have touchless contact. He can almost name whatever price he wants.

'Dad?' says Angelo.

'Yes, Ange, what is it?'

'I need some help. I am drowning. The demand for new apps and tech solutions is off the scale. I can create them – that's fine. I just don't

266

have time for any of the commercial aspects of my business. Any chance you could come on board?'

'It would be my pleasure . . . I don't need to call you gaffer, though, do I?'

Matty is privately over the moon to have been asked. He left his sons as teenagers, and now he is being asked to help one of them run his business. This will give him a sense of purpose that he badly needs after ten years inside.

Maria buys Nonna an iPad so that they can keep in touch with Italy. Everyone thinks that this will be futile, that there is no way that Nonna will understand it. However, Nonna masters the technology seamlessly, like a duck taking to water. Angelo talks them through connecting it all up to a big screen and speakers. She even becomes the family quiz master for the weekly quiz.

Marco decides early during the pandemic that the rules don't apply to him. He isn't going to stay in just because he is told to by some politicians in London. He is way too important for all of that. He and Josie regularly host parties at their flat, which is outside the rules. They have had a couple of penalty notices already but don't show much sign of caring about them.

Christina has decided to buy herself a dog, a small black and tan cocker spaniel puppy called Alfie. Immediately, her sons are relegated to second place behind the new love of her life. Matty knows all too well that the two are as thick as thieves, conspiring behind his back.

It does get them both outdoors, and they walk a lot in 2020. At first, they follow the guidelines and only go out once a day, but lately they have started to drive all over Morecambe Bay and the Lake District. Although tourism has waned over the years, the absence of visitors during lockdown is noticeable.

In the Lake District, normally plagued by vehicles, it is much cleaner and more enjoyable. The locals say that this is the best that the flora and fauna have ever looked, having not been trampled by hordes of uncaring tourists.

'It's strange, isn't it,' says Matty, 'but lockdown has made us start to appreciate what we have here in this country. The scenery is majestic, I am much more aware of the birds and the flowers, and the air feels purer with no planes and fewer cars.

'Matty?'

'Yes?'

'I think I want to go home.'

Matty recognises her melancholic seriousness; it is a difficult decision that has taken many years to slowly come to the boil.

* * *

The pandemic and subsequent lockdowns result in divergent outcomes for Marco and Josie.

The hospitality and late-night entertainment industry is the worst affected across the country. Clubs are the first to close and will probably be the last to reopen. Whereas some businesses are disrupted for weeks, the clubs face closure for years. There's an air of financial ruin hanging over the sector, as well as all the support businesses that hang off the back of it.

All the live venues are shuttered. The DJs who are legitimately on his books receive furlough; those who are grey do not and are left to fend for themselves. Some try re-invention and come up with creative on-line sessions. It isn't easy to go clubbing in your own bedroom. It keeps them occupied, but no one enjoys a fraction of the revenues that they had before.

Overnight, revenues for Marco shrink to zero. To make matters worse, Bergamot has taken future sales of £250k for this summer's proposed outdoor event, and customers are now demanding refunds. He tries to offer credit notes, kicking it down the road, but with little success. Most people have booked it on their credit cards; he is no match for their corporate recovery teams.

The problem is that Marco has already spent most of the money. He believed he was bomb-proof and was already dreaming of reaching the scale that he had seen at Coachella. He is not a person who ever conducts risk evaluation; it isn't in his nature. His dream of being a major music promoter is being snatched away from him in a cruel fashion.

For the second time in his short adult life, he is about to lose his financial stability overnight, through something that is not his fault. This time, though, he is facing financial ruin.

'Don't worry, babes. It's just a few weeks; it will be fine,' says Josie.

'Have you gone mad? I am totally screwed . . . again!'

'Nah, don't worry; my dad will sort it out.'

'Sort it out? No, he won't – he fucking hates me.'

'No, he doesn't. He just thinks you are a little impetuous.'

'I don't even know what the fuck that means.'

'Impatient, then.'

'I'm not impatient. I am fucking raging.

With Josie's business, it is completely different. It is as if someone has applied an accelerant to a fire. Her business goes completely nuts.

Suddenly, everyone is attending the YouTube university or learning from TikTok. People are locked up, but their online activity has doubled. Working from home, there's nobody to stop you being distracted by social media. People are craving escapism, being reminded of what life might be like again. They want to dream. They want Josie Wills to show them what is hot, and what is not. What they might look forward to when this is all over.

During the second lockdown, the air routes remain open between London and Dubai. It is supposed to be for people to meet work commitments and not tourism. However, that is stretched beyond belief, as just about every influencer in the world rocks up in the Emirates to enjoy the sunshine and keep the key work of influencing moving forwards.

Josie has organised the trip out to the Emirates and paid for it all herself. They are staying at a boutique hotel down on Jumeirah Beach.

She is pissed off at how ungrateful he is, and he is pissed off at everything, so they have already had plenty of tasty rows. He is out every night searching for parties, whereas she wants to stay home and look fresh. She wants to hit the gym, and he wants to hit the Friday buffets.

'Listen, babes, I am here to work,' says Josie as he emerges from his bed in mid-afternoon.

'I am not stopping you, am I?'

'No, but perhaps we could work on stuff together. You could help with the filming and stuff.'

'What, like now? You want me to work for you – is this where we have ended up? I am your fucking photographer. Do you want me to do your make-up as well??'

'In case it escapes your notice, I am your only fucking source of income at the moment.'

'Yeah, and don't you just love reminding me of that? I'm out of here. I have a meeting to attend.'

Whilst in Dubai, he discovers that Nino has moved over here and is living in an apartment nearby. He decides to give him a call and see if they can catch up. The two men meet at the far end of Jumeirah Beach, beside the newly constructed giant wheel, one of the centrepieces of the forthcoming Expo. It's ae man-made beach, with the sea bed cruelly ripped up to provide faux paradise.

There are still plenty of tourists on the beach. It is hard to believe that a global pandemic is raging across the world.

They decide to walk along the beach towards the Ritz-Carlton Hotel, perhaps for a drink.

'Thanks for meeting me, Nino,' says Marco.

'No problem, my friend. It has been quite the time with everything going on. This is also the first time that I have seen you since your uncle passed. I am very sorry.'

'Thank you. Yes, that was horrible. Did you ever find out what really happened?'

'No, and my advice is not to look too closely. He made too many enemies. It is rumoured that he put a *malocchio*, an old Italian curse, on myself and my partners. Never a good idea to throw curses around in southern Italy.'

'I suppose so. And how has the pandemic impacted business?'

'It has been catastrophic for us at the hotels. We closed them all for four months. They are open again, but the experience is not good, given the restrictions. We have lost our international market; no one is travelling now. It will take a few years to recover, I think.'

'Did the government help?'

'This is Italy you are talking about; the government only helps itself. Rome always sends the money north and never south. They think that they helped, but they made it very complicated. Of course, I invented a couple of hundred employees to claim furlough for; helped to dull the pain,' he says, with a cold smile.

'And the other side of the business?'

'Marco, you know I don't like to talk about it. You never know who might be listening, especially here in Dubai. They are world experts at listening in to conversations. But if you must know, demand is insatiable. It is going to be a golden year. The problem is that supply has increased massively, which drives the price down. It is like the oil market. Now, tell me, how is your business going? I feel for you; it cannot be easy.'

'I am not going to lie; I am in deep shit. God know when venues will reopen. I have sunk a load of cash into a planned outdoor event that is unlikely to go ahead until at least 2022. I think I am going to go bust. Everyone will laugh at me again. Poor old Marco, always the same outcome.'

'Oh dear, that does not sound good. You know that we can help you with a loan if you want – defer it until you are back on your feet again.'

'That is kind of you, though I have an alternative request to make.'

'Ok.'

'I want you to let me in on the retail side of your other business. I have so many contacts from people in hospitality and music. People who are not working but are still trying to be creative and need the buzz that supports it. Will you allow me to sell cocaine in England? Just until such time as my other business opens again,' pleads Marco.

Nino stops walking along the beach, looking out at the hazy Arabian sea towards the Palm Jumeriah. He watches a group of people tumble out of a plane, parachuting slowly down to the beach. It isn't the type of pleasure he craves, too much risk, but each to their own. His face is very serious when he turns to look at Marco.

'On two separate occasions, your mother and then your father came to see me in Calabria to discuss business. I gave them my word that I would not involve your family in the drug business. I am an honourable man; this would put me in a very difficult position.'

'Fuck them. They are from a different generation; they don't understand that the world has changed. It has passed them by, and they are weak and unable to react.'

'What has changed?'

'They think of bad drugs like heroin or ecstasy. They don't understand how normalised something like cocaine has become. It is everywhere and I need to be in charge of my own destiny. I don't want to rely on my family; I don't want to be kept by my girlfriend.'

'This is a dangerous path that you want to follow. This is not a career for everyone. Once you start, it will be hard to walk away. There are some very dangerous obstacles in your way.'

'I am desperate.'

'Desperation is never a good motivation.'

'No, wrong word; I am determined.'

'How can I be sure that I will be secure and that my role in this is not compromised?'

'I will be protected by the Williams family. Francis and Kenny will look after me.'

'Well, if you get them to give it the green light, I can live with it. If your mother or father find out, I need to remain in the shadows.'

'Thank you, *Zio* . . . I will never forget.'

CHAPTER FORTY-ONE

2022

Matty likes to take the early morning walk with Alfie. The dog is besotted with Christina but tolerates Matty on the basis that he goes on longer and more interesting walks. He also bypasses Christina's strict dry-food-only diet and slips him the odd sausage.

The two walk all over Morecambe golf course before the members come out for the day. There is a glistening slick of morning dew on the grass, which will burn off quickly. The only others around are the greens keepers, who all know Alfie and often have a treat for him, even though he likes running through their bunkers after they have been raked.

He likes to pick up a coffee down at the café just off the coastal road. Not a fancy one, just two spoons of Nescafe and some milk. As a nod to the environment, he takes his own reusable mug.

On his way back home, he stops at the gate overlooking the fields that he owns. He has owned the property for almost twelve years, and apart from renting it back to the farmer, has made little from it. He reflects on why this had been so important to him. It wasn't about the money in isolation; it was about showing Christina that he could be ambitious and successful. It was about showing the people of Morecambe that he had made it.

Was this a good motivation, or did it just highlight his own insecurities? Either way, it was symbolic of his journey in life: a small grassy field tucked away in a corner of the North West of England, on the edge of the Atlantic. To him, it had been everything; it was his world. Now, as an older man, he questions why it was so important; the world was a much bigger place.

Maybe, if he had invested more energy in keeping his family on the right path, in directing Marco in a different direction, his younger son would have been happier and more rewarded.

The council have now completely flipped their position on planning permissions. Not only have they approved the planning, but they are now making overtures about providing incentives, in terms of grants. They are also very keen to bury any adverse publicity surrounding their former disgraced Head of Planning.

Finally, there are signs that Morecambe might become an up-and-coming town. He remembers how determined he had been to make a

John G Gemmell

difference, how he could see himself getting involved in local politics. But now perhaps he should leave it to others.

Back home, Alfie happily leaves little paw prints on the floor in pursuit of his mummy.

'I stopped by the field today,' says Matty. 'You know, we need to decide soon.'

'I know. It's such a big deal; it is your dream.'

'Not really. It *was* my dream, but now it is just a fork in the road. We either carry out the development, or we sell it to a property developer. The fact that we now have planning permission has a huge impact on the price; we are going to make lots of money from it, finally.'

The two of them are up in the bedroom, sitting on the bed. Alfie is curled up in his little wicker basket, snoring happily.

'But do you really think that after all that has happened, we can live here?' says Christina. 'Every time I am in town, I feel that people have already judged me.'

'Of course we can, and next time I will come with you, and you can point them out. I will chase them down the street to protect your honour. I have lived here all my life; we can hold our heads up high.'

'When I first came here from Italy, I was running away. My brother was not a nice person, and if I stayed, it would have been a very unhappy life.

'I was just a young woman, only twenty years of age, and I thought I needed to prove myself in my new country. It was me that pushed you too hard. It is me who I blame for you going to prison.

'And now, in the blink of an eye, I find myself a fifty-five-year-old woman. If I was to meet the younger version of myself, I am not sure that I would like her very much.'

'Nonsense. Though the good news for you is that you still look every bit as beautiful as the girl that I first fell in love with,' he says, giving her a tender kiss. 'And remember, you stayed here; it would have been easy for you to go back home, but you didn't. You came to see me every week, come hell or high water.'

'When I was back in Calabria for my brother's funeral, I poured my heart out to Padre Conte. He made sense of it all for me, told me to focus on the future and the ones that I love.'

'Wise words from a wise old man.'

'I just don't know. Does the past have a place in the future?'

'Have you ever thought that you might not have been running away, you might have been running towards it? You make it sound like leaving Italy was a wrong choice, but for me, it was the best decision you ever made.

'Whether we like it or not, we are entering the final quarter of our lives. Time is precious now. The boys are grown up; they're standing on their own two feet. We make decisions for us now. Never ignore the past, but we can choose the future.'

* * *

Angelo's business has expanded rapidly over the last few years. So much so that he decides he can no longer run it out of his parents' garage. He takes out a lease on an office in Tech City in Manchester and rents a flat close by.

Revenues have multiplied tenfold, and he now has a team of eight people taking the business forward. All energetic, young creatives who make Matty feel like a dinosaur. Matty is no longer required on a day-to-day basis, but his son has made him Non-Executive Chairman as an expression of his thanks. He cherished spending so much time with his older son. He got to know him as his own man, and he knows that he will be successful in life.

In contrast, Marco has become increasingly distant and detached from his family. For a short time, when his music business took off, he was happy. Now he has regressed to the sullen behaviours of his youth – much more dangerous, now that he is an adult. Matty feels that he is losing him. He doesn't know what he is doing to earn money these days.

Unbeknown to Matty, Marco has been given the green light to start trading drugs in Manchester. The caveat is that he is to stick to his own market and not take on existing distributors. In theory, this means that he can supply his own network of musicians and DJs, as well as several social influencers through Josie.

He is determined to make up for lost time. He is now a man on a mission. If he rubs up a few people along the way, then fuck them. It means they had it coming; they got complacent. There is a new kid on the block, and nobody is going to stand in his way. He is determined that this time, nobody is going to stop him.

He quickly sets up a very efficient supply chain. He simply takes orders through WhatsApp, on up to twenty mobile devices. Orders are then delivered through an army of bored young kids on electric scooters. His key point of differentiation is speed of delivery. He likes to boast that he is quicker to deliver than Uber Eats.

Although he is back on his feet financially and has avoided catastrophe, he still carries a burning indignation about the slight to the de Luca name. If his father had been allowed to continue growing his empire, Marco would now be inheriting huge resources and could have weathered the storm much more easily.

He deeply resents his parents for their inactivity. Since his father came out of jail, he senses that they have changed, are far more self-reflective. Perhaps they have just gotten old.

He doesn't know where his brother stands, but he wants to find out, so he drops in on him at the end of the working day. He also has a need for some of his IT skills.

'There he is, the big dog. King of technology and all that stuff,' says Marco.

'Hello, Marco. Not like you to stop by.'

'Well, you know, I thought it was about time I caught up with all the gossip from my big bro. Any chance of a coffee?'

'Sure, although it will have to be instant. Hope that's ok with you?'

'C'mon, you are supposed to be Italian!'

'I have always felt more comfortable being English, to be honest.'

The office is completely open plan. There are ten identical workstations, arranged in a circle. In the middle is a meeting space for four. In the corner is a co-lab area, with wipeable whiteboards. The walls are all pared back to brick, and there is some clever lighting that can alter depending on mood or what work you want to complete. They even have a robotic carpet cleaner that works the night shift.

'So where is your office, then?'

'I don't have one. Creatively, we are all equal.'

'Whatever,' says Marco. 'Anyway, I hear it is all very successful. All those lonely nights up in your bedroom paid off. I always thought you were just wanking online to girls on the other side of the world.'

'And I am hearing that you have started in the coke game. You know, if Dad finds out, he will kill you.'

'Relax. The old man will never find out. Do your guys need any? I can sort you out, give you a good deal. Will make you more creative.'

'No thanks. I am very much in my father's camp and anti-drugs.'

'Still taking the moral high ground and looking down on your little brother? It was always the same: the golden boy, good at school, sets up his own business versus the tearaway younger brother. Well, I tell you what, I am going to be big stuff, you know.'

'Marco, what do you really want?'

'Well, it's about Mum and Dad. They have changed, haven't they?'

'Of course, they have; they are older. They have lived with Dad being in prison for ten years. They have now lived through a global pandemic. Who wouldn't have changed?'

'Yes, but growing up, they had such energy. If you took a pop at the King and Queen, you better be good because you only got one chance at it.'

'That's not the childhood that I remember. I remember them working hard to support us.'

'Well, it is mine. All the comings and goings, plotting the latest robbery, the amount of cash that kicked about the house . . . Can you imagine what your business and mine would be worth if we had received the right amount of capital from the family's business? We would be on the path to millions. And it all fell apart because two guys grassed them up.'

'Look, you are either high on your own product or have been reading too many mafia books. This is utterly absurd.'

'Thought as much; didn't expect much backbone from you. However, right now, I need you to do me a favour.'

When he had finished with his request, his older brother got up to show him to the door.

'Listen, you get to pick your friends, but not your family. I will do this for you, but after that, I don't want anything else to do with you. I will love you forever, but you are the most self-entitled little prick that I have ever met. I will be successful in life by what I do, nothing else. Now, get the fuck out of my office.'

* * *

Marco carries his rage around with him for several days until he eventually approaches Francis and Kenny for help.

'Can I ask you both a favour please?'

'Whenever you say that, I know it's not going to end well,' says Francis.

'You remember that my father was sent to prison based on the evidence of a couple of grasses?'

'You might just have told us a few times,' says Kenny.

'Well, I have decided that I am going to avenge the family's name.'

'Does your father agree with that?' asks Francis.

'Yes, he does, 100%. He has given me his blessing; says that we have waited too long. Like your father, mine is entering retirement. He wants me to head up the family now, so I need to take care of this for him as a gift for taking over control of the family.'

'Very dramatic, very Italian,' says Francis.

'Be clear – what is it you are asking?' says Kenny.

'I want to take out a contract to kill the two that put my father in jail, as our revenge.'

'That's serious stuff, you know,' says Francis coolly. 'That tends to come with a life sentence, bro.'

'No, what is serious is the shame and the hurt that my family suffered. That is much worse.'

'Well, it is not something that our family would take on directly,' says Kenny.

'But if you are that determined, we can connect you to someone who could,' says Francis. 'Although, let's be clear, we are nowhere near this one. I don't even think we will tell Dad; he won't like it one bit.'

'The old men need to realise that their time has been. We're in charge now.'

'Tell you what, big shot, why don't you come down and say that to my dad? You won't last five seconds.'

'What would the damage be?'

'Sadly, the price would be only about £30k. It's amazing what some people are prepared to do.'

'Ok, let's do it,' says Marco. 'Set up a meet, and I will give them the information that they need.'

* * *

The clubs are slowly and cautiously coming out of hibernation. They have not yet seen the rush back that happened in pubs where people flocked to reacquaint themselves with a pint. A pint of lager has taken on almost biblical status as people sit out in the freezing cold just to savour one.

Customers still inherently worry about the virus in a club environment, given the proximity to each other. The two-year hiatus for nightclubs has led to different dynamics.

The twenty-two-year-olds in 2019 are now twenty-five; they're in relationships and saving for houses. The fifteen-year-olds of 2019 are now the new customers presenting themselves at the front door, having never been in a club before and not having the etiquette handed down as part of their rite of passage. It is like a weird time warp.

Marco has started supplying DJs again to the clubs. The main problem is that he has either lost his mojo for it or has simply been seduced by making more money from dealing drugs. The clubs are beginning to question his judgement, such as supplying drill music at a mainstream Saturday night venue. The grumblings are picking up pace, and the news is making its way back to the Williams brothers.

He has also opened other supply channels beyond Nino. He is cultivating a relationship with some contacts in Liverpool. Watching the trends in America, he believes that Fentanyl might be the next big thing, and he wants to be front of the queue.

He isn't allowed to sell drugs in the clubs, but those who do are aware of the threat that his appearance has made on the scene. The playboy Italian prince doesn't cultivate an empathetic persona when he is in the clubs. He throws money about and has developed a following of young men and women who love his wild partying.

However, he has clearly angered some people. Threats have been posted online that he needs to watch his back. Images of young men dressed in black, with knives and guns, are posted on the clubs' Twitter feeds before being quickly taken down. It feels as though a war might break out at any moment. With the clubs having been closed for such a long time, a drug war is the last thing that anyone needs right now. Apart from Marco, who believes that his time has arrived.

Francis and Kenny are furious and decide to pay him a little visit in the VIP booth at My Illusion nightclub.

'Marco. This is all beginning to get out of hand. You need to take a lower profile,' says Francis.

'Fuck them, jumped-up social media wannabees. Let them try and take me on!' shouts Marco. 'I will fuck them all up big time.'

'Stop playing a pretend gangster, Marco. It is embarrassing,' says Francis.

'I want you to let me sell coke in the clubs now. I think I am ready.'

'No, you don't understand,' says Francis.' That is not how our business works. We survive in this town by running businesses that have no trouble. Do you understand? You appear to have some kind of death wish going on.'

'Fuck you, both!' he shouts as they leave. Thankfully, the music is so loud that it doesn't reach them.

Marco is left sitting furiously beside Josie. They are both nursing a glass of champagne, but neither feels like celebrating. It feels as though the relationship has been heading south since Dubai.

'Do your brothers honestly think I'm scared of them?'

'Marco, they are my family. Please don't go there.'

'Yeah, look, even you are laughing at me, just because they came in and laid down the law.'

'To be honest, I don't want to be here at all,' says Josie. 'I no longer enjoy being part of the club scene. I think I have outgrown it.'

'Of course, you just want to sit at home, boring everyone to death on TikTok about skin cream rituals and the latest diet plans, stuff that no one gives a fuck about, apart from a bunch of little girls.'

'Marco, that is so cruel. You know how hard I have worked over the last few years to make this career successful.'

Their voices have gradually escalated, catching the attention of other customers. Phones are quietly being produced to capture things if they get out of control. Nothing better than a couple of local celebrities losing their shit in public.

'Yeah, and it has been me that has been there to support you over the last few years.'

'Support me? No you haven't, you arrogant little fuck! I funded *you* when your business collapsed. *I'm* the one that had to listen to how hard you have had things. Everybody else to blame apart from yourself.'

'Yeah, but now that I am up and running again, you are not giving me much support.'

'Marco, you are dealing drugs, for God's sake.'

'So what? Lots of people do it; it's no big deal. In fact, I could be even bigger if you were to help me.'

'What are you talking about?'

'Look, you have over 400k followers now. Why can't you give them to me, and I can add them to my supply list?'

'Are you insane? What kind of credible fashion influencer would give her client database to a freaking drug dealer?'

Josie decides it is time to get out, so she grabs her phone and her bag and makes a signal to one of the security team to get her a car. She knows full well that her actions will be relayed back to her brothers. For once, she really doesn't care.

'Listen, Marco. I am out of here. Do me a favour and find somewhere to sleep tonight because I don't want you back at the flat.'

However, she doesn't go to the flat herself. Instead, she goes home to her dad's house. She has phoned ahead, so he is up in the kitchen in his dressing gown, making hot chocolate. She immediately sweeps in and bursts into tears.

Dad has a feeling that he has a long night of listening ahead.

CHAPTER FORTY-TWO

2022

Today is the day that Davy is due to make his long-awaited reveal. He has dressed up for the part: light grey trousers, with a razor-sharp crease, paired with a black roll neck sweater. A kind of lightweight gangster chic is what he is trying to pull off.

Everyone gathers in the main living room in Hillhead, awaiting the arrival of the police. It is only used for grand occasions. They all sit on a modular shaped sofa in light cream. It is rarely used, due to the high spillage risk. The windows have American-style wooden shutters, and there is a glass table (also a nightmare to keep clean), standing on a handmade Moroccan rug. It is all very tasteful; it is all very Lisa.

The doorbell rings, which signals the arrival of Brogan Reilly and Phil Simpson. They are dressed in a casual version of police uniform. It is seen as non-inflammatory to attend meetings without any hardware on show.

However, this is Davy's show, so he opts to stand in front of everyone, instead of sitting.

'Ms Brogan Reilly and Phil Simpson,' says Davy. 'So nice to see you again. This is my wife, Kathy, and you know my daughter, Lisa. And of course you know these two toerags.'

'Well, you two have certainly led us on a song and dance these last two weeks,' says Brogan.

'Sorry,' they say in unison.

'You have lost weight,' says Brogan to Stephen.

'It's amazing what worry does,' says Stephen, quietly happy and making a mental note to check the mirror.

'And you,' says Brogan, pointing at Tony, 'you seem to be dressing better than when I first met you.'

'Ah, I see you haven't lost your sunny disposition,' says Tony. 'Lisa is now in charge of my wardrobe; she is my fashion consultant.'

'Kathy, what are we thinking? Get the kettle on. Can you get tea organised for everyone?' says Davy.

'Well, Davy Gavin, you are one hell of a character. I pulled the files; you have led quite the life,' says Brogan, flushing a little.

'So can we perhaps begin?' she continues, producing a mobile phone to record what is said.

'Oh no, my dear,' says Davy. 'We need to wait for Kathy. She will be very cross if I was to start without her.'

At that moment, Kathy trundles into the living room with an old-fashioned tea trolley laden with tea cups and a plate of buns. Lisa is mortified. A tea trolley is not something that she owns, which can only mean that Kathy has brought it up from her house, a prop for the occasion. She imagines that her parents have sat up deep into the night working on the finer details of the big reveal, cackling at her discomfort. What other fresh embarrassments does her mother have in store for her?

Kathy fusses about pouring the tea, which is passed anti-clockwise, followed by the milk, the sugar and the cakes.

'Oh, Mrs G,' says Tony. 'Iced coconut buns! You are a legend.'

'And if you get any of it on the sofa, you're dead,' hisses Lisa.

'Ahem,' says Brogan. 'Lovely to be included as part of this family gathering, but is there any chance that we can get started?'

'Of course we can, my dear,' says Davy.

However, the second he says it, he is interrupted by the doorbell again. Bella comes rushing into the room, bearing popcorn.

'Sorry peeps, traffic was shocking, but I wouldn't miss this for a moment! I have been so invested in this story I couldn't possibly miss the grand finale.'

'Right, let us begin,' says Davy.

'Now, as you know, following two failed attempts on the lives of Stephen and Tony, the family decided to take control over security. An action that the police were firmly opposed to,' says Brogan, principally to get it on record.

'We spent the week down at Loch Lomond,' says Davy.

'Absolutely beautiful place. I like it a lot. Have you been there before, Brogan?' asks Tony.

'Yes, Tony, I live in Scotland. I have been to Loch Lomond. Can we continue, please?'

'I wasn't very happy with security up to that point, so I decided to upweight it and brought in a small tactical team,' says Davy.

'Oh, did you? Of course,' says Brogan.

'But I must tell you at this stage that there was a third attempt on the lives of the boys,'-says Davy, gravely.

'*What?* Are you kidding me? Why are we only hearing about this now?' says Phil. 'Brogan, the bosses will have us for this one.'

'Relax, relax,' says Davy. 'We apprehended them before they could do any damage.'

'You should have seen them! They were shitting themselves from the two SAS boys that Davy rustled up,' says Tony. 'It was great.'

'Apprehended: what does that mean, and where are they?' says Brogan. 'We are the police. They have committed a serious crime, which we need to investigate.'

'I am afraid that they managed to get away. I am really sorry – I must be losing my touch,' says Davy. 'But you will be delighted to know that we secured the long-distance rifle that they were planning on using.' He produces it in a clear plastic bag, secured with ties, with 'Exhibit A' on a cardboard tag.

'So, it turns out I know Frankie Williams from the old days,' continues Davy.

'He knows everyone, so he does. You can't even go to the shops without bumping into someone,' says Kathy. 'Sometimes I send him down for a loaf of bread, and it takes him an hour. And here is me waiting for a slice of toast. Anyone want more tea?'

The trolley makes another run, this time in the opposite direction, which is better for the yin and yang.

'So, I phone Frankie up, and it's all very interesting,' says Davy. 'He told me that the police had paid him a visit last week and asked about this. I have to say you have very good instincts, and they were right: he was completely in the dark.'

'Were they?' says Brogan.

'Yes, the person who took out the contract on the boys was Marco de Luca. His boys organised it through some underworld Manchester connections. The price was £30k I believe. Frankie is raging at them for taking such a risk.'

'Thirty grand – should we be insulted?' says Stephen.

'And I presume that you have no information on who any of these people might be?' says Phil.

'Sorry, I don't But the good news is that Frankie has been back in touch, and as of a few days ago, the contract is officially cancelled.'

'Oh Dad,' says Lisa, giving her old man a cuddle, 'that's brilliant news.'

'Hold on, hold on. There is an awful lot to process here,' says Brogan. 'I am surrounded by all sorts of crimes being committed. We are the police; we cannot just close the whole thing down and enjoy iced buns and popcorn.'

'There is still popcorn, going,' says Tony.

'Well, on the basis that your main role was to ensure the welfare of your witnesses, why not?' says Stephen. 'Did you ever find out about the initial security breaches at your end?'

'I am afraid that is still a live line of enquiry,' says Brogan.

'Which means that you don't have a bloody clue.'

'I have solved that mystery too, but I have decided that I cannot give you that piece of the jigsaw, for operational reasons,' says Davy. Tony's cheeks begin to slightly burn.

'Oh, that's not fair,' says Bella. 'Imagine spending all that time on the jigsaw, and at the very end, you discover that you can't complete it because there is a piece missing.'

'I am never that bothered about finishing it. It is about the journey and the joy of doing it, rather than the final destination,' says Tony.

'Weirdo,' says Bella.

'Thank you, both; completely unhelpful, as usual,' says Brogan. 'Can we get this back on track, please?'

Davy is relieved that he doesn't need to reveal that the person responsible for hacking the police security is none other than Angelo O'Hare. With his team's technical ability, and an appalling lack of security protocols, they completed it in under an hour. They passed the locations of both boys to Marco, and then onward to those planning the hit.

Angelo had only done so out of blind loyalty to his brother or possibly just to get him out of his hair.

'Good shout,' says Davy. 'Whilst we still have young Marco charging about the place like a loose cannon, pursuing old-school vendettas, you are not safe. So, I decided to give Matty O'Hare a call.'

'Of course you did,' says Brogan.

'Absolutely lovely fella, heart of gold. Proper old school. He was more than happy to own up to his shortcomings and the bad things he did. He doesn't bear any grudge against either of you two lads. In fact, he said it would be great to meet up for lunch sometime.'

'Sorry, I am now getting lost again,' says Phil.

Davy starts to lay out the final pieces in the puzzle.

'Well, the problem is that young Marco has become a major liability to Frankie. At first, they tolerated him, but he is now causing chaos in the clubs of Manchester. They are worried that war is going to break out unless they do something about it. There have been death threats.

'His relationship with Frankie's daughter, Josie, is on the floor. It has broken down completely. He is controlling and manipulative, and Frankie can see her confidence slipping away. He knows it is about time he does something to protect his daughter.

'At the same time, Matty is also at the end of his tether. He has had enough. He didn't know his son was dealing drugs until I gave him the news. He was apoplectic.

'Apparently, there was an Uncle Bruno back in Italy who was the same. He had a compulsive personality, fuelled by greed, and a sense of entitlement. The minute you add cocaine into the mix, the pot boils over, and everyone in the vicinity gets burned.'

'He sounds a right nasty piece of work,' says Kathy.

'And do I presume that you are now going to provide us with a solution?' says Brogan.

'Of course, my dear,' says Davy. 'Having worked with the police for most of my life, I know that the police prefer solutions to problems, so here you go. We are going to set you up with a time and location in Manchester where you will be able to stop young Marco and find him in possession of a large amount of cocaine.'

'And does the boy's father agree with it?' asks Brogan.

'Well, that has been the tricky bit. It is a real dilemma for him. On the one hand, he thinks his son is in terrible danger and prison might be the best option. However, he also knows that an Italian mother will never give her son up, So he has agreed to do it without telling his wife, and to live with the betrayal.'

'Do you know how wrong this is, on so many levels?' says Brogan.

'There is something appealing about it, though,' says Phil. 'It does give us closure.'

'Of course, there it makes sense. Just think: you resolve the problem with your breach of witness protection, the two boys here are free, you take an upstart drug dealer out of circulation, and you avoid war in the clubs of Manchester. What's not to love?' says Davy.

'Look, can you give me five minutes? I want to phone this in to our superiors,' says Brogan.

She leaves the room and heads out to the car, returning shortly.

'Well, guess what? They have told us to accept the proposal. Apparently, the directive comes from the very top,' says Brogan to Phil.

'Excellent!' says Davy. 'I forgot to tell you that I met your Chief Super yesterday for a pint. I knew him as a young pup, when he was a newbie. Always liked him; pleased he has done so well for himself.'

'Jesus, I despair,' says Brogan.

'I've had to put up with this for years, my dear. Don't worry dear, you get used to it eventually,' says Kathy.

'Why do I feel that two old rogues have played us good and proper?' says Brogan.

'Well, that's settled then,' says Davy. 'Right, Stephen, I am sure that you must have a nice bottle of malt whisky in this house. It's how we used to toast the conclusion of a deal back in the old days.'

The strange little group have somehow formed a bond over the last couple of weeks. Kathy has persuaded the police to stay a little longer and even makes them some sandwiches before they depart.

At some point in the evening, Stephen finds himself alone with his father-in-law.

'Davy, I just want to apologise for all the deception over the last ten years. You deserve better,' says Stephen. 'Also, I am not going to lie, I am not proud of what I did for Matty. I should never have become involved. You do know that I would do anything for Lisa and the children.'

'You're fine, son,' says Davy. 'Deep down, I know you love my daughter, and that's all I care about.'

'Thanks.'

'I did some bad things back in the day, stuff that I am not proud of. It was a different time back then; it was the law of the jungle. I did it to survive, to provide for Kathy and Lisa. Nothing more than that. And I would do it all over again. All you ever need in life is security and love; the rest is just interference.'

288

Epilogue

Frankie Williams has happily returned to his retirement, tending to his allotment, far from the stresses of the underworld. Francis decided enough was enough and sold the security business to another party. He is planning a move into cybercrime, so is using the time to learn all about cryptocurrency. Kenneth decided that there wasn't much point in dating a billionaire's daughter without enjoying the perks, so he has relocated to Singapore where he finds the humidity challenging.

Josie continues to grow her followers, with no end in sight of people wanting to be influenced. She now has grandpuppies, as Freddy successfully produced some offspring. Following her split from Marco, it hasn't taken her long to hook up with a very promising midfielder from Salford City, who is tipped to make a big move soon.

Lisa continues to throw herself into work and grow her business with people who meet her criteria of sustainability and inclusivity. She still makes soup for the street kitchen and has even started to make her stock from scratch. She now has another pair of hands because Stephen resigned from the accountancy partnership and is now her Chief Commercial Officer, managing the financials and finding new customers, which has taken a huge weight off her shoulders. They built an office at home so they could be more present for the children.

Cameron and Emily no longer want to go to Florida as it is bad for your carbon footprint. At SeaWorld, they saw a documentary about the orcas that made them very sad.

Bella has recently announced her engagement to Mikkel, with a wedding planned for next year, in Stockholm.

Tony has enrolled at Glasgow Caledonian University to study Social Sciences. He is boarding with Stephen and Lisa, and it is now one full year since he stole anything. He is even allowed to be the babysitter again, although matches and marshmallows are still banned.

Angelo has gone from strength to strength. He has matured beyond apps and has established a strategic partnership with a tech giant from Silicon Valley. He exists exclusively in the metaverse, preferably through an avatar. His family think this is cool, even though they have no idea what he is talking about.

Marco was found guilty of possession of Cat A drugs, with intent to supply. He was sentenced to five years imprisonment. Sadly, for him, he has decided to take his sense of entitlement into prison with him. This is not the cleverest choice he has ever made, but then clever is not really his forte.

Matty and Christina made their decision at the crossroad in their life. They decided to create a new life, free of all the baggage. They sold the house in Morecambe and the development site and moved to Italy to take up home in the Villa de Luca. This was to the absolute delight of Nonna, who now knows that it has a proper succession plan. The plan is to fully reopen the orchards and turn the property into an agri-tourism hotel where people can enjoy authentic hospitality, support the land and finally see the real Calabria. Christina faithfully goes home to England every couple of months to visit her younger son in prison, oblivious to the deception that put him there.

Davy thoroughly enjoyed his brief return to the front line. It was never the violence that he enjoyed; it was being in control that gave him the buzz. Sadly, for him, it was no more than a swan song. Kathy firmly put an end to any notion he might have had of another shot at the title. So, it is back to the bowling club for him, where his membership number continues its trajectory upwards, twenty at the last count. At least the drama gave him a story to share with the boys, a story that ripens every time he tells it.

Nino continues to operate successfully in the watery shadows of the Eastern Mediterranean, which, for him, is the only way to survive.

Milton Keynes UK
Ingram Content Group UK Ltd.
UKHW022106271023
431481UK00005B/55